Star Watch

Book One of the
Star Watch series

Written By

Mark Wayne McGinnis

Cover design by:
Eren Arik

Edited by:
Lura Lee Genz
Mia Manns

Published by:
Avenstar Productions

ISBN-10: 0986109851
ISBN-13: 978-0-9861098-5-0

To join Mark's mailing list, jump to:

http://eepurl.com/bs7M9r

Prologue

```
Alchieves System
Planet Trom, Cloud-Port E5926
```

"Another SkyTrans captain just reported in ... his engine's out of service until further notice."

"Another? Shit!" Security Commander Larkbadder barked. "Not today of all days. Not today."

"Well, that's what happens when six million people all try to migrate within the same three days. The engines are old and poorly maintained. We're lucky they've held up as long as they have," Transportation Minister Dullard said unapologetically, without looking up from his terminal.

Larkbadder watched as the frustrated transportation minister, overweight, overstressed, and clearly overworked, tapped at the input device in front of him. There were twenty such terminals clustered about in the middle of the tower. All of the workers manning them, with the exception of Dullard, who'd just relieved its previous occupant, were *mechers*—AI controlled bots. The metallic mechers looked and sounded somewhat like Tromians, but were ridiculously tall—seven feet at least—and could rotate their heads a full three hundred and sixty degrees. For the most part, mechers were the most annoying Tromian creation ever conceived.

Larkbadder now stood at the observation window, fifteen hundred feet above the open-air concourse below. Like ants, thousands of Tromians—men, women, and children—were hurrying from scores of port-annex doors directly below him, onto the concourse platform. The traffic control tower was perched high above every other structure on the cloud-port periphery. Larkbadder walked to an adjacent observation window. With hands on hips, he looked out and shook his head. Below, throngs of people continued to push and shove, frantic to escape—to secure a seat on a SkyTrans engine. How many brawls, fistfights, and numerous other altercations had his officers had to break up over the last few hours? Things were teetering on the verge of out and out riots down there.

A mammoth–sized SkyTrans engine sat directly across the concourse, about a mile's distance away. Steam hissed and spat from a thousand or so individual relief valves positioned all over the mud-colored engine's hull. To his left, thirty miles of the concourse platform disappeared into the clouds, as another ten SkyTrans engines began taking on passengers. Each of the monstrous-sized vehicles was a quarter of a mile long and fifty yards wide.

Temporarily cozied up to their berths, the SkyTrans engines took on as many passengers as regulations would allow: about one hundred thousand souls each … often that number was pushed an additional thirty thousand. *And they wonder why these old engines give out*, he thought.

The transportation minister joined Larkbadder at the window. "You sticking around?"

Larkbadder looked at Dullard as if he were crazy. "Of

course I'm sticking around." He realized he'd replied with a little more fervor than intended. "It's not like I have anywhere else to go ... may as well stay here and see what happens," Larkbadder said. But his calm demeanor was in true contrast to his actual state of mind. He was scared ... for anyone that didn't get away from Trom. Truth be told, he was just as terrified what would become of himself.

"How about you ... when are you scheduled to ..." Larkbadder didn't finish; instead, using his chin, he gestured toward the closest SkyTrans engine.

Transportation Minister Dullard looked uncomfortable with the question, as if a deep, dark secret had come to light. Then his shoulders relaxed and he let out a long breath. "Late tonight. My wife and daughter are meeting me here. We're on the last engine to leave Trom. I only hope—"

Larkbadder cut him off, "You'll be gone in plenty of time. Plenty." He turned and gave the transportation minister a positive, upbeat look. "No Pharlom ships have entered this sector, let alone our planetary system. Plenty of time."

The truth was, Larkbadder knew that at least eighteen Pharlom vessels had been detected coming into the sector and were making fast progress toward Alchieves space, their own ten-planet solar system. Over the past twenty years, no one had given the Pharloms much thought. True, they'd been Trom's worst enemy before then, but the mighty Craing had kept them at bay—made it virtually impossible for years to wage war against a neighboring system—while Trom provided mined minerals and other raw materials, not to mention slave labor and crew personnel, to the ever-growing Craing interstellar fleets. But then suddenly, the Craing fleets were gone. Defeated in another part of the galaxy ... somewhere. Their celebration was short-lived, though. For as bad as the Craing Empire was ... and it certainly was terrible, the Pharloms were worse. Now they would take advantage of Trom's vulnerability, as well as that of the neighboring planets. At least the Craing, typically, didn't rape and pillage. Now, it was only a matter of time before Pharlom boots hit the ground and God help anyone still around Trom when they did.

A horn's final call sounded from the nearest SkyTrans engine. As the tower windows trembled, Larkbadder felt the familiar deep vibration course through virtually every part of his body. He watched as another gargantuan vehicle slowly moved away from its mooring. A new vibration filled the air as its big ion drive began to rev up. He watched the engine move away—picking up speed. Then it was gone ... lost in the clouds.

Chapter 1

Sol System
Planet Earth, Central Valley Scrapyard,
San Bernardino, CA

Jason watched Dira floating in the pool. Hot this time of year in San Bernardino; he knew it was only a matter of minutes, *hell ... seconds*, before he'd join her. The kids were back with their mother in D.C., and the silence, without their youthful boisterousness filling the air, was a welcome change of pace. He picked up a paperback he'd started, but it wasn't holding his interest. He looked for the other vinyl float and spotted it, deflated, submerged at the bottom of the pool. *Damn kids ...*

The strap of Dira's bikini top was unclasped and, after two weeks, there was little hint she'd ever had tan lines. Who'd have guessed a Jhardonian woman's skin would turn even more violet when sunburned? His eyes were back on Dira and the perfect curvature of her remarkable backside.

"Why don't you stop looking at my ass and come in?"

"The other float is at the bottom of the pool," he said.

"I'll scoot over ... there's room." She managed to keep her top pinned between her upper arms while scooting several inches to her right. She patted the now six inches of open space on her float.

"There's not nearly enough room for me."

"Lie on your side, we'll make it work," she said, smiling. She released the tension on her bikini top and gravity did the rest. "Oops," she said, feigning surprise.

Jason enjoyed the eyeful and said, "Okay ... maybe in a few minutes." He got off the lounge chair and headed for the back of the house. Dira's eyes followed him. He knew that she knew what he was trying so desperately to hide—that he was going bat-shit, stir crazy here. "Can I get you anything?"

"Nope ... I'm good," she said.

Jason looked out over the scrapyard's seemingly endless expanse of rusted-out old cars, buses, and even the remains of a downed jet fighter. The yard belonged to his father Perry and his grandfather Ol' Gus before him. Jason shielded his eyes against the sun, as if saluting, and squinted toward one particular grouping of old vehicles off in the distance. *There they are.* A faded yellow school bus and, next to it, a red, now actually more faded pink, 1961 Cadillac convertible. He debated if he should go below today. Down several hundred feet below the surface was where it all started, over two years ago. Jason rubbed the scruff on his chin and thought of his young daughter, Mollie. Four life-altering events had happened to Jason and Mollie within a matter of minutes: One, they came face-to-face with a cyborg, right here in the scrapyard, an alien he knew today as Ricket. Two, Mollie was shot by that same, albeit startled, alien. Three, with Jason clutching her lifeless body in his arms, Ricket led them to a hidden elevator shaft. Together, they descended to a dried-up underground aquifer. Four, he first set eyes on *The Lilly* and, somewhere within the bowels of that magnificent spaceship, Mollie and Jason were whisked into *Medical*; Mollie was placed into something called a MediPod … where, still lifeless from a plasma bolt to her heart, she was miraculously brought back to life.

Jason turned back toward the house, which was open to the outside. The eight-foot-high sliding windows were now secured into a recessed cubbyhole off to one side. Nan, his ex-wife, had designed the house pretty much from scratch … she said her blueprints would allow the outside decking, and the inside living environment, to merge. Jason padded into the kitchen, opened the fridge door and let its cool air envelop him.

His father, the admiral, had also returned to the scrapyard, when the war with the Craing ended; he was prepared to retire here … ready to finally restore his old '49 F1 pickup truck. But within a few months he'd found an excuse to head back into space … he too had gone stir crazy.

"Please close the refrigerator door, Captain Reynolds."

It was the unpleasant voice of the household AI. She was reprimanding him—again. He contemplated shooting her, but realized he wasn't certain where the actual computer core was located in the house. Perhaps in the basement? No, this was not a typical house, by any means. It was a house comprised of alien, *Caldurian*, technology. Like *The Lilly*. His heart sank every time he thought of her … of how she was now nothing more than space dust.

Jason pulled a bottle of OJ from the top shelf and let the door swing shut.

He'd no sooner brought the bottle to his lips when he heard the familiar melodic ringtone of his internal Nano-Com. Part of a Caldurian nano-technology package, Jason, and most of the other crewmembers who had served on board both *The Lilly* and the *Minian*, had it installed within their physiology and could communicate with virtually anyone within thousands of miles' distance.

Out of habit Jason brought two fingers to his ear. "Go for Captain," he said, already knowing the incoming NanoCom call was, in fact, from his father.

"Enough is enough."

"I beg your pardon?"

"You've been rambling around that place long enough. There's only so many hours you can lay in the sun … or whatever the two of you are doing down there."

"You'd be surprised how entertained we've been; able to keep our—"

"Fine … I'll take your word for it. Put away the pool toys, pack a few things, and lock up the house. The paperwork's come through."

"I didn't submit any paperwork, Dad."

"None of that *Dad* shit … it's Admiral. Your leave has officially been revoked and you, as well as Dira, are back on active duty, as of right now."

Jason tried to keep the smile from his lips, knowing full well his father would be able to hear it in his voice. Sure, with *The Lilly* gone, things would now be different. Perhaps they'd give him one of the U.S. Craing heavy cruiser conversions … it really didn't matter. "What exactly do you have in mind for me?"

"Just get up here and stop wasting time, Admiral Reynolds." The connection ended.

"Admiral? What the hell's he talking about?"

Jason looked up to see Dira standing in the family room, watching him. "Do I have time for a shower … Admiral Reynolds?"

"Sure, take as long as you want … a command decision … apparently I've been promoted."

She rolled her eyes and headed toward the master bedroom. He thought about the whole admiral thing. He'd fought against receiving the promotion for over a year—but now, for some reason, it seemed to fit. He was forty now. Time to let other officers head into battle ... and play the wild adventurer.

* * *

One thing for sure about military life, you can fit just about anything you need into a standard issue duffle. Together, Dira and Jason made their way through the maze of junk cars, piles of scrap metal, and stacks of rusted root beer-colored wheel rims. Like himself, Dira was back in a spacer's jumpsuit. Inevitably, his eyes leveled on her walking several paces in front of him. For goodness' sakes, she even made a jumpsuit look sexy.

As if reading his mind, she glanced back over her shoulder and gave him a scolding look. "Knock it off, Admiral ... none of that." She made an abrupt turn, passing between the old, faded caddy and the school bus. She found the hidden access button beneath the front right wheel well and gave it a definitive slap. The bus's narrow double-doors opened and she disappeared up the metal stairs. Jason took one last look around the yard before following her inside.

The bus was basically a shell—no rows of bench seats, nor driver's seat or steering wheel. Jason watched as Dira hit another access button and the floor began to descend. The elevator shaft was dark but if you looked hard, the walls were lined with a myriad of old hubcaps, automobile doors, and side panels. Twenty years earlier, Ricket and his grandfather had spent weeks ... months ... making the hideaway below safe. It was Ol' Gus who'd first discovered what was hidden there. Buried beneath a hundred years of dirt and sediment, *The Lilly* rested, unobserved. Ricket, too, lay buried—somewhere outside the ship, his bionic brain core partially scrubbed.

The lift came to a jarring stop. They'd reached the bottom of the shaft. Jason pulled open the metal lift gate and the two headed off into the tunnel before them.

By the time they hiked the distance through the winding passage, eventually emerging into the wide expanse of the aquifer proper, both were breathing hard.

Jason's heart missed a beat, so used to seeing his ship—*The Lilly*—sitting right there, in this hiding place so very few knew about. He pushed a recurring feeling of loss aside … just as he'd done a hundred times before. They headed toward the center of the aquifer where a small transport vessel sat, illuminated by high, overhead hanging lights; it was a Caldurian shuttle—the *Perilous*.

Off to the right were stacks of recently-constructed environmental compartments, containing complete living quarters for no less than a hundred crewmembers; also, a large mess hall and a laboratory-type facility, as well as other amenities. Everything one would need to survive down here—probably indefinitely, if necessary.

A solitary figure emerged from the rear of the shuttle and headed down the gangway. It was Lieutenant Commander Grimes. She, along with a group of other Navy **Top Gun** pilots, was assigned to *The Lilly* a year and a half earlier, then later transferred over to the *Minian,* the senior-most pilot of its fleet of advanced Caldurian fighters and shuttles.

"Captain Reynolds, it's so good to see you again. Hey, Dira … you're certainly looking well-rested."

"Lieutenant, good to see you too," Jason said.

Dira gave Grimes a hug. They were friends and it had been quite a while since Dira had served with the fleet in any official capacity. Not since she'd returned home to Jhardon—a planet ravaged earlier by the Craing. Her father, the king of Jhardon, was recently killed and her mother, the queen, seemed at death's door from illness. It looked as if Dira, actually a princess by birthright, would be required to step in as ruler. But all that changed when Ricket was able to procure a MediPod and had it delivered to the royal palace. It still took several days of wrangling on Dira's part to convince those at her mother's bedside to allow such alien technology to come anywhere close to the dying queen's frail body. In the end, reason, and the all too imminent death of their beloved queen, made them grant Dira permission. Her mother soon recovered and immediately went to work changing the monarchy to a more democratic form of government. Not interested in politics in the least, Dira was then free to return to the Alliance—to Jason—and resume her work as a medical doctor ... a job she truly loved doing.

They wasted no time getting aboard the shuttle. Grimes took her seat in the cockpit while Dira and Jason sat in the front seats, directly behind her, in the cabin. With the cabin open to the cockpit, Jason watched Grimes at the controls. She entered in the coordinates—to an area directly above the scrapyard on the surface—and activated a phase-shift. Everything flashed white. Jason looked out the observation window to his left and now saw the scrapyard a hundred feet below them, and his house nestled on the east side of the vast property. Grimes pulled back on the controls and the *Perilous* rapidly headed away from the surface. Within seconds, they'd reached Earth's upper atmosphere.

Chapter 2

Alchieves System
Pharlom Command Warship

The Pharloms, as a race, were distinctive in looks and mannerisms. Even the Craing, who had come across thousands of different species and races over the centuries, had placed the Pharloms at the very top of the list—as one of the most bizarre.

Leon Pike, a human, was born to two Earth parents who'd joined a younger Commander Perry Reynolds, some twenty-seven years earlier, to crew aboard an amazing Caldurian vessel named *The Lilly*. Leon's parents were now long dead … and his home had always been open space. At only twenty-six, he went by the title of Merchant Trader, but in truth he was up for hire for any number of trades: intergalactic guide; bounty hunter; even a trader of black-market goods … on a rare occasion—if the terms were acceptable. But that didn't mean Leon lacked a strong moral compass. Yes, he was a man with few personal allegiances, but the ones he did possess were quite strong. Leon didn't steal from or cheat his friends, and he did his best not to sleep with their wives. He may have broken the latter rule several times lately, but he

14

had made a conscious vow—a decree—to never, ever, let that happen again. That was four days ago.

Leon held no allegiance to the Pharloms—none whatsoever. Being here now, on the command vessel's bridge, sitting next to Mangga, the fleet's Grand Overseer (equivalent to the rank of admiral), had been one big error in judgment.

Leon wasn't entirely sure, but he thought Mangga was looking at him. The Pharloms did not have faces, per se, in terms of the typical two eyes, nose, and mouth. They did have a head, but it looked more like a piece of granite than something organic. Composed of hundreds of sharp ridges, and just as many valley-like indentations, there simply was no way to know where, exactly, a Pharlom was looking. Although, of late, Leon thought he saw an eye, of sorts, located in the mid-section of Mangga's head. So, nodding in that general direction, he gave back a tight-lipped smile and a curt nod.

Leon tried to remember the course of the events that had put him here. That hiccup had come about using Dirinian middleman Jericho Goll, another human, but obviously one lacking any semblance of a moral compass of his own. Jericho had set the whole thing up—had come to Leon with what he'd described as a quick, in-and-out, two- or three-day planetary guide gig. An unnamed third party needed to traverse the ten-world Alchieves solar system. Not a simple process. Leon, though, had done it several times—mostly smuggling bendalli weed to the locals. The Tromians, who'd been raided many times over years past, had constructed close to one hundred space cannons that were now located throughout their solar system. Most were perched on satellite moons, but some also free-floated in space. Just one of the gigantic weapons could annihilate a trespasser ship. Leon knew the access codes, which allowed any given ship a free pass without harassment. And that's how he'd gotten himself into this present fix.

Leon actually liked the Tromian people. They didn't deserve this … whatever *this* was. Probably a raid, one he'd be responsible for. He pushed feelings of guilt from his mind and tried to concentrate on the hovering hologram at the center of the bridge. They had just entered the Alchieves solar system and were approaching the first access point. Within seconds, the Pharlom destroyer would be hailed. If the access code relayed back wasn't correct, this ship, and others in this fleet of eighteen, would be fired upon.

Leon debated if he should just go ahead and give them an incorrect code … let the pieces fall as they may. Hell, perhaps the Pharloms' shields could fend off an inevitable, retaliatory bombardment. Not likely … Leon never heard of ships surviving Tromian cannon fire, once unleashed.

And now was the time—the communications officer was informing the Grand Overseer of the incoming hail. The timer had been initiated. He would have less than forty-five seconds to enter the proper nine-digit code.

"You will provide the code now, human," the Grand Overseer ordered.

Leon stared back at the Pharlom leader. He, like other Pharloms, was big and imposing. Like brown-colored stone men, they all wore black and had armor plating secured over their chest, lower torso, and upper thighs. Their hands, their most human-looking aspect, held a cluster of eight fingers—digits—and like the rest of their physiology's makeup, was more mineral-based than fleshy. Their every movement produced the sound of stone grating against stone. That sound, multiplied times ten as the bridge crew constantly moved about, was getting beyond irritating.

At twenty-six, Leon felt he had a good many years

ahead. He certainly was not ready to die, either at the hands of these raiders, or by Tromian cannon fire. He stood and walked around the bridge perimeter to the communications officer. He leaned over and began entering the code onto a touchpad device. He had this, the first access point code, memorized. Actually, he had the code for every access point memorized—each of the ten different sets of geometric symbols. Once the last symbol was entered, a return Tromian transmission indicated they'd received clearance to proceed.

Leon knew the next challenge for the Pharloms would be staying hidden from Tromian sensors. He'd be surprised if they weren't detected already.

"Eighteen ships won't go undetected from this point on, Grand Overseer," Leon said, as he returned to his oversized chair, back on Mangga's left.

"Yes. We most definitely have been detected."

"Then the rest of the codes won't help you … they'll lock us out," Leon said, suddenly feeling uneasy.

"We only needed access into the solar system … this first set of codes. The only ones we did not possess. I thank you for your help in that regard. Now … no more of your services will be required."

"But how will you—"

The Grand Overseer cut him off, sounding annoyed. "I suggest you not speak, nor bring further attention to yourself. Remember, you are our guest here … cause problems and you'll be eliminated."

Leon sat back and kept his mouth shut. The center hologram was active—showing various planets and moons and, strangely, the all too quiet floating cannon platforms—moving past them in the silence of space.

The only thing Leon could come up with was he'd given them an additional few moments for the element of surprise.

It seemed a lot of trouble for all the effort. Truthfully, he didn't know what these people thought ... what they considered important, or not. They were raiders ... pillagers of worlds. Everyone had heard of the Pharloms. They would ravage at will all the planets within this solar system. Leon only knew he needed to get off this ship, away from the Pharloms, as soon as humanly possible. Leon recognized the tiny, light-blue world at the center of the hologram. So that was their destination ... Trom. As the planet grew larger, so too did the levels of excitement of the bridge crew. This was what they lived for.

"Um ... I need to use the facilities."

The Grand Overseer ignored him.

"I really need to go—"

"Quiet!" The Grand Overseer turned in Leon's direction then back toward the hologram. He spoke to the crewmember on his side. Leon remembered his name, something like Garbon ... or Carbon. Whatever his name was, he stood up and gestured for Leon to follow him. Before leaving the bridge, Leon gave a half-hearted wave to the Overseer. "I'll be right back."

"You're fortunate the Grand Overseer likes you," the bridge officer said.

Leon simply nodded at that, not sure being liked by the Overseer was such a good thing.

They turned and entered another corridor. The air was humid, hot and sticky. And the deck was gritty beneath his feet—as if there was a beach nearby and nobody had remembered to wipe their feet. The corridors were wide, like the chairs, and everything else, too, aboard this Pharlom ship. Leon pegged the Pharlom walking in front of him to be several thousand pounds ... easily. The problem was guesstimating where his heart was located. How the hell could he even ball park it? So he didn't try. He studied the placement of the body armor and saw where each section of armor was loosely strapped in place. Perhaps in battle they tighten these things up a little. Leon also paid attention to ridgelines of his rock-like skin. Big sections, like continents—like tectonic plates that moved on their own, as the big creature walked. In between those rocky plates would be his only access to the soft organics within. With well-practiced efficiency, Leon pulled a slender-bladed knife from a hidden sheath at the back of his collar. Garbon ... or Carbon must have detected the movement because he slowed, turning his large girth around to face Leon. Leon didn't hesitate—he drove the blade of his knife up at an angle where his armor gapped open—in between the lower torso and his chest tectonic plates ... once ... twice ... three times.

Chapter 3

Alchieves System
Pharlom Command Warship

Leon jumped back as the Pharlom creature staggered, stumbled, and fell face forward onto the deck. He was fairly sure the huge creature was dead, even before hitting the deck. He was also fairly sure the racket from its fall could be heard all the way back to the bridge. Leon moved quickly, removing an energy weapon side arm from the Pharlom, who now looked more like a pile of rocks than anything else. He hesitated, looking both ways, up and down the corridor, preparing for others to come running at him any second. No one came. Leon examined the weapon in his hand. It was immense—suited for someone with fingers the size of bananas. He placed two fingers over the trigger and tested his grip. It would have to do. Leon took one last look at Garbon, or Carbon, or whatever the hell his name was, and hurried down the corridor.

He knew exactly where he needed to go. One thing in Leon's favor—the Pharloms typically designed their vessels with only one primary deck. They didn't like stairways. You wouldn't find an elevator on board, either—their enormous weight prohibited its usage. The ship was an oblong sphere, so Leon kept moving down the curved corridor toward its wider stern section. Eventually he knew he'd run into the flight deck. There he'd find a ship. Unfortunately, though, the Pharloms weren't much on using smaller, individual-type space vessels. Their girth alone prohibited them from getting in and out of small spaces. But Leon did notice there were other vessels about when he'd first arrived, more like excavation and utility vehicles stored within the ship's flight deck. He wasn't sure if any of them were space faring, and only hoped he'd have time to find out.

Leon felt through the soles of his shoes the unmistakable pounding of multiple Pharloms on the move up ahead—the deck vibrated as if dual pile drivers were approaching. A klaxon alarm blared and he heard the computerized voice of an AI. His internal nano-devices were already translating, as the sectional coordinates of his current position were given out. He looked for somewhere to hide—a hatchway or an intersecting corridor … anything. What he found was neither right nor left, but overhead, where a wide support girder ran the width of the ship. *How do I get up there?* From the deck to the beam, he guessed, was about ten feet. Taking large, quick steps backward, he took a deep breath and ran. He angled toward the side bulkhead and jumped, using his right foot to push off halfway up the bulkhead. That gave him the extra few inches he needed to reach up and grab the girder with the fingertips of both hands. He hung there, swaying back and forth for several seconds, expecting to see Pharloms come into view around the curve of the corridor any moment. He managed to pull himself high enough that he could reach one hand up, and over, the cross beam, which gave him enough of a secure handhold to pull his torso and legs up. The girder was no more than nine inches across but it was wide enough for him to lie down sideways. Leon had no sooner pulled his legs up on the beam when three Pharloms appeared. He knew from experience they were all out running. Any other species would see him lying up there, pretty much in plain view—but these rock people didn't have a neck to swivel. They slowed … here were the coordinates the AI had most recently indicated for his position. They passed by beneath him and thundered on. As soon as they were around the bend, he jumped down and continued toward the stern.

More Pharloms were looking for him. Twice, Leon needed to repeat the same maneuver—jumping up, grabbing onto, then lying on an overhead support girder. Eventually, he was certain, they would see him. He figured he'd already traversed a quarter mile when he heard, in the distance, noise coming from the flight deck ahead. He slowed his pace and stayed close to the bulkhead. At a wide hatchway, he peered around the corner.

Leon had wondered about his relatively easy escape—the lack of any real initiative by the Pharloms to apprehend him. All that was answered now. The Pharlom ship was no longer in space; in fact, from what he could see through the wide open doors of the flight deck, they were already on the ground. Beyond the doors was the misty-blue world of Trom. They'd landed at the edge of a city. From his perspective, Leon guessed it was the capital city of Cammilon. No less than two hundred Pharlom soldiers, each loaded up with immense packs, and equally immense energy rifles, were methodically heading off the ship onto Trom soil. The invasion there had begun.

Leon was not new to war … to battle. As early as his teens, he'd been involved in the Craing War … personally killing hundreds of Craing, or those they'd sent into battle on their behalf. He'd also been wounded and nearly killed. As a Seaman in the Allied forces, he'd served under several commanders, most notably Admiral Perry Reynolds. He was taken under the admiral's wing from age seventeen on, and had learned much, until the small destroyer he was assigned to was hit by three consecutive plasma blasts and forced to make an emergency crash landing onto a desolate, pretty much uninhabited planet nicknamed Genocide 5, or more commonly Gen5. Leon, the only survivor on board the mangled destroyer, suffered a broken arm and ankle. Gen5 became his home for nearly a year. Marooned, he learned to hunt the local game, which he called *rippers*; nastily mean, rodent-like creatures, with abnormally large canines … they were an acquired taste. After thirteen months, his NanoCom saved him. Since all communications equipment on board the ship was destroyed, he not only needed a space vessel to come within range of the desolate planet, he needed, too, to connect with someone also fitted with a NanoCom. As it turned out, Sean Doogin, a scraggly old U.S. petty officer who'd gone AWOL from the Allied forces five years earlier, rescued him. Leon, in no hurry to return to fighting the Craing and feeling more than a little abandoned by his Allied cohorts, partnered up with Doogin for two years. He was introduced to a life he'd had little awareness of previously. Much of space's commerce took place in what was referred to as the Gray Sleeve. There was nothing for the right price that couldn't be acquired via the Gray Sleeve. A dark underworld where, to Leon's surprise, one could not only make a good living but have the adventure of a lifetime in the process. Sure, it was dangerous. Doogin found that out six months earlier, when he was killed fleeing the premises of a Bagram officer's living quarters. He'd become quite fond of the officer's wife and both were killed that evening. Leon inherited Doogin's somewhat beat up ship, called the *SpaceRunner*. Twenty-five years old, the ship had good bones, was ridiculously fast, and had some cool state of the art features. At the moment, Leon wished he weren't still a light-year's distance away from his ship.

The Pharlom soldiers were gone—headed for the city. The planet would be ravaged for its natural resources, but first cleansed of its inhabitants. From what Leon knew of the Tromian people, they were good traders, avoided war, and definitely didn't deserve what would be happening here.

Leon brought his attention toward the vehicles parked along the periphery of the flight deck. They were all large—beat-to-shit excavation tractors, along with several general transportation vehicles. One was definitely space worthy: an old Alliance delivery scout. He'd flown aboard the same type of shuttle countless times when serving in the military.

Just then Leon realized he wasn't alone on the flight deck. He heard the ratcheting sound of a projectile weapon being readied. The Pharloms still used what was the equivalent of a machine gun type weapon, and a large one was now pointed directly at his head. He raised both hands—one of which was still gripping the overlarge plasma pistol.

Without thinking, Leon dove to his right, behind a grouping of stacked, large metal canisters. The Pharlom immediately began firing. The ear-shattering noise, from large caliber projectiles ricocheting off the metal canisters, the deck, and the bulkhead behind him, was near deafening. Leon half crawled, half ran out from his hiding place into the open. He was dead, anyway, if he stayed there another few seconds. Holding the pistol in both hands, two fingers over the trigger, he fired in the general direction of the Pharlom. The weapon bucked in his hands with incredible force. *This is an impressive weapon*, he thought, trying to reel in his aim while he ran. The Pharloms weren't the quickest bunch when it came to close-combat fighting and that was Leon's saving grace. He dove again, as more rounds sparked off the deck plating where his feet stood only two seconds earlier. Leon continued to fire, even as he landed hard on the metal surface. He kept his fingers tightly pulling on the trigger and, like chipping away at a boulder with a hammer, big chips of the creature's rocky exterior fragmented off, flying into the air. He brought his aim up to the rocky creature's head area and continued firing. Its bowling ball-sized head exploded into a dust cloud and the Pharlom's body clanged down in a stony heap onto the deck.

Leon was already up and running toward the delivery scout. The entrance to the vehicle was through a side hatch. It was open and Leon ran inside without slowing down. Making an immediate right turn he stood at the controls. There were no pilot or copilot seats and the controls were a jury-rigged mess. Obviously configured for a Pharlom's big hands, it took Leon several moments to figure things out. With the primary drive whirling up to speed, Leon pulled back on the controls, got the old delivery scout up off the deck, and turned in the direction of the open bay doors. He goosed the small ship forward, out into the Trom sunlight.

There were fifteen or so other ships, positioned on the landscape below him, on the outskirts of the city. Hundreds of Pharlom soldiers were advancing through the streets. Leon brought the delivery scout into city space, not really knowing why he didn't simply escape … head for the upper atmosphere. Perhaps it was because he, himself, felt partly responsible for the Pharloms being here. He looked down through the observation window and saw Tromian resistance—men and women firing on the approaching soldiers … making a stand. A woman—a mother and her two small children—ran from a building. They were holding hands and clearly terrified.

"No ... don't go that way!" Leon yelled aloud. But it was already too late. All three ... the mother and her two small children, turned the corner and ran headlong into the path of three Pharlom soldiers. They were struck down with heavy stone fists and, like insects, stomped on with gargantuan boulder-like feet as the Pharlom soldiers then continued moving further into the city.

Chapter 4

Alchieves System
Delivery Scout, Planet Trom, Skies Above
Cammilon City

Leon soon realized he wasn't alone in the sky above Cammilon. Another Pharlom warship, this one a small attack marauder, was systematically firing its primary plasma weapon down into the city below. Several miles away, a tall building, which had withstood several direct strikes already, suddenly fell—massive edifice pieces crashing onto the crowded streets.

He watched as more and more Tromians frantically poured into the streets from neighboring buildings. Leon's anger turned to fury. There had to be a way to help ... to do something!

He kept the rickety delivery scout hovering, several hundred feet up, in an alleyway between two skyscraper buildings, as he continued to watch the marauder. Every second he stayed hiding ... doing nothing ... hundreds, if not thousands, were being massacred. He had an idea—one possibility—bouncing around in his head, but he quickly shooed it away. It was insane … suicidal. But nothing else was coming to mind. What *was* working for him, in his favor, was the fact that his nano-devices would allow him to communicate with that Pharlom marauder. He could probably pass himself off as one of their own. The Pharloms had proven to be fairly dim-witted. Added to that, he was flying one of their vessels. But would he be granted permission to enter their flight deck?

Currently, the attack marauder was concentrating its weapon fire on a distant bridge. Vehicles, not unlike automobiles back on Earth, were stationary—a massive traffic jam pileup. People were running, trying to escape the inevitable. Similar to the destruction of the tall building moments before, the center of the bridge disappeared in a flash, causing the supporting ends of the structure to precariously lean in, then to fall forward into the river below. All that remained was a spiraling plume of black smoke.

A decision was made on the spot; Leon needed to get on that marauder. Somehow he'd commandeer it and do what he could to protect this besieged city. He was likely to get himself killed in the process … there was very little doubt about that.

He spent the next minute trying to figure out the delivery scout's communications system. After three separate tries, he reached the marauder's communications officer. Access to the flight deck was granted, but he'd need to hurry … they were leaving as soon as the city was leveled.

It was then that Leon saw her. Eight stories up on the building to his left—through an open window—was a slender Tromian woman. She looked to be younger than him, perhaps a university student? With a small satchel slung over one shoulder she stood still, watching him. He could tell she was trying to determine if he was friend or foe. A gust of wind billowed her long blond hair—her eyes stayed locked on his. Then her lips moved—she was saying something. Somehow, above the incessant noise outside, Leon knew exactly what she was conveying: *Help me ... please help me.*

The momentary distraction caused him to lose track of the attack marauder. Leon looked back at the destroyed bridge, then over to the horizon—there, several high up cloud-ports were ablaze—billowing black smoke trailed off like distant smoke signals in the wind. There was no sign of the ship. As a shadow darkened the delivery scout's cockpit, Leon realized the marauder was directly overhead. Suddenly, he could smell a change in the ozone and the hairs on his arms stood on end. An instant later a bright blue plasma bolt, crackling like thunder, shot down from the attack marauder above. Leon watched as the building to his left began to vibrate and shake violently. The young woman was screaming now and reaching for something to hold on to. Leon accelerated the delivery scout forward, away from the building—he thought he heard her scream something after him. He accelerated out of the narrow alleyway and, once clear of the buildings on both sides, ratcheted the controls all the way to the left, made a sharp U-turn, and reentered the same alleyway. The delivery scout had its sliding hatch door facing in now, toward the building under attack. It was clear the structure was disintegrating from the inside out. Fire spewed out from at least half of the nearby windows.

Leon goosed the scout craft forward while he desperately searched for the same window and the young woman with the blond hair. She wasn't there. *Did she succumb to the white-hot plasma blasts—did the floor she'd been on already collapse?* No! There she was ... running back toward the same window. Leon wasn't in the right location. In one fluid maneuver, he had the delivery scout scoot forward three windows ahead, hugging to the side of the building. With the delivery scout hovering in place, Leon was quickly out of his seat and leaving the cockpit. He slid open the hatch and there she was—no more than five feet away. Angry flames flared as if grabbing for her, reaching up and around her from behind.

"You'll have to jump!"

He didn't need to ask twice. Arms outstretched, she leapt into his open arms. Her forward momentum plowed them both backward into the delivery scout and down onto the grimy deck. She lay perfectly still in his arms for several long moments. With her head buried in his chest, Leon could smell a faint scent of smoke in her hair. His eyes traveled down to her bare arms, which were still tightly wrapped around him. She pulled back and lifted her face away from his chest. With their faces now just inches apart, she looked into his eyes. *God, she's more beautiful than I'd first thought.* Something was clanging against the top of the delivery scout. They were being bombarded with debris raining down from above.

"I need to get us out of here."

He pushed her aside with a bit more force than intended. He scurried into the cockpit on all fours and, without looking, punched the controls forward. All he could do was hope there was nothing obstructing their forward movement. At virtually the same moment, the building … her building, behind them, began to collapse.

The attacking marauder moved methodically away, seeking another target. This time its sights were set on what looked to be a hospital, or perhaps a school. The young woman stood next to Leon now, in the cockpit. Tears filled her eyes as she took in the devastation before them. She turned to look at him. "Can't you do something?"

Leon glanced over to her. *You mean more than saving your*

life? But he kept his thoughts to himself.

She turned around and assessed the dirty, small vessel. "What is this thing? Some kind of trash pickup vehicle? What are you? A garbage man?"

"No! I stole this from the Pharloms."

"Like ... on purpose? You stole a trash vehicle? One that has no weapons and probably can't even leave this atmosphere?"

"Hey ... there were slim pickings at the time."

She turned back toward the mayhem in front of them. "We have to stop them ... kill every last one of them."

If he'd had any doubts about taking her with him ... into the marauder, they were now gone. She would die to protect her home. "Hold on to something, we're going to steal another ship."

She looked back at him questioningly, then simply nodded. The attack marauder was still close. Leon brought the delivery scout up vertically, until it was parallel with the bottom of the Pharlom vessel, which, he now discovered, was a larger ship, especially at this close proximity, than he'd previously realized.

"Where the hell is the flight deck?" he questioned out loud, scanning from one end of the vessel's outer hull to the other.

"There!" she said, extending a graceful arm, pointing higher up, toward the upper section of the marauder.

She smiled and looked excited. She looked courageous! *My kind of woman.*

He brought the delivery scout up, closing the gap between the two vessels. The bay doors were already open and he could see significant activity pulsing inside, where no less than thirty large hulking Pharlom soldiers milled about. Both Leon and the woman took a quick step backward, trying to stay out of sight.

The flight deck was a relatively open space. No fighters or drones around, contending for a parking space. Leon selected a relatively unoccupied area, deep within the bay. He set the delivery scout down and shut off the scout's drive. They looked at each other. Leon shrugged. "Just so you know, this is probably the stupidest thing I've ever done ... and I've done more than my share of stupid things."

"Then why don't you stop talking about it and go actually do something? People are dying out there." He noticed she was holding his Pharlom pistol. It looked ridiculously large in her small hand.

The delivery scout's hatch was still open from when he had rescued her. He stepped back into the rear section and tentatively approached the opening. He peeked out. No one was paying much attention to them ... yet. He held out his hand. "I'll take that."

Reluctantly, she placed the energy weapon in his hand. "I can show you how to shoot that, if you need me to."

"Thanks, I think I'm good," he said, not sure if she was serious or just pulling his chain.

Two Pharlom soldiers now looked their way. They dropped what they were doing and began to approach. Leon turned to her, putting his index finger over his lips. Thinking better of it, he pointed toward the back of the hold, mouthing: "Get back there and make some noise. I'll need a distraction."

She looked at him with that same questioning expression. He flashed her a big smile and raised his eyebrows.

She rolled her eyes but did step further back into the delivery scout's hold.

Leon moved forward into the cockpit and stood sideways behind a narrow bulkhead. It didn't do much to hide his six-foot-two frame, but it would have to do. He heard the young woman clamoring around, slapping the walls, talking loudly— everything she could think of to bring attention her way.

The first Pharlom reached the delivery scout's open hatch, his big rock face unreadable. He stepped into the scout and made room for his Pharlom friend to join him. Immediately, their combined weight made the vehicle pitch precariously at an angle. The two Pharloms staggered, but still managed to stay on their feet. Neither took his attention away from the noisy, lunatic humanoid female standing less than ten feet away.

The barrels of their guns came up—both pointed in her general direction. Leon noticed they were holding the same projectile-type rifles fired at him earlier. He didn't want to think what those weapons could do to this beautiful woman. Leon stepped into the open, his own plasma weapon raised. Gripping the pistol in both hands, he fired, then kept on firing. Five plasma bolts ripped into the head of one Pharlom; then five plasma bolts ripped into the other. Leon repeated the same firing pattern, going back and forth three more times. Almost simultaneously, their heads blew apart—two dust clouds hanging in the air. Leon and the young woman instinctively stepped back to avoid the falling pile of rocks.

She glared at him. "Why did you wait so long to shoot? I thought I was going to die right here in this trash—"

"Hey, I just saved your life ... again. A simple thank you would suffice."

She shook her head at him, exasperated.

"By the way, I'm Leon ... Leon Pike. What's your name?"

"Hanna ... we need to get out of here."

Chapter 5

Sol System
The *Minian* — Open Space

A fter several months away, it felt good to be back on the *Minian* again. Jason left Grimes on the flight deck— she'd relayed his father's instructions that both he and Dira were to report to his ready room—pronto. As they exited onto the ship's twenty-third deck, there seemed to be full crew on board, and Jason found himself returning salutes as he passed crewmembers every minute or so. Being aboard, though, was also bittersweet. So much of the *Minian* was similar to *The Lilly* in design. Sure, this ship was substantially larger—with its forward to aft length reaching a little over one mile. It was also much newer—embracing more advanced Caldurian technology. Much of the vessel, the last time Jason was on board, he'd yet to explore.

The energy-based hatch to the captain's ready room was open and Jason heard his father's familiar baritone as he leaned in, knocking on the bulkhead.

"Don't be shy, get in here," his father bellowed.

Jason, with Dira in tow, entered the ready room and

found his father, Ricket and Granger, the tall Caldurian, seated at the conference table.

Granger had a smug look on his face. As tall as any human, Caldurians were similar in looks to the triangular-shaped headed Craing. With large eyes, they pretty much fit several stereotypical depictions of aliens in movies.

Each of the integrated displays, situated around the large compartment, displayed a different planetary system. Jason recognized about half of them; others, he was fairly sure, he'd never seen before.

"Have a seat."

Jason and Dira did as instructed.

"Hello, Captain ... it is good to see you again. And you, as well, Dira," Ricket said.

Dira replied first, "You're looking well, Ricket. I like your new uniform."

Jason then noticed they were all wearing new uniforms. Gone was the dreary, drab gray one, and everyone was garbed instead in navy blue, with a lighter blue piping around the sleeves and collar. The uniforms also looked substantially more formal.

Jason, surprised at seeing Granger even wearing a uniform, asked, "You're officially part of the crew?"

His father answered for him. "Granger's officially an Alliance officer. We all are. With the exception of a small fleet being provided for Earth's defense ... about thirty thousand ships, the Alliance fleet has been strategically dispersed throughout the Allied worlds ... with no less than one hundred and eighty thousand warships."

"That was very generous of you," Jason said.

"Not generous at all. Maintaining a fleet that size does not come cheap. It's an expense that needs to be distributed among all Alliance members."

That made perfectly good sense to Jason, but he noticed his father still hadn't answered his question. Jason tried again, "So, Granger ... what exactly is your job ... your command?"

"We'll get to that in a moment," his father interjected, looking annoyed at Jason's persistence.

Jason and Dira exchanged a quick glance. She, too, was leery of the Caldurian. On the positive side, he was a genius and knew this ship like no other. But he'd proven to be not only opportunistic, but also untrustworthy. He'd even provided Caldurian technology to the Craing for some stint of time.

The admiral picked up on Jason's less than pleased expression, but continued on anyway, "As I mentioned, your paperwork has been processed and fast-tracked. You are officially vice-admiral within our Allied forces. Congratulations."

Jason nodded and said, "Thank you, I think. I'm not sure what that higher rank entails, but I'll do my best ... whatever that is."

"What do you mean?" his father asked.

"Even a vice-admiral basically holds down a desk-job position. I'm assuming I'll oversee, or help oversee, some of our Allied fleet assets."

His father chuckled at that. "You ... a desk job? How long do you think that would last? A week? Maybe two? No. Your services are required in a different regard." The admiral paused, as if to collect his thoughts. "Look ... things are different now. While the Craing Empire is no longer a threat ... no longer even an empire ... their vast interstellar military today contributes the bulk of the Alliance fleet. With that said ... there are monumental situational changes happening throughout the galaxy ... beyond that, I can't be concerned. The Milky Way has quickly become a galactic mess. Infighting ... piracy ... old conflicts, wars reigniting. It all comes down to interstellar instability that affects the Allied worlds. We don't want another Craing situation … not ever."

Jason shrugged. "What can you do? I mean, is it our job to police the galaxy?"

The room went quiet as the admiral continued to stare intently at Jason.

Then realization set in. "Oh, come on … you can't be serious?"

More silence. Ricket was looking down at the table. Granger was smiling.

"I'm policing the galaxy … a fucking policeman?"

The admiral, not doing a very good job hiding his own amusement, said, "Policing is your description, not mine. It needs to be done and it needs to be done now."

Jason saw Dira in his peripheral vision and she too was amused. *Why is this so funny to everyone else?*

"Why go to the trouble of giving me a promotion if I'm just going to be an interstellar Barney Fife?"

Even his father laughed out loud at that. "Look, this actually is serious business. Probably the most important posting for any Allied officer. The Alliance's wellbeing, as well as Earth's, depends on how well you do your assignment. We'll be providing you with tremendous resources to ensure that you have exactly what you need: ships, crew, security forces … you name it. You'll also be captaining the *Minian*."

That was unexpected. Jason began to grow more interested. "I still don't understand my whole vice-admiral-promotion thing."

"You'll be gone for weeks, maybe even months at a time. I want you to have the authority to make big decisions. Decisions not only affecting the Alliance, as a whole, but also the wellbeing of individual alien worlds. You'll have in-field responsibilities I wouldn't particularly envy. No, Star Watch will have to operate as close to an autonomous force as possible for it to be truly effective."

"Star Watch?"

"Yes, that's what we've named the armada."

"And how many ships are we talking about?"

"Twelve ... plus the *Minian*. Three light Craing cruisers, and nine heavy Craing cruisers."

"I'm just surprised you're not keeping the *Minian* here for yourself."

"I'll be fine. I'll now be stationed on the Drac-Vin vessel ... the *Assailant*; she will become my command ship."

Jason had forgotten about that ship. Almost as technologically advanced as the *Minian*, the vessel possessed two extra capabilities—both visual and sensors invisibility. She was also the same warship Ot-Mul, the deceased Drac-Vin leader, once captained.

"My suggestion to you, Vice-Admiral, is keep your rank on the down low. Maintain your former captaincy title for the crew."

"And what about me, Admiral? Where will I be stationed?" Dira asked.

Jason turned toward Dira—he'd totally capitalized the conversation, leaving her out. "I'm sorry, Dira. I should have—"

"She's a big girl, Captain ... let her talk for herself," the admiral said. "To answer your question, Dira, you too have been promoted. You've been elevated to the rank of Lieutenant Commander in charge of the *Minian*'s onboard medical hospital."

"Thank you, Admiral. I won't let you down."

"I'm sure you won't. My only worry is that your obvious close relationship with Vice-Admiral Reynolds will get in the way. Needless to say, you'll need to be discreet. I'm not in a position to tell you to break off your relationship ... just don't flaunt it in front of the crew."

"Yes, sir."

Jason brought his attention to Ricket. "You're coming with us?"

Ricket smiled. "I wouldn't miss it. As I understand the parameters of Star Watch's directives, not everything involves space policing. As your science officer, I hope to assist in the exploration of new worlds ... and to reestablish what the Caldurians first began."

Jason shook his head. "And what was that?"

"The habitats, what you refer to as the Zoo. I'd like to add portal access to other ... still undiscovered ... environments. I would find great pleasure in doing that."

"Well, you've certainly earned any posting you desire, Ricket. That sounds like a terrific, admirable, quest." Jason turned his attention back to his father. "Who will you have leading the security forces?"

"I can't do everything for you, Captain. Other than Ricket, Dira and Granger, you'll need to pick and choose your own leadership team. By the way ... you have a day to accomplish exactly that. There's a nasty bit of inter-planetary strife happening on Trom in the Alchieves system."

"We'll be ready," Jason said.

"Good ... now get out of here ... we have other business to discuss."

As Jason and Dira exited the ready room, it occurred to him he still hadn't been told what Granger's duties would entail.

Chapter 6

Sol System
The *Perilous*, Planet Earth — Nearing
Boulder, CO

Jason, sitting next to Grimes in the cockpit of the *Perilous*, had a full day ahead of him and was ready to get an early start. They'd reached the North American continent on Earth, specifically Boulder, Colorado, just as the rising sun highlighted the ridged Rocky Mountain foothills.

While much of the United States had turned the corner in containing the zombie-like *peovils*, in this part of the country—Colorado, Utah, Wyoming, and New Mexico—the *peovils* were still causing havoc. Not only were they becoming more violent, they seemed to be getting smarter, and more resourceful, too. It all started when Ot-Mul, at that time a Craing fleet commander, dispatched a series of attack drones to hundreds of locations around Earth. The drones released large spider-like creatures called molt weevils that systematically hunted, captured, and eventually cocooned their prey ... primarily humans. With billions, nearly half the world's population, taken by the dreadful alien beings, the molt weevils finally began to die off. But that wasn't the end of it—about half of those poor souls still living within the cocoons would become something else completely—something even worse than the molt weevil ... half human half molt weevil, the zombie-like ... *peovils*. Millions of them still wandered the Earth, alone and in packs; they never slept, and their hunger for human flesh was rarely satisfied.

Grimes brought the shuttle down in the parking lot of a shopping mall, directly in front of a Target store. Through the observation window, Jason noticed the lot was half-filled with pickup trucks and other four-wheel drive vehicles; all seemed covered in mud and grime.

"Stay with the shuttle. This shouldn't take long."

"Aye, Cap," Grimes said, reaching for a paperback book lying atop the control panel.

* * *

Three good ol' boys, dressed in faded camos and holding M16s, watched as Jason approached the store's front entrance. The center one spat something brown toward Jason's feet.

"Hold it right there," the spitter said.

Jason did as he was told. "I'm here to see Billy Hernandez. The man I believe you work for."

"He's busy. 'Bout ready to kick off another hunt this morning."

"That's fine ... I just need to see him for a minute," Jason said.

The three men looked similar. All had full beards, matching Denver Broncos caps, and dressed alike in Army surplus duds, although each man, obviously, had never served a single day in any branch of the U.S. military.

Jason, thus far, had avoided using his NanoCom to contact Billy. He wanted their meet-up to be face-to-face. The man on the left pulled a walkie-talkie from a pocket, brought it to his mouth, and uttered something unintelligible. While waiting for a response, he too spat something brown, again, in the rough direction of Jason's feet. The man to the far right brought out a small tin of Skoal and held it up … an offering. Jason shook his head. He watched the man place a good-sized pinch of the tobacco into his mouth.

The automatic doors behind the three bearded men slid open. Billy appeared, looking distracted, but became all smiles once he spotted Jason. Billy had been Jason's best friend for the better part of ten years. Like Jason, he too had been a Navy SEAL. Jason first recruited Billy, then numerous other SEALs, on to *The Lilly*; most had served under Jason's command at some time or another.

"Captain!"

"Sorry to just drop in like this, Billy."

Billy pulled Jason into a bear hug; the big Cuban-American smelled of both cigars and sweat. Pulling apart, Billy said, "You here to lend a hand? We could definitely use someone like you—" He then saw the *Perilous* and reassessed Jason, dressed in a spacer's jumpsuit.

"Oh, no … tell me it isn't so? Tell me you haven't come out of retirement?"

Jason shrugged. "I'm back in space. Commanding the *Minian*. Seems there's a big need for intergalactic law enforcement … something called Star Watch."

"And you're here to recruit me?"

"Something like that."

Billy gestured toward the parking lot and they moved away from the three men. It began to drizzle but that didn't stop Billy from lighting up a fresh cigar. "You know, I'd follow you anywhere, Cap ... but I'm right in the middle of this nightmare. Fucking zombies coming down at night ... right into the locals' homes and what they're doing isn't pretty. Sometimes whole families are ... anyway, I need to finish this."

"Figured as much. Had to ask, though. They're lucky to have you," Jason said.

"With luck ... we'll get the upper hand on things around here within the next few weeks. I'll catch up to you then."

"And Gunny?" Jason asked.

"She's here. Been at my side the whole time. We're a good team. There's no way she'd leave now—"

He stopped talking when he saw the tall muscular woman with dark skin exit the Target. She had a large duffle slung over one shoulder and was heading in their direction. Billy took a long drag on his stogie. "Crap."

Jason opened his arms wide and gave Gunny Orion a hug. After several moments, she pulled away and, looking guilty, glanced over at Billy—her boyfriend now for close to two years.

"I'm sorry, Billy."

"Come on ... you love it here. We're doing good work together. I thought this was what you wanted," Billy said, shock registering on his face.

"No, Billy ... *you* love it here. I can't take another second in this place. It's dirty and the zombies are disgusting. I'm going back with the captain. If he'll have me?" She looked over at Jason, her eyebrows raised.

He studied her broad, attractive face. All of her skin actually held an intricate pattern of tattooed geometric symbols. She'd been his right hand on the bridge for as long as he'd been in space. She was a former Marine and not one who'd accepted gender-biased limitations. Although Orion looked

Earth human-like, she was actually from a planet called Tarkin. She'd originally served on board *The Lilly*, with his father and, prior to that, she had been quite famous on Tarkin— some sort of sports figure, from what Jason had heard.

"It just so happens I'm in need of someone competent at tactical. But you sure you want to leave here, Gunny? I don't want to get between things for you two."

Both Orion and Jason looked at Billy. "You go … I can't leave. People depend on me."

Orion leaned in and gave Billy a long kiss on the lips. "I'm sorry, I really am. But you'll know where to find me … right?"

Billy slowly nodded. He looked at Jason. "Take good care of her."

"I will." Jason shook his friend's hand goodbye.

* * *

Back in the *Perilous* again, their next stop was on the other side of the planet. The last time Jason was there, he'd visited both Pyongyang, the *Kumsusan Palace of the Sun*— sometimes called *Kim Jong Un Palace*—as well as Ryongsong residence … where Jason and his team had stormed the young North Korean leader's private residence.

But today, the *Perilous* was heading north, into the Paegam region in Ryanggang province. It was there, along a wide plateau, surrounded by northern Korea's highest mountains, that hundreds of rhino-warrior beasts had made their home. The land, annexed at the end of the Craing War, was where Traveler … the de facto leader of his tribe, had chosen to reside with his species. Traveler, and some of his kin, had fought at Jason's side many times in the past. The beast somewhat resembled an African rhinoceros, with his thick gray hide

44

and two substantial horns protruding from his forehead. But all resemblance stopped there. Rhino-warriors, whose two home planets were destroyed in the Craing War, walked upright; they were typically seven feet tall, and weighed close to one thousand pounds. If their physiques weren't intimidating enough, the rhino-warriors' weapon of choice was a Thor-like heavy hammer that weighed hundreds of pounds and could easily flatten a man to the size of an Egg McMuffin with one blow. From everything Jason had heard, the rhinos were happy here—plenty of game to hunt, and, for the most part, the locals gave them a wide berth.

Grimes brought the *Perilous* down close to the treetops. Like a sea of green, the tall evergreens were thick and lush. He had yet to spot any roads, or even the ground, for that matter. Then, abruptly, the trees were gone, revealing a wide, hilly plateau crisscrossed with azure streams, which seemed to culminate into a distant lake. Then, off in the distance, familiar dome shapes appeared. Rhino-warriors hand built the mud structures as communal centers, as well as individual domiciles. Gray smoke billowed into the air from several small fires and from a larger fire at the center of the camp.

Grimes maneuvered the *Perilous* down within twenty feet of the ground and followed the winding path of a stream until they reached the encampment. She found an open area, just west of the big, blazing bonfire, and set the shuttle on the ground. Jason mentally prepared himself for making another sales pitch, but looking out at the beautiful landscape, he had little confidence he'd be taking Traveler, or any of the others, up into space today.

Grimes opened the back hatch, and Jason and Orion, both unarmed, descended the gangway. A semi-circle of male and female rhinos encircled the shuttle. Most were unarmed, though several gripped heavy hammers in their hands.

Traveler stood apart from the others. He held a heavy hammer and was clad in his typical battle attire—a short leather skirt with a thick leather breastplate.

Jason and Orion walked to Traveler and stopped six feet in front of him.

"It is good to see you again, my friend," Jason said.

Traveler did not answer, at first. Over the years, Jason had learned to read the rhino's subtle facial expressions, and at this moment, Traveler was not happy.

"You come now?"

Jason didn't understand. Was *now* significant? Was today some kind of special rhino holiday they'd interrupted? "I'm sorry ... is this a bad time?" Jason asked.

"Why have I been left here?"

"What do you mean? This is the land you personally selected for your people. From what I've heard they are happy here."

"They are happy. I am not. I thought you understood that I was to return to my own home within HAB 17?"

"You don't want to stay here ... among your own kind ... to lead your people?"

Traveler gazed in the direction of his tribe. "I relinquished my role as leader one week after arriving here. In the anticipation that you would come for me ... take me back to my home on HAB 17."

"I'm sorry, Traveler. I didn't realize that's what you wanted. You know that *The Lilly*'s been destroyed?"

Traveler's shoulders visibly slumped.

"But hey ... that's okay ... Habitat 17 still exists; we can access it from the *Minian*. On the *Minian* it's called HAB 170."

Jason recognized Traveler's happiness with that news. "Listen, I will gladly relocate you to the habitat ... but I'm here to ask if you will still ... um—"

"Yes, Captain Reynolds, I will fight at your side. Together, warriors again!"

Chapter 7

Sol System
The *Perilous*, Planet Earth, Paegam region in Ryanggang province, North Korea

---

As it turned out, Traveler wasn't the only one leaving. Two hundred and fifty or so other rhinos also wished to return to HAB 17. Traveler wanted to leave right then, with Jason; the others would be picked up, via numerous shuttles, sometime later in the day.

Jason had one more, the most important, stop to make. Grimes entered the restricted airspace above Washington, D.C., and got clearance to land on the White House's east lawn. To say Washington was hit hard by the infestation would be a profound understatement. Millions of people along the Eastern Seaboard had succumbed to the molt weevils. The large, multi-legged creatures moved like lightning and had their victims in their clutches within seconds of any encounter. After that, it was mere minutes before a man, woman, or child was enshrouded in a cocoon of web-like material. Within a matter of days, Washington, D.C. was reduced to a ghost town. Even now, most streets and sidewalks were deserted of traffic. Government offices, for the most part, were still unoccupied. Earlier inhabitants of the White House, Capitol Building, and other federal buildings, had all been taken. With that in mind, it wasn't far-fetched that Nan, Jason's ex-wife, had risen from her entry-level cabinet position, secretary of inter-stellar relations, to become the acting president of the United States. The public, as it turned out, loved her ... wanted no one else to lead the country, or even the world, out of its most desperate situation.

"Hang loose, I need an hour," Jason said, getting to his feet.

"We're fine ... go ... spend time with your family," Grimes said.

Jason was met at the bottom of the gangway by an armed contingent of five U.S. Marines. In the distance, no less than fifty heavily armed Marines surrounded the outer perimeter of the presidential property. Jason fell in stride with the small escort team and was ushered toward the nearby white residence.

Left by the Marines at the rear entrance, he entered the White House through a back doorway. The very first sound he heard was that of a baby crying. Jason smiled. *Kid's got some lungs on him.*

Compared to the nation's capital in general, the White House was bustling. Jason had visited six times over the past few months, since the birth of his son, and it was good to see so many people back in the business of running the country.

Jason found his way to the West Wing and the Oval Office. He walked over to the large redwood desk and looked about the empty room. A middle-aged woman peeked her head in from around the corner. "Good morning, Captain Reynolds ... She's upstairs ... nursing."

"Thank you, Ms. Pollard."

Jason followed the slender woman down several hallways

until he found the stairway leading to the family residences above. Gone now were the sounds of a baby crying … replaced, instead, with the voices of two young girls arguing about something. Nan, seated in an armchair, his son in her arms, was adjusting the top of her blouse, tugging it back into place.

"He won't eat. Maybe he knew you were coming." She stood and handed him the light-blue bundle. A small pinkish head peeked out one end of the blanket. Small eyes widened when they locked on to Jason and the infant made soft, happy cooing sounds. Nan leaned in and kissed the top of young Michael's head, then kissed Jason's cheek. "It's good to see you again … we've missed you. You doing okay? Heard you're heading back into space."

"Yes and yes. Doing fine and yes, decided it was time to get back into the mix of things. Seems my father's found something for me to do. Some kind of space marshal position."

"I heard," she said with a smile. "Wyatt Earp of the final frontier …"

"How are the kids?"

"Go see for yourself; they both were excited when they heard you were coming by today."

"In a moment," he said, unable to take his eyes off his son. He was beautiful. Amazing. Jason wondered what the future held for the little guy. Would he follow in his father's and grandfather's footsteps, venturing out into the far reaches of space? Or, perhaps, follow his mother's path and become a future world leader?

"Dad!"

It was Mollie, running into the presidential master suite. She wore a yellow dress and had her long hair parted neatly down the middle. Jason quickly handed Michael off to Nan and prepared for the incoming hug. Mollie, her arms wrapping around him, asked, "Where have you been? Why do you always stay away so long?"

"I was just here last week, kiddo. Before that, you spent two weeks with me in California ... aren't you sick of me yet?"

"No! I want you to come live with us ... here in the White House."

"Yeah ... that's going to happen," Nan said sarcastically.

Just then Jason noticed Boomer standing in the doorway. She was dressed in jeans and a sweatshirt—her hair pulled back in a tight ponytail. Jason and Nan exchanged a quick glance.

"She hates it here. She's also mad at you for making her live here," Nan said.

"She's also mean to the help ... she plays tricks on people. She's not very nice, Dad," Mollie added, making a scowly face in the direction of Boomer.

Jason continued to stare at his obviously unhappy little girl. He knew it when he first sent her away to stay here with her mother. Mollie and Boomer shared the same DNA and were actually the very same person. But, over the past year, since a bizarre time realm mishap that resulted in there being two identical Mollies, their individual personality traits produced two entirely different young girls. While Mollie was much like her mother, Boomer (who'd renamed herself) was ... well ... hard to describe. It was as though she was meant to travel in space. Even at ten, she was an adrenalin junkie ... not so unlike her father. She didn't particularly get along well with kids her own age, and was fascinated by martial arts. Taken under the wing of close-combat instructors aboard *The Lilly*, she'd become scarily competent throwing knives, among other things.

"Are you going to just stand there making mean faces at me, or can I get a hug?"

Boomer squinted her eyes at him, attempting to make as hateful a glare as possible.

"Knock it off, Boomer," Nan said, irritated. "You were just saying this morning how much you missed your father."

With that Boomer spun on her heels and left the doorway. Nan rolled her eyes. "Kids ... everything has to be so dramatic."

"I'll talk to her."

"Good ... she's driving us all a little crazy."

Jason found Boomer in her bedroom. It was a fairly stark room, compared to Mollie's. There was no sense of permanence. She'd never really settled in. Boomer sat on her bed and pretended to read a book.

Jason sat down next to her. She didn't look up. "What are you reading there?"

"A book; what does it look like?"

He continued to gaze down at her. He let her smart mouth go ... for now. "I wanted to tell you, I'm heading back into space for a while."

"Good. I hope you stay away a long time. Maybe you and Dira can build a house on another planet and have lots of little kids and—"

"That's enough of that!"

She continued scowling, her face mean. She continued to pretend to read.

"I'm now captain of the *Minian* ... you know?"

That got a reaction. She was doing everything she could to keep a smile from her lips.

"Seems Ricket is excited about bringing new habitats into the Zoo ... He mentioned something ... I'm trying to remember what he said."

Boomer's eyes were now the size of small dinner plates. "What? Tell me what he said!"

"Just something about needing help in the Zoo ... it's really quite large, you know ... huge, in fact. I told him I'd help him find an assistant."

Her arms wrapped around his neck before he'd even finished the words. Her muffled voice rose up, her face buried in his chest. "I'm going with you? I can come with you, Dad?"

He looked down at her upturned, hopeful face. "Of course you can. I've already talked to your mom. If you want, you can live with me on the *Minian*."

She wiped away several tears and became all business. "Okay ... I'll need to bring Dewdrop ... That's not even an option."

"It's your droid ... that's not a problem. But understand, you'll be attending school. You'll also have—"

"I know, a new nanny ... someone like Petty Officer Miller. I miss her, Dad."

"I know you do. She cared about you and Mollie. We'll find the perfect person. Now let's get your things packed up together. It's time to go."

Chapter 8

Sol System
The *Minian*, Open Space — Nearing
Jefferson Station

Jason reviewed his virtual notebook on the trip back to the *Minian*. The admiral, it seemed, had been busy since he'd left for Earth—he'd already sent out Jason's marching orders for the following week.

"So, any idea where we're off to first, Cap?" Orion asked, filling the narrow space between the cockpit and the cabin behind it.

Jason, sitting in the copilot's chair, shifted to face her. "There are pockets of instability, including planetary infighting, piracy, and even several imminent world invasions. Obviously, the most egregious acts are apt to bring the greatest instability to the Alliance, and they are flagged as high priority and will be our top destinations."

Orion looked over at Jason's virtual notepad and he expanded the hovering holographic image so she too could see the report.

Jason continued, "There are two worlds in jeopardy. Trom,

typically a peaceful world, with much in the way of natural resources, is being invaded by the Pharloms, who sound
more like local thugs or bullies, out to flex their muscles now
that the Craing are no longer a threat. The Pharloms have a
small fleet of warships and are poised to land on Trom ... or
have already."

"And the other one?"

"The other planet in jeopardy is the Dacci Commonwealth. They're in the path of an approaching fleet of ships
from something called the Sahhrain."

"Oh ... I've definitely heard of the Sahhrain," Orion said,
her expression serious. "Dark is the word that comes to mind.
Their spiritual beliefs require them to live their lives in a solitary way. They don't have much commerce with outside star
systems and they're said to possess powerful supernatural
abilities."

"Well, it looks like they've kept to themselves for the last
twenty years. There's not much we know about them, other
than they have a fleet of no less than fifty warships ... their
home star system is desolate." He read on, noting that the
Sahhrain system had five planets circling a burnt-out sun.

"But why are the Sahhrain interested in the Dacci Commonwealth?" Orion asked.

"Greater access to the far reaches of the universe. Look
here," Jason said, pointing to a familiar spiral symbol. There,
within the Dacci Commonwealth's star system, was a Loop
wormhole. Both Jason and Orion knew from past experienc-
es these fixed location wormholes, interspersed throughout
the universe, were the Craing's primary means of far-reach-
ing interstellar travel. One reason they'd maintained such a
profound advantage and influence over their enemies for so
long.

"If the Sahhrain get access to that wormhole," Jason said,

"they'll be far more difficult to rein in. We don't want another Craing Empire-type escalation."

* * *

Jason eyed Earth's distant white moon and the shimmering cluster of lights beyond it. As they approached, details of the sprawling space base became more apparent. There were four sprawling military platforms for Allied combined fleets; dozens of moored warships were in maintenance there, for one thing or another. But the real attention-grabber was the newly-constructed *Jefferson Station*. As the recognized seat of the Alliance, all big decision-making policy took place there among the Allied worlds. Grimes slowed the *Perilous* as *Jefferson Station* filled the forward observation window. The station went against all preconceived, conventional, design principles. With that said, it was beautiful and inspiring, yet immense and intimidating at the same time. Jason had visited the station on several occasions and still found it captivating. There was the center hub disk, or saucer, spanning a thirty-mile radius, where the primary station's populace conducted business and also resided. Encircling the hub, almost twenty miles out, was a thick outer ring, which had its own ten, constantly rotating, encircling, round rings spaced evenly along the structure. Jason thought the smaller, perpendicular rings looked somewhat like little Ferris wheels.

Both the *Minian* and the significantly smaller *Assailant*, now the admiral's command ship, were parked several miles off in space. In the distance beyond was the bulk of the fleet—including several meganaughts, ten or more dreadnaughts, and hundreds of both heavy and light former Craing cruisers.

"We've been cleared onto the *Minian*'s flight deck, Captain," Grimes said.

"Take us in, Lieutenant."

* * *

Jason entered the *Minian*'s bridge with Boomer following two steps behind. The *Minian*'s AI announced, "Captain Reynolds has entered the bridge."

Once again, Jason was reminded of *The Lilly*—so similar, yet quite different as well. The *Minian* was larger—far more advanced. Heads turned in his direction, then to Boomer. She immediately moved to the command chair and sat down, her feet not quite reaching the deck. She placed her arms on the armrests, sat back, staring at the bemused faces, and said, "There's a new Captain Reynolds on board ... as you were, people."

That brought chuckles and several salutes. Jason winked at her and brought his attention to the forward right console where Granger, Ricket, and Bristol were involved in a heated discussion. The console was open, obviously going through some sort of modification.

"Hello, Captain," Ricket said. Both he and Bristol were on the deck, lying on their backs, holding handheld test equipment. Granger was seated in a chair in front of the console.

"What do we have here?"

Ricket sat up, then stood. "Captain ... we understand we'll be underway soon. In an attempt to get the *Minian* operating optimally, we've gone ahead and installed several upgrades."

"Doesn't look like you've been successful," Jason said, peering into the inside of the console; its wired bundles, he'd learned in the past, were called PhasePath Conduits.

"Hi, Orion ... report to your post!" said Boomer. Jason turned to see Gunny Orion entering the bridge as Boomer still play-acted captain.

"Aye, Captain," Gunny replied, sounding appropriately official and saluting the ten-year-old.

Jason brought his attention back to the others.

"This was a cluster-fuck from the get-go."

Jason took a step back as young, pimply-faced Bristol scooted out from underneath the console and sat up. Bristol was far from a military person. In fact, his past was check-ered at best ... brother to a psychotic pirate, Captain Stalls, who, among other things, was a mass murderer. But with all Bristol's faults, the least of which were a bad temper and a foul mouth, his past genius had saved countless crewmem-bers' lives, including Jason's. So Jason was willing to tolerate some of Bristol's shortcomings.

"Just tell me what's going on here. Our timetable for de-parture has been pushed up. We have to go."

"It's another of Granger's new Caldurian upgrades," Bristol said.

Jason looked down at Ricket; maybe he'd give him a straight answer.

"It's a problem tied to the communications system and the whole interchange wormhole process, Captain," Ricket said, referring to another aspect of what the technological-ly advanced Caldurian vessels were capable of, including their unique means to travel virtually unlimited distances across the universe. That ability was accomplished through a unique, permission-based communication to an elusive being of higher-consciousness known now as the interchange. The interchange was not a single being but several, or many; Ja-son wasn't sure how many. His only point of contact with the interchange was through an aquatic, wormlike being called a Drapple, who could be contacted through one of the on-board Zoo habitats. Staying within the Drapple's—and the interchange's—good graces was monumentally important, as it didn't dole out permission to move unhindered across the universe arbitrarily. Those bestowed with this ability had to adhere to certain moral constraints. The simple fact that his three crewmembers were messing with something so important, especially before a crucial mission, was crazy.

"Are you telling me we've lost the ability to call up an interchange wormhole?"

All three shook their heads in unison. "No no," Ricket said, "but Granger's upgrade does seem to have instigated a negative byproduct."

"What?"

"A significant time delay, Captain ... it seems now to take close to an hour from the time we've communicated our interchange wormhole in-and-out coordinates request to when the wormhole actually appears."

"So we've gone from something that worked perfectly fine ... took mere minutes to accomplish, to now taking an hour? That's ridiculous ... not to mention, the long delay could put both ship and crew in potentially dangerous situations!"

"I assure you, Captain ... I will continue to work on this issue ... I promise, it will be resolved—"

Jason cut Granger off mid-sentence: "We will be leaving *Jefferson Station* as soon as an interchange wormhole can be called up. Ricket, you have the coordinates to Trom in the Alchieves system. I expect this mess to be cleaned up by the time I return." Jason spun around to see Boomer sitting wide-eyed in the command chair. "Come on, Boomer ... we need to get you situated."

Chapter 9

Sol System
The *Minian*, Open Space — Near Jefferson
Station

With Boomer doing her best to keep up with her dad, she and Jason found Jack lumbering along, using a long mop handle to steer a rolling bucket in between the fifteenth row of habitats, deep within the *Minian*'s Zoo. Jason interrupted the old caretaker's duties to let him know he'd be responsible, as he'd once been on *The Lilly*, for Boomer's care—a minimum of several hours every day.

Looking around her surroundings, Boomer couldn't remember the last time she'd been this excited. She listened as Jack balked at the request, exclaiming how little time he had to babysit her, but Boomer, unoffended, knew Jack was only being Jack ... grumpy. She knew that Jack was actually quite fond of her—liked her company. From what she'd already seen of the *Minian*'s Zoo, he'd need her help. She figured it was easily ten times the size of *The Lilly*'s Zoo. And though the same habitats once accessible from *The Lilly* were here as well, there were hundreds of others she'd yet to have an opportunity to explore.

Her father hurried off to other duties on the ship's bridge, leaving Boomer with Jack. Attending to something, she wasn't sure what, Jack left with his mop and bucket. *There are droids far better suited for these types of chores*, she thought … but Jack wasn't big on technology. She slopped the end of the mop onto the deck, half-heartedly dragging it back and forth, then dunked it back into the bucket. She was having trouble keeping her attention on the boring job at hand. Up ahead was a section cordoned off with what looked like strung yellow tape like she'd seen on TV—where a murder had taken place. She pushed the long mop handle forward, steering the bucket to an open habitat. The common transparent portal window was, surprisingly, deactivated—allowing her to take a step into another world. A warm breeze touched her cheeks and she heard the sounds of small insects, no more than a few feet away. But something wasn't right. In all the hours spent working around the habitats she'd never found a portal left open. She was well aware of environmental contamination concerns—both for the *Minian* as well as the Zoo. The access panel to the left of the portal was blinking with a series of red lights. Boomer's heart rate elevated and she debated if she should call out to Jack. But there was something familiar about the habitat's otherworldliness— the humid air, dense tropical trees, and the thick foliage. She turned and looked back at the seemingly empty Zoo corridor behind her and, coming to a quick decision, stepped further into the habitat. It all looked familiar.

Ten feet to her front was a dense wall of ferns, taller than she was. About to turn away and return to the Zoo, a distant noise caught her attention. There was a rustling off in the distance, deep in the overgrown foliage. Birds screeched and took flight all around. Suddenly, an animal burst into the open and Boomer only had time to see something big and black barreling down on her. Paralyzed, she stood immobilized as it leapt for her. Bowled over onto the ground, her face was slathered by a giant blue tongue.

Boomer laughed with delight as the six-legged drog licked her face, making yippy, excited, whining sounds.

Boomer yelled, "Alice! Stop ... licking ... me!"

With that, the drog leapt off her, running around in circles—going right then darting left. All six legs moved simultaneously, in their strange, unnatural, rhythm. Boomer sat on the ground and watched Alice's crazy happy antics. She hadn't seen her favorite pet since *The Lilly*. Then she had a sudden insight, realizing their clever ruse: Her father quickly dropping her off; Jack acting annoyed; the open habitat. It was all pre-staged—to reunite her with Alice. Coming from behind her, she heard her name called.

"Boomer!"

She turned around and saw Dira, Rizzo—one of her father's young Navy SEAL friends—and Jack standing in the corridor, smiling back at her.

"You all tricked me?"

Dira, laughing, stepped in and gave Alice a scratch behind her ears. Rizzo smiled and waved. "We've got to get back; good to see you again, Boomer." Rizzo and Dira hurried off down the corridor.

"Thank you, Jack ... I really missed Alice."

Jack half-shrugged, scratching at his white scruffy beard. "It's no big deal. Just thought you'd want to see her again."

Boomer got down on her knees and wrapped her arms around the drog's midsection. Placing her head on her back, she cooed, "You're a good girl, Alice."

Jack walked over to the access panel. "You can come back and play with her later. Boomer, I need to get this portal closed ... its been held open a lot longer than it's supposed to be." He gestured for Boomer to join him in the corridor as he entered a code into the access panel. Boomer, watching Alice seated on her back haunches, gave her a goodbye wave while the portal window was reactivated. She heard the familiar three beeps and the portal window appeared again like solid glass.

"The captain tells me he wants me to give you more responsibilities," Jack said, looking serious. "He thinks you're ready for it. To be honest ... I'm not so sure."

"I am ready!"

"Uh huh. Well ... okay ... come with me. We'll start right now." He strode down the corridor, not waiting for Boomer, while talking over his shoulder. "With Ricket's help, I've begun work on several of the more distressed habitats in the Zoo ... some have gone long periods of time without any attention ... what's necessary in maintaining and retaining viable eco-systems."

Boomer, catching up and walking by his side, took in the various habitats they passed along the way.

"Although there are some habitats that are more self-sufficient ... ecosystems needing little in the way of oversight ... there are others, like Alice's HAB 209 back there, that require significantly more attention. Animals of all different species need to be fed ... cared for. If that doesn't happen, you know the result?"

"They die."

"Yes, that's right, they die. And I won't have that on my watch."

Boomer continued walking by Jack's side until he slowed. They reached the end of the corridor and stopped in front of a habitat. "This one is in bad shape. Ignored from way back, when the *Minian* was under Caldurian control, before Granger had ..."

Boomer finished Jack's sentence for him, "Before Granger stole the *Minian* from them, right?"

Jack didn't respond to that. He pointed to the habitat. "Unattended for over a year, all indigenous animal life perished. Starvation, the primary issue. This is HAB 7 and I want you to see firsthand what happened here."

"What is it you want me to see in there?"

Jack moved off to the access panel and began entering the code. She kept her eyes on HAB 7's portal window. It looked dark and foreboding inside, as if a storm was brewing. Like any moment the skies would open up and pour down a deluge of rain. She realized that this habitat seemed different, too. Where other habitats were naturally primitive, untouched by civilization or environmental changes—this one clearly showed evidence of some habitation by intelligent life. Dreary-looking in the darkness, there were ancient ruins scattered across the distant landscape.

"What is this place, Jack?" she asked.

He entered the last digits of the code and immediately three beeps sounded. Preparing to enter the open habitat, he reached out his hand to Boomer. "Come with me."

Together, they crossed over the threshold and entered HAB 7. Taking no more than ten steps, she heard the portal reinitialize. They were now trapped in this dreary place until Jack reentered the code.

Boomer looked back over her shoulder and found the nearly hidden metal box containing the inside access panel. It started to drizzle. "Jack, are you sure we should be in here? Maybe we should wait for Ricket. He's a scientist."

"I'm more than qualified to be here, young lady," he scoffed.

But she knew he wasn't. He was older, and looked to be having trouble walking on the uneven terrain. The last thing she needed was for him to break a hip, or something … and she didn't know the code to get them out of here.

"Jack, I think we should activate our suits," Boomer said, her senses alert.

"Why?" he snapped.

"Well … it may be dangerous. Please?"

"All indications are we're entering a dead environment. Now look here, Boomer, I felt it necessary to show you the importance of what we'll be doing in the coming days … show you the ins and outs which come with your new responsibilities. Most importantly, what happens when a habitat is not properly cared for. This place is an example of that kind of neglect."

Jack tripped and went down on one knee. He slowly stood back up, but looked unsteady.

"We're initiating our suits, Jack … we have to!"

He looked at her and let out a breath. "Fine. I'm not sure I remember how, though."

She watched as Jack used his thumb and forefinger to pinch two small indentations on both sides of the small, metallic device worn on his belt. It took him several tries. She let out a slow breath, trying to be patient. Everyone on board the *Minian* was required to wear a SuitPac device, which was relatively new Caldurian technology to both *The Lilly* and *Minian's* crew. The SuitPac transformed itself before her eyes as small sections, segment-by-segment, expanded and followed the contours of Jack's body. The last section to unfold enveloped his head in an oblong helmet. Within the span of two to three seconds every inch of Jack was encased in a hardened battle suit. Boomer then initiated her own SuitPac and several seconds later was staring back at Jack through the visor of her helmet. A myriad of semi-transparent numerical and symbolic Heads-Up Display, HUD, indicators danced in front of her eyes. Boomer was well acquainted with the amazing functionality of a battle suit. A suit that was, in all practicality, a self-contained space ship unto itself.

Rain poured down from above. Somehow the suit's visor compensated for the torrent of water and her vision remained crystal clear. "So what did you want to show me, Jack? The weather is getting pretty bad."

Jack pointed in the direction of a half-walled circular structure. Time and the elements had left the dark block walls worn and eroded. Then Boomer saw the droid. Half buried in the gray sand, it looked similar to her own droid, Dewdrop.

Jack nodded, as if anticipating Boomer's next question. "Part of the problem here. All the feeding and caregiving droids that serviced this habitat are like this ... inoperable."

Boomer stopped in front of the droid and knelt down. She used her hand to wipe sand away from its buried lower, triangular-shaped torso. It was facing downward, toward the ground. She carefully slid her hands beneath its body, and flipped it over onto its back. Startled, Jack reached his hand out, touching Boomer's shoulder, and coaxed her to back away. They stared down at the open cavity on the droid's now-exposed torso. The droid had deployed a plasma weapon in that small open cavity on its chest area. Boomer thought of Dewdrop, who had a similar hidden cavity, with a weapon configured inside it—just like this one. She peered up at Jack, then at the droid. "This droid's been in a battle ... look, there's scorch marks all over it."

Jack looked nervous; unlike Boomer, he wasn't the slightest bit familiar with combat situations. "Come on, we should now return to the portal."

But Boomer was no longer looking at the droid—or at Jack, either, for that matter. All her attention was focused on the figure standing atop one of the toppled pillars—less than fifty feet away. Dressed in white, from head to toe, the material of his garment whipped behind him in the stormy wind. The surrounding darkness flashed white when lightning streaked like jagged tree branches across the sky. In that bright instant, Boomer saw two similarly dressed figures standing close behind the man on the pillar.

Jack looked down, scared and ready to run. Boomer was more curious than scared. Why weren't those men showing up on her HUD, she wondered. Where were their life-icons?

The man on the pillar jumped down and, along with his three companions, headed directly for them. Jack grabbed Boomer's arm and pulled. "We need to get out of here ... right now!"

Boomer knew she was well equipped to handle herself. The battle suit was nearly impregnable and she had plasma weapons integrated at both her wrists. She readied herself for possible action.

Jack moved behind her as the first of the men drew close. He was dressed, she imagined, like an Arabian nomad would be dressed; most of his face was veiled—only his eyes and long hair were left uncovered.

"Stop right there," Boomer commanded into the roaring wind, holding out her wrist, prepared to fire.

She watched the man's eyes. When he moved it was quick as lightning. He now stood inches from her. When he lifted his hand and touched her visor, her battle suit began to retract, segment by segment, back into the small SuitPac on her belt. She turned to see Jack lying on the ground ... he looked dead.

Chapter 10

Sol System
The *Minian*, Open Space — Near Jefferson
Station

The *Minian* was scheduled to depart in forty-five minutes. Jason, sitting in his ready room, alongside recently
promoted Commander Perkins, his XO, was doing a final review of the onboard roster. Perkins, a man in his mid-thirties,
was preppy looking, his straight blond hair usually perfectly
combed. Jason found his second-in-command something of
a do-gooder … everything by the book. It had caused conflicts between them in the past, but in the end, Jason figured
his XO was a good balance for his own shoot from the hip
style of command.

"So this is it … this is final?"

"Actually, not quite, sir. One final inbound shuttle is entering the flight deck now. Last minute additions … including your new petty officer, who's assigned to Boomer."

From what Jason understood, the *Minian*, for the first
time that he was aware of, had a full crew complement.

"So we have two thousand and forty," Perkins said, looking at his own virtual notebook. "The bulk of security forces consists of thirteen hundred and fifty specially-trained,

highly lethal, men and women, from a hybrid Marine, Navy SEAL contingent; they are commonly referred to as *Space Sharks,* or simply *Sharks.* There's also the non-officer onboard crew, consisting of six hundred men and women, mostly brought in from recently decommissioned ships."

Jason was well aware of the latter fact. He'd lately been inundated with requests from other fleet commanders who were looking for new posts for their best people. With the long Craing War over, a thing of the past, ships were being decommissioned, their crews retiring, either back to Earth or to homes on other planets. Without a present war to engage in, there simply wasn't the need for such a large military presence.

"We have sixty-five officers spread out across multiple departments," Perkins added.

"A lot of people," Jason said. He'd reviewed the list numerous times and it still seemed like an overwhelming number of crew on board. His largest command responsibility to date.

"And that's just the *Minian*'s crew. The armada includes three light Craing cruisers and nine heavy Craing cruisers. That's roughly another two thousand."

Jason was being hailed via his NanoCom. He gestured for Perkins to hold tight.

"Go for Captain."

"You still have a place for me?" Billy Hernandez asked.

"You, yes ... your stinking cigars, no," Jason said, glad to hear his friend's voice. "So what happened? Got tired chasing zombies?"

"Something like that. Um, Cap ... I'm here with Lieutenant Garret. It seems there's no room here for this old sea dog."

Jason checked the time. "I'll be right down, I need to

make a quick stop first ... try not to get your panties twisted into a knot."

* * *

Jason exited the DeckPort on Deck 7—where the ship's security forces barracks were situated. He found Lieutenant Garret's office; Billy stood in the center of a group of men nearby. Jason tapped his knuckles on the lieutenant's open hatch and entered the compartment. Garret was seated at his desk, reviewing a virtual notebook. Without looking up, he said, "Just take a seat ... be with you in a moment." Jason instantly didn't like the man. Stocky, with broad shoulders and an extreme flattop haircut, the ruddy-faced lieutenant looked near to Jason's age.

Jason remained standing and waited for Garret to look up. Eventually he did.

"Oh! Pardon me, sir. Didn't see you lingering there."

Jason checked his watch. "I don't have a lot of time so I'll make this short and sweet. Hernandez will hold a leadership position here."

"With all due respect, sir. Billy ... as well as your other men including Jackson and Rizzo ... is not trained at the same high level as my Sharks. I can work Rizzo and Jackson into shape ... but not for leadership roles. This isn't a good fit for Hernandez."

"Is that so?"

"Aye, sir. I realize you two go way back. You're friends and all. But—"

"Stand up, Lieutenant. You've already disrespected me once. Don't disrespect me again."

Garret made a face, hesitated a second, then slowly rose to his feet. He made a nasally sound—a quick huffing noise through his nostrils.

"You're a real tough guy ... I can see that, Lieutenant." Jason glanced back through the hatch at the growing crowd watching them from the barracks. "Tell me. Are you as tough as your men ... your Sharks? Or are you just a big talker ... a blow hard?" Jason checked his watch again. He had ten minutes to get back to the bridge.

"Look. I'm sorry if we got off on the wrong foot, Captain. I guess, I'm just not used to being micromanaged when it comes to my men."

"Yeah, well things are done differently on my ship. Keep in mind, they're not *your* men any longer, they are mine. But I'm going to give you an opportunity to put your money where your mouth is. I noticed you have a gym and a sparring ring set up here."

"Sharks are rarely idle ... you're free to come down and use it, sir. Perhaps we can put a program together for you. Get that waistline of yours tightened up a bit."

Jason knew his middle wasn't quite as firm as it had been several months ago, but it hadn't yet reached the point he needed to loosen his belt a notch either.

"Get yourself into that ring. Don't change your clothes, don't remove your boots," Jason ordered.

"Me?"

"Yes, you ... right now."

There it was again, the nostril snorting. This time, a smirk came along with it. "No problem, Captain."

Garret came around his desk and walked past Jason, keeping his eyes locked on Jason's. Apparently, their heated discussion hadn't gone unheard. All Sharks in that section of the barracks, easily one hundred men, plus a few women, made an open space for the lieutenant to walk through. There were hoots and hollers and pats on his back as Garret moved through the crowd toward the gym. Jason held back a moment and waited for Billy to join him at his side.

"What exactly are we doing here, Cap?"

Jason looked at his watch again. "I have six minutes. You want a place here, among these men?"

Billy nodded. "Sure."

"Show Garret what an old SEAL has left in his tank."

"Yeah, you sure?"

"We're burning daylight here … I'm sure."

Jason watched Billy head off between the Sharks, boos and insults following him. The gym was not large enough for everyone to enter so Jason had to muscle his way in between big, muscular bodies. The ring was a hexagon—the ultimate fighting-type configuration—used for mixed martial arts: boxing, karate, wrestling, Sambo, Muay Thai, Brazilian jiu-jitsu, and judo, and of course standard military close combat training, to give a few.

Garret was standing in the middle of the ring, warming up—dancing around like a prizefighter. On the other side of the ring, Jason spotted Rizzo, and Sergeant Jackson, the enormous African-American Army Ranger who'd also served on *The Lilly*.

Again, Jason checked the time. He had about two minutes before the *Minian* was scheduled to enter into an interchange wormhole … he needed to get back on the bridge. He reflected on the last time a ship entered that area of space and the subsequent loss of the *Assailant* … and his father along with it.

The two men fist bumped and looked toward Jason. The surrounding tightly packed Sharks, one hundred or so, went quiet. They too watched Jason. He looked at Billy and nodded once.

Garret threw the first punch, while Billy was still partially turned away. His fist connected with the side of Billy's head, and Billy went down onto all fours. It appeared to shake his Cuban friend. Garret didn't wait for Billy to regain his wits. Using the rigid toe of his left boot, Garret kicked Billy in the ribs, then, with the heel of the other boot, he kicked down at the back of Billy's head. The crowd groaned in sympathy to what must have been an agonizing blow. Now sprawled flat on his stomach, Jason saw Billy blinking his eyes, trying to clear his head. Smiling and striding around Billy's prone body, Garret slapped at his fellow Sharks' outstretched hands. Big mistake, Jason thought. Billy got back to his feet and staggered a bit, but back was Billy's confident smile.

Jason waited for what he suspected was coming. What he himself would do. Billy ratcheted his upper body around in a quick, fluid motion and, like a released spring, his lower body uncoiled—delivering a powerful, spinning back kick that connected directly with Garret's solar plexus. Now, as Garret doubled over, Billy, half-stepping to the side, delivered a short heel-stomp to the back of the man's left knee. Garret let out a high-pitched yelp and began to fall backward. Billy, anticipating it, finished him off with a solid uppercut to the chin. His dead weight flopped down to the mat, unmoving.

It took sixty seconds for Garret to come around. Jason crouched over his prone body and watched his face, waiting for Garret's eyes to blink open, the haze to clear.

"Listen to me, Lieutenant Garret. You now report to Lieutenant Commander Billy Hernandez. He outranks you and I expect you to show him the proper respect ... respect you failed to show me. I advise you not to underestimate my men again. Any one of us could have laid you out flat ... including me."

Jason stood and handed Billy a small gray box. "Here are your new collar bars—these men now report to you."

Chapter 11

Alchieves System
Pharlom Attack Marauder, Planet Trom,
Skies Above Cammilon City

H anna was right—the plasma blasts most certainly were bringing unwanted attention in their direction. Leon took a quick look out of the open hatch and saw five Pharloms ... no, six ... from different locations around the flight deck, heading their way. All were armed with projectile rifles. *Terrific.*

Leon scooped up one of the weapons, dropped by the dead creature on the delivery scout's deck, and handed it over to Hanna. He grabbed the second one for himself, still keeping a firm grip on the plasma pistol in his other hand.

"This way ... keep up!" he yelled, already moving outside the hatch.

Hanna stayed close on his heels and together they ran toward a rectangular opening on the deck—surrounded on three sides by a thick metal railing. The first to reach it, he didn't hesitate heading down a recessed, wide-tread stairway. Gunfire rained from above; shrapnel ricocheting around them prompted Leon to hold back and reach for Hanna's hand.

"Keep going!" she barked, swatting his hand away and

passing him on the stairs. They descended to a lower level and hurried forward into what he figured was a parts depot for the vehicles above. Running flat out now, they headed forward toward the bow. Leon spotted an oily reflection but didn't have time to warn Hanna. Her front foot upon hitting the patch of grease skidded out from under her, sending her sprawling sideways. She went down hard, Leon with her. Together, they slid across the deck, plowing into metal shelving. Leon whacked his head on a protruding metal flange—some kind of replacement mechanical part. Lying on his back, blood came away on his fingers as he probed the open gash above his right ear.

Hanna, laid out several feet away, stirred and moaned, "What the hell happened?" She lifted her head up, her wheat-colored blond hair covering much of her face.

"You slipped and took us both down."

Before she could respond, they heard the heavy clanging of Pharlom footfalls on the stairway. Leon looked around for their weapons—both were sent flying during their tumble. But it was too late, anyway. Looking up, he saw the muzzle of a Pharlom projectile weapon, only inches away from his face.

Hanna sat up and pushed her hair from her eyes. "It was a stupid plan, anyway," she said, looking defiantly at Leon.

Her scrappy attitude made him smile, even as he glanced up at the seven Pharloms, now in a huddle around them. Still smiling, Leon said, "Take me to your leader," slowly rising to his feet. He shrugged and said, "I've always wanted to say that."

* * *

Their hands were bound behind them. Seated on the ground, their backs rested against the hull of the same attack marauder. They were a mile above the surface of Trom, where the marauder had landed on one of the immense, gravity-defying cloud-ports. All but one of the SkyTrans transport engines remained moored, several miles away. The open concourse before them was pocked with craters, some ten feet in diameter.

But it was the bodies, the smell, and the ever-present sound of buzzing flies that held Leon's attention. Men, women, and children lying inert … scattered around as far as the eye could see. Too many to really count. Nearby, a small girl, probably no older than five or six, clutched a blue doll in her tiny lifeless hand. To his left were various damaged port structures, and the control tower, though still standing, had a large, forward window blown out.

"What are they going to do with us?"

Leon felt the warmth of Hanna's upper shoulder against his own. Although her hair again covered much of her face, he could see her eyes, looking sideways at him.

He gestured forward with his chin. "I think they've set this cloud-port up as some kind of concentration camp." In the distance, fencing had been erected. When he squinted his eyes he could see movement on its far side. He suspected there were thousands upon thousands of prisoners held there.

"Why don't they just kill us? What could they possibly want with us?"

"Slave labor, for one thing."

"One thing? What's the other?" she asked, her attention heightened and her brow creased.

Leon grimaced.

Instantly, her expression mirrored his. "Oh no … no way? How could that even be possible? They're like made of stone … do they even have the … necessary equipment to do such a—"

Leon shook his head, really wishing he'd omitted that last bit of trivia. "I don't know anything for sure. Rumors, really. Probably all made up."

"What kind of rumors?" she spat back.

"I don't know … just that the Pharloms are … well, let's just say they're highly passionate." He looked into her wide eyes. "It's not something you'd live through anyway. And hey … from what I've heard, they're not particularly oriented toward any one species or any one gender."

Hanna continued to stare at Leon for several seconds. "Well, that's at least something." She too grimaced.

"Hey, it's not going to come to that. We'll find a way off this rock … somehow," Leon added.

"Well, I hope you think of something soon, because they're coming for us."

A low-flying open transport fast approached. A Pharlom was at the controls while two others, armed, stood on the wide cargo-like deck behind him.

A guard appeared out from the attack marauder's hatch and poked Leon with his rifle. Leon and Hanna got to their feet as the flatbed cargo vessel pulled up, setting down onto the concourse tarmac. Now close enough to see, he noticed the flatbed wasn't empty. A stack of seven-foot-long metallic bodies lay strapped together toward the back of the transport. He knew what they were—*mechers*—AI controlled robots. Tromians used the robots to do just about everything they didn't want to do themselves. But they were poorly designed. He'd seen a strong wind topple them over. He'd also seen them trip over their own two metallic feet. But now, seeing those still bodies bunched together, he felt an odd sympathy for them. For, at the end of the day, they remained simple mechanical bots. They didn't deserve to end up this way, nor did the Tromian people.

Next they were manhandled onto the transport and told to sit down. Quickly underway, they headed toward the distant fence Leon had spotted earlier. Within a minute the transport rose higher into the air to clear a twenty-foot-high gate. Hanna, on her knees next to Leon, stayed quiet as thousands upon thousands of Tromians noisily milled about below. Above the whirling sounds of the transport drive were the sounds of misery: children's cries mixed with the sobs and pleadings of both men and women.

Hanna turned toward him. "You have to do something … anything, Leon."

Leon saw hundreds of tent-like barracks, row upon row of them, toward the outer periphery of the encampment. If he were to make a move, it needed to be in the next few seconds. Noticing the two Pharlom guards were facing forward, away from them, he felt fairly confident he could take out one, just like he'd done on the Pharlom command ship. But two … and the pilot?

The moment came and went. The transport suddenly dropped, descending into the fray below. Pharlom guards approached as the vessel landed and thick, rocklike hands lifted Leon and Hanna onto their feet and half dragged, half pushed, them towards a tent larger than the others.

"Let go of me, I can walk!" Hanna screamed at the guard pulling her along. Leon was thrust forward into the air and landed hard on the ground. A second later, Hanna landed down next to him. A guard stood over her, blocking out the bright sun. A black and ominous silhouette, he tilted his head to the side, as if assessing her as she lay there.

Tent flaps flew open and another granite-skinned Pharlom approached them from behind. Leon, now in a seated position, angled his body around to face him. This one was big, wearing a red sash angled across his chest, atop his body armor. He slowly shook his large, bowling ball head.

"No ... not until she's processed, Gratto," he said.

"Yes, Warden Derl," Hanna's guard replied, stepping away from her.

"Remove their bindings and bring them inside," the warden commanded. He turned and disappeared behind the flaps of the tent.

As Leon and Hanna were pulled to their feet, the bindings pinning his arms behind his back were freed. He rubbed his sore wrists. Masses of Tromians stood around them, their eyes full of fear and desperation as they watched in silence.

They were pushed into the tent, into the dimness within it. Leon blinked several times, his eyes adjusting to the inside gloom. They were herded to the rear of a line of prisoners. Leon took in his surroundings: The size of a circus tent, it was far larger-looking than it appeared on the outside. Several hundred prisoners were being processed in multiple moving lines. Armed Pharlom guards stood along the periphery where long tables were set up, with Pharloms seated behind them.

Twenty minutes later, Leon and Hanna reached the front of the line. The Pharlom wearing the red sash sat before them. The guard next to him pointed some kind of a device at Hanna, possibly a camera. It made a mechanical clicking sound. He set the device down and picked up another one—a gun. Leon sprang forward but the guard to his right grabbed his arms firmly in his massive hands. Hanna inhaled audibly and looked down at her chest. A small red dot appeared. Blood.

She stayed on her feet, seemingly unaffected by whatever was shot into her. Leon's photo was taken and then he, too, was shot in the chest. They'd been tagged, like animals in the wild—so they could be tracked. He touched the place where he'd felt the sting and felt a small lump beneath his skin.

Their two guards had them moving again. The big tent had another opening, off to the side, and another line had formed there. One of the guards grunted and gestured for them to follow the other prisoners, then left them.

Hanna's arms were crossed over her chest. Her head down, she'd become quiet.

"Hey, we're going to get out of here," he said. "I promise."

They crossed from one tent into another … smaller, but just as dark inside. A middle-aged Tromian man, who seemed to be in charge, stepped away from a group of prisoners and approached them. "Hello, I'm Security Commander Lark-badder." His eyes narrowed as he looked at Leon.

Leon looked back at Larkbadder in disbelief—*of all the people to run into.*

Larkbadder looked triumphant. "I knew I'd catch up to you, Pike … eventually."

Chapter 12

Sol System
The *Minian*, Zoo Habitat 7

Boomer fell to her knees at Jack's side. His battle suit, too, had been retracted. Tears flooded her eyes as she shook him. "Jack! Jack!" Looking up at the nomad in white, she screamed above the howling wind, "You killed him! Why would you kill him?"

The nomad's eyes stayed on hers for several beats, then moved toward Jack. "He is not dead. He is simply unconscious." The nomad turned his attention to the two similarly dressed beings several steps behind him. "Bring her." The nomad leader headed off toward the distant ruins, not looking back. One of them grabbed her arm and pulled her to her feet. He then hiked her up over his shoulder, like a sack of potatoes, and followed in the direction of the leader. Upside down, she watched the other nomad drag Jack's unconscious body back to where the now-invisible portal window was located.

* * *

Boomer had apparently lost consciousness somewhere along the way. She had no idea how she'd gotten to this place. Lying upon layers of soft blankets, unmoving, only her

81

eyes took in her surroundings. Muted, amber light filtered down from somewhere above. Subdued voices echoed nearby. Merely ten years of age, she instinctively knew this was a hallowed, spiritual, place. They had brought her to the ruins and she was fairly certain she was underground. More ancient pillars and stone block walls reminded Boomer of the Jefferson monument back in Washington D.C. but this place was older—much older. She didn't feel she was in any immediate danger. Her thoughts turned to Jack. Had the nomad spoken the truth ... was Jack indeed alive?

Boomer slowly lifted her head and brought herself up on one elbow. Two realizations occurred to her simultaneously: Her spacer's jumpsuit had been replaced with nomad robes, and she was not alone.

"Where are my clothes?" Boomer asked the nomad leader, seated cross-legged several feet away from her.

He didn't answer. His constant stare was unnerving. As she'd been trained, she assessed her opponent. He was unarmed, leaning back on his arms, which were stretched out behind him. He was vulnerable.

She sprang to her feet with both fists clenched. Without hesitating, she kicked out with a bare foot, instinctively curling her toes back, prepared for the balls of her toes to make solid contact just beneath the nomad's nose. The move was something she'd practiced hundreds if not thousands of times before. All her training had been customized to fit her small, ten-year-old frame—designed for someone of small stature and physical strength to make the greatest impact possible. She knew that an up-and-forward strike to the nose, done with sufficient force, would first impact the lower, then the upper, lateral cartilage—both fracturing and driving the splintered nasal bone up and back into the frontal sinuses, then into the brain itself.

The expected impact didn't come. The nomad seemed to vanish right before her eyes. Boomer, now off-balance, fell forward. She tucked in her head and like a rolling ball rose back on her feet, ready to strike again. She spun around to see the nomad was reseated, back where he was only seconds before.

"Please be seated."

"Where are my clothes? Why am I here?"

The nomad sat up straighter and gestured for Boomer to take a seat on the blanket in front of him. She considered another attack but knew it would produce the same result. The truth was, the man had amazing abilities and she was intrigued.

She sat, but continued to glare at the nomad.

"I am Prince Aahil Aqeel ... please call me Aahil."

"I don't care who you are. I want to get out of here."

"You are free to leave at any time. You are not our prisoner."

"What did you do with Jack?"

"Your friend is fine. The being you know as Ricket has retrieved his unconscious body from where he was placed, near the portal into your vessel."

"Why didn't you just take me there too? Why ... am ... I ... here?" she asked, fighting back tears.

Up to that point the nomad's face remained mostly covered—only a small band open—from where his large brown eyes stared back at her. Now, seeing him up close, she realized his skin had a blue tinge to it. He reached around to the back of his head and released the veil-like cloth covering his face, letting it fall free around his neck. His face was long and handsome. A scruffy beard covered the lower part of his face and, seeing his grin, Boomer noticed he had perfectly straight white teeth.

"You have questions. That is understandable. All will become apparent over time. Most important now is that you understand that you, Boomer, have searched for us, for me ... not the other way around."

"That's crazy! You're crazy. I don't know what you are talking about. I wasn't searching for anyone. I'm just a kid ... I don't even know you." She said the words but instinctively knew they weren't true. She hadn't known before that she'd been in search of ... *something*, but realized now his words were ringing true.

She spoke without thinking, "I want to learn how you do that ... how you move like that."

He seemed to take that in, giving it some thought. She looked to her left, then to her right. A circle of twenty men and women now surrounded them. Startled, she gasped, *How do they do that?*

Like Aahil, long black hair hung down their backs and each had the same bluish skin tone. "We are the Blues," Aahil said. "This gathering is the Council of One. The elders of the Blues."

Boomer glanced around the circle. They didn't seem all that elderly ... most looked about her father's age—some even younger. She looked back at Aahil and gasped again. He was now wrinkled and silver-haired ... very old. Bent and hunched over, the weight of many years behind him, he reached out a withered claw of a hand and gestured toward the council. "They could look more like this ..."

The entire council, in the fraction of a second it took her to glance around the circle, had changed their appearance. They were children now—about her age. Bemused, they smiled.

But sadness pulled heavily on her heart and she didn't understand why. Unlike Mollie, she didn't think of herself

84

as particularly emotional. She thought of herself more like a young warrior than a typical little girl. But in that very moment she was filled with dread ... a despair she'd never imagined existed. She stared back at Aahil and wiped tears from her cheeks. He'd turned again to his former age. He rubbed at the scruff of his beard, his eyes displaying a mix of compassion and something else ... *understanding*.

"Listen to me carefully, Boomer ... terrible things are about to happen. What you are feeling is anguish ... the residual effects of an unimaginable evil, emanating from within our own universe, our own galaxy. The Dark has awakened."

"What does that mean ... what's the Dark?"

"Your people refer to them as the Sahhrain." Aahil paused for a moment, his expression serious—he leaned back and his face fell into the dark shadows. "The Sahhrain are a superstitious, and patient, people ... they have waited thousands of years for what is occurring right now. For the coming of their true master ... the one from an alternate realm that will deliver them to a promised afterlife. Know that the Blues do not share these beliefs."

"Is the afterlife like heaven?" Boomer asked.

Aahil abruptly shook his head. "No ... nothing like that. More like the opposite. This is a people that prefer misery. Perhaps not as much for themselves, but certainly to all others. Inflicting pain and suffering brings them closer to their master. The concept of happiness is insulting ... vile, to the Sahhrain. There is no place in the universe for this emotion. The day of reckoning is now upon them, foreseen thousands of years ago. To that end, total annihilation of life ... all worlds within this realm are to be systematically destroyed. It is their charge."

"How do you destroy a whole universe ... isn't that impossible?"

"Their master has the key … a key he will bring with him when he arrives."

"But won't they, the Sahhrain, die too … do they want to die?"

"They don't see it that way, Boomer. Dying is a human concept … no, they think of it as a cleansing. A necessary cleansing before they can move on to *Ahmm Topor* … the miserable purgatory that awaits them."

"Well, what am I supposed to do? I don't understand. You should be telling this to my father. He can fight them. He can fight anyone."

"Your father can do many things. He is a strong man and, like you, a warrior for good. But to go up against the Dark, the Sahhrain, will take far more than your advanced star ships and powerful weaponry."

"What will it take?" Boomer asked.

"The ability to fight them at their own level; to move across rooms in the blink of an eye; to enter into an opponent's consciousness—see what they see. And, in the case of the Sahhrain, to fill the darkness with light."

"Could I do those things?"

Aahil looked at Boomer with compassion in his eyes, then over to the Council of One. Boomer watched as some shook their heads no while others nodded assent, albeit hesitantly.

"It will be entirely up to you, my young friend. To enter into the training, the mastery of *Kahill Callan*, is no small matter. In fact, failure to complete even the first level … would result in your death."

"I wouldn't fail," Boomer said. "Wait … how many levels are there?"

Aahil continued to stare at her. "It is time for you to return to your life aboard your ship."

"But when will I return? How will I know what—?"

Boomer's words hung in the air. She felt a subtle breeze and a presence behind her, even before she turned around. But nothing was there. Perplexed, she turned back to Aahil. He was no longer alone. A woman was seated next to him— her eyes unwavering from Boomer's. Boomer fidgeted, not liking her intense scrutiny. *Why's everyone so serious here?*

The woman spoke, "Your training has already begun, Boomer: The first stages of *Kahill Callan*. Rest assured, you won't be alone ... in fact, I will be with you."

Right then Boomer noticed the woman was wearing a *Minian* spacer's jumpsuit. Confused, Boomer opened her mouth to speak, but no words came to her.

"For you, Boomer, this is all new. But not for us ... we have awaited your arrival for some time now," Aahil said. "This is Capri Sharan, but you, and everyone else aboard your ship, will know her as Briar Mansfield. Boomer, the Sahhrain are stirring ... like an awakening beast from a deep sleep ... and the Sahhrain are hungry."

"Hungry for what?"

Aahil continued to stare intently at Boomer; then, letting his eyes move to the other council members and to Capri Sharan, he replied, "Our very souls."

Chapter 13

```
Sol System
The Minian, Medical
```

J ason was furious as he stared down into the small observation window at Jack.

"He's unconscious, but there doesn't appear to be anything, at least physiologically, wrong with him. He'll most
likely awaken sooner rather than later," Dira said. She stood
at the MediPod control panel and did something to cause
the MediPod, like a clamshell, to slowly separate and open.

They had missed their scheduled departure, voyaging
through a newly formed interchange wormhole. Not that
their delay compared to the fact that Boomer was missing.
Jason looked around the Medical facility's vacant MediPods,
and into its adjoining compartment of empty beds. He answered an incoming NanoCom call, bringing two fingers up
to his ear.

"Go for Captain."

"Did I not mention the situation on Trom has turned
ugly?" the admiral asked, irritated.

"Seems we have a crewmember who's gone astray. As
soon as we find—"

The admiral cut him off: "Well, I'm sure I don't need to

tell you the crewmember needs to be disciplined. This is too important ... Damn it!"

"We're on it. Truth is, if it were anyone else, I'd have left 'em behind."

"Who is—"

"I'll give you one guess," Jason said.

"Boomer," the admiral replied.

"Bingo. Problem is, the AI's not detecting her presence on board ... obviously, that's making me more than a little nervous." Jason's eyes focused on Dira, who looked back at him sympathetically.

"So my granddaughter's missing? Where the hell is her drone ... Dewdrop or Teardrop?"

"It's Dewdrop and it's still in our quarters. She left it behind when she went to work in the Zoo. And before you say anything, yes ... we suspect she's still within one of the habitats. That's where we found Jack, the caretaker, unconscious. But her life readings aren't showing up there, either. In fact, the other habitat we suspect she might be in shows no life readings whatsoever." Jason noticed Jack starting to come around. "I'll get back to you, Admiral." He cut the connection and moved closer to the one occupied MediPod. Jack's eyes were open and Dira was giving him some water.

"Where's my daughter, Jack?"

Jack pushed Dira's hand away and leaned up on one elbow. "She's not in the Zoo? The last thing I remember, she was mopping the deck; then playing with Alice ... things beyond that are hazy."

"We were looking for the two of you. By chance, Ricket found you."

"Where ... where was I?"

"Lying face down, in a habitat close to the portal window."

"I don't remember." Jack rubbed his eyes, looking confused. Jason felt his irritation growing to the point he could imagine himself pulling Jack out of the MediPod by the lapels of his stupid green coveralls and—

"Dad?"

Jason spun around to see Boomer, standing next to a woman he'd never seen before.

"Boomer! Where have you been?"

Boomer and the woman exchanged a furtive glance and the woman replied, "Captain, in all likelihood, this is my fault."

"And just who the hell are you?" he asked ill-humoredly.

"I am Petty Officer Briar Mansfield. I'm the replacement ... here to watch over Boomer."

Jason took in her uniform, and some pieces began to fall in place. He assessed the attractive woman standing alongside his daughter. Her reddish brown hair was pulled into a bun at the back of her head. Several strands had escaped and she nervously pushed them behind an ear with long, tapered, fingers. Almost as tall as Jason, Petty Officer Mansfield was slender and angular looking—more runway-model than Naval NCO.

"Where have you been, Boomer?" Jason asked.

Without hesitation, she said, "Briar found me leaving the Zoo ... I wanted to show her the habitat ... to play with Alice ... I'm really sorry, Dad."

"Once back in the Zoo corridor, the AI informed us where ... where to bring her," the petty officer interjected.

Something didn't add up, in Jason's mind—why didn't the AI know where Boomer was?—but now wasn't the time to pursue it. "I want that little bundle of trouble watched at all times. If not by you, then by her droid. This ship is beyond immense. Too easy for a ten-year-old to get lost ... to get into trouble."

"I understand, Captain."

"Can I show her where our quarters are … where she'll be living, Dad?" Boomer asked, as though nothing had happened.

Jason nodded. "Fine. But I'm not done with this, kiddo. We need to talk later." He gave them both a stern look and motioned them to be on their way. He watched them leave and turned back to Dira, now helping Jack from the Medi-Pod.

"I'm sorry, Captain. I'll keep a closer eye on her in the future," Jack said, contrite.

"Yes, you will. And like you just heard me say, she's not to be left alone until further notice."

Jack nodded and walked toward the exit. He slowed and turned back toward them. He shook his head, as if he'd thought better of saying something more, and left.

Now alone, Dira moved to Jason's side and placed a hand on his arm. She was smiling as she looked up at him. In that moment, the irritation he felt toward Jack and his daughter dissolved. She glanced toward the entrance to Medical and, with a mischievous expression, pulled him closer and kissed him. The next moment, she pushed him away; heading into the adjoining compartment, she asked over her shoulder, "Don't you have a ship to command, Captain?"

* * *

Jason entered the bridge and headed for the command chair. He noticed Granger and Bristol still working on the communications console—specifically, the interface to the interchange. At least now everything seemed buttoned-up, as no exposed cabling was visible. They were seated and discussing in low tones something they were viewing on a small virtual display.

Ricket entered the bridge, just as Jason took a seat.

"Captain, I believe we have rectified any time-delay issues, calling up an interchange wormhole," Ricket told him, now standing at his side.

"So what are they doing?" Jason asked, looking over at Bristol and Granger.

"They still believe we're not taking full advantage of the latest Caldurian code ... right now, we're pretty much back using former old levels of software."

Jason saw Bristol nervously glance in their direction— *what's wrong with him?*

"Fine. But know we can't afford any problems when it comes to interchange wormhole travel. Thousands of lives hinge on this technology operating flawlessly. I hope they realize the importance of that."

"If they don't, I'll remind them, Captain."

Jason scowled in Bristol's direction. "If things are working, they need to stop futzing with it until we return to *Jefferson Station* and can spend a few days there in maintenance."

"They know that, Captain. They're just using this downtime discussing how to avoid a potential problem next time."

Jason turned to Orion, seated at the tactical station. "The rest of our armada?"

"They're waiting on us, Cap."

"Seaman Gordon, have you established new communication with the interchange?"

"Aye, Captain ... on your command, I'll provide the in-and-out coordinates."

"Do so now, Seaman."

"Aye, Captain," Gordon replied.

Jason took in the large, surrounding, three hundred-and-sixty degree virtual display positioned overhead. Though often split into multiple virtual segment-feeds, currently, the display showed one contiguous view of local space. With its high resolution and 3D perspective, to anyone not familiar with advanced Caldurian technology the top of the *Minian*'s bridge would appear to be a spectacular, wide-open perspective to open space.

"Captain, the interchange's wormhole is forming thirty-six hundred miles out and coincides with the specified *in* coordinates," Seaman Gordon reported.

"Ensign McNeil, please take us out and away from *Jefferson Station* space. Put us at the mouth of the wormhole coordinates," Jason said.

"Gunny, we need to assume we'll be entering into a combat situation with the Pharloms. Inform each of the armada ship commanders to sound battle stations now."

"Yes, Captain."

As the seconds passed, the distant interchange-created wormhole began to take shape. Colorful static discharges—like bright bolts of lightning, and reaching miles into space—encircled an oblong, pitch black orifice.

"Gunny, add a logistical view to the display."

"Yes, Captain."

A new feed segment came alive on the above display, showing the Earth and the moon, *Jefferson Station,* as well as the various space platforms. Icons in yellow represented the *Minian* and other armada vessels. A blue icon, further out in space, indicated the position of the interchange's new wormhole. Within fifteen seconds, they reached the mouth of the wormhole.

Ensign McNeil turned in his seat and looked toward Jason.

"Go ahead ... take us in, Helm."

Chapter 14

```
Alchieves System
Planet Trom, Cloud-Port E5926
```

"And what are you, the welcoming committee?" Leon asked.

Larkbadder continued attending to a scrape on Hanna's elbow. He'd cleaned it with water and wrapped it with a clean strip of cloth. "Infections need to be avoided here. As you can imagine, conditions are unsanitary. There are no medications … no treatments, other than the most basic ones," Larkbadder said, directly to Hanna.

"Thank you," she replied, touching the makeshift bandage on her arm.

Larkbadder had brought them to his own barracks tent, which seemed no different from the many others scattered around the encampment. "There are no more available cots, so you'll need to share these with others." He gestured to two nearby cots, placed adjacent to each other. "These two are available during the day … the prisoners are out working while the sun is up."

"Work? What do the Pharloms have everybody doing?"

Leon asked, taking a seat on one of the cots—then bouncing on it—as if testing for its level of comfort.

"There's no shortage of work ... shoveling latrine trenches, filling food bowls; those are among the preferred duties."

"And the not-so-preferred?" Hanna asked.

"Dealing with the dead. There are still thousands of bodies needing to be stripped of jewelry, then carted off to the bio furnaces," Larkbadder told her.

Leon knew what a bio furnace was. They were a common component of war. He pictured the quasi-portable structure he'd seen on a distant, alien battlefield—basically consisting of a wide chain-mesh conveyor belt, leading into an enclosed, ten-by-ten-foot compartment. The ceiling, also ten feet high, contained a solid bank of high-powered plasma generators. Once a body ... or bodies ... was fed into the compartment, it took less than three seconds to become atomized. No muss, no mess.

"Who decides who does what around here?" Leon asked.

"Each barrack has its own prisoner representative."

"And that is you, I'm guessing?"

"Yes. For this barrack, as well as for the camp as a whole."

"How do we get out of here? You have to have thought about it ... perhaps put a plan together?" Leon asked.

Larkbadder didn't answer right away, cautiously looking both left and right. He sat down next to Hanna on the cot and leaned forward. "At the beginning of the attack, when the Pharloms were first detected in Trom space, pleas for help were sent ... to our neighboring systems ... as far as central Allied command. They assured us help would come. But that was some time ago. Apparently our inclusion within the Alliance has less importance than we thought. So ... we're on our own." Larkbadder looked dejected. "Anyway, almost immediately after being imprisoned here attempts were made to escape. I'm sure you've noticed we're situated atop a cloud-port thousands of feet above the surface of the planet of Trom. So the only viable means of escape is to steal, or hijack, a ship."

Leon shrugged. "So steal a *flippin'* ship."

"It's been tried ... more than once. Such attempts were monumental failures. The prisoners were apprehended and..." his voice trailed off.

"What?" Hanna coaxed.

"The apprehended prisoners were assembled in front of the others and made an example of."

Both Leon and Hanna continued to stare at Larkbadder.

"Use your imagination ... leave it to say the Pharloms entertained themselves throughout the night ... until they were satisfied. I just happened to be one of the prisoners selected to cart off what was left of their remains to the bio furnace. Those mental images will stick with me till the day I die."

"So you've given up?" Hanna asked.

Leon was surprised—she had asked the same question he'd been ready to ask himself; his appreciation for her ballsy attitude just kept on growing.

For the first time, Larkbadder let a smile cross his lips. "I'm not sitting here talking to you, Pike, because I like your company. I don't. You're a miscreant ... there's a bounty on your head in this system, and I wouldn't be surprised to hear that you were wanted in other systems as well."

Hanna looked straight at Leon now. Her expression was hard to read.

Larkbadder continued, "With that said, if there's anyone who can get off this rock, it's you. And just maybe, you can bring back help."

"That, or he'll leave this system and never look back,"

Hanna said.

Leon placed a hand on his chest. "Your lack of trust in me cuts right to the heart, Hanna." Though he made light of her comment, it actually stung. He may very well be a miscreant, as Larkbadder put it, but he was loyal to those he cared about—sometimes. He turned back to Larkbadder. "Other than the Marauder, I didn't notice any other vessel."

Larkbadder's smile returned. "And there you have the crux of the problem. The Pharloms may be thick … dull-witted, but they're smart enough to ensure no other escape attempts are even remotely possible."

"Shit."

"Exactly."

"So why did you think he could be of any help?" Hanna asked.

"Your friend has a unique ability … like how he was able to divert a freighter, filled to the brim with Dramgolian Ail … metric tons of the stuff … a six-month supply, to this planet. Let me tell you both, the one thing you don't mess with is a Tromian's Dramgolian Ail. You're actually quite famous here, Pike. I'd suggest a disguise, but …" Larkbadder looked around the barracks and shrugged, "not much chance of that."

Hanna's expression now was much easier to read: a cross between disgust and disbelief. "Let's get back to escaping," Leon said.

"As the Security Commander heading up that case, your unique communications abilities became apparent. Not only can you speak in any alien language, you take on its dialect, too … you sound like a native."

What Larkbadder was referring to was Leon's use of his internal nano-devices and his NanoCom's translating capability. He had to admit, they'd provided him with more opportunities than he ever could have imagined.

Larkbadder stood and hurried over to the tent's outer fabric—he peered through a small gap in the material.

Leon had been hearing noises coming from outside. Obviously, Larkbadder heard them as well.

"What is it?" Hanna asked.

Larkbadder continued to watch whatever was happening outside. "Pharloms preparing a campfire." He turned toward Leon. "Just like last time. My guess … some have attempted another escape. There are six men and one woman; all have their hands bound behind their backs. From the looks of the collected Pharloms, they're feeling uncharacteristically jovial."

Hanna looked like she was going to be sick. She pointed a finger at Leon, as if she were holding a pistol. "I don't really know who you are and, to be honest, I don't really like you very much, but if you can help get us out of here, I'll do anything for you … Hell, I'll have your baby."

"Slow down, cupcake … we just met." He stood and joined Larkbadder at the small open gap and peered out. "How much time?"

Larkbadder said, "Last time they waited until dark. But the natives are looking restless. My guess? An hour … maybe less."

"Can you stall them? You have access to the dude with the red sash … the warden?"

"I intervene, even in the slightest, I'll be bound up and thrown in with the others. We've learned to keep our mouths shut, or pay the consequences."

"Can you think of any other reason you'd need to speak with him … perhaps some camp liaison issues?"

"Overcrowding. I could ask for a meeting to discuss more barracks."

"If I'm going to be slinking around in the dark, I'd feel a lot better knowing he, and some of the others, were distracted. Maybe you can start a small commotion?"

Larkbadder scowled at that, then nodded. "Look, the communications depot is located on the far side of the big tent you were first brought into for processing." He crouched down next to his cot, pulled back the blanket, and came up with a metal pipe, about a foot long. "If you're going to do this, you'll need a weapon. Take this."

Hanna stood up, grabbing it from Larkbadder's hand before Leon could. "I'll take that."

"What do you think you're doing?"

"I'm coming with you," she said.

"Like hell you are. If I get caught, that's one thing. There's no point in both of us risking our lives. Sit tight and let me handle this," Leon said, reaching for the pipe.

"I don't trust you … certainly not with my life. No, I'm going with you and there's nothing you can do or say to change my mind."

Chapter 15

Sol System
The *Assailant*, Open Space — Near
Jefferson Station

Admiral Perry Reynolds was awakened twenty-five min-utes after finally falling asleep. He'd returned to the *Assailant* totally exhausted. Too many pressing matters ... post-war grievances, tensions regarding how to redistribute military assets among Alliance members, the need to con-tinue to protect Earth, and the near-extinction of humanity there.

He continued lying in bed, listening to the gentle, re-petitive tone. The AI's voice came alive. "Admiral Reynolds, you have an emergency situation that requires your attention. Captain Underwood awaits your response."

I'm too fucking old for this shit! He let his mind drift back to the nearly refurbished F1, sitting back at the scrapyard. *Why couldn't I have just left it alone ... stayed retired?*

The admiral rubbed his tired eyes and, pulling aside the bedcovers, swung his legs over the edge of the bed. He found his robe, lying at the end of the bed, and stood. "Let him in."

Captain Underwood hurried into the admiral's cabin looking desperate. He, too, looked as if he'd been rousted early from sleep. One of the older officers in the fleet, Underwood was almost completely gray on top, tall, and in relatively good shape. "Admiral, we have a situation."

"I gathered as much, Carl. Tell me what couldn't wait—"

The captain cut him off: "I'm sorry, Admiral, but the shit's hit the fan in quadrant 5626."

The admiral shook his head. "I don't have any idea what that means."

"It's the Sahhrain, Admiral … they entered the Dacci Commonwealth system three hours ago … casualties are already in the hundreds of thousands." The admiral was well aware the Sahhrain were like no other adversary. Driven by ancient rituals, superstitions, myths, and folklore, the Sahhrain were consumed with a dark, evil belief system that crossed into the afterlife.

He had already determined the Sahhrain needed to be dealt with. They were the next mission, after Trom, for Jason and his Star Watch armada.

"How many Allied warships are battle-ready at this moment?"

"Here at Jefferson Station?"

"Yes."

"Close to one hundred, Admiral."

He contemplated on that figure for a moment. The *Assailant* had recently undergone retrofitting, allowing for interchange wormhole travel. If they wanted to get to the Dacci Commonwealth system ASAP, his ship would be needed to open up an interchange wormhole. She was also, next to the *Minian*, the most powerful warship in the fleet. With the ship's cloaking capability, she was nearly impossible to defeat.

Underwood said, "In anticipation of your command, I've taken the liberty to ready the fleet, sir."

"I'll be commanding the operation from the *Assailant*, Captain. Have the fleet ready to move within the hour."

"Very good, sir." Underwood quickly left his quarters.

The admiral walked to the observation window. In the distance, blue and captivating—Earth shone bright amid the contrasting blackness of space. He pushed away the growing feeling of dread that recently had begun burrowing, like slithering dark snakes, into his consciousness. He wondered, as he gazed at his home planet, if this might be the last time he'd ever see Earth.

* * *

Similar to what the admiral was doing, thirty-eight light-years away, Lord Vikor Shakrim *was* gazing out through a large, elongated, observation aperture toward another distant planet—a planet devoid of any coloration with the exception, perhaps, of pale gray. One of the least populated of the Dacci Commonwealth system of planets, it was the most similar to his own home world, Sahhrain. Wind, perpetual sandstorms, and other harsh conditions had fashioned his people into what they'd become ... certainly resilient ... but also patient. Feeling his excitement elevating, Shakrim checked himself. Neutral ambivalence toward others, those not of Sahhrain lineage, was the sacred state of mind to hold, as prescribed by his early forefathers, and set down in their holy primogenitor writings. But over the years, the millennia, most Sahhrain had transposed all vestiges of such ambivalence toward other races into unadulterated hatred, smacking of evilness.

His muted reflection, staring back at him on the glassy surface of the observation window, told of his lack of sleep. Deep creases around his mouth, a sunken hollowness to his cheeks, were noticeable. The pallor of his skin—the color of the distant gray planet—had recently turned several shades darker. Lord Vikor Shakrim, standing straight, took two steps backward, allowing his full reflection to come into view. At six-foot-eight, he had a striking form. As dictated by his rank, he wore the customary, reflective-gold breastplate, which somewhat enhanced his own chiseled pectoral and abdominal musculature. His black stretched uniform, molded to the contours of his flesh, glistened as black as the dark space beyond. And black like his hair—pulled straight up, angled back, thick and coarse like Brillo, it was formed into a cone-shaped mound. The only indulgence of color came from the inside lining of his cloak, revealing when he moved bright glimpses of scarlet red.

Enough of this! Shakrim reluctantly pulled his eyes away from his reflection, turned, and hurried from his simply adorned, albeit ample, living quarters. In the passageway three crewmembers immediately stopped in their tracks, and bowed their heads. He ignored them. He also ignored the many figures, like grotesque artistic reliefs, displayed on the bulkheads throughout the ship. Mostly heads and upper torsos—enemies of the Sahhrain—were positioned as though some incredible force had pressed their form into one side of the bulkhead. They now peered forth, each covered in metallic black, in suspended animations of both agony and despair. Shakrim passed by almost a dozen mummified alien forms before reaching the bridge.

Lord Shakrim entered the bridge with purpose. His sudden black and gold appearance, the momentary flashes of red, brought crew activity to a momentary standstill. Heads bowed as Shakrim strode to the center of the triangular-shaped bridge. Three of the ship's senior officers stood at the center console, referred to as the board, where a high-resolution display provided a comprehensive, logistical presentation of space and the planets within the local solar system.

The three officers were obviously in the middle of something—probably strategizing. With a casual swipe of his hand, Lord Shakrim cleared the board to black. With another wave, he brought forth a live feed of the planet below, Corplin-Re. Standing erect, hands on his hips, he assessed the gray world. He used his mind—his telekinetic powers—and the image below began to enlarge, to zoom in, at a faster and faster rate. The three officers quietly watched his superior telekinesis abilities at work. All Sahhrain possessed similar mental powers, in varying degrees: the ability to move small objects—ten to fifteen feet. But it always required the use of hands—a wave … a gesture with two hands, or some kind of physical motion, or action—to manipulate the objects. Lord Shakrim needed no such antics. His telekinetic powers were far superior to those of others on the ship, or in the entire fleet, for that matter. He wasn't limited, either, to mere ten- or fifteen-foot manipulations—he was able to mentally move very heavy objects a mile's distance. He continued to focus, zooming in on the planet until the feed showed him exactly what he was seeking.

"Lord Shakrim, as you can see, our army has constrained the local Dacci populace. What resistance we encountered from their paltry military effort has also been dealt with. We also have control of the Loop wormhole here in Dacci space—"

"I'm well aware of all this, Commander Hilt … If I want to hear you prattle annoyingly, I'll ask you to." Lord Shakrim continued to stare at the feed. A straight line of attacking Sahhrain *shieldsmen* warriors, each dressed identically in black battle suits, had *enhancement shields* worn on their left forearms. These small shields worked uniformly with the shieldsmen's own telekinetic powers—amplifying them—

creating a directional pulse or wave that virtually paralyzed nearby opponents.

He watched as the marines maintained a tight formation. The embattled Dacci, small and insubstantial-looking in comparison, attacked indiscriminately from all sides. Some fired handheld plasma weapons, while others resorted to throwing stones. Shakrim zoomed back some to get a better, wider perspective. Thousands upon thousands of Dacci bodies lay lifeless on the ground. He smiled and nodded his approval. Shakrim knew better ... they were not dead. No, death would come to them, but very slowly ... hours, maybe days, from now. Mere killing was far too easy. The Sahhrain were infamous for inflicting rituals of unending suffering ...

Chapter 16

Alchieves System
The *Minian*, Bridge

___

The *Minian* exited the interchange wormhole at the out-skirts of the Alchieves star system. Within minutes, the rest of the armada followed suit. Moments later, the wormhole began to slowly fade, eventually disappearing completely from view.

"Talk to me, Gunny," Jason said.

"Looks like the Pharloms have arrived in force," Orion replied back from tactical. "No less than fifty warships of varying size and strength, and more are still arriving, as we speak. All have plasma weaponry and advanced shielding capabilities. A formidable fleet, Cap. Looks like there's several stationary transport-type vessels here as well."

"Well, we're not here to start the next interstellar war … let's see if we can try a little diplomacy first. Seaman Gordon, hail their command ship."

"Aye, Captain." Several minutes went by, "… um … no response, sir," Gordon said.

Jason studied the logistics segment on the overhead display. Most Pharlom vessels were farther within the system, closer to the Trom world, approximately six hundred million miles' distance from their current position. Ten warships were positioned closer and in a line at the edge of that system. "What are those, Gunny?" Jason asked, gesturing toward a series of red icons distributed around the planetary system.

"Cannon platforms ... big mothers, too, Cap. I'm guessing those things pack a major wallop."

"Any way to know if the Pharloms have taken control of them?"

"Not really—"

"Totally disagree," Bristol interjected from the forward port side of the bridge. "I just pinged one of their sensor interface ports ... though what I can see of the code is minimal, I am seeing a reassignment of their command and control parameters. You can bet they are now Pharlom-controlled guns."

"I stand corrected, Captain. Looks like Bristol's right," Orion said.

Jason nodded, his eyes still on the display. "Show me the command ship."

A pulsating ring surrounded one of the warships, the one closest to Trom.

"It's the heaviest of the lot, Captain," Orion said. "It has shields comparable to those of our Craing cruisers, yet significantly better firepower."

"Sir, I finally have a hail response ... a Grand Overseer ... Mangga ... apparently he's the fleet commander."

"Thank you, Seaman Gordon ... on screen."

It took several moments for Jason to figure out what the hell he was looking at. Perhaps a pile of rocks? Jason glanced toward Orion—she shrugged and looked as mystified as he felt.

"Hello ... I am Captain Jason Reynolds of the Allied Star Watch vessel, the *Minian*. Who am I addressing?"

The pile of rocks shifted and turned. "You are addressing Grand Overseer Mangga. What do you want here?"

"You've entered Allied space and have taken predatory action against an Alliance world. I want you to pull your forces back ... do it now. Then we can discuss reparations for the damages you've caused within this system."

"And who are you to dictate to me, human garbage?" the Pharlom leader replied in his deep gravelly voice.

Jason felt his irritation growing. Not knowing where Mangga's eyes were, or if he even had eyes, was disconcerting. "What I am ... is the Law ..." Jason smiled. "There's a new sheriff in town and I'm giving you ten minutes to pull your forces back."

Again the gravelly voice boomed, "I do not need to pull my forces back, human refuse. Leave this system now, or be annihilated."

"Listen to me, Mangga ... I don't want to destroy you, or your fleet. Honestly, I really don't. There's been far too much of that over the last few years. But be advised, don't let the size of our armada deceive you; I assure you, you are outmatched in every way that counts."

"Leave here, human. This is your final warning."

"We're not going anywhere ..."

Orion interjected, "Captain, the Pharlom ship is charging weapons."

Before Jason could say anything else, five consecutive plasma bursts erupted from the bow of the Pharlom command ship.

Jason reached for the chair's armrest. "Damage report," Jason yelled.

"It's not us, Captain ... it was one of the two large transport ships," Orion said.

Jason saw that a new segment had been added above and he was now looking at significant space debris from one of the two transport vessels.

"Apparently the two ships were being held captive, Cap, and one of those transports was just fired upon … not destroyed, but has sustained heavy damage. With close to one hundred thousand passengers on board, the casualties could be high."

Jason wanted to atomize the Pharlom warship. The command to do so was on the tip of his tongue. He looked at Orion and then back to the screen. "And the other one … how many are on board?"

"Even more, approximately one hundred and thirty thousand passengers."

Jason looked up to the display. He pictured himself taking a sledgehammer to the pile of rocks sitting there. He managed to somewhat rein in his emotions. "Orion, go ahead, make that command ship our bitch."

"Gladly, Cap."

In a flurry of plasma fire, small explosions erupted along the exterior hull of the Pharlom command ship.

"She's currently weaponless and her drives are toast … I'd be happy to finish her—"

"No … that's fine for now. Okay … do the same thing to the ten closest Pharlom warships."

Orion faced her tactical board and momentarily spoke a series of commands. Another flurry of plasma fire erupted from the *Minian* as well as six other Star Watch armada warships—each contributing to the rapid-fire attack. "No return fire, Captain. All of the closest enemy ships are disabled. All other Pharlom vessels are keeping their distance."

"We've made our point to Mangga and his fleet. I think

what's needed now is a little face-to-face time," Jason said, through clenched teeth—realizing that probably wasn't the best choice of words. The Pharlom Grand Overseer didn't really have much of a face. There was a loud roar of noise—much of which were insults—coming from Mangga. The pile of rocks was standing and looked to be stomping.

"Stand by, Grand Overseer Mangga, your vessel's about to be boarded."

He turned toward Orion. "Find Traveler and a few of his friends. Have Billy assemble a team of no more than ten. And roust my XO ... tell him he's needed on the bridge."

"Yes, Cap," Orion said.

Jason surveyed the bridge, looking for Ricket. Less than four feet tall, he was often easy to overlook. Ricket entered the bridge and headed directly for the command chair. Jason had given up a long time ago trying to figure out how he did that ... how he seemed to show up just when he was needed.

"Yes, Captain?"

Jason was still shaken. "Ricket, I have a special project for you."

"Yes, Captain."

"Communications with Trom went dark some time ago. We need to know what's going on there. It's evident an insurgency of Pharlom forces is already on the planet. I need to know if there are survivors and, specifically, where we can find them ... perhaps communicate with them. It looks like we'll be preoccupied here for the immediate future."

"I suggest we send a series of probes, Captain. Once we have more information, more data, I can better suggest a methodology for communicating with any survivors."

"Good. I'll check in with you later." Jason rose, hurrying to his feet.

"Captain, Traveler requests you meet him at the entrance

to the Zoo. He says he doesn't know his way around the *Minian* yet."

He's not the only one, Jason thought to himself. When things settled down, he really needed to spend time exploring the rest of his ship. "I'm on my way. Have Billy and his team meet us there as well."

Commander Perkins entered the bridge, blinking away sleep from his eyes. "I am ready to relieve you, sir."

"Thank you, Commander, I am ready to be relieved." Jason waited for his XO to approach so he could talk to him in a lowered voice. "Orion will bring you up to speed. I am not looking to go to war here, Commander. Fire only if fired upon. Use your discretion. Measured force only, is that understood?"

"Perfectly, sir."

"For now, have the armada sit tight here. Be prepared to bring the *Minian*, via a series of phase-shifts, to the Pharlom command ship's coordinates. I'm taking an assault team onto their vessel … have a little powwow with their commander."

Jason gave Perkins a curt nod and headed for the exit.

"Good luck, Sheriff," Orion said to him with a smile.

* * *

Jason found Traveler, plus three other rhino-warriors, standing at the entrance to the *Minian*'s Zoo. Rhino-warriors First Reflection, Hangs to Ground, and Few Words stood with him. Hangs to Ground, aptly named for his remarkably long, almost touching all the way to the deck, member, grunted recognition at seeing Jason. What first grabbed Jason's attention was the young girl, staring up at Traveler. Boomer! Her scolding finger pointed up at Traveler in the middle of some sort of reprimand.

"You need to wipe your feet when you come in here to the Zoo, Traveler. Who do you think mops the deck? I do."

Jason held back a comment and let Traveler take his medicine. The beast looked somewhat dejected. Traveler glanced over to Jason but only got a commiserate shrug in response.

Boomer saw her father and smiled brightly. "Dad!" She ran over and gave him a hug.

He looked down into her large brown eyes. "Hey, little one, where's your ..."

"I'm here," came a woman's voice.

Petty Officer Briar Mansfield peered around the bulk of Breeds Often. She gave Jason a little wave.

"I'm showing Briar what my duties are in the Zoo."

"That's good. You're doing your studies ... your school work, too?"

"We did that this morning, Captain," the petty officer answered, replying for his daughter.

"That's excellent ... why don't you run along now, Boomer. I've got some business to attend to with Traveler and the others here." He watched Boomer, who first assessed the team of rhinos, and then Billy and his assault team, who'd just entered. Her interest in such things did not elude him. She was a smart, plugged-in, little girl.

"Come on, Briar, I want to show you the Shintoh Gloths."

Jason waited for them to disappear from sight before turning toward Billy.

"What's on our plate today, Cap?" Billy asked.

Rizzo and Sergeant Jackson were among Billy's assault team and Jason acknowledged them with a nod of his chin. "We're dropping in on a Pharlom command ship. They've invaded this Allied star system and we need to convince them to leave."

"That sounds very diplomatic, Cap. Should we bring

chocolates, maybe some flowers?" Billy asked him, with a lopsided grin.

Jason didn't respond, he was being hailed by the bridge.

"Go for Captain."

"Captain, we've completed our phase-shifts. We're in close to the Pharlom command ship ... we're actually well inside their shields."

"Thank you, XO. Have Gunny update our HUDs with the Pharlom ship's layout ... no, never mind; it just came through. I'll be in touch."

Jason saw Billy's helmet visor open, a wet and soggy stogie protruding from the corner of his mouth. He caught his eye and Billy removed the cigar, placing it into one of the many small compartments on his battle suit. Jason perused the overlay of the Pharlom ship's layout on his HUD. He found the bridge and a section of the ship large enough for his team to phase-shift into.

"Everyone ready?" he asked.

Chapter 17

Alchieves System
Pharlom Command Warship

In a white flash, Jason collectively phase-shifted his assault team into the Pharlom command ship. Ensuring they were all were accounted for, he turned his attention to their surroundings. Steam rose everywhere, making visibility difficult.

"What is this place, Cap?" Billy asked.

"Not sure. I do know the Pharloms have thick, mineral-based, epidermal layers. Like rock. Perhaps they need moisture ... like some kind of wetting treatment so they don't completely dry out."

Jason noticed grittiness beneath his boots—as if he were walking on a layer of sand. The area was large—easily sixty to seventy feet square. Bench-like seating was built into the surrounding bulkheads. As he approached one of the bulkheads, he saw evenly spaced openings in the bench.

"Looks like you dropped us into the shitter, Cap," Rizzo remarked humorously.

Chuckles came over the open channel from the rest of the team. Jason even heard Traveler grunt, which was as close to a chuckle as it got.

Jackson said, "Exit's over here." He waited for Jason, and together they moved through a wide corridor, which eventually led into an even wider one. The steam had dissipated and according to Jason's HUD overlay they were close to the bridge. As he waited for the rest of his team to emerge from the steamy bathroom, a klaxon began to bellow.

"Looks like it's show time," Billy said.

"Yeah, so much for our element of surprise," Jason replied, watching the movement of life-icons at the bottom of his HUD. In addition to showing their own team's fourteen blue icons, no less than twenty alien icons could be seen, approaching them—five from the bridge and fifteen from the far end of the corridor.

"We've got the others, Cap," Billy said. In a flash, half of Billy's team phase-shifted away while he and four others headed on down the corridor.

Pharloms from the bridge were the first to enter the wide corridor. Jason wasn't prepared for their size. Even taller than the rhinos, they moved surprisingly well, considering their hugeness. There was something unnerving about the grating sound they made as they moved forward, like large rocks being rubbed and scraped together.

Traveler and the three other rhino-warriors were the first to come into contact with the emerging Pharloms. Plasma fire erupted and Hangs to Ground took several energy bolts directly to his face. He went down, fast and hard. Jason raised his multi-gun, ready to take down the rhino's attacker, but Traveler had already rushed forward, blocking his aim. With his large arm outstretched, winding around counterclockwise and gaining tremendous centrifugal force—the business end of Traveler's heavy hammer connected with the Pharlom's bowling ball-sized head, shattering it into a large puff of dust.

The corridor was now ablaze with plasma fire from all

sides. Distant sounds of battle came from further away, where others of the assault team were also engaging the enemy.

Jason fired into the mid-section of an approaching Pharlom. Fracturing rock chips, the size of baseballs, broke away from the alien's hulk, but didn't seem to slow him down much. Soon, more Pharlom combatants found their way into the battle. From behind him, a massive, eight-fingered fist connected with Jason's helmet. Even with the advanced Caldurian dampening technology built into his battle suit, Jason saw stars and staggered. Another blow, this one from the front, hit him below his chin. The force of the punch propelled him off his feet. He landed on his back, further down the corridor, and lost his hold on his multi-gun. From out of his peripheral vision he could see it, lying out of reach on the deck. The once seemingly large ship corridor now seemed small—packed with too many fighting combatants, each engaged in his own personal altercation. Two Pharloms towered over Jason, pointing their large plasma pistols at him. Reflexively, Jason raised and extended both arms. Plasma fire spewed from his battle suit's integrated wrist guns. Without any conscious thought behind it, he aimed both guns toward their heads. He kept on firing until first one, and then the second, head blew apart.

"Shoot at their heads!" Jason yelled into the open channel.

"You just figuring that out now, Cap?" Billy replied.

Getting to his feet, Jason saw that the skirmish was coming to an end. Piles of rock chunks filled the space around him. In addition to Hangs to Ground, two of his assault team members were also down. According to Jason's HUD, and their three still-active life-icons—each was injured … but still alive.

"Rizzo, you and the others guard the entrance. Billy and

Traveler … you're with me." Jason moved toward the entrance to the bridge and saw that the hatch was securely closed. With a quick check of his ship overlay, he phase-shifted the three of them into the bridge.

They flashed into the very center of the near-circular bridge compartment, landing within the bright contours of a large holographic display. Jason saw a distorted partial image of the planet Trom displayed on Traveler's back. The three took several steps forward, out of the flickering projection's range, and took in the unconventional layout of the bridge. As if standing on a stage-in-the-round, the bridge officers and crew around them were situated in a circle.

Jason said, "Nobody move!"

According to a pop-up tag on his heads up display, sitting directly across from Jason was Grand Overseer Mangga. Billy and Traveler walked around the inside perimeter of the bridge consoles, ensuring that no one made any abrupt movements. Jason approached Mangga, who'd awkwardly risen to his feet. Mangga's face was featureless, and Jason felt slightly cheated he couldn't visually catch a shocked expression at their sudden presence.

An explosion of sound erupted behind him. Startled, Jason spun around to see Traveler lifting his heavy hammer away from a collapsed section of console. The Pharlom who'd been sitting at that station now lay on the deck, apparently unhurt. Traveler turned toward Jason. "He moved."

Jason turned back toward Mangga. "I am Captain Jason Reynolds, of the Star Watch vessel *Minian*. You were warned, and now I'm commandeering your ship and placing you under ship arrest. You will issue an order of surrender to your fleet."

The Grand Overseer began to speak, "Another will take my place … my Pharlom fleet is ten times the size of yours—"

Jason held up a hand, stopping Mangga mid-sentence. With two fingers up to his ear, Jason listened to Perkins, back on the *Minian,* relaying recent events in space.

"Captain, as soon as the *Minian* phase-shifted, the armada was attacked."

Jason wasn't in the least surprised to hear that. "Go on."

"The space cannons took us by surprise; we've sustained moderate damage to three ships."

"And the Pharlom fleet?"

"Apparently Bristol was working on something. I'm not really sure what."

Bristol's squeaky voice came on the line: "Captain, I hacked the cannons. It's really not that complicated."

"So what happened with the cannons? You do know I'm sort of in the middle of something here ... right?"

"The cannons have been firing non-stop. They're beasts, those things!"

"What the hell are you talking about, Bristol?"

"The Tromian cannons ... they're taking out Pharlom ships. I reprogrammed them. Hell, all the cannons in the system are on a rampage."

"Well, stop them! Those weren't my orders. I've got things under control here. Perkins, you still there?"

"Yes, sir."

"Stand down and wait for my command. Keep an eye on Bristol." Jason cut the connection and turned his attention back to the Grand Overseer. He let out a breath ... *things were so much easier when you could just annihilate an enemy.*

"Cap!"

Jason turned toward Billy. He was pointing a finger in the direction of the large holographic display in the middle of the room.

Debris, like countless colossal meteors, was falling from

numerous pummeled Pharlom warships, and beginning to strike Trom's outer atmosphere. Bristol's actions were, inadvertently, causing more damage to the planet than even the Pharloms intended.

Jason opened a new NanoCom connection. "Orion! Lock on and take out that debris."

"I'm already on it, Captain."

Jason heard the *Minian's* powerful plasma weapon pounding away through the comms connection. "We definitely won't be able to get them all. The planet's already suffered substantial damage."

Chapter 18

Alchieves System
Planet Trom, Cloud-Port E5926

Leon and Hanna moved from one barracks tent into an-other, doing their best to stay out of sight of any pa-trolling Pharlom guards. Good news for them, most of the Pharloms were now congregating outside for the evening festivities—where hordes of prisoners were gathered around a raging bonfire. Leon picked up his pace, seeing that dusk was quickly turning to night.

"We need to move it along ... why are you dilly-dallying back there?" he whispered over his shoulder.

"I'm two steps behind you. What do you want me to do? Walk on your shoes?"

They reached the far-side opening in the tent closest to the main tent, sited about ten feet away from where they stood. As he pulled the fabric of the tent apart to peer out, the distant sounds of Pharlom activities grew louder. He looked both ways and, seeing it was clear, opened the flap of the tent wider. "You go across first ... I'll follow you."

Hanna nodded, not looking particularly comfortable with the switch. She looked out, verified the coast was clear, and quickly darted across to the main tent's opening, ten feet away. Ready to sprint across himself, Leon hesitated. Two armed Pharloms had come around the corner and were approaching. He saw Hanna's pretty face peering back out from the flap on the main tent. She didn't seem to notice the two Pharloms, which astounded him, since they weren't exactly light footed. *If she makes any sudden movement, or opens the tent flap—she's as good as dead*, he thought.

With the guards less than fifteen feet away, Hanna opened the tent flap several inches wider and stuck her head out. Leon bit his lip in frustration. She was probably curious to see what he was so interested in. The flap movement caught one guard's attention and he reached for his holstered energy weapon. Leon cursed under his breath. He looked around for something substantial to use as a weapon. There was nothing. One of the guards disappeared into the tent, while the other, his weapon drawn, stood less than five feet away from Leon.

He decided just thinking about what to do wasn't getting anything accomplished. He moved from the folds of the tent flap out into the space between the tents, pulling the long stiletto from his back collar. He'd had success with this maneuver once before … why reinvent the wheel? Again, he observed where on the guard's back the armored sections were gaping open. In the dim darkness it was more difficult to see just where the ridgelines on his rock-like skin were located, where Leon should stab him.

Leon heard Hanna's desperate pleading coming from inside the main tent. He stabbed the Pharlom guard in the back, applying the same slightly upward angle he'd used on board the Pharlom ship. The tip of his knife hit, what felt to him like solid rock, and stopped—he'd cleared the armor but missed the ridgeline. The Pharlom guard spun around with remarkable speed, his plasma weapon already pointed at Leon's stomach.

"What are you doing? Why are you here?" the gravel-ly-voiced guard asked.

In that split second, something interesting occurred to Leon. His earlier assumption was right about Grand Over-seer Mangga and the peculiar positioning of one eye. As with Mangga, there was the same tiny glistening—a minis-cule amount of teardrop moisture—coming from an area one would expect to find the nose, on the large round head. Leon jabbed the knife up and forward, targeting the tiny glint of moisture. First the tip, then the whole stiletto blade, slid into the narrow orifice, like a sword into a scabbard, plunging into the Pharlom guard's cranium. In a thunderous avalanche, the guard dropped to the ground.

Leon rushed across. The Pharlom guard inside the tent appeared as dead as the one lying just outside. Dust swirled in the dim light as Hanna, still clutching their fought-over pipe in one hand, stood over the pile of rocks on the dirt floor. The guard's head was shattered and there was something else. Several feet away, an elongated length of *something* quivered on the ground.

"Is that what I think it is?" Leon asked, not able to take his eyes off it.

Hanna, too, adjusting her torn clothes, was staring down at the castrated, though still-erect, member. "He was going to ..." her words trailed off. Shrugging, she added, "It just snapped off when I hit it ... I guess desperate moments require desperate actions."

"We have a similar saying where I come from," Leon said, more than a little impressed with her resourcefulness. Looking at her, he said, "We need to keep going ... come on." He took her free hand and together they hurried further into the main tent.

They passed by the same long tables when they were first admitted into the prison camp. Gone were the lines of prisoners, the guards, and the Pharloms seated at the tables. Off to the left, the front flaps of the tent were wide open and Leon saw several guards standing outside, their silhouettes black against the amber flames of the distant bonfire. They slowed, crouching low below the table tops. A man's screams reverberated in the distance.

True to Larkbadder's word, there was another opening close by ahead. They approached slowly, keeping low to the ground; they could see inside that it definitely was a field communications depot. Two Pharloms sat in the darkened space—their heads and upper torsos illuminated in the console-display lights. What caught Leon's full attention were the near-hysterical voices coming from the communications equipment. Apparently, the cavalry had indeed arrived and all hell was erupting above, in space. There was something garbled being said about fragmented ships ... ships that were going to impact into Trom. One of the Pharloms got to his feet, knocking his large chair over in the process. Both Leon and Hanna backed away, taking cover as he scurried through the opening, then out the front entrance of the main tent. The lone Pharlom sat with his back to the opening. Leon considered the pipe in Hanna's hand and the knife still held in his own. He gestured Hanna to stay put, and half-crouched, half-crawled into the confined space. Five or six different communication channels were currently broadcasting, all emitting tones of desperation. In their noise, Leon inched closer till he was right behind the seated Pharlom. He studied the broad exposed area directly below his head— not so much a neck—but not his shoulders either ... here he easily spotted the distinct ridgeline on his rock-like skin. Holding the hilt of his knife in both hands Leon carefully positioned the tip of the blade and jammed it forward—he used the palm of his other hand to hammer the hilt of the knife and drove the blade all the way in. The body crumbled off the chair onto the floor.

"Do you hear that?" Hanna asked.

Leon, getting into the vacated chair, turned his head and listened. There were faint screams coming from outside, and the loud, still frantic, racket from the communications equipment. "What ... what do you hear?"

"Listen! One of those voices isn't Pharlom."

He listened more carefully and heard that she was right. Somewhere mixed in the barrage of voices, a calm, pleasant voice was speaking. Hanna walked the length of the ten-foot-long console, coming to an abrupt stop at its far end. "It's here ... it's coming from this station."

Leon tried to move his chair but gave up when he discovered how heavy it was. Both crouched low over the console, their faces mere inches from each other, as they tried to figure out the communications equipment in front of them.

"Try this," Hanna said, moving a big metal lever, better suited for gigantic Pharlom fingers. The voice went silent.

"No, that turned it off," Leon said. He then spotted what looked like an adjustable microphone, a grouping of switches and controls clustered nearby. He set the lever back the way it was and began selecting other controls, while speaking into the microphone. The third attempt did the trick.

"Yes ... I can hear you. My name is Ricket, of the Star Watch ship *Minian*. To whom am I speaking?"

Leon and Hanna looked at each other, wide-eyed, and smiled. She pulled his face into hers and kissed him on the lips.

Ricket's voice was back. "Hello? Are you there?"

"Yes! We're here. We're prisoners on Trom … at a camp located on one of the cloud-ports, actually."

"Listen to me carefully. A battle has ensued in Trom's outer space. Fragments of destroyed ships are descending down toward Trom. What is your location?" Ricket asked.

"I don't know for sure—"

A bright light outside the tent streamed into the dark communications depot. Thunder pounded overhead, then a fiery *something* tore through the top of the tent.

The concussive explosion thrust Leon into the air and across the tent. The super-heated air around him seemed to suck in and then expand out in a great gale-force rush. The tent disintegrated into fiery embers that rose into the air like dust in the wind. He got to his hands and knees and looked around their surroundings. Everything was black—including his own clothes—his hands. It was then that he saw Hanna's body, not far from where he'd been blown. He moved to her side and, as gently as possible, turned her onto her back. Her clothes were gone—had been completely blown away. He looked down at her once beautiful face and gasped. There was now very little left of it. He heard something coming from the blackened hole that was once her mouth … she was trying to say something.

Chapter 19

Alchieves System
The *Minian*, Bridge

___

"Report, XO," Jason said, hurrying back into the *Minian*'s bridge.

Perkins stood up from the command chair and moved out of the way. "As you now know, Captain, while you were on the Pharlom command ship, our armada was attacked by four more warships. Three of our ships suffered minor damage, while another, a light cruiser, sustained considerable damage. Repair crews have been deployed. Captain, I want you to know, our response was intended to be measured ... as ordered. But Bristol's reprogramming of the Tromian space cannons changed all that. Multiple Pharlom ships were subsequently hit ... destroyed ... others badly damaged."

"So what's the status of their fleet now?"

"We know that the earlier orders from Grand Overseer Mangga to surrender were indeed relayed out to what remained of the fleet commanders ... maybe out to twenty-five warships. But it seems most of those remaining fleet commanders are now operating autonomously—attacks are still occurring."

Ricket joined Perkins at his side. "Captain, the planet below is being bombarded by debris." Ricket gave a sideways glance in the direction of Bristol, who was uncommonly quiet.

Jason redirected his attention to Bristol, saying, "You sure screwed the pooch this time, Bristol." For once, Bristol didn't retort with a snarky reply.

Orion turned in her seat. "I've got virtually every one of the *Minian's* plasma cannons working overtime, Cap, but we still can't take out all the ship debris; a lot of junk is making its way through Trom's atmosphere, impacting on the surface."

"And one more thing, Captain," Ricket said, "we've made contact with someone being held at one of the Pharlom prison camps. He's asking to be rescued."

"How many prisoners?"

"Comms went down suddenly in the middle of the conversation, Cap, but prior to that we found out thousands are being held on the same cloud-port he's a prisoner on, but there are other cloud-ports and he suspects there are other camps," Ricket said.

"Cap, I'm gathering that information now ... the locations of the other camps," Orion said, working at her post, her back to him. She turned around, and added, "Okay ... yes, here it is ... there's three other camps situated on separate cloud-ports. Apparently, the Pharloms haven't done much with the planet itself. Other than the damage being incurred there from falling debris, there's not much to worry about in that regard. The other thing, Cap ... the Pharlom guards are still in control of the cloud-ports. They're heavily armed and making a stand."

Jason thought for a moment. It looked like Billy's Sharks,

restless and needing something to do, were going to see some action. "Here's what I want to happen. XO ... have Billy phase-shift Shark teams out to the rest of the Pharlom fleet. I want the rest of their warships' weapons permanently disabled."

"Aye, Cap."

"Also ... let's have Billy assign other Shark teams to take back the three cloud-ports. Tell him the Pharlom guards are heavily armed and trenched in for the long fight."

* * *

Billy and his one hundred and forty-four Sharks phase-shifted to the cloud-port coordinates provided earlier by Rizzo. He had been held up on the *Minian*, meeting with Lieutenant Garret, who would be commanding the space-based assaults. Although there seemed to be minor residual resentment from both Billy's kicking his ass in the ring, as well as Billy taking over his command of the Sharks, Garret seemed to be handling it—taking it in stride. If nothing else, he was a professional. Billy reviewed how he wanted Garret to use coordinated, synchronized phase-shifts into the enemy ships. Orion would provide the tactical drop locations. Garret was reminded of the Star Watch directive ... this wasn't about obliterating all life forms on the Pharlom ships. "Take control of the situation ... neutralize the threat by disarming the enemy ships ... then get out ... that's all."

Billy spoke over the open channel to his six teams: Lion, Tiger, Zebra, Bear, Cobra, and Rabbit. "Lion and Tiger, move off to the relative west, Zebra and Bear, east. Both teams be ready for flanking maneuvers on my command. Cobra and Rabbit ... we're in the middle. Go ... everyone move!"

Billy watched as the four teams of twenty-four split off

in two directions and headed away toward the far sides of the cloud-port. "Let's go," he said, heading down the center of the concourse toward the mass of distant tents.

Rizzo, Rabbit's leader, joined Billy and his Cobras, matching his quick stride jog, step for step. Billy turned his head to look at Rizzo. "What's wrong with you, team leader?"

"Rabbit?"

Billy smiled. "What?"

"You did that on purpose … we've got lions, tigers, co-bras, bears … and my team are the rabbits?"

Billy's reply was interrupted, "Incoming!"

"Looks like four hovercraft en route. Each loaded with piles of rock," Seaman Goodwin of Cobra team announced. The words had only just left his lips when a stream of plasma bolts from one of the hovercraft hit him straight on in the visor.

"They've got mounted heavy guns on those crafts!" Rizzo said.

Billy yelled for everyone to hit the ground. He looked over at Goodwin and then at his row of small life-icons on his HUD. Goodwin's icon had turned light gray—he was dead.

"Listen up," Billy said, "those guns can breach our suits. We need to take them out first." Billy suspected that their visors were the weakest link in their armor, and Goodwin was the unfortunate recipient of a very lucky shot.

The four hovercraft had come to a stop about eighty yards away and he saw moving piles of rock jumping down from the open flat beds of the crafts and forming a line across the concourse—a line that would block any further progress toward the camp behind them.

"Rabbit team … I'm setting your drop location twenty yards behind them. Be careful what you're shooting at. We'll have them in a crossfire … just remember, Cobra will be in your line of fire as well." Billy gave Rizzo a nod.

Rabbit team got to their feet and Billy used the group phase-shift function to shift them all at once.

In a flash, the team disappeared and then reappeared on the other side of the Pharlom combatants. Almost immediately, Rabbit team engaged the enemy.

"Move up, Cobras!" Billy yelled into the open channel. His team sprinted forward and when close enough, began firing at the clusters of rock-like guards.

"These fuckers can take a licking," Sergeant Jackson said, four men over from Billy.

"Remember … head shots. Otherwise you're just wasting your plasma."

Billy heard chuckles over his comms at that. Two more of Cobra team went down from their big guns. Both shot in the visor. "Take those guns, damn it!"

The battle raged on for another five minutes. One by one, the Pharlom guards went down and their big hovercraft mounted plasma guns were captured. In the end, five Sharks were dead.

"Teams report," Billy said.

"Lions and Tigers in position" … "Zebras and Bears in position."

"Be prepared to split your teams … phase-shifting to improve your positions."

Billy ordered his teams onto the flatbed hovercraft and together they flew off toward the front gate of the camp. As they approached, Billy saw more Pharlom guards standing in a line. It looked as though they had set up a perimeter around the inside of the fence.

At forty yards out, Billy said, "Teams get ready … on my command."

He looked at the three other crafts, including his own. Four Sharks had taken up positions behind the large mounted plasma guns. They had to use two hands poised over a gargantuan trigger. Hovering several feet off the ground and moving at about thirty miles an hour—side by side, the hovercraft approached the camp's front gate.

"Take out the gate," Billy ordered. "All teams attack ... I repeat ... all teams attack."

The four mounted guns came alive at once and the tall gate and nearby fencing blew apart. As his armada of flatbed hovercraft entered into the camp, Billy noticed something for the first time. There was a raised tower, built on stilts, at the center of the camp. Atop it was a substantially bigger plasma cannon and it was firing non-stop from its unimpeded vantage point.

One to the left and one to the right, two hovercraft exploded in obliterating balls of fire—instantly killing no less than forty men.

Billy, and every other Shark, jumped from the hovercraft and made for cover—which consisted primarily of the rock pile bodies of the dead Pharlom guards.

"We're not going to last long with that cannon up there, Billy," Rizzo said. "I'm taking it out."

"Have at it ... take Jackson with you."

Two flashes, one right after the other, and Rizzo and Jackson were gone.

Billy continued to fire his multi-gun at three Pharloms making slow but consistent forward progress in his direction. The tower cannon roared and more explosions erupted—this time off to the east. *Hurry up, Rizzo ... we're losing good men here.*

The big gun went silent. Then, "Weapon neutralized," came Rizzo's voice on the open channel.

It took another twenty minutes before the last of the Pharlom guards either died fighting or surrendered to the Sharks.

Chapter 20

```
Alchieves System
The Minian, Bridge
```

Jason, via NanoCom, listened to Billy give his recount of the battle to take the cloud-port.

"Good job, Billy. I know you lost some good men today, but you kept prisoner fatalities to a minimum. I'll be down there in a few. Oh ... and rest up. You've got three other cloud-ports to take later on today. Hopefully there'll be fewer casualties."

Jason cut the connection and turned toward Orion. "Let's set a heavy cruiser down on the cloud-port and work out viable means to start transferring prisoners back to the surface. We'll take the *Minian* down to the cloud-port below and meet ... what was the prisoner's name?"

"It's Pike. Leon Pike, Captain," Ricket said.

"Fine. Let's go meet Mr. Pike and liberate some prisoners."

* * *

The gravity-defying cloud-port was immense ... a mile or so wide and easily thirty miles in length. Earlier, Jason ordered McNeil, at the helm, to bring the *Minian* down onto the cloud-port's open concourse. Billy and his team already had the camp secured and the surviving guards placed in custody. Dira and her team of doctors and medics were then dispatched to the scene. The cloud-port was still being hit pretty hard by falling debris and the prisoner death toll had risen into the hundreds.

Jason, too, wanted to get down to the cloud-port, but he needed to take care of some business first in his ready room. According to a high-priority interstellar memorandum from *Jefferson Station*, soon after the *Minian*'s departure, his father had taken the *Assailant*, along with a small armada, through an interchange wormhole, out to the Dacci system to confront the Sahhrain. *What the hell was he thinking?* From what Jason had learned, the Sahhrain were on a whole different level from other combatants, such as the Pharloms, or even the Craing for that matter. The truth was, the Sahhrain made Jason more than a little nervous. And now to make things even more worrisome, the admiral hadn't reported in. Subsequently, two separate drones were dispatched through interchange wormholes over the last few hours and neither was heard from either. Jason reread the memorandum and something else occurred to him—did the Sahhrain now have access to interstellar wormhole travel? No ... he remembered ... even the slightest operational or crew type alteration detected by the *Minian*'s AI prompted immediate security safeguards—safeguards that had been put in place for just such a scenario. He let out a breath. *Jesus, Dad ... what the hell have you gotten yourself into?*

Jason was being hailed. "Go for Captain ... what's up, Billy?"

"Captain, there's a Leon Pike out here who wants to speak to you."

"Who?"

"Remember … the prisoner that first made contact with us?"

"Yep … tell him to hold tight, I'm on my way."

* * *

Jason and Ricket exited together from the *Minian*'s rearmost hatchway, via one of the five big ship's airlocks. As they walked down the gangway, Jason took in the scene around and below him. Hundreds, if not thousands, of identical-looking tent structures, barracks, filled the long concourse lying beyond where the *Minian* was parked.

Dark smoke billowed into the air from scattered fragments of falling ship wreckage—some small, and some the size of a school bus. Jason caught Star Watch uniforms interspersed throughout the hordes of prisoners.

Ricket pointed toward a cluster of people, about one hundred yards away. "There, Captain."

Jason leaned forward and squinted his eyes. How Ricket was able to see anything that far a distance out amazed him. In Ricket's past, before regaining full-organic beingness, he'd been a cyborg—a state he'd endured for close to two hundred years and the consequence of an old Craing religious process, called the *Transformation of Eternity*. Ricket, potentially, could have lived for thousands of years. But just last year, new Caldurian MediPod technology made it possible for him to shed his mechanical aspects. But recently he'd begun to reintroduce certain internal technology into his physiology that went far beyond the standard nano-devices Jason, and select others on board the *Minian*, shared. Was Ricket, inadvertently, migrating back toward his earlier cyborg existence?

Eyebrows raised, Jason gave Ricket an appraising look.

Ricket smiled. "Come, they wait for us, Captain."

Together, they hurried down the gangway and entered into the throngs of people. Jason noticed a pen setup for Pharlom guards—now they were the prisoners. Rizzo was ushering two more Pharlom guards into the same pen at gunpoint. He gave Jason a quick wave and continued on with his duties.

By the time Jason reached the field medical station, he and Ricket had been stopped by dozens of prisoners. All had questions: Where should I go? How do I find my husband, my wife, my child? How do I get back home? Jason's hatred toward the Pharloms grew in magnitude with each one's desperate plea. At this point, he wanted to find Traveler's hammer and pummel every last one of the Pharloms into dust.

Jason's heart skipped a beat seeing Dira's pretty face up ahead. She was directing other medics toward several Tromians lying on cots. They looked to have the most serious injuries—primarily burns. As they approached, Dira saw Jason, bringing a brief smile to her face. Then she was pulled over by a man to another patient ... a young woman.

"Just as soon as the next MediPod becomes available, we'll transport her and get her fixed up," Dira said to the man.

"No ... Now! She needs a MediPod, right now ... can't you see her suffering?"

The man had a grip on Dira's upper arm and positioned his face mere inches from hers.

Jason stepped in and put his own hand around the man's shoulder. "You need to back off, sir."

The man turned toward Jason and jerked his shoulder away. "Look at her ... look at the pain she's in!"

136

Jason looked down where the man pointed and saw what once may have been a beautiful young woman. Her blond hair was matted with blood, and most of her face was charred black with second and third degree burns. Her eyes were closed but she was awake. Jason saw that her hands were tightly clenched with white knuckles.

"I'll give her more pain meds," Dira interjected. "As bad as she looks, she's in no danger of dying. But others are."

"What's her name?" Jason asked.

"Hanna," Leon said. "I don't know her last name, or if she even has one."

It was then Jason realized the man was human ... human ... and from Earth. And one more thing, he had internal nano-devices. "Who are you?" Jason asked.

"I'm Leon Pike ... the one who called you guys."

"Yes, you spoke with me, Mr. Pike," Ricket said.

Leon looked down at Ricket, noticing him for the first time with recognition registering on his face. "Yes ... thank you for helping—"

Jason cut him off, "You served aboard *The Lilly?*"

Leon, obviously taken aback by the question, held Jason's stare. "How do you know that?"

"Because, until recently, she was my ship. There's not too many people walking around wearing the kind of Caldurian nano-devices you're equipped with."

Leon let out a slow, long breath, keeping his eyes on Hanna. He nodded, almost imperceptibly, and then looked back at Jason. "You're one of the admiral's sons ... I'd heard him talk about you ... both you and Brian. At that time you were still back on Earth and had no idea your father was even alive."

"So what happened?" Jason asked.

"A mission ... the destroyer I was on was attacked by a

Craing cruiser. Three plasma blasts and the ship was done for ... we had to ditch onto the nearest planet. Long story short, the ship was toast and I was the only survivor. It was over a year before I was rescued. Considering the Allied forces never took the time to look for me, I decided I'd forgo my obligation to return to military duty. In their eyes I was dead anyway."

"But you're not dead, and now I have to figure out what the hell to do with you."

Hanna moaned. Her eyes opened and, in that instant, Jason realized he'd seen those same eyes before.

Suddenly, the world beneath their feet didn't just shake, it dropped out from under them. Screams came from all directions. Anyone standing before was now either scrambling for something to hold on to, or was already on the ground.

"What the hell was that?" Jason asked, looking out at the sea of people who, like himself, were thrown down onto the hard surface of the concourse.

Chapter 21

Sol System
The *Minian*, Zoo Habitat 7

They were seated on thick blankets, back in the same subterranean ruins—in the same room as before. Candles were lit and flames flickered, causing shadows to dance on the stone walls and ornate columns. There was a faint sound of wind blowing above—off in the distance.

"Drink this," Briar said.

"What is it? It looks gross."

"Just drink it, Boomer ... the less you think about it the better."

Boomer held the steaming cup up to her nose. "It smells rank."

Briar nodded. "As much as you can ... come on, be a big girl."

Boomer knew she should have told her father ... spoken to him about the nomads and who Briar really was. And now she wanted her to drink this—whatever it was ... tea concoction. "Will the changes to me be *reversimle* ...?"

"You mean reversible?"

"Yeah. Can I reverse things if I don't like what it does to me?"

"No."

"Maybe I should think about this ... talk to my father first."

Briar leaned back and stared at Boomer for several seconds. "As a *Kahill Callan* master, one, in time, learns to make potions. The Blues have many different potions for many different things. The liquid you're holding in your hands ... that mixture of herbs, minerals, and alien organic compounds, is called *Jahhlorine* ... a transformation potion, which came from various planets, all around the galaxy. It took many lifetimes to accumulate and very little of it remains. You could not put a dollar amount on its value, especially since so many have died—not only to procure this potion, but in keeping it safe for over a thousand years. This is your one chance, your one opportunity, Boomer. You have been chosen, but you must make the ultimate choice whether or not to continue on yourself. I know it's not an easy decision. And I won't lie ... things will never be the same for you."

Boomer stared into the cup's liquid and felt its hot, swirling mist on her cheeks. She put the cup to her lips and hesitated. Her eyes looked over the upper lip of the cup, holding Briar's own. She slowly went ahead, drinking up its smelly contents, till not a drop remained.

She gasped. "That was really, really gross. I think I might hurl."

Briar took the cup from her. "Don't throw up, Boomer ... think about something else. About your training." Briar looked into the now empty cup.

"Did you have to drink this stuff, too?"

"Yes ... I was older than you and I wasn't able to swallow more than a few sips. I'm not sure anyone's ever consumed a whole cup before … yuck, it's disgusting."

Boomer laughed and put a hand on her stomach. "I really feel like I'm going to be sick."

Prince Aahil Aqeel entered the room without making the slightest noise. Boomer watched him approach, as if he were gliding. Perhaps it was the potion … maybe she was hallucinating? She placed the palm of her hand on her forehead and closed her eyes. "I feel funny."

She opened her eyes again to see that the prince was now seated next to Briar. Both were smiling.

"Do you feel better?" Aahil asked.

"I think so. What happens now?"

Aahil did not reply right away. His smile was gone, replaced by a worried expression. "Boomer, your training is now more important than ever. And it must be expedited … quickened."

"Why?"

"The Sahhrain are why. They are advancing again. And something else: They have taken your grandfather."

"You mean my grandfather, the admiral?"

Aahil nodded.

"I need to tell my father … he'll rescue him," Boomer said, starting to get up.

"In the end, we believe only you can stop the Sahhrain. And only after more training."

"Me? That's crazy … I'm just a little kid. No! My father will do it."

"Captain Reynolds will need your help. Boomer, the Sahhrain have great powers … powers beyond technology. Only one with Kahill Callan training can accomplish what will be necessary."

"You are a master of Kahill Callan, right?" Boomer asked.

"Yes, I am a Tahli warrior."

"And Briar, are you a Tally warrior, too?"

"It's pronounced Tah-lee. And yes, just recently ... but my training is still not complete; I still have much to learn from the prince here," she replied, glancing at Aahil.

"Then why do you need me? I don't understand," Boomer said.

"Even before you took the potion, Boomer, you had amazing powers of your own. Perhaps from the events that transpired during your time realm ordeal last year ... I do not know. But the potion will only enhance what was already preexisting within you. You, Boomer, are the one we have been looking for ... you are our one last hope to alter what has been foreseen as the end of all that is good ... the end of temperance throughout the universe. You too will become a Tahli warrior; you will make a stand against the evil one, called Lord Vikor Shakrim."

"Even his name sounds scary," Boomer said, looking apprehensive.

"Even he is unaware of his own true powers ... his potential, and his profound influence on things to come within the galaxy."

"How do you know all this ... like about what happened to me with the time realms and what's going to happen in the future?"

Briar said, "In time, you too will possess this ability, Boomer, as your training progresses. But it's the Council of One that guides us and provides prophesies to us. They led us to you, Boomer. Again ... you are our true one hope."

"What if you've made a mistake? I don't feel comfortable with everything you said," Boomer said, feeling overwhelmed. She wanted to leave now; get away from this place ... these people. She wanted her father.

Aahil held something up for her to see. "This is an enhancement shield. It is the weapon of a Tahli warrior. The Sahhrain have a very similar device." Aahil flipped the small, curved triangular shaped, hubcap-sized object over, showing Boomer its underside. He slid his left forearm into two straps there, so the shield would stay securely on his arm. Briar reached behind herself and came up with another shield. She also fitted two straps onto her left forearm. They stood, removed their sandals, and walked to the middle open section of the room. They bowed their heads at each other and quickly took up a fighting stance.

They now had Boomer's complete attention and she no longer wanted to leave.

Briar was the first to strike. She swung a kick out with her right foot, towards Aahil's head—a roundhouse kick, like Boomer was familiar with. Aahil easily stepped away from it and countered with his own sidekick, which connected with Briar's exposed right-side torso. So forceful was the blow, Briar was elevated several feet off the ground. Boomer caught Briar grimace as she sailed through the air. But she didn't fall. She used the shield … got it pointed beneath her and somehow propelled herself up into the air, where she flipped back around, landing lightly on her feet.

"What?!" Boomer yelled, excitement now clearly evident on her face.

Briar was on the move again; this time, she used her shield to attack. With both hands behind the shield she pointed it directly at Aahil's head, and punched it forward. In that instant, the shield produced a violet, wave-like, distortion—one that shot toward Aahil, but was deflected by his own shield at the very last moment.

Aahil countered with a shield blast of his own, directed toward Briar's feet. She fell toward the ground, but again, at the very last second, she propelled herself upward, regained her footing, and attacked. Now both warriors were strictly using their shields—firing distortion blasts, one after another. Sparks flew as distortion waves were intersecting in front of them.

Boomer noticed while Briar was getting winded, her auburn hair wet and matted to her forehead, Aahil looked as fresh as when he first started out. Much of the time he wasn't even looking at his opponent, he was looking over at Boomer.

"You, too, will learn the fighting ways of a Tahli warrior, Boomer," Aahil said. "You then will be a master of Kahill Callan in your own right." Still looking at Boomer, Aahil deflected several more distortion blasts from Briar, then used his shield to propel himself upward, into a backward flip, and landed on the back side of Briar. She was taken by surprise and it cost her. He used his shield—not only to elevate her several feet into the air—but to also restrict her movements. She looked paralyzed. Only her eyes moved and she blinked in succession several times until Aahil released her. She fell to the floor, hard, landing on her backside.

"Ouch, that hurt, Aahil!" she exclaimed, getting to her feet and rubbing her rear end.

Aahil continued, "Tomorrow your training begins, Boomer. By then, the potion will have altered your body's physiology enough so you can start working out with an enhancement shield."

"I get one of those?" Boomer asked, pointing to the enhancement shield on Briar's arm.

"Yes, we have one for you. Boomer … tonight you will notice certain things … changes. Do not be alarmed. Briar will be able to answer all of your questions. She will be your Kahill Callan instructor."

"You won't be teaching me?" Boomer asked.

"No. You will face-off with me only when Briar has

taught you all that she can. And only when you can defeat her in battle. And that may take quite some time."

Chapter 22

Alchieves System
Planet Trom, Cloud-Port E5926

The ground dropped beneath them again, this time even farther than the last time.

"Captain, I believe at least one, perhaps several, anti-gravity generators on this cloud-port have become disabled ... perhaps from falling debris," Ricket said, already back on his feet. "I need to get to those generators ... perhaps they can be repaired."

Jason stood. His main concern was with those in the field medical station. Dira was at Hanna's side, along with Hanna's deserter companion, Leon. The ground rumbled again and everyone stood braced, apprehensive.

"Hey, Captain ..."

Jason turned to see Billy, jogging in his direction, accompanied by a Tromian. Both were stumbling every few steps due to the increasingly turbulent shaking.

"What is it, Billy?"

"This is Security Commander Larkbadder; in addition to being kept a prisoner here, he's in charge of security, here and on other cloud-ports. He says one of the anti-gravity generators is giving out."

Jason glanced over to Ricket, who nodded appreciatively.

"What can we do, Security Commander ... can it be repaired?"

Larkbadder was already shaking his head. "That's where I've just come from. The anti-gravity generators are positioned around the periphery of the cloud-port. Ten of them, twenty feet down. Each one is encased in a protective vault that's supposed to be impervious to all environmental mishaps, or even to enemy attacks. But the drive section of a falling spacecraft striking a generator was far and away more than anyone planned for." Larkbadder pointed to a particularly dark plume of smoke rising into the air several miles away.

"Can the other generators compensate for the damaged one?" Ricket interjected.

"Well, that's what they're doing now ... but the added strain is taking its toll. Soon, like you felt from that big drop, the other generators are going to give out."

"How much time do we have?"

"It could be hours or it could be minutes."

"Look, there's thousands of people on this floating rock ... I suppose we can try to squeeze them all onto our ship, and onto other vessels," Jason said, not looking too confident.

"No, Captain ... I don't think we have enough time to do that. I suggest we move everyone onto the one remaining SkyTrans vessel. It needs a little maintenance, but it's capable of staying airborne. And since it's already prepped to take on passengers, we can get everyone on board much sooner."

As if on cue, the ground began to shake again, then dropped several more feet. Jason felt a familiar *quick-drop-in-an-elevator* sensation and steadied himself. "I think you're right, Commander; let's get them on board that SkyTrans,

ASAP. Is there any way to broadcast ... like a PA system?"

Larkbadder looked toward a cluster of buildings, along the outskirts of the cloud-port. "Yes, but I'll need to get up to that tower over there."

Jason looked around out at the mass of bodies. This could easily turn ugly. The last thing they needed was a stampede. He needed every last man he had for crowd control. He turned and found Pike. "You, Mr. Pike, go with the security commander to the tower. Help him with whatever he needs."

Leon looked down at Hanna with a worried expression.

Dira said, "I'm transferring her to the *Minian* now. Go ... there's nothing more you can do for her."

Leon didn't look particularly pleased but left with Larkbadder anyway.

"I want the *Minian* airborne within the next five minutes. There's no way we're going down with this rock." Jason turned to Dira. "We need to transfer all the injured into the *Minian*'s hospital and use one of her holds for overflow."

"I'm a step ahead of you, Captain. If you'll make an exception to the no-phase-shifting-on-board-ship rule, we can start phase-shifting the injured over, using our crew in battle suits."

"Yes, go ahead; do whatever needs to be done."

"Captain."

Jason was quickly getting overwhelmed. "Yes, what is it, Ricket?"

"Has anyone actually verified that that SkyTrans can stay aloft? I mean, if the cloud-port should start falling?"

Jason continued to stare down at Ricket until the booming voice of Larkbadder distracted him.

"Attention. Attention all Tromians. Soon you will be directed where to go. You will be leaving this cloud-port. Gather what belongings you have and stay together with your families. Standby for further notice."

Billy was still communicating with the *Minian* as more and more of the crew, mostly military from the *Minian*'s barracks, but other crewmembers too, headed down forward and rear gangways.

"Okay, Cap ... I need to get our Sharks in place for crowd control."

"Go ahead. Let me know if you need me for anything," Jason said. Rizzo was kneeling at Dira's side and she was telling him to be careful as he gingerly slid two arms beneath Hanna and slowly stood. He nodded to Dira. A second later, in a white flash, they phase-shifted away.

"Captain?"

Jason looked down to see Ricket, staring up at him. "Oh ... I'm sorry, Ricket. You were saying something about the SkyTrans?"

"Yes, are you certain it can actually stay aloft?"

"Why wouldn't it be able to?"

Ricket pointed to the huge, dirt-colored, transport vehicle, stationed at the side of the cloud-port. Jason slightly turned his head. "Is it ... tilting a bit ... or is that my imagination?"

"Yes. It is somewhat off-kilter, Captain. I believe the constant, abrupt dropping and the numerous tremors have had an adverse affect on the SkyTrans's mooring. Look, the SkyTrans is not actually aloft at the present moment; its entire weight is resting on the concourse."

"That can't be good," Jason said. "What do you need from me ... how can I help?"

"We need to inspect the vehicle's cockpit, as soon as possible."

Jason looked at the big transport engine and tried to guess where the cockpit might be.

"I've uploaded the SkyTrans's schematics overlay onto our HUDs, Captain. I have the phase-shift coordinates already loaded," Ricket said.

"Good. Take us on in, then, Ricket."

* * *

Ricket phase-shifted them into a circular vestibule area on the second level. Jason didn't know what he expected the inside of a SkyTrans to look like, but this wasn't it. The transport engine had obviously been ridden hard for many years. Looking at his HUD's translucent schematic overlay, he saw there were actually five levels, none much different from this one. Small porthole windows lined both sides of the expansive cabin, providing just enough light to see—but barely. The seats were metal, somewhat like aluminum. There were at least one hundred rows, crossing from port to starboard, segmented by wide aisles every ten seats or so. As he looked back toward the stern of the vessel, the seat rows seemed to go on forever.

The deck was littered with trash, and he imagined it didn't smell all that great either. A single worn shoe lay at his feet.

"Captain, the cockpit is through here."

Jason spun around, noticing Ricket was gone. They were close to the bow of the vessel and there was only one hatchway, located off to the side. Again, he heard Ricket's voice.

"I think we have a problem, Captain."

Jason moved through a narrow, almost tubular, corridor, entering what had to be the SkyTrans cockpit ... or, more accurately, the bridge. It was wide, spanning the width of the vessel, but not very deep. Several consoles were positioned at the front of the compartment and the controls looked dated—mostly mechanical levers and switches. Ricket stood and immediately fell as the ship began to violently shake.

"What is it, Ricket?" Jason asked, heading over to him and helping him up to his feet.

Ricket pointed to a series of four-in-a-row meters. "We have no battery reserves, Captain. Getting the SkyTrans drives up and running will be impossible."

"Batteries, like in an automobile?"

Ricket looked somewhat confused. "Similar ... I suppose."

"Then can we jump-start this old ship ... like from the *Minian*?" Jason asked him.

Chapter 23

Dacci System
Planet Dacci, Glist Mining Crater AB14

Lord Vikor Shakrim stood with his hands on his hips, his cloak flapping in the steady, swirling updraft. He looked to the far horizon. The surface of Dacci was like no other world—its rich concentration of unique, many radioactive, minerals, one of a kind compounds, metals with bazaar magnetic properties, all contributed to a surface that glowed a ghostly blue—most noticeably in the early evenings, or, like now … in the early morning dawn. His mind turned to Admiral Reynolds … he'd come close to killing the Allied forces commander and he had to give the old human his due … he'd withstood incredible pain … both mentally and physically. Not to mention the humiliation—always an important, contributing factor, to achieving optimum results. Had Shakrim gleaned all that he could from Reynolds? It was hard to say. One thing was for certain … the admiral was broken … and he would never be the same.

Below the metal catwalk on which he stood was a crater of unimaginable proportions. Too many miles across to see its far side with any real clarity, Lord Shakrim concentrated instead on the spiraling roadway that traversed the gapping orifice all the way down to its bottom. Machines moved and jittered about below at the crater's furthest depth, looking more like small toys than the massive, earthmoving equipment they actually were.

"Glist." He spoke the word out loud as he looked to the two thousand-year-old enhancement shield secured on his left forearm. Movement caught his eye. Big yellow containers, carrying the rare blue-glowing mineral, were now making their way up the steep, near vertical, rising and curving roadway. Even from this distance, the ore shimmered in the early morning light. The Sahhrain leader embraced feelings of exhilaration. An unadulterated spasm of power filled his consciousness, for it was this strange mineral compound, found only here in its purest form, and nowhere else in the universe, that would give him the ultimate potential for power. Blue Glist would propel his future far beyond even his wildest dreams. Dreams of spreading the darkness ... for only with darkness could *Rom Dasticon* rise and take ahold within this realm. This was no fable deity or religious imagining, as so many even among the Sahhrain believed. *Rom Dasticon* was real—the true Sachem, and Lord Vikor Shakrim's only master.

Unconsciously, he let his fingertips trail along the shield's engraved contours. He felt the energy from the Glist pushing back, repelling his subtle touch. He uttered the word again, "Glist."

Below, the steady procession of ascending container vehicles had stopped.

"What is the hold up?" Lord Shakrim asked, without looking at the group of nervous Dacci mining officials standing on either side of him on the catwalk.

"There ... an empty container vehicle heading down into

the crater … has apparently clipped the leading ascending container vehicle. It's only a temporary jam-up, my Lord."

Lord Shakrim let out a hot breath and turned toward the young Dacci man, who was naturally good-natured. His wide, green eyes stared hopefully toward Shakrim. Shakrim didn't like being looked at by lesser beings. "You will do well to remove your gaze from me, Dacci imbecile."

"Yes, my Lord."

"What is being done to alleviate the problem, Dacci? Minutes count. A delay here causes a delay in my enhancement shields being manufactured. That is unacceptable."

"Soon, I promise, a repair team will arrive and evaluate the problem. Please be patient, my Lord Shakrim."

"No … you, personally, will evaluate the problem."

The Dacci man smiled apologetically and held out his hands, a gesture that conveyed there was nothing he could do here, so far above the accident thousands of feet below.

On the catwalk, a quiet hush befell those around Lord Shakrim as the Dacci man seemed magically lifted into the air—up off the catwalk—as though he were caught in a tractor beam. Shakrim adjusted the direction on his enhancement shield's face and the Dacci man began to move outward, over the gaping mouth of the crater. As Lord Shakrim increased the shield's power, the violet distortion emitted became more visible.

The Dacci man's surprised murmurs turned to pleas for help, then changed to desperate screams. He flailed his arms and kicked, as if trying to gain purchase on some invisible step or ledge. Shakrim's typically sour expression was now one of mild bemusement.

The Dacci man's flailing eased some as he was lowered deeper into the crater, nearing the accident site. At five hundred feet above the container vehicles the Dacci man's progress halted in mid-air. He looked up and found Lord Vikor Shakrim standing on the catwalk far above him. The Dacci man's facial expression, just beginning to show hopefulness of a positive outcome, turned to grimaced bafflement.

With a casual gesture of his right hand, Shakrim pointed to a small, quickly moving hover truck, far below. An assessment crew had arrived.

At that same moment, realization struck the Dacci man—his services were no longer required. The violet distortion field faded into a mist ... then was gone. The Dacci man dropped in silence ... his body landing into the open container bin.

Lord Vikor Shakrim placed no further attention on the goings on below. He looked up and found several visible stars, and thought of his Sachem, *Rom Dasticon*, the most powerful force in the universe ... *though not this universe*. His eyes roamed across the heavens above, as if he were looking for something specific. Which, abstractly, he was. Somewhere out there was the ship that would bring his Sachem forth—here, into this realm. The ancient writings foretold of this phenomenon; his visions, too, had shown it to be true. The vessel, called the *Minian*, would bring to him the *Rom Dasticon* from the farthest depths of the multiverse.

* * *

Boomer ran barefoot among the broken, eroding ruins within HAB 7. Her lungs burned and the ever-present gritty wind caused her eyes to sting and water. Gone was her spacer's jumpsuit—gone was the set of small throwing knives she typically kept hidden. Today she wore the lightweight garments of the desert nomad. And today, she carried the weapon of the Tahli warrior: a smaller-sized enhancement shield, worn snugly on her left forearm.

Briar Mansfield was running next to her and Boomer was mustering everything she could to keep pace with this Kahill Callan master's long fluid stride. "Use the shield to propel you; direct its energy down and backward, like this." Briar's own shield, which she'd reversed on her arm to face downward, moved back and forth, corresponding in cadence to her running stride. Boomer watched as Briar pulled far ahead, her strides easily twenty to thirty feet long. She soon circled around, running back to Boomer's side.

"The shield uses, enhances, your own highly-focused thoughts," Briar told her. "Thoughts have a vibration rate. You must talk to the shield ... communicate with it ... feel the vibrations moving back and forth between you and the shield. Remember, your shield is a part of you ... not a separate thing."

"Well, it's not doing any of that crap for me. I think my shield is broken. I think you gave me a broken shield ... that, or maybe this one's just a stupid toy," Boomer said, irritated.

The two slowed and came to a stop at what looked, to Boomer, like remains of a stone bridge, which abruptly ended over their heads, twenty feet up.

"What is this place?" Boomer asked, trying to catch her breath.

"It's just an old aquifer. It once used to flow water to other parts of the city."

"What happened to the city?"

"Thousands of years ago it was a beautiful place ... a Shangri-La. It was destroyed during the third rising."

"Third rising?"

"The Sahhrain's third rising."

"How many risings have they had?" Boomer asked.

"They are on their fifth ... some fear that they won't be

156

defeated this time—that they've finally come into their own time."

Boomer wasn't sure she understood all Briar said, but nodded her head just the same.

"Here, give me your shield, Boomer ... let me take a look at it."

Boomer slid it off her arm, handing it over to Briar.

"You haven't graced it yet."

"What do you mean? Graced it?"

"When you put it on, or take it off ... you thank it for its gifts ... for the gifts it bestows on you." Briar took the small shield and placed her own palm on its outer surface. "Shalla ka la rohlm."

Boomer repeated Briar's words, "Shalla ka la ... rohlm?"

"That's right. It means *gratitude into the light*."

"You try it." Briar handed it back.

Boomer smiled, placed her palm upon its surface, and feeling somewhat silly, said, "Shalla ka la rohlm."

Had she just felt something? A tingle ... an almost imperceptible electrical charge?

"You ready to go again?" Briar asked.

"I'm ready," Boomer said, slipping the shield over her hand and onto her forearm. For sure, this time she did feel *something*. Boomer didn't wait for Briar; she sprinted forward, along the worn path, trying to get at least some kind of head start. She positioned the shield face down and let it move back and forth, the way Briar had done. She reflected on her thoughts, being vibrations, and tried communicating, actually talking, to the shield. Her next stride took her completely by surprise: She'd leapt a twenty-foot distance in the blink of an eye.

Chapter 24

```
Alchieves System
SkyTrans Transport Vessel E911v, Planet
Trom, Cloud-Port E5926
```

The cloud-port fell several more feet before jolting to a stop. Both Ricket and Jason were thrown to the deck.

"Would that work ... using the *Minian* to recharge the batteries?" Jason asked.

"No, Captain ... but that did give me another idea that has promise."

Jason got to his feet and waited for Ricket to continue.

"The energy storage device this engine uses is dated technology ... quite inefficient, really. The SkyTrans propulsion system utilizes one large ion drive. Hmm, I'll need to manufacture a flash power source, in the *Minian*'s phase synthesizer ... something that won't take long to make."

"Ricket, this cloud-port is about to fall. We have only minutes—"

"Yes, Captain. Please meet me in the engineering section of this vehicle ... I will be there within seven minutes." With that, Ricket closed his helmet's visor and flashed away. Jason went to the port observation window and looked down at the concourse below. Large groups of people were moving into designated areas in front of the various SkyTrans loading ramps. He heard the voice of Security Commander Larkbadder broadcasting directives from the PA system. Jason looked directly across to the tall control tower, on the other side of the concourse, where he figured both Larkbadder and Leon Pike were probably standing at this moment. His thoughts went from Larkbadder to Leon, who seemed like a strange man. Not entirely unlikable and, if he was entirely honest with himself, he wasn't so sure he'd have reacted any differently after being marooned on an alien planet for a year. *So what to do with him?* He had qualities that could be useful. And he knew this sector of space better than any of them.

Jason heard Larkbadder's voice again and realized hordes of people were moving—rushing forward, toward the ramps. *Crap!* He'd let the time run away! He brought up the SkyTrans schematic overlay and pinpointed engineering's location. It would be a tight squeeze, but he found a location suitable to phase-shift into. About to phase-shift away, Jason was hailed.

"Go for Captain."

"Captain … I'm reading highly-elevated heat signatures from four other anti-gravity generators. They're red-lining, Cap!"

"We're working on it, Gunny," Jason said, looking back out the window. At first he didn't see any sign of the *Minian*, but he then spotted her about one thousand feet above. "I'm hoping it won't come to this, but be prepared to phase-shift anyone wearing a battle suit back onto the *Minian*—save as many as possible, if this rock falls."

"I think most would phase-shift off themselves, Cap …

but, yes, we'll ensure our people get off the cloud-port."

Jason cut the connection and phase-shifted to the Sky-Trans's opposite end. As dingy and grimy as the passenger and bridge sections of the SkyTrans engine were, he found engineering far worse for wear and neglect. Steam hissed and sprayed from too many broken, or cracked, pipe openings to count, and the air was thick with humidity. Pipes of every size surrounded him. Large boiler-type containers took up nearly the entire compartment space. Corrosion and sediment gave everything an archaic, on the verge of crumbling apart, feeling. *How old is this thing?*

Jason, again using the schematic overlay to locate where the ship's actual drive mechanism was located, found it was farther back, more toward the stern. Heading twenty steps down a narrow passage, amid a jungle of more pipes, he found it. The massive drive system took up most of the stern section of the vessel—surprisingly, it looked to be partially mechanical-looking, strange for it being an ion drive. Here too, everything was all dripping with condensation; it sat idle. Jason thought it would be a miracle if the thing even turned over.

The SkyTrans began to rock back and forth. Jason had the same sinking feeling in his gut and waited for the cloud-port to stop falling. Eventually, it did … but the rocking motion continued. They were running out of time. *Where the hell's Ricket?*

Jason saw the flash of something and Ricket's life-icon appeared on his HUD, along with Bristol's. Jason walked forward and came to a set of steps leading up to a metal catwalk.

"Here, Captain."

Jason found Ricket, kneeling down by a black, nondescript enclosure the size of a typical Navy-issue footlocker.

He seemed to be trying to figure out how to open it. Bristol was holding an advanced-looking, toaster-sized piece of equipment that looked completely out of place in these surroundings.

Bristol, seeing Jason approach, handed him the device. "Hold this."

Bristol's disregard of respecting military protocol came as no surprise to Jason. The truth was, Bristol didn't actually hold a military post on the *Minian*. He was more of a consultant than anything else. Brilliant as he was, Jason found even a little bit of the guy went a long way.

"Just get out of the way and let me do it," Bristol said to Ricket. "I don't see how you can do anything with those little Craing fingers of yours … Move!"

Ricket backed away, giving him space at the enclosure. Bristol moved his hands around a flange, one hand going left, the other going right, his fingertips probing its underneath side. His left hand abruptly stopped. He moved his right hand to the same corresponding position on the other side of the enclosure. He gripped his fingers and there came an audible unlatching sound. Bristol pulled up on the enclosure, and its upper half came away in his hands. "Out of the way … I'm putting this down right where you're standing."

Jason stepped back as the top half of the enclosure slammed down onto the catwalk.

Ricket moved quickly, taking the toaster-sized device away from Jason, and kneeled at the open enclosure. Bristol pulled a satchel around to his front that he wore over one shoulder. Inside it were a myriad of wires and cables and other small devices that Jason was clueless about.

"Use the ano-adapter to splice—"

"I already know that, Ricket. Why don't you just let me do it?" Bristol barked, nudging Ricket to the side with his scrawny shoulder.

Jason lost his balance as the SkyTrans began rocking violently. He found a horizontally running pipe, at head level, to grab on to. And then the shuddering started. Like little micro-falls. Ricket and Bristol looked up and around.

"Don't stop!" Jason commanded.

That earned Jason a backward glance from Bristol as he and Ricket quickly returned to whatever it was they were doing inside the enclosure.

Jason answered an incoming hail, "Go for Captain."

"We need to get you three out of there, Cap!" Orion yelled into his NanoCom.

"And leave thousands of Tromians to fall to their deaths? I think we've almost got it. Ricket and—"

"Then you don't know … the cloud-port … Captain, it's free falling!"

"What?"

"Free falling!"

"Okay … read off the altitude as we fall. We'll phase-shift out if we have to."

"You're at twenty-five thousand feet, and falling … twenty-four …"

Jason saw Ricket and Bristol were done—Bristol reaching for the top of the enclosure.

"Leave the fucking thing … we're free falling. Ricket, get this thing kicked over!"

Ricket looked up at Jason, his eyes wide behind his visor. "We can't do that from here. We need to get back to the bridge."

"Twenty-two thousand … Twenty-one thousand …"

"Then get us there!" Jason spat out.

Ricket continued to stare up at him. "The overlay schematic … Captain, there are … people crowded into the bridge."

"Eighteen thousand ... seventeen thousand ..."

Jason didn't hesitate and phase-shifted the three of them into the bridge compartment. Typically, Jason found that a phase-shift into solid mass would always displace the mass—the phase-shifter taking precedence over what was there. In the case of a phase-shift onto organic material, as would be the case here, the phase-shift process could be catastrophic to the recipient. Like a sudden impact akin to being hit by a car—organic material, such as a person, rarely walked away from it.

The flash occurred and bodies flew everywhere—screams filling the air.

"Fifteen thousand ... fourteen thousand ..."

"Everyone out of here! Now!" Jason yelled. Several Tromians, lying immobile on the deck, were either dead or unconscious. Scared, and moving way too slowly, the crowd began to clear out of the confined space.

"Thirteen thousand ... twelve thousand ..."

Jason pushed a man out of the way and looked for Ricket, but found Bristol instead. He was crouched down at the center console; Ricket's legs protruded from beneath it. He heard Ricket on the open channel: "Try it now!"

"Ten thousand ... nine thousand ..."

Bristol threw a large lever forward, and the SkyTrans began to vibrate ... but now it was a constant, rhythmic, vibration ... the drive had come alive!

"Seven thousand ..."

"We're still falling!" Jason yelled.

Ricket joined Bristol and both were busy at the controls. Jason wondered if it was time ... time to abandon and move his people from the SkyTrans and off the cloud-port. He wondered if he could really abandon the tens of thousands of Tromians on the cloud-port to meet their dire fate on the rapidly-approaching surface below.

"Five thousand ..."

Outside the forward observation window he saw the cloud-port falling away from their SkyTrans—plummeting faster toward the surface of Trom.

"I'm getting us out of here!" Jason yelled.

"Five thousand and sixty ... Five thousand and fifty ... Five thousand and forty ... Hey, Cap," Orion said, relief in her voice, "at your current rate of descent, you'll be able to land that thing and survive."

Ricket and Bristol glanced over to Jason ... both smiling.

Chapter 25

Alchieves System
Planet Trom, Cloud-Port E5926

Leon, grasping on to a vertical support beam within the cloud-base's control tower, was having a hard time staying on his feet. The distant SkyTrans, already separated from its berth, was only somewhat staying aloft on its own, slowly moving away from the falling cloud-port. For the last several minutes, Leon, without any notable success, tried using his internal NanoCom to request assistance from the *Minian*, while Larkbadder conversed with one of the tall, AI-controlled, *mecher* robots at the back of the tower.

Larkbadder looked concerned, his voice rose as he continued to interrogate the robot. He looked over to Leon, "We're in free fall … we're about to smash down onto the surface."

Leon nodded. "I know that! I've been trying to get someone's attention … anyone's, actually."

They'd opted to stay in the control tower even as the last stragglers hurried up several gangways onto the SkyTrans. Then, the free-fall began, and even walking was nearly impossible. Leon looked through the smashed-out observation window and could see the quickly-approaching planet's surface below them. He estimated the cloud-port they were on was no more than ten to fifteen thousand feet above the surface and was falling fast. Which meant they had mere minutes, if even that, to survive.

Leon turned away from the window and let out a controlled breath. "So, what is the bot saying?" he asked, not really interested.

"Basically ... that we're fucked."

That made Leon smile, in spite of the dire situation. Clumsily, the mecher stumbled its way over to Leon and introduced itself. "Hello, I am Trommy5."

"Uh huh," Leon said, turning away. He looked down toward the concourse below, trying his NanoCom again. He felt a hand tug on his shoulder and spun around. "Hey, just back off ... okay?" Leon said, expecting to see the annoying mecher.

But it wasn't the mecher. Billy Hernandez, Sergeant Jackson, and Rizzo stood there in their battle suits. "We need to go ... now!" Without another word Billy and Rizzo moved in close and wrapped their arms around Leon and Larkbadder.

Larkbadder almost pulled free. "That one too! Don't leave that bot!"

Jackson hesitated, but then, coming to some sort of mental resolve, went ahead and wrapped his arms around the tall, awkward, mecher. The six phase-shifted away, fifteen seconds before the cloud-port splashed into the largest of Trom's oceans below.

* * *

Leon, years earlier, spent time on *The Lilly*; he was assigned to her for sixteen months, so he was familiar with the beautiful aesthetics provided on a Caldurian vessel. But the *Minian*, at least one hundred years newer, took him by surprise. Sure, she was huge—over a mile long—but her symmetry and graceful lines ... the attention given to every detail, to the smallest degree, stunned him. Typically, starships were all about utility. But the *Minian* was much more than that; almost feminine in design, the ship had curves and padded bulkheads; muted colors were used throughout ... everything was flush and integrated ... impeccably constructed. As Leon walked the long corridor, he was quite sure she was one of the most advanced starships in the galaxy.

They had phase-shifted into the flight deck. Billy and Rizzo immediately sprinted away, having to attend to other emergencies. Jackson, big as any NFL linebacker, was their escort and walked several paces in front of Leon and Larkbadder. The mecher, Trommy5, was noisily clanging along behind.

Jackson, his visor raised, turned his big head back toward Leon. "Hey, man, the hospital is right there, off to the right. I'll take the commander and the ... um ... bot down to the barracks. You're supposed to be escorted, so let me know when you're done here."

Leon nodded, slowed to a stop and watched them as they headed in the direction of a nearby DeckPort. Leon watched as Larkbadder looked unsure about entering into the elevator-like opening. Only this opening wasn't solid—more like a constantly moving distortion field—one that would transport the user to any deck on the ship ... as long as the user had a clear intention of where he wanted to go. There were more conventional ways to use the DeckPort for the novice, as well, and Leon continued to watch as Jackson, undoubtedly, explained the other methods to Larkbadder and the bot. Eventually, Sergeant Jackson grabbed both Larkbadder's and Trommy5's wrists and together they stepped into the DeckPort. Leon knew the instant they stepped from this level they would step out onto another level—just as if they'd walked through a door.

Leon turned toward the doublewide hatchway on his right and entered the *Minian's* Medical area. Easily five times the size of that on *The Lilly*, this hospital had several large, adjacent compartments. The first one was equipped with numerous MediPods, all seeming to be in use, and there was a laboratory, of sorts, on the left. A more conventional hospital layout, with railed beds, also all in use, was off to the right. Medical personnel scurried here and there, some escorting injured Tromians to MediPods or, next door, into hospital beds.

At the far end of the compartment, Leon spotted a flash of violet skin. He headed off toward the exotic-looking doctor ... *what was her name? Oh yeah ... Dira.*

She was obviously the one in charge here. Leon watched as she gave instructions to one of the med techs. "This one's almost done ... get the elderly lady in the recovery room prepped." The med tech hurried off. Dira did a double-take when she saw Leon approaching.

"Mr. Pike. Heard you almost went for a swim in one of Trom's larger oceans."

"Well, I do like to make a splash ... but opted to keep breathing a while longer."

"You're here to see Hanna?"

Leon nodded.

"You found her," Dira said, gesturing toward the Medi-Pod behind him that he'd just passed.

Dira gestured for Leon to join her at her side. They both peered down into the small elongated window at the top

portion of the MediPod's clamshell-like top. Leon first noticed Hanna's straw-colored long hair; several strands had
fallen over her still face, her expression peaceful.

"Is she okay? Will she—"

"She's fine. That is, at least health-wise," Dira said, glancing back to Leon.

"What is that supposed to mean?"

Dira's reply was interrupted by the approach of Captain
Reynolds. Leon estimated him to be around forty, and physically very capable. As tall as Leon, he had dark hair and eyes,
and didn't seem like the typical skipper. Definitely didn't do
things by the book and, from what he'd observed, was friends
with much of the crew. They were loyal to him and he to
them. And there was definitely *something* going on between
him and Dira.

"How is she?" the captain asked, looking into the small
window on the opposite side of the MediPod.

"Hello to you, too, Jason," Dira said.

Jason smiled and held Dira's eyes for a moment … "Hello, Dira." His eyes shifted to Leon. "Mr. Pike."

"She's fine. I can let her out of this thing now," Dira said,
reaching for the MediPod's control tablet.

"Wait just a minute, Dira," the captain said—his eyes still
on Leon. "How well do you know this woman?"

"Know her?" said Leon. "I don't … not really. I saved her
life … rescued her from a falling building. Since then she's
helped me kill plenty of Pharloms. I assumed she was a university student on Trom." Leon shrugged, letting the captain
know that was all he knew.

Jason turned as a skinny guy in his late teens, or early
twenties, approached. His face, perpetually scowling, and his
beak-like nose, gave him a birdlike quality. Pimples, several
ripe for the picking, clustered around his chin and nose.

"Bristol … thanks for coming," the captain said.

"I was busy; what do you want?"

"I want you to take a look at this woman."

Leon didn't know what to make of that statement. What could this scrawny kid have to do with Hanna? But then he saw it too. Probably the same thing the captain had previously noticed. Beautiful Hanna, lying in the MediPod, and this homely kid shared something between them. They both had the same eyes. Mostly it was the same distinctive light blue color, but something else too: the structure of their brows and cheekbones. Their resemblance, in that regard, was uncanny.

Bristol peered down into the MediPod, little changing in his sour expression. "Yeah … so what?"

Hanna opened her eyes and looked around her surroundings. Initially, fear showed in her expression but then understanding—perhaps she remembered what happened to her on Trom—being transported here to the *Minian*'s hospital to be treated for severe burns.

She looked to her left first and saw Dira, then her eyes moved to Leon's. She smiled. Turning her head she looked out through the other window and saw Bristol. Hanna's expression turned to confusion and then … intense emotion, as her eyes, so similar to the skinny young man's above her, brimmed with tears. Her hands came up, covering her mouth, and she began sobbing within the confines of the MediPod.

Chapter 26

Alchieves System
The *Minian*, Medical

The clamshell slowly separated, coming to a stop once fully opened. Jason watched as Bristol continued to stare down at the MediPod's lone inhabitant.

Hanna, composed to the point she'd stopped crying, swung her feet over the MediPod's side and down onto the deck. Dira held out her hand, giving added support to Hanna, who slowly stood. She turned and, finding Leon, a fleeting smile returned.

Jason didn't like surprises—when it came to Bristol. His brother, a murderous pirate currently spending the rest of his life imprisoned in what used to be HAB 12 on *The Lilly*, single-handedly killed too many crewmembers, and almost killed Mollie and Nan, and Boomer, more than once. So if this woman was involved with Stalls or Bristol, Jason needed to know the particulars.

"Hanna," Dira said, "this is Captain Reynolds. He'd like to speak with you."

Hanna looked at Jason, using her fingertips to brush

back stray hairs from her face. "Hello, Captain. Thank you for saving me … for saving us."

He watched her, particularly how she avoided making eye contact with Bristol who, only moments before, drew such an emotional response from her.

"Please excuse my abruptness, but I'm sure you understand that the security of my ship is paramount."

She nodded.

"What's the story with you and Bristol?"

With a quick glance, Jason watched Bristol's reaction to the question. Hanna's eyes darted to Bristol, who also stole a glance in her direction. Neither said anything, but Bristol's face had flushed bright pink.

"What's with the third degree, Captain?" Leon interjected. "Why don't you give the poor girl a second to—"

"Mind your tongue, Mr. Pike … Need I remind you, you are a guest on this ship?"

Leon didn't answer, but he didn't argue either.

Jason turned to Bristol. "Who is she to you?"

Bristol used a fingernail to probe at his pimply chin. He shrugged. "I think she's my sister."

Jason saw tears begin to well up in Hanna's eyes again. "I thought you were dead, Bristol. They said you were dead."

Bristol crossed his thin arms over his chest. He was clearly uncomfortable with the situation and, by the way he was biting his lip, looked on the verge of tears himself. Jason let the silence hang in the air.

Abruptly, Hanna took two steps forward and threw her arms around Bristol. She cried into his neck. He slowly pulled his arms free and hugged her back. Jason and Dira exchanged a quick glance.

When they separated, Jason raised his brow, a silent prompt for one of them to explain.

Hanna said, pointing, "I haven't seen him, my younger brother, Bristol ... in six years. Actually, he's my half-brother."

Bristol's sour expression was back. "Look ... it's no big deal. We share the same father ... making me and Stalls her half-brothers. We had different mothers."

"I spent the first twelve years of my life a captive at Flatigan Castle ... my brother's lair. My mother, abducted from her home planet, was held captive by the elder Captain Jerome Stalls," Hanna said, disdain in her voice. "My mother died four years ago, during childbirth ... she was well into her fifties."

"Stalls said I have another half-brother, somewhere, too," Bristol said.

"I don't know anything about that. Hell, we all could have dozens of half-sibs out there," Hanna retorted, dismissively.

Jason said, "You understand, any connection a crewmember, or a crewmember's family, has with the Stalls clan needs to be scrutinized."

Hanna nodded and looked at Bristol. "So Eston is still alive?"

Bristol somewhat grimaced. "No one calls Stalls that ... But, yeah, last we checked."

"I need to see him," she said flatly.

"That's not going to happen," Jason said.

"If you're thinking I'm going to help him escape, think again. I detest the man. But there's something I need to ask him. It's a matter of life and death."

"Life and death for whom?" Jason asked, sounding suspicious.

"I can't tell you that right now."

Convenient, Jason thought. "And Bristol here doesn't know the answer? The two were together when we crossed paths in open space. Both together ... causing mayhem ... pirating ... plundering."

She shot Bristol a disapproving look. "Captain, you can come with me; five minutes with Eston ... Stalls, is all I need."

"What makes you think he'll tell you what you need to know?" Jason asked, his curiosity now somewhat piqued.

"Because like it or not, we're family."

Jason rubbed his forehead and shook his head. "I'm sorry, this is sounding like a lot more trouble than it's worth."

Hanna seemed to consider her next words. "Have you heard of the Sahhrain?"

That certainly got Jason's attention. Considering his own father was most probably abducted by them, maybe killed, he was now very interested. "Yes, I've heard of them."

"They are an evil ... terrible people. Make even the Craing look like little angels."

"Go on," Jason said.

Hanna glanced back toward Leon then continued, keeping her eyes on him. "Three years ago the Sahhrain attacked a deep-exploration vessel and abducted its crew. One of the crewmembers is a scientist ... and ... well, he's my husband," Hanna continued, looking steadily into Leon's eyes. "I'm sorry I didn't tell you this, Leon ... I don't even know if he's still alive. But I have to find out. Rescue him, if I can."

Leon shook his head. "You don't owe me any explanation ... and no one blames you for trying to find your husband," Leon said.

Jason watched the exchange. Putting the pieces together, he realized something was going on between the two. "Let's get back on track here; talk to me about Stalls' connection with the Sahhrain. What is it Stalls can provide?"

"As far as I know, he was the only person given unfettered

access into Sahhrain space. They loved the guy ... he's like an honorary Sahhrain. He provided them with both Allied and Craing secrets ... for years ... things that gave the Sahhrain military superiority."

"Again ... what is it you need to ask Stalls, specifically?"

"Isn't that obvious? I need to find out where my husband is ... if he's even still alive."

The captain seemed to consider that. "Bristol, get your sister and Leon set up in suitable quarters. I have pressing business to attend to, so we'll meet again in an hour." With that, Jason left Medical.

* * *

Jason routinely checked back with his XO to see if there were any new developments regarding the missing *Assailant*. Worried about his father, he was tempted to simply set new coordinates to that of his father's same interchange wormhole out-point location and face whatever awaited them on the other side. But, with multiple subsequent lost probes, and thousands of *Minian* crewmembers' lives at stake, he needed to come up with a safer, well-thought-out strategy.

Jason headed toward his ready room and decided to check in on Boomer. He hadn't had the chance to see her since the previous day. He used his NanoCom to hail her but there was no response. He tried to hail Petty Officer Mansfield but then remembered she probably hadn't had the opportunity to have her Caldurian nano-devices installed yet. It was a daunting procedure that required an overnight stint in a MediPod. She'd undergo a complete change in physiology: nanites would be introduced into her bloodstream, then nano-devices into her brain. After that, a regimen of hyper-learning modules would be uploaded, all in all giving her incredible healing attributes, broad communications capabilities, and a wealth of technical and ship-related knowledge.

Jason slowed and said aloud, "*Minian*, provide the physical location of Boomer."

He waited for the AI to respond.

"Captain Reynolds, Boomer is no longer present on the *Minian*."

"How about Petty Officer Mansfield?"

"Petty Officer Mansfield is no longer present on the *Minian*."

"Their last-known onboard coordinates?"

"The Zoo, specifically outside of habitat 7."

Damn it! He'd suspected as much. Jason told Boomer to stay out of that habitat and he'd told Mansfield the same thing. He broke his own onboard rule and phase-shifted directly into the Zoo's entryway.

He took in the numerous corridors before him and tried to remember which one contained HAB 7. He hailed Jack, the Zoo's caretaker.

"Um … hello?"

Jason was well aware that Jack was *old school*. He doubted he used his internal NanoCom very often. "This is Captain Reynolds, Jack. Where are you?"

"Right now?"

"Yes … where are you located? I need to talk to you."

Jason cut the connection. Jack was already hurrying down the fourth corridor. He waved a hand, as if his bright green coveralls weren't indication enough that he, indeed, was the one Jason sought.

"Yes, Captain … what is it? Is there a problem?"

"I'm looking for Boomer and Petty Officer Mansfield."

"Well, they're in here every day … Boomer works here, remember?"

"Yes, I know that, Jack. Can you take me to HAB 7?"

"You gave explicit orders for her to stay out of there," Jack replied.

"Yes … is it this way?" Jason asked, already heading toward the first corridor, pretty sure HAB 7 was down that way.

"All the way to the end, Captain." *This place is immense,* Jason thought, as he reached the habitat and waited for Jack to catch up. "Open it up, Jack."

Out of breath, Jack moved over to the access panel and began to enter in digits. "I'm not sure why they'd go in here … you were very clear."

Three beeps and the portal window disappeared. "If I'm not back in fifteen minutes, contact Billy."

Chapter 27

Sol System
The *Minian*, Zoo Habitat 7

Jason entered the misty-gray environment of HAB 7. His fingers found the SuitPac device on his belt and he pinched the two small indentations on its sides. Within seconds, his battle suit expanded out, covering his body. He wanted to make full use of any information his HUD could provide. He quickly found that various readouts and indicators were all over the place—as if he'd entered some kind of Bermuda Triangle, where nothing made much sense. Jason's primary interest focused on the bottom section of his HUD where life-icons, if they should appear, would reveal the proximity of anyone relatively close. Although he thought he saw two icons flash on when he first initialized his suit, it was only momentary, and now nothing was showing. He adjusted the HUD's sensitivity for any life readings out to a distance of ten miles, but nothing showed ... not even small, indigenous creatures.

Light drizzle had turned to rain and then, suddenly, to a full-blown torrent, coming down in buckets and making visibility difficult. In the distance, Jason could see what looked like ancient ruins so he headed in their direction. Again, he used his NanoCom to hail Boomer but heard nothing back. The wind had picked up and the rain was now hitting him straight on. Typically, his visor would compensate for that, but not now, not here.

Footprints, actually more like small oblong pools of collected rainwater, were his first indication of life about. There were three sets of tracks, all moving in the same direction, deeper into the collection of fractured columns, large stone blocks, and the remains of a crumbled, cobblestone road. *Movement*. Jason quickly spun left, but nothing was there, other than more remnants of the ancient ruins. He used his hand to wipe moisture off his visor and this time he definitely saw something. Two figures, dressed like nomads, were in the midst of a battle. Twenty feet up, on what once must have been the foundation of a great building, Parthenon-like, the two combatants moved with incredible speed, agility and grace.

Jason hurried forward, while setting phase-shift coordinates. He visually spotted a location, behind a row of six seven-foot-tall columns, and in a flash phase-shifted. He landed sixty feet away from his intended site. Instead, he found himself standing on the opposite side of the foundation, behind yet another set of columns.

One hundred feet away, the two nomads fought on, ignoring the near hurricane-like winds and heavy rain. Both were using some kind of weapon ... more like a small shield, attached to one arm. Periodically, bright purplish distortion waves emanated from their shields. The shorter of the two nomads, the size of a typical Craing, seemed a more proficient fighter than the taller one, but both were amazing as they used their shields to push off from the ground—sometimes doing back flips, landing behind each other and attacking; other times, they used the distortion waves to knock the other off their feet.

Jason, keeping low and well behind one of the columns, tried to adjust his HUD to zoom in on them. It took him several tries but eventually it worked—to the point he'd magnified the fight scene by three. Startled, his breath caught ... he continued to watch the smaller of the two figures and waited for her to turn in his direction. Her face was partially covered, but not the eyes. Boomer's eyes.

He felt he should be angry. She'd lied to him ... deceived him. But he wasn't. So what was he feeling? Pride? What his little ten-year-old was capable of was nothing short of astounding. Boomer was a warrior, in the truest sense. And with that insight came something else: Sadness. What had happened to his daughter?

There was a momentary blip, a quick flash, where life-icons typically appeared on his HUD. Jason spun around to see three nomads quickly approaching him from behind. All three wore shields and all three were full-grown men. The middle one, the tallest, used his shield-weapon and, in an instant, Jason was propelled off his feet—thrown against the column directly behind him. Seeing the others raise their shields, Jason ducked sideways, just as the distortion waves hit the column, causing a fountain of sparks. He raised his arms, triggering his suit's integrated wrist weapons to fire. Momentary relief came when he saw two of the nomads were struck, albeit only on their shields. *How did they move that fast, to block my plasma fire?* He reset his weapons from stun to their second-most lethal setting.

Jason continued to move fast, now running for the cover of a fallen column. Another distortion wave hit him and knocked him off his feet. Even before he hit the ground, Ja-

son was firing backwards. This time, he hit one of the nomads, who hadn't had time to block it. The nomad was not
getting off the ground. Jason, now on his back, flipped sideways as more distortion waves came again. Even without a
direct hit, he felt their power and that was enough to propel
him to spin away and rise to his feet. He scurried forward,
zigzagging, until he'd circled around and could make out
their blurry silhouettes against the pewter-colored sky.

"This is bullshit," Jason said out loud. He attacked, both
arms raised and not letting up on the firing mechanism. Distortion waves came back at him but they immediately dissipated in his own plasma fire. *Good to know.* Another nomad
went down, leaving only the taller one standing. He moved
with no sense of urgency … almost casually. His shield always held in just the right place to deflect Jason's plasma fire.
Jason took another distortion wave to his solar plexus. In
spite of the battle suit's protection he nearly doubled over.
The nomad drew closer, continuing to release wave after wave
of bright violet wave-pounding distortions. Unable to return
fire, Jason was forced to endure the blows as they came at
him. The nomad stood directly over him now. He raised his
shield again, but suddenly halted.

The barrel of a multi-gun was pressed against his temple,
Billy's finger on the trigger. "Move and I'll blow your fucking
head off."

The nomad did not move. Jason got to his feet and, despite countless bruises, knew he'd survive.

"What's going on here, Cap?"

Jason didn't answer. His attention was on the two approaching nomads … one about four feet tall.

"Dad?" Boomer ran to him and wrapped her arms around
his middle. "What are you doing here?"

He took another look at the tall nomad he'd just fought,

then retracted his battle suit. The wind-driven rain quickly drenched his spacer's jumpsuit. He dropped down to one knee and looked Boomer in the eyes. "You have some explaining to do."

Boomer's face reflected her guilt. She looked over at the other female and, for the first time, Jason realized it was Petty Officer Mansfield. His anger returned. "What the hell is going on here, Mansfield?"

The tall nomad man spoke, "I'm sorry ... I did not realize who you were ... this place distorts one's senses ... please let us get out of this weather, Captain Reynolds. We have much to discuss and there's little time."

Jason caught Billy's eye and nodded. Billy brought his multi-gun away from the nomad's head, still keeping it pointed at him near waist level.

"Who are you and what are you doing with my daughter?"

"I am not your enemy ... we ... are not your enemy. Your daughter is here of her own free will and she is in no danger."

"That doesn't answer my question. Who are you and what are you doing with my daughter?"

"I am Prince Aahil Aqeel; please call me Aahil. I will explain all that you wish to know, below ... out of the weather."

Jason stood and pulled Boomer in close. "Stay close to me, Boomer."

"Dad ... these are my friends—"

"Don't argue!"

Aahil turned away and walked back in the direction he and the others had come from. The two nomads Jason shot, he'd presumably killed, were no longer where they'd fallen. Billy fell in directly behind Aahil, with Jason and Boomer following. Mansfield joined Boomer's side, holding Jason's less-than-friendly stare.

"Hold your opinions of me until Aahil speaks."

"Speak again and I'll shoot you where you stand," Jason said.

Chapter 28

Sol System
The *Minian*, Zoo Habitat 7

They entered a narrow gap between two immense blocks of stone—a gap that would have been impossible to see unless one knew specifically where to look. They descended single file down worn and rounded stone steps. The only illumination came from lit torches, secured to metal brackets mounted high up on the walls.

Jason's irritation grew as they descended lower. How long had Boomer been coming here? Why did she feel it necessary to hide her doings from him? *Because I never would have allowed it.*

Boomer, walking in front, looked over her shoulder and smiled back at him. He smiled back before remembering he was supposed to be mad at her. His expression turned to a serious scowl but she'd already turned back away.

They'd reached the bottom of the stairway, and entered into a large subterranean room. Multiple columns stood like sentinels against the side walls. A small fire burned at one end of the room, its smoke disappearing into a soot-covered opening above. The floors were covered in brightly colored rugs; numerous large pillows lay scattered around for seating.

"Please sit there, Captain," Aahil said, gesturing toward a space on the floor closer to the fire.

Jason, Boomer, and Billy sat together, while Aahil and Mansfield sat across from them.

"I'm sure you have many questions … and I will answer all of them. But first, we must drink hot Pandonian tea and let our minds quiet."

Billy shot Jason a quick sideways glance but held his tongue. Jason's eyes were on Mansfield. He'd trusted her with the safety, the very life, of his daughter. Her deception was far worse than that of Boomer—who'd, undoubtedly, been manipulated.

Two elderly women, wearing the loose-fitting robes of nomads, approached—one with a wooden tray, piled up with stacked bowls, the other carrying an ancient-looking kettle of some sort. Bowls were accepted all around and steaming tea was poured.

"You're going to like this stuff," Boomer said, holding her own cup out for filling.

The women left the way they'd come. Aahil raised his bowl, said words Jason didn't understand and, curiously to him, they weren't translated by his internal nano-devices. The nomad leader drank from his own bowl—closing his eyes and obviously enjoying the hot liquid.

Boomer elbowed her dad and said, "Drink … it's rude not to."

Jason did as told and sipped from his bowl. The fruit-tangy brew was delicious. He'd be hard pressed to come up with something that tasted any better. He took several more sips and found Aahil smiling at him.

"I'm glad you find Pandonian tea to your liking."

Jason put his bowl down and looked across to the woman, seated on Aahil's left. "Start talking, Mansfield. Who the hell are you?"

"This should be good," Billy murmured under his breath. Jason saw he had an unlit stogie in his mouth.

"My name is not Mansfield. It is Capri Sharan ... I am not a U.S. military petty officer ... although there is a Petty Officer Mansfield in the U.S. military ... and she's currently on an extended vacation. I assure you, she is well and will be returning to her home base shortly."

"So you're an imposter ... I put that together myself ... but why? Why go to all this trouble and why with my daughter?"

It was Aahil who answered his question. "Do you really need to ask? Did you see your daughter sparring in the ruins? Did you see the way she moved, the way she anticipated her opponent's actions?"

Jason nodded, but didn't say anything.

"It's been a mere few days since she began her training, Captain. She has already eclipsed the ability of the one training her." Aahil hesitated long enough to give Capri an apologetic look. "Few students of this ancient martial arts can aspire to the level Boomer has already reached in a few days. It's as if she's once again remembering something familiar rather than learning something new."

"Why her? Sure, she's a natural warrior, but that's not news to me."

"Anyone can learn to fight ... to battle, Captain. She has powers that go well beyond anything you can imagine."

Jason looked down at his daughter, who was now playing with her bowl ... uncomfortable with the conversation. "Boomer is an amazing child, but she should be allowed to be just that ... a ten-year-old girl."

"Not with such high stakes looming, Captain. Please ... let us talk of the Sahhrain—specifically, the one named Shakrim ... Lord Vikor Shakrim."

"I already know about the Sahhrain ... we're in the process of taking them on next, now that the Pharloms have been successfully dealt with."

"Captain, the Sahhrain are not the same foe as the Pharloms, or the Craing, or any other alien species you've come into contact with. You see ... they are misery incarnate. They live to replace light with pain and darkness. Their rise has been foretold ... this is their time. And they have a leader who, all too soon, might be far too powerful for anyone to defeat."

"Anyone can be defeated," Billy said. "Many thought the Craing undefeatable. Look at them now."

"As I said, Lieutenant Commander Hernandez, the Sahhrain are not the Craing ... warships and advanced technology will not be enough. Not entirely, anyway."

"Where does my daughter fit in with all this?" Jason asked.

"The time will come when she must stand before Lord Vikor Shakrim ... it has been foretold."

Jason shook his head and snickered. "That's not going to happen. I don't care what kind of powers you think she has ... she's ten!"

"Almost eleven," Boomer said back, as if that would change everything.

The elderly woman was back, refilling Jason's and Billy's bowls. He took another sip, then nearly spat the hot liquid out. Instead he swallowed and felt he was about to be sick. "What was that?"

"Tastes rank, huh?" Boomer asked, nodding her head.

Jason looked about him, noticing there were now others

in the room. More nomads—most looking as ancient as the ruins they were all seated in.

"This gathering is the Council of One. The Elders of the Blues."

Jason noticed all the Elders had a slight bluish tinge to their skin. Same with Aahil ... but not Capri Sharan. His mind was becoming foggy—the room beginning to spin. He saw Billy flop backwards, onto a large pillow, his cigar dropping to the rug. Then Jason felt himself fall—falling—falling into darkness.

He found himself awake, standing amongst many others. A battle of epic proportions was being fought all around him. Strange beings, wearing partial battle suits, were holding spears and small shields, like Boomer and Mansfield had worn earlier. Their hair was coarse, worn in a peculiar cone-shaped bun—pointed upward and back. The air was filled with ozone, and bright violet waves of distortion came from virtually every direction. Dead men ... men with blue-toned skin lay motionless at Jason's feet.

The sounds of battle came alive in his ears: screams of agony; the sounds of spears puncturing flesh—and an ever-present humming sound emanated from energy shields. The Blues were being massacred. Although they too possessed similar energy shields, the Blues weren't a match for the larger, more powerful, Sahhrain.

Jason realized he knew who they were—who all of them were, and why they were fighting. The Blues fought for their very existence—the right to live—while the Sahhrain only fought for their leader, for the honor of serving their lord. Jason reached for a spear on the ground, wanting to help stop the maniacal beasts. But his hands moved through the spear, as if it were made of air. He was *there* but not really there.

The last of the Blues were vanquished—a massacre taking

place right before his eyes and there was nothing he could do to stop it—stop the outcome, fatal to so many thousands of these blue-skinned men. Their bodies were still warm; steam, coursing off their dead flesh, rose in the air, as the corpses piled up on the battlefield.

A procession approached him from up ahead. A group of Sahhrain soldiers marched in his direction, in double-row formation. They halted and separated, widening the space between the two rows. In the distance, Jason caught a reflection of polished gold and bright scarlet. The Sahhrain leader hurried forward, moving between the double ranks of soldiers.

More than Jason's height, he was easily seven feet tall. More than his obvious strength and prowess, the Sahhrain leader emitted a marked sense of confidence. Similar to what Jason had experienced in the past, with an alien species called the Mau—he was filled with dread and despair.

Jason turned to see more Sahhrain soldiers approaching from behind. Two of them held one of the surviving Blues, by his arms. He knew, somehow, that this was the Blues' leader. Jason moved to get out of the way but found they'd walked right through him—as if he weren't there. Which, apparently, he wasn't.

The Blues' leader was brought before the Sahhrain leader … his own image reflected back in the polished gold breastplate, two feet in front of him. His arms were released and he staggered to stay upright.

Jason's realizations continued. He knew just where he was and who the Sahhrain leader was: it was Lord Moch Righ, and he was witnessing something that had happened hundreds of years earlier.

The leader of the Blues was up in the air now—both hands clutched at his throat—as though trying to unleash himself from an invisible stranglehold. His feet kicked wildly as muffled, agonized, and choking sounds filled the air. But Lord Moch Righ was not looking at the dying Blues' leader—he was staring directly at Jason.

Jason woke up.

Aahil was now seated at his side. "Captain Reynolds, what you witnessed—"

Jason cut him off, "I know what I witnessed. At least, what I *think* I witnessed."

"Lord Moch Righ lived four hundred years ago. He was powerful, nearly vanquishing an entire race of people ... my people."

"Then he was defeated?"

Aahil slowly nodded. "At great cost to the Blues. We were saved by a master of *Kahill Callan* ... a Blue, with unparalleled strength, who defeated Lord Moch Righ in a daylong battle."

"Who was he?"

"She ... someone named Uma ... Uma Carice."

Jason realized Boomer was now sitting at his other side. She took his hand in hers.

"I need to do this, Dad."

Jason wanted to discard what she was saying outright, but he couldn't. "I suspect you do ... but that doesn't mean I have to like it."

Chapter 29

Alchieves System
The *Minian*, Captain's Ready Room

Jason made the decision to bring the *Minian* within three light-years of the *Assailant*'s last interchange wormhole coordinates. Not entirely sure if the distance proved far enough away for them to avoid the same fate that befell his father's small armada, but waiting around ... doing nothing, in light of recent developments and the new insights given him, made the risk not only worthwhile, but advisable and imperative.

Although the Pharloms had been dealt with—sent back to where they'd come from ... Trom would still require their protection until more Alliance forces could arrive, with a more quasi-permanent contingent. Jason decided to split up his armada of twelve warships. He'd leave six on Trom, and take six with the *Minian*. They could rejoin with his half of the Star Watch armada later.

Jason paced the deck of his ready room, his unsettled thoughts probing—first on his missing, probably deceased, father. Then on to that perpetrator of darkness, Lord Vikor Shakrim; then on to his own daughter, Boomer, who, as preposterous as it seemed, especially to him, would someday go up against that very same evil.

How could he allow that? How could he put the weight of so much on Boomer's small shoulders? And what were the chances that the *Minian*'s small armada could stop the progression of the Sahhrain forces? He needed to approach their options from multiple directions. He checked the time—1500 hours. It was time.

Ricket was the first to arrive and take a seat. Jason took a seat next to him at the head of the table. The rest streamed in, also taking seats. Jason looked around the table at Billy and Orion; his XO, Perkins; Dira and Rizzo; the commander of his top-gun fighter pilots, Lieutenant Commander Grimes; the Caldurian, Granger; Bristol and Hanna; Leon Pike; and, sitting to his right, Boomer. The last person to enter the compartment and sit was Capri Sharan.

Capri's invite was the last one he'd issued, and Jason still wasn't completely confident in his decision to include her here, among his core team's ranks. In the end, he knew he had little choice in the matter. She was the go-between person for Prince Aahil Aqeel and Jason's Star Watch force. He'd just have to get over what was, in his mind, her deceit and treachery.

"Thank you, everyone," said Jason, "for coming at such short notice. Look around … this is our core leadership team … those who have been selected to go against the Sahhrain, and its leader, Lord Vikor Shakrim, before there's the necessity of all-out war. One of the directives of Star Watch is to help avoid getting the Alliance into another long, drawn-out, engagement … another horrific war."

Leon held up a hand.

"What is it, Mr. Pike?"

"No offense, sir … but my plans don't include sticking

around here. I'm sorry, but I have a ship to get back to. I have a life of my own."

"Nobody's going to force you to stay, Mr. Pike. But I'm hoping that your plans will change ... some of you still have a need to know what others in here already know."

On cue, three people entered the ready room: Prince Aahil Aqeel, and the same two elderly women—one carrying stacked bowls, the other a hot, steaming kettle.

"This is Prince Aahil Aqeel, for those not aware of who he is. In several moments you will know more, know who this man is, and know what we're truly up against. I suspect each of you will have your own unique experience."

Jason watched as all the bowls were passed around the table, and the mysterious hot liquid was poured into each. Confused faces first looked down at the steamy bowls of liquid set before them, then over at Jason. "Drink up."

* * *

With the exception of Jason, Boomer, Billy, Capri, and Aahil, everyone else was out cold, their heads resting on the table in front of them.

Aahil remained standing, leaning against a bulkhead. He'd dismissed the two nomad women earlier. For a moment, Jason and Aahil held each other's stare.

Boomer tugged on Jason's sleeve. He leaned over so she could whisper into his ear.

"Grandpa is still alive."

"How ... how do you know that?"

"Petty Officer ... oops, Capri—told me right before we came in here. She said the prince knows where he's being held."

Jason didn't know whether the news was factual or not,

but even the chance of it being true struck him hard. He blinked away the moisture welling up in his eyes and smiled. "I hope that is true, little one."

Dira stirred—wiggled her nose and opened her eyes. She sat upright and looked toward Jason. Concern creased her brow. He wondered what she'd just experienced ... what vision she'd seen? He wanted to reach across the table, take her hands in his. More, he wanted to hold her in his arms and bring her close. Looking at her—her amazing, beautiful face ... Jason wondered how he'd been so fortunate to deserve her love. Her lips parted, as if poised to say something, then closed.

The others, too, were coming around. Granger was the first to speak. "Captain ... you must be very careful how you proceed from this point on."

"Yes, Granger we will—"

"No!" Granger interrupted. "What I'm saying is there's more to this than you know. More than visions—or the knowledge that was imparted ... conveyed to us ... from them."

Jason waited as the Caldurian assembled his thoughts.

"My people ... the Caldurians ... were not unaware of the risings of Sahhrain. We were there to help bring them down the last time ... sent the few that remained into hiding. Captain, you should have informed me of this situation as soon as you first became aware of it."

"Why ... what is it you know?"

All eyes were on Granger, watching as his agitation grew. "The *Minian's* Zoo habitat ... HAB 7 ... in there lies the ancient ruins of the Blues."

"I already know that."

Granger glanced over to the prince. "The Blues and the Sahhrain, their cultures are a tangled web going back several millennia or more. What you do not know is that for many generations it was the Blues who were the dark force ... the Sahhrain, their tortured slaves. There, beneath the sands of that world within HAB 7, are stone tablets, many feet tall. They tell the story ... the story *and* the prophecy."

Capri said, "He's right, Captain. The Blues ... my people ... have indeed had a dark past."

Jason noticed Capri Sharan no longer looked like a human from Earth. Her auburn hair was now black and her skin tone as blue-tinged as Prince Aahil Aqeel's. Apparently, she too was capable of changing her appearance, or at least others' perception of her appearance, at will.

Both Leon and Hanna exchanged baffled looks.

Capri continued, "The Blues have evolved over two thousand years. We wanted to make reparations for our ancestors' actions toward the Sahhrain. The Blues traveled to, and colonized, other planets ... more livable environments, compared to the harshness you see within HAB 7. They, the Sahhrain, of course were freed ... given their own world to inhabit, along with access to our own advanced technologies. But the more kindness and reparations we offered, gave them over lifetimes, the more profound the Sahhrain's hatred toward us, and others, became."

"And so today we have the Sahhrain ... this time they're more capable than they'd ever been in the past ... and they are hell-bent on moving farther out into the galaxy?" Jason asked.

Capri and Aqeel glanced at one another. Aqeel said, "What you do not know is that the Sahhrain now have control of a Craing Loop wormhole which is located there in Dacci space. It will only be a matter of time before they figure out how to reconfigure it for their own interstellar travel."

"That cannot be allowed to happen," Jason said flatly. Although Jason knew the Craing's previous method for traveling out to hundreds of light-years' distance, it would only be to fixed, other Loop wormhole, locations. Nothing that provided the kind of travel flexibility that their own interchange wormhole travel provided. But still ... the Sahhrain would possess a new means to spread their darkness ... like a deathly plague spreading across the galaxy.

"Captain," Granger said, sounding impatient, "back to the tablets ... the prophecies. They speak of the final rising of the Sahhrain and bringing forth, from the spirit world, their great Sachem, *Rom Dasticon*, the most powerful force in the universe."

"Come on ... that's just elaborate fables ... it was a different time ... you can't take everything to be—"

Granger cut back in, "They speak of a mysterious 'chariot in the sky' that will deliver this most powerful force, this *Rom Dasticon*, from an alternate dimension ... alternate universe. At face value, sure, this does sound like a simple fable, but considering the *Minian* has that same unique capability, to traverse into the multiverse, we must consider that Lord Vikor Shakrim may be coming for this very ship ... his mysterious *chariot in the sky* ... to thus deliver forth his all-powerful Sachem."

Jason said, "Well, that may be a stretch ... if he even knows about the *Minian*." But he started to wonder—was it possible Shakrim did possess knowledge of the *Minian*'s capabilities? Was there really some omnificent power, residing somewhere within another realm ... in some alternate universe? If so, wouldn't the *Minian* be the perfect vessel to deliver Shakrim to that reality, making the Sahhrain virtually undefeatable? He didn't think so, but now, thinking more seriously about it, he wasn't completely certain.

"Captain, I implore you to keep the *Minian* as far away

from Lord Shakrim as possible," Granger reiterated. "You need to get this ship out of this sector at once!"

"No, Granger ... I'm not going to hide from Lord Shakrim, or anyone else, for that matter. In fact, we'll be taking the fight right to him. Our Star Watch armada will join with the Blues ... with Aahil and his fleet of sixty warships."

Aahil said, "We have a limited amount of time to catch Lord Shakrim, who's currently away from his fleet. Our sources tell me he, along with his personal guard ... a force of twenty-five Sahhrain warriors called the *Chosen Spears*, are in the Dacci planetary system. He's there obtaining an exotic mineral, called Glist, for manufacturing even more powerful enhancement shields for his forces. Apparently, it's an operation he's taken personal control over. While he's on the surface, his fleet, consisting of five hundred warships, is on standby in Dacci space. If there ever was the right place and time to take down Lord Vikor Shakrim ... it would be there, on the planet near those deep Glist mines." Aahil nodded toward Boomer, who nodded back to him.

Jason didn't want to think about Boomer facing off against Lord Shakrim. To him, the idea was still preposterous. But he also knew that getting close enough to confront Shakrim, with his unique powers, not to mention his Chosen Spear warriors, would require a more drastic approach.

Billy said, "I still don't get why we don't just take out the whole Sahhrain fleet. Hell, we can get enough Allied ships here within a day or two, then send an army down to the surface to neutralize Lord whatever his name is."

Jason thought about that for a moment and then thought about his father's explicit directives. "That's not what we do now, Billy. That's not the directive for Star Watch. No one wants another war, and we're not here to start one. No ... we need to cut the head off that serpent and hope the Sahhrain fleet, with a little prompting from our combined forces in space, will return home—their tails between their legs."

Billy said, "And this Lord Shakrim? He's just one guy … right?"

"Hardly," Aahil said. "In the past, with his highly acute intuition … he's always avoided personal attacks. No matter how many teams are sent to remove him from power, he's gone, like smoke in the wind, long before our forces are close enough."

"So he's a coward?" Billy asked.

"No … not a coward. He is a great warrior … unbeaten, in fact. Again, his highly acute intuition makes him extremely lethal in combat. His physical size … his unmatched prowess with an enhancement shield, makes him a formidable—"

Jason cut him off, "And you want me to put my daughter up against that?"

"Who else but a little girl could get close enough to engage him? He would simply evade another assault team. Captain, all we ask of Boomer is to temporarily constrain him … paralyze him … just long enough for us to move in to capture him."

Frustrated, Jason turned toward Leon: "How about you? You on board now to do your part?"

Leon returned Hanna's direct stare and slowly nodded his assent. "I suppose … what is it you'd need from me?"

"You say you have a ship … something a typical space trader might possess? Maybe even the kind of spacecraft an interstellar pirate might own?" Jason asked.

Leon smiled. "You could say that. It's fast and it's got all the bells and whistles one would need to avoid certain … situations."

"Like getting caught by those you've ripped off in the past?" Hanna asked flatly.

Jason didn't give him time to answer. "We'll need two things from you ... first your ship, then you need to make friends with Stalls. Stalls will need to feel comfortable with you."

Leon's brow furrowed.

"We'll put a team together to accompany you into HAB 12, where Stalls is currently imprisoned."

"It's not HAB 12, anymore, Dad," Boomer corrected. "Here on the *Minian* it's HAB 331."

"Fine, then, HAB 331. Hanna, Leon, and Bristol, all of you will go ... and I'll assign an assault team to accompany you, for your protection. I'm hoping your combined family bonds will help motivate Stalls to assist with this mission ... that, and we're providing an opportunity for him to get out of that hellish habitat ... even only temporarily. You'll bring back Stalls and, upon your return, prepare for the next mission into Dacci space."

Jason looked back down at Boomer. "In the meantime ... you have a lot to prepare for yourself, little one. There's not a lot of time." Jason turned his gaze toward Capri and then toward Aahil.

Capri said, "She has progressed significantly with her training. We will need more time with her, but I promise you, Captain ... Boomer will be ready in time."

"When did you say we'd get my ship?" Leon asked.

"As soon as you get back from that habitat. By the way, where is it ... is it relatively close?"

"Relatively," Leon replied. "Hidden here within the sector. I'll provide you with the exact coordinates."

"Good. When you return from HAB 331, we'll fetch it," Jason said. "You'll be piloting the mission that will get Boomer in close to Lord Shakrim." Jason glanced down at Boomer and let out a breath. "That team will include Capri, Boomer, and Captain Stalls, along with someone highly competent to watch over him. Remember, Stalls will be your ticket in … without him … without his connections with the Sahhrain … there'll be no way to safely enter Dacci space."

Granger continued to glare at Jason. Ignoring him, Jason looked down at Ricket. "You have been uncharacteristically quiet during these proceedings, Ricket. What are your thoughts?"

"I'd like to see the tablets Granger speaks of."

Chapter 30

Dacci System
The *Minian,* Bridge

Ensign McNeil, at the *Minian's* helm, calculated that the safest distance away from Dacci space and the Sahhrain fleet would be some fifteen light-years from their current position near the planet Trom. Seaman Gordon, at the communications board, made the necessary requests for an interchange wormhole.

Jason, seated in the command chair, reviewed his virtual notepad and the ever-accumulating requests from other sectors within the galaxy for the assistance of Star Watch—reiterating the need for their new interstellar policing services. The admiral had been right on, foreseeing the need for this kind of rapid-response force ... but would their current armada, small as it was, have sufficient power and might? Especially since he didn't see the Sahhrain being curbed or defeated easily, as the Pharloms had just been.

"Captain, the wormhole has stabilized," McNeil said.

"Go ahead, take us in, Ensign."

Jason stood and looked up at the wraparound overhead

display. Before them sat the looming mouth of the wormhole. He turned and saw the distant planet of Trom, now fading behind them. It would be years, maybe decades, before the Tromians recovered, rebuilt, from the devastation incurred from the Pharloms' invasion. Jason wondered how many similar scenarios would unfold like the destruction on Trom, now that the Craing weren't around maintaining restrictive order.

"Entering the interchange wormhole now, Captain."

Jason sat back down and brought his attention to what lay ahead. The *Minian* entered the wormhole first, followed soon afterward by the reduced armada of six Star Watch warships.

They exited the far side of the interchange wormhole into complete darkness.

"Status, Gunny?"

"Captain, we've entered one of the least celestially-populated zones in this sector ... or in the galaxy, for that matter."

Jason peered up into the near-total blackness. Usually, there were thousands, millions, of tiny, flickering pinpoints of light nearby. Sure, off in the far distance, starlight was seen—but nothing even remotely nearby—except for a bright solitary, lone star system.

"We're well outside normal sensor range, Cap," Orion said, "but the *Minian*'s sensors, which are extremely sensitive and sophisticated, are picking up numerous warship signatures—over five hundred of them. Most definitely the Sahhrain fleet, and probably the much smaller Blues fleet, too."

"Seaman Gordon, hail the Blues ... have them provide us coordinates to intersect with their fleet."

"Aye, Captain."

"Please bring up the logistical view, Gunny."

A new segment was added forward, on the overhead display, providing an icon-based representation of the only nearby star system. He saw the distant position of the Blues' fleet, set somewhat away from the much larger Sahhrain fleet.

Ricket broke the silence. Jason hadn't seen him enter the bridge. "As you can see, there are actually three separate star systems there, Captain ... although, from this distance, there seems to be but one. You have the Sahhrain system, furthest away from us, with five planets, circling a burnt-out sun. Their only heat and light comes from the two neighboring solar systems ... their world is not as warm as Earth, but surprisingly habitable ... say, similar to the state of Alaska on your planet."

"And the other two solar systems?" Jason asked.

"The Blues' system is nearest to us, at our present position, but the furthest from the Sahhrain. Technology-wise, the two are comparable. Militarily, they're almost comparable ... although it seems the Sahhrain are on the verge of changing that. A buildup of many new warships, the recent siege into the centermost part of the Dacci solar system, and the plundering of Glist, on the planet Dacci. The Dacci star system, Captain, is considered the center of the galaxy and the oldest planetary system known."

Jason looked at Ricket, standing at the side of his command chair. "What do you know about the Blues?"

"Captain?"

"How did they know Boomer was on board and that she was the one ... the one who's mentioned in the prophecy? And how could they possibly know the *Minian* had a Zoo habitat portal into that dreary world of theirs?"

Ricket contemplated that for a moment. "I too have wondered those things, Captain. It is why I want to see those ancient tablets firsthand. That planet, which is actually called

Harpaign, lies there, within the Blues' solar system."

"I didn't realize that ... but why not just access the planet directly from our HAB 7?"

"Captain, Zoo habitats are, in all actuality, alternate, typically small, several hundred-square-mile multiverse representations of the actual planet, in its own dimensional reality. Each habitat is typically set at a different, much older, point in time than our own."

"So, you're saying, in order to ensure we're dealing only with their true reality ... we need to go directly to Harpaign?"

"I would say so ... Captain. But there is something else ... something I have not yet figured out."

"What is that?"

"Prince Aahil Aqeel and Capri Sharan and the other nomads ... how did they enter HAB 7? Remember ... only through a portal does one access one of the Caldurian closed habitats."

"That's an excellent question, Ricket. One ... we need to ask them as soon as possible."

"They are no longer on the *Minian*, Captain. I ventured into HAB 7 right before coming here. I walked amongst the ruins. I found the gap and the subterranean room, but there was no sign anywhere that anyone had actually been in there for hundreds of years."

Jason froze. "That's not possible." His thoughts flashed to Boomer. "*Minian* ... locate my daughter."

"Boomer is no longer on board the *Minian*, Captain Reynolds," the AI replied.

Jason stood. "What was her last known location and who was she with?"

"Within the Zoo habitats ... she was located directly outside of Habitat 7. She was accompanied by Prince Aahil Aqeel and Capri Sharan, as well as her droid ... Dewdrop."

Damn it! They'd taken her to complete her training. *But why take her away from the* Minian *or* HAB 7? At least she had her droid with her. He'd often witnessed its loyalty for her wellbeing. Boomer had proven herself remarkably capable, surviving situations against near-impossible odds. *Okay, Boomer … I have to trust you know what you're doing. You just better come back safe … and soon.*

Chapter 31

Dacci System
The *Minian*, the Zoo

Leon stood at the back of the bustling crowd of crew personnel within the *Minian*'s Zoo corridor. He marveled at the vast compartment's collection of alien world habitats. He looked over to several nearby near-transparent portal windows. These strange environments held hundreds of alien worlds—bizarre alien species. A few of which were currently staring right back at him.

Hanna joined him at his side and smiled. "Pretty cool, don't you think?"

"Huh? Oh ... yeah, I guess. But I think more than a few creatures are sizing me up as a potential meal ... it's kinda creepy."

Hanna laughed at that. "Thank you again for doing this, Leon. It means a lot to me. I know this little excursion isn't just for me ... Stalls will potentially be their passport to enter into Dacci space. But I do need to find my missing husband, too, so I hope, with Bristol's help, Stalls will be willing to help me."

"Why wouldn't he? You *are* his sister ... right?"

"Stalls is an opportunist and a psychopath, among other things. We were never close ... he's always been abusive ... even when younger. He'll only help me if there's something in it for him."

"Sounds like a terrific fellow."

"Anyway ... thank you."

"Don't mention it." Leon changed the subject: "The way Ricket explained it, we should be able to get in and out of there in a matter of hours. That new little ship looks more than capable of getting us where we need to be." Leon nodded toward the highly streamlined craft, taking up much of the corridor in front of them. He was impressed, not only with its size, but how it was manufactured—right here on the *Minian*, apparently, and all within the past twenty-four hours. Ricket explained earlier that this was the third such craft he'd manufactured—this one the most advanced and his favorite; for that reason he'd christened it the *Charm*.

"We're all going to fit inside that thing?" Hanna asked.

"With room to spare," a voice countered back, from the group of military people standing at the side of the *Charm*. "Hi ... I'm Lieutenant Commander Grimes," she said, approaching them. "I'll be your pilot today."

Leon took in the small-framed, compact fighter pilot, guesstimating her to be no more than five foot two. She wore her hair short, in a bob style, with bangs—*cute*. She looked highly competent. Some vulnerability showed, though, in her expressive brown eyes. They held each other's stare for a fleeting moment. Leon felt Hanna stiffen at his side.

"Why not just do that ... phase-shifty thing?" Hanna asked.

Grimes smiled at the question. "The habitats," she gestured with her hand to the surrounding portals, "these environments are replicas of various planet surfaces. They exists within the multiverse … they're not actually residing on the other side of the windows. You can't phase-shift from the *Minian*'s Zoo into a habitat. Once inside that's a different story … your battle suit has an actual reference point."

"That makes sense … and why so many people to pick up one marooned pirate?" Hanna asked, surveying the six or seven armed men standing nearby in their battle suits.

Grimes said, "It's always better to be prepared … this particular habitat has a most-unfriendly environment. Too many Serapin Terplins."

"Serapin …?" Hanna asked.

"Serapin Terplins … think *Jurassic Park* raptor. Then add on a foot or two in height and color the beasts bright blue. They communicate with each other and, from what I hear, there's even a few that fly."

One of the battle suit-clad men approached. Leon recognized him from the sky-port back on Trom. "We're ready, if you are."

"Thanks, Rizzo," Grimes said. "Rizzo is leading our assault team. They'll keep us safe and make sure Stalls doesn't try any funny business."

Rizzo smiled and nodded, first at Leon, then Hanna. Hanna smiled back and pushed her hair away from her face. Leon noticed Hanna was still watching as the young SEAL returned to his men.

A voice came from behind. "What are we waiting for?"

Leon turned around to see Bristol walking toward them, eating what looked like a slice of toast. His eyes were on the *Charm*. Grinning, his mouth full of half-chewed bread, he said, "Cool … he built another one."

* * *

Once everyone was on board the small craft, Ricket showed up outside the *Charm* and entered what seemed an almost endless code into an access panel, located at the side of HAB 331. Then, with only a little back-and-forth maneuvering within the corridor, Grimes eased the *Charm* through the now-open portal. Viewing him through a starboard observation window, Leon saw Ricket, in the corridor, wave as the ship slowly departed the *Minian* and entered the habitat.

Rizzo sat next to Grimes in the compact cockpit, while the rest of the assault team, along with Hanna and Leon, sat in the cabin directly behind. Seated in the front row seats, Hanna sat between Leon and Bristol. Leon, as well as the others, could see into the cockpit and out its front observation window. A sandy, desert-like environment lay outside, with a range of jagged, rocky mountains ahead.

"How you going to find him?" Leon asked.

Grimes maneuvered the *Charm* several hundred feet up in the air, moving onward. "We already know where he is. He's fitted with a tracker ... but the *Charm*'s sensors will detect his location even if he's found a way to remove it."

"So, then, where is he?" Hanna asked.

Bristol extended a skinny arm and pointed to the 3D display hovering in front of Grimes and Rizzo. "That red dot there ... that would be your first clue."

Leon really didn't like Bristol—always a *smartass* remark—the shitty attitude. *Why do these people put up with the guy?*

Leon felt the little vessel pick up speed, now on course toward the red icon. He glanced toward Hanna and saw the anticipation on her face. His attraction to her had only grown over the past few days, but her having a husband definitely changed things. That, and the fact that he knew she was trouble. He'd met others like her before ... and his inner voice was telling him, screaming at him, to stay clear. Too many secrets—too many hidden agendas ... and again, that whole missing husband thing.

They passed the rocky cliffs and soon a gorge of sorts came into view. Smoke billowed into the air and Leon could see bright red lava flows streaming in various places along the chasm.

"How the hell did he do that?" Rizzo asked, leaning forward and looking downward as they passed over what had to be quite a magnificent obstacle for anyone attempting to traverse from one side of the chasm to the other.

Grimes said, "You got me ... he wasn't supposed to be able to leave this desert and mountain-ridged area. From what Captain Reynolds told me, although he's armed with a multi-gun, he was left stranded on that high mountain ledge back there ..." She laughed. "He didn't even have clothes to wear ... thanks to the captain."

"Yeah, heard that, too," Rizzo said. "Okay ... looks like we're getting close ... go ahead and bring us down."

Leon noticed on the display there were a significant number of orange icons showing up, moving in a line, with a sole red icon, also moving.

"I take it there's other inhabitants here?" Leon asked.

"Besides the Serapins ... there's a bunch of ancient Craing warriors running around on this side of the volcanic chasm. This habitat is based on a small slice of the Craing world of Halimar ... but as it appeared thousands of years ago," Bristol said. "I've been to this shit hole ... the sooner we do what we came for, the better."

Rizzo, his visor open, seemed to think Bristol's comments humorous. The *Charm* landed on a flat, seemingly endless field of green grass. From Leon's perspective, it resembled any number of places back on Earth—Kansas, Ohio, or eastern Colorado. Rizzo got to his feet. "You three ... once outside initialize your SuitPac devices. It may look safe out there but, I assure you, it's not."

One by one, everyone disembarked through the rear hatchway. Hanna stepped away from the ship and looked around. "It's nice here."

Rizzo leaned close to her and pinched the SuitPac device at her belt. Immediately, a segmented battle suit covered her head to toe. Leon saw her shielded eyes take in the icons and various readouts displayed on her HUD.

"You'll get used to it all," Leon said. "It looks a lot more intimidating than it really is." He triggered his own SuitPac. The first thing he noticed were quickly approaching orange icons.

Rizzo said, "You three ... stay down on the ground and keep out of the way." He, and the six others on his assault team, quickly spread out, their multi-guns raised.

In the distance, Leon heard an increasing clattering noise. The ground began to vibrate beneath his prone body's battle suit. Then, on the horizon, he saw something. He worked his HUD settings and zoomed in. It was a line—easily twenty-five small chariots, all charging forward, each manned by a small Craing. And these chariots weren't being pulled by horses, but by blue-colored beasts, the Serapins. And they were all charging in their direction.

At the center of the charge, and slightly ahead of the others, was a larger chariot, being drawn by two equally larger Serapins. A human, wearing a leather breastplate, held the reins.

Bristol, directly to Leon's right, said, "No fucking way ... Stalls!"

Chapter 32

Dacci System
The *Minian*, Zoo Habitat 331

Leon got to his feet and watched as a single, straight-line formation of chariots charged forward, with no sign of slowing. Churned up chunks of grass, small rocks, and dirt clods were sprayed into the air from pummeling, powerful, Serapin claws—adding to the almost cinematic effect of the oncoming spectacle. Long, wet strings of saliva hung from open, gaping jaws … embedded with unusually long, and undoubtedly sharp, teeth. Suddenly, and not a moment too soon, the pirate captain reined in his two charging Serapins and, in a dramatic, climatic show of piloting control he, followed by the other chariot drivers, pulled hard on their reins and brought their chariots to an immediate skidding halt, no more than thirty yards from where Leon and the others were standing.

Rizzo and his team had their multi-guns held high: the stocks of their weapons up against their shoulders, their muzzles pointed at the new arrivals. Similarly, twenty-five Craing warriors stood with their arms outstretched, bows fully drawn, with arrows poised for flight.

It was a show worthy of applause. Especially since it was all for show. Leon figured Stalls must be well aware that arrows would have zero impact on their battle suits. He must also be fully cognizant that the assault team's weaponry would bring down his little Craing army in mere seconds, if it came to battling. No ... this was all for show.

Bristol was the first to retract his battle suit, soon followed by Hanna. Next, Leon retracted his suit as well—not wanting to show he was any less brave, even in the face of all those arrows, still pointed in their general direction. Leon stepped to Hanna's side. "Good God, I guess that smell is something one gets used to," he said under his breath, gesturing toward the twenty-six jittery, steaming hot, Serapin beasts. But Hanna's attention was fully on the tall man, now stepping down from out of the rear of his chariot. As he turned away from them for a second, Leon saw him from behind and noted he had a long, black ponytail hanging down to the middle of his back. As he now approached, Leon saw Stalls smile. But his smile wasn't what one would expect from someone seeing a long lost relative, or even a good friend, again. No, he wore a smile of contempt and arrogance. His self-importance was almost tangible, something Leon almost could reach out and touch.

Bristol took a hesitant step forward, doing his part in meeting his approaching, far bigger, half-brother. Stalls' eyes never left Bristol. When close enough, Stalls swung a fierce backhand that connected with the left side of Bristol's face. The skinny, overtly nerdy, younger man fell to the ground in an awkward tangle of arms and legs. Rizzo and his men, their weapons raised and poised to fire, quickly moved forward.

"Hold on ... it's all right!" Bristol yelled. "Stand down ... I probably had that coming."

Rizzo retracted his visor into his helmet, his face clearly

showing his anger. "Touch him again and I'll be happy to burn you down to an oily stain on the ground."

Stalls' eyes briefly left Bristol for Rizzo. Recognition showed on his face. It was apparent today's encounter wasn't the first time they'd come in contact with each other. Stalls' smile returned, and, ignoring Rizzo, he extended his hand down to Bristol, who took it and pulled himself up off the ground.

"Little brother. How nice of you to drop by for a visit. You should have called first; I would have prepared a feast in your honor. For you and for our young sister," he said, now turning his gaze in Hanna's direction.

Leon watched with fascination as the family drama unfolded. *This is never going to work.*

Stalls maintained his grip on Bristol's hand and pulled his younger brother in close. "It is good to see you, Bristol. I might even forgive you … in time." He released Bristol's hand and turned toward his half-sister. "Hanna … look at you … you're all grown up … a woman in every way." Stalls took a step back and eyed his sister up and down, head to toe, then back up again. "And what a woman you are!" He stepped forward quickly, pulling her close. Her arms remained at her sides as she disappeared into the big man's enfolding embrace.

Only a few feet away, Leon thought Stalls smelled nearly as foul as the Serapins. He saw that Hanna's eyes were closed, more like clenched, as she waited for her older brother to release her. Leon noticed Stalls looking over at him—assessing him from over her shoulder.

"And who do we have here?" Stalls asked, finally releasing his hold on Hanna. He gestured for the Craing men to put down their bows. Rizzo then said, "Stand down," to his team as well.

"That's Leon Pike," Hanna said in a flat voice. "Be nice to him. He might be your ticket out of here ... if you don't screw things up."

Stalls stepped away from Hanna, but maintained a hold on both her wrists. "What is this man to you, Hanna? I don't like him ... I don't like the way he looks at you."

Hanna flashed a quick glance in Leon's direction but didn't say anything.

Stalls released one of her hands, slowly bringing his fingertips up to her face. She flinched. Stalls hesitated, then continued on, using the back of his fingers to gently stroke one cheek. She tried to pull away but his solid grip on her other arm held her in place. "Such a pretty face ... you always were so ..."

Seeing the revulsion on Hanna's face, Leon couldn't simply stand by. He looked over to Rizzo, who also seemed ready to make a move. Leon said, "Hey, why don't you let her go, Stalls. We have some important things to discuss."

Stalls acted as if he hadn't heard Leon—continuing to gaze at his sister—first tilting his head one way, then the other.

This guy really is a sicko, Leon thought.

Stalls spoke softly, almost in a whisper, "Don't you think it's disrespectful to come into someone else's backyard and start making demands? What do you think I should do about him, Hanna?"

Leon shook his head. "Look ... I'm not going to ask you again; let her go."

Bristol, looking nearly as uncomfortable as Hanna, said, "Come on, Stalls ... knock it off ... okay?"

Leon, watching, saw it coming—it was nearly imperceptible. He'd learned a long time ago, when waiting for an opponent's first move, you notice two things: their eyes and their breathing. It was subtle, but he'd definitely caught it. Stalls' eyes twitched—ever so slightly—and he'd taken in a breath, and held it. Stalls yanked Hanna to his right while punching out with his left fist toward Leon's face. Leon was ready for him. Stalls' punch was fast, very fast. But not fast enough to tag him. Leon dodged it and stepped to the side. He also brought up the long knife he'd earlier pulled out from the back of his collar, and pressed it beneath the fleshy area of Stalls' outstretched chin. *So much for Jason's directive to make friends.* Perhaps Stalls detected the attraction between him and Hanna … thinking Leon had encroached on his familial territory, or something. Hell, there was no reasoning with psychotics and it was obvious this old pirate was more than a little crazy.

"Move … even twitch … and the tip of this blade will be tickling the middle of your brain. Do you understand?"

Stalls stayed perfectly still, keeping his eyes focused steadily on Leon.

The pirate smiled; this time, a broad, showing-all-his-teeth kind of smile. He laughed and said, "Maybe I do like you … you're devious and probably ruthless."

Leon, slowly, brought the tip of his knife away from Stalls' chin. Stalls' smile remained as he assessed first Leon, then the rest of the assault team. He rubbed his hands together, like a hungry man ready to eat. "This is going to be good. I can tell … this is going to be monumental, isn't it?" he asked, now looking at Hanna.

"If you're done with the theatrics, I'll tell you," she said, the slightest touch of humor in her voice.

"No … I want to savor this. You will join me … all of you … for dinner. My camp is nearby—"

"I know where the camp is," Rizzo interrupted. "Remember … this isn't my first trip to the circus, Stalls."

* * *

They sat around a blazing fire, within a clearing the size of two side-by-side football fields. The surrounding evergreen trees were tall and dense, not dissimilar to some big pines indigenous to northwest America. The *Charm* was close by and Rizzo's men kept a vigilant guard on both the ship and the passengers seated outside.

Leon didn't know the complete story ... how Stalls ended up in this habitat, but it seemed obvious to him he'd made the best of it. He had to give the pirate that much credit.

"I really should still be mad at you, little brother. Your captain left me stranded on a bluff, hundreds of feet from the ground. Did I mention he'd taken my clothes? Do you have any idea what it's like to scale down the side of a mountain with no pants?" That evoked laughs all around, except from Hanna.

"At least you had a weapon," Bristol said.

"It lasted a few weeks ... and I killed a lot of Serapins. But then the battery pack, and the spares, too, all petered out. The beasts continued to come ... mostly at night. I knew there was just one hope for my survival ... to get across that volcanic gorge. I'd seen fields of green from atop the bluff; I knew I had to get across it ... somehow."

"How'd you manage that?" Rizzo asked. "Hell ... I tried to do it myself, and that was with a battle suit on. More than a few on our team went up in flames crossing that chasm."

"Patience and timing," Stalls replied. "Every three days, there's a lull in volcanic activity. It only lasts a few minutes, so you need to move fast. I tried four separate times ... only the last time, I was successful."

Leon watched as the group talked and ate—some kind

of meat and gravy stew that was actually not too bad. As near to normal as Stalls was behaving now, Leon had no doubt the man was never far from once again becoming the lunatic he'd witnessed earlier. He saw the natives keeping an eye on himself and the other newcomers, but even more so on Stalls. He didn't see admiration in their eyes; he saw fear.

"And the Craing warriors?" Leon asked, gesturing with his hand to the surrounding encampment.

"Oh ... that's a story for another time. No ... it's time we spoke of why you're here and what you so desperately need of me."

Leon's expression turned stern. "You seem fairly content. You've made this your home ... you're a king among hundreds. We may have been mistaken. Truth is, I no longer think we should have come here. I apologize ... we shouldn't have come."

Hanna, who'd stayed quiet since her ordeal with Stalls back in the field, looked over to Leon with a startled expression. Rizzo and Bristol looked equally disconcerted.

"Don't trifle with me, Mr. Pike. You need me ... for something ... and it's going to get me out of here." Stalls appeared on the verge again and close to erupting, which was exactly where Leon wanted him.

"First, you're going to help your sister ... provide her with the information she requires. Then we can talk about getting you out of here and what else we need from you."

Stalls tossed his half-eaten bowl of stew onto the ground and looked over at Hanna. He smiled at her and said, "You think I don't know exactly what you're dying to ask me? Why you've come along on this little habitat foray?"

"Is he ... alive?" she asked, her eyes downcast, staring steadily into the flames.

Stalls waited for her to look up at him. Obviously, he

liked to taunt … no … he liked to torture. "Hanna, the man you married is not the same man who managed to survive the Sahhrain prison camps."

"What does that mean? Why can't you just answer the damn question?" Hanna was standing now, her fists clenched.

Stalls let out a long breath, as if the whole conversation had become overly burdensome. Leon considered retrieving his knife.

"What it means is your husband, Ridert, is no longer the same man taken from that exploration vessel three years ago. He's lost an eye, for one thing, although he looks surprisingly dashing with his eye patch—but the changes go far deeper than that. In fact, he's now the leader of Lord Vikor Shakrim's very own Chosen Spears imperial guard … the truth is, he's nearly as cunning, might I dare say as evil, as Lord Shakrim himself. We've shared Targonian spirits together on several occasions. As much as it pains me to say this … the casual observer might go so far as to even call us friends."

She jumped on him. Her screams echoed out into the night. Fists pounded down onto Stalls' head and shoulders. Her knee came up and connected to his nose. Blood spurted and poured freely down and over his lips. The sounds of his laughter began to ebb and, with one quick flick of his hand, Hanna was knocked to the ground. She stayed down and sobbed. Leon put a hand on her back, tried to help her up, but she shrugged him off. Getting to her feet on her own she ran to the *Charm* and disappeared inside.

Stalls looked up at Leon. "So tell me … what services do you require of me?"

Leon wanted to kill Stalls right then … this second … and someday he'd make that happen. He hesitated before answering, "You mentioned Lord Vikor Shakrim."

Chapter 33

Dacci System
The *Minian*, Flight Bay

Jason stood at the massive, arched bay opening on the *Minian*'s starboard flight deck. He felt the subtle effects of the invisible energy field—used to maintain the integrity of the ship's internal environment—a barrier against the vacuum of space beyond. There, in the distance, was the twinkling starlight of three planetary systems. The flight deck was quiet, with the exception of maintenance droids—attending to the Caldurian fighters, numerous pilotless fighter droids, and a handful of shuttlecraft.

Jason continued to stare off into distant space. His father, perhaps his daughter, too, was out there ... somewhere. In both cases, Jason felt responsible for their situations. So now he'd have to wait. The team had already set off to HAB 331, to find and bring back Stalls. Something he was more than a little leery about. Stalls was ever the sly egocentric, and Jason was well aware what the ex-pirate was capable of ... something he'd reminded Rizzo about, and more than once.

Jason decided to take advantage of the downtime. He

needed to discover more about the Sahhrain and the Blues, before confrontations between them came to pass. The best way to do that was to visit Harpaign, the desolate world in the Blues' solar system.

Ricket arrived with his battle suit already initialized. He stood at Jason's side in silence for a moment, and together they looked out toward the distant stars. Jason eventually said, "This will be somewhat dangerous, Ricket. As you well know, the *Pacesetter*'s probably undetectable to any vessel we'll be coming into contact with ... with that said, still we'll be skirting a hostile fleet."

"I do understand that, Captain. But the planet Harpaign, for the most part, is sparsely populated. As miserable as the weather is within HAB 7, it seems to have worsened even more over time. A most undesirable environment."

"You know where to go ... where to locate these ancient tablets?"

"I believe so, Captain. I've uploaded all the pertinent information to our HUDs and to the *Pacesetter*." Ricket gestured to the fighter stationed nearby.

Together, they headed over to the sleek, dark red Caldurian vessel. Jason felt the familiar rush of adrenalin as he approached his most-favored fighter ... it was fast and remarkably intuitive. He'd learned to pilot vessels like her only after his own hyper-learning stint in a MediPod, two years earlier, and the thrill of piloting a small, highly-maneuverable ship, like the *Pacesetter*, was now in his blood. He waved Ricket toward the inset ladder.

"Up you go."

The canopy was open and Ricket took the front-most seat, while Jason sat in the seat directly behind him. The canopy closed and the cockpit came alive with multiple holographic 3D displays, which hovered just above their dual dash control boards. Jason listened to the soft voice of the AI, providing ship status information over his NanoCom. All was well—the *Pacesetter* operating at a hundred percent.

Jason quickly reviewed the latest uploads from Ricket on his HUD, skimming some items, giving others more attention. They'd be traveling to the far side of Harpaign. Since the *Pacesetter* was equipped with phase-shift capability, their actual travel time in space would be limited. He viewed the suggested plot coordinates, optimal phase-shifting points, along their upcoming flight. Phase-shifting allowed for jumps across great distances in space, thousands of miles— but there were limitations to how many phase-shifts could take place within a given block of time, without providing adequate time for the system to recharge. In this particular case, the *Pacesetter*'s AI had calculated seven phase-shifts, while providing hands-on, sub-light flight in areas of space that were the least congested with alien spacecraft. He entered a few adjustments to their plot coordinates and reduced the plot screen down to a small icon window on his HUD.

"Ready?"

"Ready," Ricket replied.

Jason, though well aware the *Pacesetter*'s AI was more than capable to fly the little space fighter with little or no assistance from the pilot, nevertheless preferred a hands-on manual mode. He was also aware that at this stage of interstellar flight, pilots were never really flying on their own ... human reaction time was far too slow, too inaccurate. Although the pilot's hand movements on the controls were followed, they'd been anticipated by the AI, along with thousands of other, best-guess decision scenarios, where the AI actually made all the intricate, necessary micro-adjustments to fulfill the pilot's commands. Safeguards were in place where the AI could override a pilot's faulty, or dangerous, decision making

... but most of those safeguards were deactivated by Jason early on, as his skill at the controls heightened, and his *need* for *riskier* maneuvers increased.

Jason heard the fighter's powerful drive start whirling at a higher pitch as he brought the *Pacesetter* up off the flight deck. He punched the controls forward and the fighter rocketed out, beneath the *Minian's* expansive flight bay archway, into open space. He immediately went through a series of forward and backward loops, sideways turns, and various combat maneuvers he'd been thinking about since the last time he'd been behind the controls. As his excitement elevated, Jason became more and more aware of the AI's voice in his ear, letting him know that he had deviated from the prescribed flight plan. Reluctantly, he slowed the *Pacesetter* down, straightened out her trajectory, and returned to the plotted course.

"You all right up there, Ricket?"

"I'm fine, Captain. That was quite invigorating."

"I guess I needed to get it out of my system. Okay, we're coming to our first phase-shift coordinates in ten seconds."

Jason waited for the telltale phase-shift flash. It came and in that same instant, they were propelled thousands of miles closer to their destination. The flash came again, and then again, and then again. With each phase-shift, Jason watched as their physical perspective, in relation to the Blues' solar system, was altered. Jason halted the automatic, preset phase-shift program, and peered out through the canopy.

"Captain, Sahhrain warships are present here, within this system."

Jason saw that the bulk of activity, hundreds of ships, was still within the nearby Dacci system. But Ricket was right— no fewer than thirty Sahhrain vessels were near.

"Let's get a little closer," Jason said. He configured the

Pacesetter for another phase-shift, one that would place them fairly near Harpaign.

Flash.

Jason involuntarily clenched his teeth. "Crap!" He'd maneuvered the *Pacesetter* within two phase-shifts of the planet, but far too close to three Sahhrain warships. *And that's what happens when you manually override an AI.*

"Can you confirm we're not showing up on their close-range scans?"

Ricket didn't answer for several moments. "What's probably a more important question, Captain ... is why didn't these three vessels show up on the *Minian*'s or the *Pacesetter*'s long-range scans?"

"That is a good question," Jason said. "Odd-looking ships ... can't say I've ever seen anything like them," he added, using his HUD to magnify one of the warships. It was battleship gray and comprised of five pyramid-shaped superstructures, each connected to a pentagon- shaped center hub. In a sense, the ship appeared star-shaped.

"Captain ... these warships are not of Sahhrain design. But from the communications chatter I'm picking up, they are, indeed, now Sahhrain fleet vessels. Probably absconded ... much the way the *Assailant* was."

"Speaking of which ... any sign of her?"

"The *Minian* hasn't picked up her signature within any of the planetary systems here, Captain. But these vessels are large ... large enough to bring the *Assailant* on board ... hide her from detection."

"And there's no way of knowing how many of those ... snowflake-looking ships ... there are?"

"That is incorrect, Captain. I have altered both the *Minian*'s and the *Pacesetter*'s sensor databases to include the three vessels' unique, variable-spectrum Teclar waves ... ingenious as the process was that hid them, we'll now be able to detect all these vessels."

Jason was only partially listening to Ricket. His attention was on the holographic display and the light-blue icon now blinking. Below the icon was a single word: *Assailant*.

"Are you seeing what I'm seeing, Ricket?"

"Yes, Captain. I suspect we'll be making another course change?"

"It's right here in this star system ... I'm not letting that ship out of my sight. Hold on while I set new phase-shift coordinates."

"Yes, Captain."

Chapter 34

Dacci System
The *Pacesetter*, Open Space

"Captain, I have determined the vessels are of Parlek Orion origin."

"Parlek Orion?"

"Not from this galaxy. Only recently, actually right before the end of the war, the planetary system was conquered by the Craing. It seems the Sahhrain have since taken ownership of their fleet."

"In another galaxy? How the hell would that be possible?" Jason peered into the forward section of the *Pacesetter*'s cockpit, where Ricket sat. A full minute elapsed before an answer came back.

"Captain, the Sahhrain are utilizing the local Loop wormhole ... from my estimate, this wormhole, the one here in nearby Dacci space, has its outpoint near the Parlek Orion Empire ... I'm sorry, Captain, I did not have this information available for you before."

Jason let that set in. That changed everything. It went well beyond the purview of Star Watch. No longer a simple matter of policing a localized uprising … the situation had elevated, becoming instead an interstellar threat that would require the might of the full Allied forces.

Jason spent the next few minutes on comms, speaking with his XO back on the *Minian*. Perkins was instructed to send a formal correspondence back to Jefferson Station, one that would provide the pertinent information and convey the now-elevated threat level of their situation. Jason wondered who was the ultimate decision-maker at command, now that his father was gone.

"Captain, on the far side of Harpaign is another Parlek Orion vessel. It is positioned exactly where the *Assailant* is being held."

Jason stared at his own console display. "I see a ship icon there … but there's no indication it's one of the Parlek Orion vessels."

"With my internal nano-devices, the vessel's unique signature is unmistakable," Ricket added.

Jason again peered into the forward cockpit … *just how much new tech has Ricket added into that little head of his?*

"One more thing, Captain."

"Go on."

"The admiral's life-icon, albeit critically faint, is there too."

Jason immediately considered bringing in a rescue team. He called up a new flight path overlay layer onto the display. He tried several different scenarios, utilizing the absolute longest phase-shifts possible, from the *Minian* to their current position. He then calculated the time necessary for the assault team to be assembled and dispatched: Forty minutes, plus or minus.

"Can you guesstimate the admiral's condition … how much time he has?"

"Not accurately, Captain. I've been working on that and my best-guess prognosis would be ..." Ricket went quiet.

"Spit it out, Ricket!"

"Minutes. Mere minutes. He's dying, Captain. I am very sorry."

Jason was already looking at new overlays—ones that would bring the *Pacesetter* to the far side of Harpaign and to the alien vessel. "Ricket, contact the *Minian* ... have Billy assemble an assault team and ensure they're dispatched in the next few minutes. Ensure, too, that Dira is part of their team."

"Yes, Captain."

Flash.

"Perhaps we should wait for the assault team, Captain."

Flash. Flash.

After the third phase-shift Jason answered, "You've done the calculations ... you know as well as I do that my father won't survive in the amount of time it'll take Billy and his team to arrive here."

"We'll just have to be extra stealthy ..."

* * *

Boomer was thrown off-guard, taking a distortion wave directly to her stomach. Doubled over, she was brought down to her knees. Tears came to her eyes, blurring her vision. Sensing, more than seeing, she assessed their movements—they were readying for another attack. She straightened and kept moving. She could now use her shield in ways others hadn't, coming to rely on it like she relied on her own limbs. It was now a part of her ... *it was her*. The shield, with its three curved sides, was basically triangular, its curved edges approximately one inch thick. It was the shield's three-sided edging that Boomer first became interested in—had explored—realizing their unique design, potentially, made the shield capable of yielding so much more. Each of the three one-inch edges was independently accessible and varied from the other two. Understanding their dynamics made all the difference, when it came down to why Boomer was now capable of doing things with the shield that even Prince Aahil Aqeel could not do.

The prince was here, among four other Tahli warriors—each a *Kahill Callan* master. They moved with lighting-fast speed—sometimes coming together in a combined attack—other times, singularly.

Boomer cartwheeled left, using the shield's three edges independently, to push and pull her spinning movements away from a newly assembled two-man attack. Violet distortion waves filled the space where she'd previously been only milliseconds earlier. Her cartwheel morphed into a running forward flip that put her near the base of a large tree. Her leading foot's next step landed high up on the tree's trunk, and instinctively she angled her shield down in such a way that she could continue running straight up the side of the great towering redwood.

Branches burst into sawdust around Boomer, as countless distortion waves shot up at her from below. *Crap! Where do I go from here?* At thirty feet up, her shield no longer pushing back against the ground and propelling her upwards, her ascent began to slow. Two distortion waves hit her at the same time—one hitting her in the buttocks, the other in her upper back. With only simple nomad's garments on for protection, the pain ... like white-hot lightning bolts ... paralyzed her. She fell ten feet, landing across one of the few remaining, lower-level, horizontal branches. The slam to her chest forced all the air from her lungs. She tried to gasp but couldn't—still paralyzed from too many distortion wave strikes.

The sounds heard earlier in the forest were now still as Boomer lay face down, straddling the tree branch. She felt the bark's roughness on her hands and left cheek; the coolness of it. She slowly regained the ability to breathe again. Before she could fully fathom what the cracking, splintering sounds were, she was already falling to the ground.

Boomer fell, landing face down atop the same broken branch. Exhausted, and wondering if she'd broken something important, she stared at the accumulation of pine needles all around where she lay. What her father didn't know was that these gifted nomads could travel between the Zoo habitats, as well as other places, other realms, with relative ease. They had purposely picked this dark and remote forest to continue her training.

Five sets of legs were standing nearby, and she wondered if she would ever be good enough ... capable enough, to do what these nomads kept asking of her. She didn't want to keep disappointing them—disappointing Aahil.

"Get up, Boomer."

"I can't."

"Get up now ... you cannot quit."

"I'm too tired. I don't want to do this anymore. I want to go home."

Boomer heard a female's voice, several steps back behind the others, say, "She's too young ... too immature. We should let her return to her ship."

Boomer recognized Capri's voice. She knew what she was trying to do. What was the word ... manip? ... manipulate her. It wasn't going to work. She'd given all she had and she just wasn't good enough. If she were, she wouldn't be lying facedown on the ground.

"I have a gift for you, Boomer. You may not want it now,

though ... since you've quit."

Boomer tried to focus on Aahil's particular set of legs. "What is it?"

"It's two thousand years old and derived from a material found in only one small place in the galaxy."

Boomer lifted her cheek off the ground and peered up at Aahil. He was holding out a wooden box, cradled in his two hands.

"Is it in that box, or is it the box itself?"

"It's in the box."

Boomer sat up and crossed her legs. "Can I see it?"

"Will there be any more talk about giving up?"

"Probably."

Aahil and the others laughed out loud at that. "Then you still know how important you are ... to what we're trying to accomplish?"

"Of course I do."

Aahil knelt down and set the large box on her lap. "Open it."

Boomer rubbed at the scrape on her cheek and looked down at the intricately engraved wooden box. There were scenes of a battle carved into it. Strange men with spears and shields and words she couldn't read. She opened the box.

"Grace it before you touch it, then do so again afterwards," Aahil said.

Boomer removed her own shield from her wrist and looked up to Aahil. She saw the tension in his face ... tension, and something else. Some sadness showing there, too? "This was yours, wasn't it?"

"I suspect I was merely meant to hold on to it until you were ready."

"Shalla ka la rohlm." She placed her hand on the faintly blue-hued metal. Abruptly, she took in a breath as the shield's electric charge coursed through her palm and up her arm. "Shalla ka la rohlm."

It was bigger than her training shield; she now traced the shield's engraved surface with her fingertips, while physically and mentally exploring its essence. It was alive and as she connected with it ... delved deeper into it—it too, reached back ... exploring deep into her own inner consciousness.

"Can I try it?"

Chapter 35

Dacci System
The *Pacesetter*, Open Space

The *Pacesetter*'s final phase-shift put Jason and Rick-et close enough in to see the distant Sahhrain's Parlek Orion ship with their naked eyes. The vessel was larger than others they'd seen—closer in size to a meganaught, versus a heavy cruiser.

"Tell me everything you can about that ship and its crew, Ricket."

"Well ... as you can see, Captain, it is a substantially larger vessel. It is named the Gallium. Akin to other of their ships, its shields emit variable-spectrum Teclar waves, making the vessel invisible to virtually all far- and close-range sensors. Similar to other Parlek Orion ships, there are five pyramid-shaped superstructures on it, but this huge ship is designed with large flight bays and has a number of vessels moored inside ... including the Assailant."

Jason goosed the Pacesetter's drive and approached the large warship. "Is their technology capable of detecting the Pacesetter?"

233

"No, Captain ... I have been monitoring multiple Gallium comms channels ... we have not been detected. With that said ... still, we should not get much closer."

Jason quickly slowed and stopped further progress of the small fighter.

"Captain, a vessel is leaving the Gallium ... it's the Assailant."

"The admiral?"

"Still on board the Gallium," Ricket said.

Jason spotted the familiar silhouette of the Assailant emerging from one of the pyramid-like superstructures. It accelerated and, within seconds, was gone. Jason wondered if Lord Vikor Shakrim was on board. Had he just missed an opportunity to end the uprising ... and to save Boomer?

"Your father is being held within the topmost structure of the ship at its current orientation. If we are going to do something ... we ... should move quickly, Captain."

Ricket, already anticipating Jason's next request, displayed the Gallium's internal schematics. An ever-so-faint blue icon pulsed on and off, approximately midway within the top superstructure.

"There are significant Sahhrain forces all around his position—"

"Yes ... I can see that," Jason snapped, viewing thirty to forty active red icons all around his father's location. "What about this area here?" he asked Ricket, outlining a circle upon the virtual display with his fingertip.

"That is a sub-reactor chamber. It's duplicated within each of the superstructures."

"Large enough to phase-shift into?"

"Individually, or in the *Pacesetter*?"

"Either," Jason said.

"It would be a tight fit for the *Pacesetter*, but yes, room enough. The problem will be the radiation. There's a reason there are no life-icons in, or near, this location, Captain. Our battle suits won't provide us with sufficient shielding, but the *Pacesetter* would ... at least, maybe, for several minutes."

Time was their enemy at this point. They couldn't bring the *Pacesetter* any closer in to the *Gallium*, and individually phase-shifting from this far a distance in open space—both there and back ... while hefting an ailing admiral along the way—didn't make much sense either.

"Would the sub-reactor's radiation hide our presence?"

Ricket didn't answer right away. "Maybe."

Jason smiled at his reply. "At least you're honest. We'll need to try. If I do things right, the Sahhrain will never know I'm there. Before they realize it, the admiral, locked in a cell one moment, has disappeared in the next."

Jason set new *Pacesetter* phase-shift coordinates and, without any hesitation, they flashed away.

In an instant they were thrown into an amber-hued darkness; the fighter's running lights illuminated the confined curvature of the sub-reactor chamber.

An alarm pinged. The *Pacesetter*'s AI announced, "External radiation levels are exceeding safe parameters."

Jason expected to have more time. "You'll have to take the *Pacesetter* out of here ... come back when I have the admiral."

"Yes, Captain."

He thought he heard relief in Ricket's voice. He rechecked the *Gallium*'s layout once more and his father's location. "See you later!" Jason flashed away.

* * *

Jason phase-shifted into what seemed to be an onboard

brig. The lighting there was intense—so intense he used his HUD settings to make the necessary compensation to his helmet's visor. He'd landed within the confines of a long corridor, which provided access to multiple prison-like cells. His father lay on the deck of a cell directly in front of him. He was still wearing his admiral's jumpsuit, but it was bloodied and torn—hanging open, exposing his chest. White chest hair mingled with blood that was caked thick in splotches where he'd obviously been poked, more likely stabbed, with something sharp.

Jason stepped closer and was immediately halted by an energy field of some kind. He phase-shifted to a position two feet inside his father's cell. Worried, Jason thought the admiral looked dead. Jason watched for some movement of his chest, to see if he was breathing. He let out his own breath, seeing on his HUD that the admiral's life-icon, dim as it was, was still there—but was blinking on and off—indicating his life signs were fading. Jason had little time to save his father.

The admiral coughed and his eyes opened. "Get out of here … go!" the admiral ordered, his voice barely above a whisper.

"That's not going to happen." Jason quickly retrieved a SuitPac device from a pocket compartment at the side of his thigh. He affixed it to his father's stained and bloodied belt and squeezed the two side sensors. Within two seconds, his father's body was covered from head to toe inside a battle suit and, most important to Jason, was being medically attended to by the suit's advanced Caldurian life support functions. It was no MediPod but it was something. Hopefully it would keep him alive until Dira could physically attend to him.

His father's voice, sounding stronger now, said, "They've taken my ship … they have the *Assailant*."

Jason helped him stand, supporting him with his arm

under his father's arm and going around his waist. "I know that. We'll worry about that later."

His father looked from side to side. "Where's your team?"

"There wasn't time ... Ricket and I pretty much stumbled upon this ship and on you. For now, we're on our own."

"You're an idiot ... you know that, right?"

"Uh huh ... I've been told as much."

Jason hailed Ricket. Nothing. He brought up his HUD's long-range logistic layer and looked for the *Pacesetter*. "Holy crap!"

"What is it?" the admiral asked.

"It's Ricket ... he's piloting the *Pacesetter* in open space. He's got three bogies on his tail ... being fired upon ... looks to have taken damage." Jason continued to watch the unfolding scene on his HUD. *Why not simply phase-shift ...?*

"Captain!" Ricket's voice was faint behind loud static.

"Go ahead, Ricket."

"*Pacesetter* is damaged ... th as ap ... repe ... this ... a trap." The connection went dead.

Enemy life-icons were quickly converging toward their location. "We need to get out of here," Jason said, looking into his father's visor. The admiral's eyes were half-closed and unfocused. *Shit!* He brought up the ship's layout again on his HUD and looked for a place to go.

Sahhrain forces were now within the brig's corridor and heading their way. Jason glanced in the direction of noisy running feet. He'd seen the Sahhrain once before—in his inner vision. In actual life they were no less imposing: tall and muscular—they wore their hair swept up and back in some kind of bun affair. Surprisingly, they were bare-armed and wore breastplates similar to those worn by ancient Roman warriors. Each held on to a long speared weapon and had a small shield, like Capri's and Boomer's, affixed to his opposite forearm.

The brig cell's energy force field vanished as the warriors approached. Two Sahhrain raised their shields toward Jason and his father. Jason initiated the phase-shift a half-second too late; first seeing the violet distortion waves and then feeling their painful effects, Jason and his father flashed away.

* * *

Jason awoke fifteen minutes later, feeling as if he'd been run over by a truck. Weightless, floating in open space, he tried to remember where he was ... what had happened. It all came back to him in a rush ... *the Sahhrain soldiers ... Ricket ... my father.* Jason abruptly turned, first left then right, and saw the admiral's battle suit floating mere feet away from his own. He reached out and pulled the prone figure in closer, turning his own body around to look into his father's visor.

"This was your rescue plan? To phase-shift us out into open space?"

Jason's relief was written all over his face. His father attempted a weak-hearted smile. "Yes, I'm still alive, son. What do we do now?"

"Hang tight for a moment, Dad."

Jason turned around again and found the *Gallium,* far off, in distant space. He tried again to hail Ricket. *Nothing.*

Something caught his eye—a fleeting reflection of light—perhaps from the not-so-near sun. Jason magnified the area of space around him with his HUD. Wreckage. Two ... no, three separate clusters of wreckage. Two fighters—both of alien design, with no life forms present. He zoomed in on the farthest-out cluster of wreckage and immediately recognized pieces of hull—dark red pieces of hull. It was the *Pacesetter*, no doubt about it. Jason looked for a life-icon within the same area—but didn't find one. He spoke to his battle suit's internal AI. Not liking the sound of her voice, it was something he rarely did. "AI ... scan for Ricket's DNA, as far out as your sensors permit."

"Scanning now ..."

"Never mind, AI ... his life-icon just appeared." Approaching at high speed, Ricket's life-icon was moving forward on a direct intersecting vector. In the distance, a small ship, an alien fighter, was fast approaching.

"What the hell?" Jason muttered aloud.

The fighter was mangled to such an extent Jason wondered how it was capable of maintaining space flight. Deep, blackened craters pockmarked much of the vessel's hull; its canopy was gone, and one wing had been sheared off. Sitting within the cockpit was a lone inhabitant.

"What the hell did you do to my fighter?"

Ricket stared back at Jason—his large eyes visible behind his battle suit's visor. "I'm sorry, Captain. I did my best to save the *Pacesetter* ... but Sahhrain fighters took me by surprise. All communications and phase-shift capabilities suffered damage."

Jason looked again at the wrecked ship Ricket was sitting in. "How'd you get in there?"

"Before the *Pacesetter* exploded I phase-shifted into one of the attacking, although heavily damaged, fighters. As you know, upon phase-shifting two organic beings cannot occupy the same space. The pilot was ejected into open space— his body thrust up and out through the now-destroyed visor. Ever since, I've been searching for you ... hoping you had phase-shifted somewhere near the proximity of the *Gallium*. How is the admiral?"

Jason, impressed with Ricket's ingenuity, looked over at

his father. "He's stable for now. But he's really in need of medical attention soon."

"Prior to the *Pacesetter*'s destruction I was in contact with the *Minian*. Billy and his team are en route—should be close by now."

Chapter 36

Dacci System
Planet Dacci, Glist Processing Plant

Lord Shakrim listened as they walked together. The dark hazy mist, swirling below their knees, obstructed their feet from view—as if they were walking through a deep black cloud. Although unseen, Shakrim's Chosen Spear guards were close at hand—never far from their master.

The Dacci man, the foundry plant's general administrator, was tall for a Dacci and surprisingly confident. Shakrim let him prattle on because he was pleased with what he was hearing—pleased with the evident progress made here and back at the mines—two hundred miles to the east.

"Bulk extraction of Glist is ahead of schedule, my Lord. Yields are excellent." Together, they continued to walk side by side between towering ion furnaces, stoked to burn blazingly hot and bring the raw Glist into a molten state.

Up ahead, magnificent great vats, shaped like ladles, brimmed with glowing blue, liquefied Glist. One after another they tipped over, pouring down the molten form of the mineral into multiple rows of V-shaped troughs. Thousands of tiny energy bolts, like azure-colored lightning, continued to travel up and down the molten metal, until the vats were emptied out; then, tipping back into an upright position, they were ready to be refilled.

"I am quite pleased with your progress, administrator. You will be rewarded handsomely for your good work here."

The plant administrator continued walking, slightly bowing his head to show his gratitude.

They'd reached Shakrim's favorite part of the foundry. The shield molds. It was where the amazing material, Glist, took shape—already combined with rare, exotic, catalysts which would, eventually, bring the now-molten material back into a hardened state. Here, they stopped and stood before a massive, waist-level metal block—upon which were square, individual molds. Lord Shakrim stared at the hundreds of empty molds before him. Then he saw the Glist. Small veins, previously undetected, now glowed blue as the Glist traveled toward its intended targets. Like a giant circulatory system coming alive before his eyes, the shield molds began filling. This part of the process was slower and necessarily so, in order for the molded shields to harden correctly. As he watched, Lord Shakrim let his mind wander back to his recent time spent with Admiral Reynolds. He'd learned much from the Allied forces commander. More than that human probably realized. He'd learned that the writings were, in fact, true—that the *chariot in the sky* would be delivered to him. That singularly amazing ship ... the *Minian*, which traveled in an alternate dimension, an alternate realm, would soon be his. Only then would he be able to bring forth his Sachem, *Rom Dasticon*. Only then, together, could they spread utter darkness to the farthest reaches of the universe.

Lord Shakrim had no sooner left the admiral's side, aboard the human's own command vessel, when the news reached him: The admiral had been rescued. That was expected ... part of the plan to bring the *Minian* here. *It's all so, so, close to happening now.* The attack would come soon ... an attack no one would be able to defend against.

Lord Vikor Shakrim looked up from the slowly filling molds and gestured toward the distant darkness. A man with an eye patch appeared from the haze, wearing a similar metallic breastplate, although one made of silver instead of gold; a new enhancement shield was affixed to his left forearm.

"Ridert. Have you done as I've asked?"

"I have, my Lord."

"All of them?"

"Thirty-six, total."

Lord Shakrim tilted his head toward the shield molds.

"Each one has been given the latest, most powerful, enhancement shield. They do not know what they've done to be given such an honor."

Lord Shakrim scoffed at that. "Has an arena been prepared, Commander Ridert?"

* * *

Within a mile of the foundry, thirty-six Sahhrain warriors readied themselves for battle. Who they would be pitted against was unknown to them. What they did know, what they had been told, was that there was no higher honor—that this one event would eclipse all other events in their pasts, and all the ones to come. Periodically, they stopped to admire the powerful new shields now gracing their forearms ... letting feelings of pride play with their heads.

What they did not know—but what all others within the Sahhrain fleet did know—was that they were disgraced ... had failed catastrophically at their individual posts. The human Allied commander, Admiral Reynolds, had been rescued, right beneath their noses. They would need to suffer a price for such negligence—be made examples of.

Lord Shakrim's arrival was completely clandestine; only his loyal Chosen Spears were aware of the true situation. The *Assailant's* arrival above the arena was unobserved—since the ship was cloaked—invisible to the naked eye as well as all sensors. It set down fifty yards from the makeshift arena. Seconds later, the gangway was lowered. Magically, Lord Shakrim walked into view—as if appearing out of thin air.

Shakrim took in the hastily erected arena, laid out within the last few hours. True to regulation, the equilateral, decagon-shaped area spanned seventy-five square yards. It was simple, lacking even the most standard properties, such as varying, strategically placed, obstacles. Makeshift bleachers were positioned around three of the four sides of the area, where close to five hundred Sahhrain, many of them warship officers and commanders, sat quietly.

Thirty-six warriors now held, in addition to their enhancement shields, long spear weapons, called pratta-shafts. Standing in a circular formation, they bowed at the approach of Lord Vikor Shakrim. They hadn't expected him: the most incredible honor imaginable! But his sudden presence, now unwaveringly apparent, foretold their death sentence. No one, ever, had survived a battle against the Lord Commander.

Murmurs arose from the crowd as Lord Shakrim entered the boundaries of the decagon arena. It was near dusk and the setting sun's reflection sparkled and shimmered off his gold breastplate. He came to a halt ten feet in front of the tight formation of thirty-six Sahhrain warriors. He saw fear on their faces; he felt their growing desperation.

Commander Ridert, now at his side, handed Lord Shakrim, already wearing an enhancement shield, a pratta-shaft. While he adjusted its fit on his arm, Shakrim looked over at his now-cowering opponents and said, "Fight with honor … give me all that you have. Fight like you've never fought before … your very life depends on it … fight to the point you will do anything, and everything, to survive. Fight to kill me. Do so, and I will allow one of you … the very best one … to be allowed to live."

Shakrim let that sink in and there it was … hope. He'd given them a glimmer of something unexpected. They would fight with more intensity now … they would kill each other. *How easily they are manipulated*, he thought. He looked into the stands at the Sahhrain seated around them. He spoke loud and clear: "You are witnessing today the cost of failure. There is not one amongst you who couldn't, just as easily, be standing here before me. You will not be warned again."

Lord Shakrim finally gave a cursory bow in the direction of the warriors before him. They broke from their formation—away from each other—taking up defensive stances, their pratta-shafts held high, and their enhancement shields rightly positioned in front of them. Each was highly trained in the Sahhrain's own, albeit similar to that of the Blues, version of *Kahill Callan* martial arts. The warriors moved quickly—several stayed clustered together, in small groups, surrounding Shakrim on all sides.

He kept his eyes on the lone warrior in front of him, knowing he would not be the first to attack. Shakrim already knew who that would be. Twenty feet directly behind his back, Shakrim felt the warrior there try to suppress his thoughts, hide them … but it was a futile effort. A warrior's pratta-shaft was far more than a simple spear. It was the only weapon capable of piercing through an opponent's distortion waves. It instantly matched any vibration it came into contact with. The spear came fast, directed towards the back of

Shakrim's head. He used his telekinetic powers to alter the spear's flight by less than four degrees—just enough, though, to change its trajectory, bypassing his own head—instead, hitting the warrior who stood before him. The pratta-shaft's tip imbedded itself into his chest, killing him instantly.

Using the edge of his shield, along with telekinesis, Lord Vikor Shakrim catapulted into the air, high above the warriors now charging toward him from up ahead. He sensed their thoughts … knew when they'd make a move. He spun around, now landing at their backsides. He swung his pratta-shaft in a wide sideways arc, its razor-sharp tip decapitating the nearest warrior; then, letting the weapon's momentum carry it around his own body, in mid-swing, he changed his grip and threw the shaft with a forceful, forward thrust. It flew unhindered for thirty feet, entering the abdominal cavity of a charging warrior, then exited him and entered into the chest of the warrior who was standing ten feet behind him. Both fell to the ground, dead.

As in most Sahhrain close-contact battles, the pratta-shaft, typically, was lost early on. Inevitably, it was the warrior—armed only with his enhancement shield—solely left to endure a prolonged battle.

Right then, no less than five pratta-shafts were in the air, all headed toward Shakrim. He dodged one and used his shield to block another. The next three missed as he again leapt high into the air—his black and red cloak billowing out dramatically behind him. The crowd abruptly cheered in unison.

Violet distortion waves, brighter and more powerful than any of the others, continuously pulsed and streamed out from Shakrim's enhancement shield. Surviving Sahhrain warriors attempted to block the devastating waves, but could not. One after another, they were catapulted high into the air—several even into the stands. Two warriors were held stationary, paralyzed, ten feet up in the air, as the one-sided battle raged on below them.

Shakrim continued to move with amazing speed and agility—never staying in one place long enough to get hit by a flying pratta-shaft or, more frequent, the continual barrage of distortion waves. One by one, Lord Shakrim pounded these waves into his opponents. Bodies lay motionless within the arena, and several outside it.

He stopped now and saw there was no one left to fight. He had taken no injuries himself. He was barely out of breath. Finally, he let his eyes level upon the two suspended warriors. He released them and they both fell to the ground. Slowly, they regained the ability to move around, and warily stood, facing him. He assessed them both.

"Your fight with me is done. The one who can defeat the other lives."

With that, Lord Vikor Shakrim strode from the arena toward his now-visible ship. The crowd cheered as the only two surviving warriors took up fighting stances.

Chapter 37

Dacci System
The *Perilous,* Open Space

The *Perilous* arrived in ten minutes. Within that time-span, Jason watched as his father's life-support indicators moved from stable to critical. One of Grimes' young fighter pilots, Lieutenant Tom Burn, occupying the pilot's seat, phase-shifted the shuttle close to them, and, within seconds, Jason was joined by Billy—who, after phase-shifting into open space, appeared nearby.

"There's not a lot of room in there, Cap, so we need to transfer the admiral into the *Perilous* the old-fashioned way."

The back hatch of the shuttle opened as the small ship backed toward them. Inside, everyone wore battle suits. Dira, standing in front of the others, gestured for Jason and Billy to maneuver the admiral's inert form toward her. Then she, along with several other sets of hands, grabbed on to the admiral's body and brought him on board.

First Billy, then Jason, got on board. Jason turned outward, to face the nearby fighter. "You okay to fly this pile of scrap back to the *Minian*? It's a bit tight in here."

"Yes, Captain ... I believe I'll be fine," said Ricket.

Jason gave a mock salute and stepped away as the rear hatch lowered and secured into place.

Jason looked out the rear observation window and saw that Ricket and his battered fighter were now heading off in the opposite direction of where the *Minian* was located—he was heading toward the planet. *What the hell's he doing?* About to hail Ricket on his NanoCom, his attention was pulled away.

"We need to get the battle suit off the admiral!" Dira yelled into an open channel.

Burn, at the controls, yelled back ... "Thirty seconds to decompress the cabin ... hold on."

Dira leaned anxiously over the admiral's unconscious body as he lay on the deck; even through her visor, Jason could see concern. He was pretty sure it matched his own grim expression. He purposely tried not to think about his father's worsening condition—how close the admiral was to death's door.

"Atmosphere's restored!" Burn announced.

Jason remotely accessed his father's battle suit HUD settings and disengaged the suit. It immediately withdrew, back into the small SuitPac device affixed to the admiral's bloodstained belt. Dira gasped, seeing the caked blood on his exposed chest.

"What the fuck did they do to him?" she asked to nobody in particular. She disengaged her own battle suit and quickly went to work, injecting him with a small device of some kind and then affixing three other, larger, devices onto his exposed skin. After that, she reengaged the admiral's battle suit and, leaning back against the bulkhead, met Jason's eyes.

"I'm not going to lie to you, Jason ... he's in a very critical condition."

"What did you do for him?"

"Gave him an amped-up nanites injection that will go directly to the distressed areas within his body. I also placed his body into a semi-stasis ... cryogenic ... state."

"Will he live? Were we in time?"

Dira stared back at Jason for several moments before answering. "You didn't know? I'm sorry, Jason ... your father's not alive. From what I can tell, he's been gone for several moments now." She reached out and placed a hand on his shoulder. "There's still hope. We'll be back on the *Minian* within minutes ... let's see what a MediPod can do for him."

Jason was fully aware what miracles a MediPod could perform. Mollie did die, shot in the heart by a plasma bolt, and he had only five minutes to get her body into a Medi-Pod. He made it, but barely. How long now had his father been dead? Four minutes ... five?

"Burn! How close?" Jason yelled toward the ship's forward cabin.

Three bright flashes, one right after the other, occurred before he actually heard his answer, "We're there! Suggest you phase-shift directly into Medical."

Simultaneously, Dira and Jason initialized their battle suits. Jason took ahold of his father, wrapping his arms around his upper torso, and the threesome flashed away.

* * *

They phase-shifted directly into Medical. Jason, a nearby med-tech, and Dira hefted the admiral's not-so insubstantial girth into the closest MediPod. Somewhere in the back of his mind Jason was keeping track of the time elapsing. His father had been dead for close to seven minutes ... plus or minus—well beyond the maximum allowance of five minutes.

As Jason stared down at his father's face, visible through the MediPod's small porthole, he silently wondered if now was the last time he'd be able to see him.

Dira kept busy at the MediPod console. He saw her reposition one of the small display screens away out of his view.

"No ... that's okay ... I want to see it."

Dira tilted her head in a way that spoke volumes—saying, in effect, *you won't like what you see.*

She repositioned the angle of the display so Jason could again see the royal-blue virtual representation of the admiral's body. A myriad of moving life-indicators, and other readouts, flashed across the screen at alarming rates. The one thing not moving, the one essential thing to show some movement, was still—his father's heart.

Dira, noting Jason's expression, said, "We'll just have to wait and see. There's substantial internal injuries here. It looks as if various organs have been ... individually targeted ... and electrified. I've heard of this kind of invasive, selective-type torture before. Victims feel unbelievable levels of pain. If you'd gotten him here ..." she paused while continuing to work at the console. "I'm sorry—"

He cut her off, "You don't have to say that for my benefit. I'm not a child. I can keep track of time and I know it's been too long. He's dead and he's going to stay that way."

Dira crossed her arms over her chest and stared back at him. "So now you're a doctor too? You're going to start giving me the patient's prognosis?"

"Just stop it." He turned to leave. "I need to make arrangements."

Dira's words caught him before he left Medical: "And exactly when did you start keeping track of the elapsed time?"

His temper flaring, Jason spun around, ready to unleash his anger. But Dira wasn't even looking at him. She stood at the console, an almost placid expression on her face as she worked the controls. "Your father was administered to within that crucial five-minute period, or do you not remember I was there ... attending to him? We got to him in time." She slapped the side of the display screen so it swung around, now facing him. Irritated by her attitude at such a difficult time, what he saw on the screen didn't register at first. "What?"

"Look at the damn display!"

Jason wondered how he could have missed it. Not only was *it* moving, steadily beating, the virtual representation of his father's heart was bright red. He looked at Dira in wonder. "He's alive?"

"He's alive."

* * *

Boomer felt sick. Realization finally set in. Really set in. This wasn't going to work. She was only ten years old and she'd been fooling herself into believing she'd be able to accomplish what they all expected of her. What was she supposed to do now? Pretend? Simply act as if she were on board with their stupid idea of her going up against this Lord Shakrim guy? He was going to kill her ... rip her into little pieces, all the while laughing at her pathetic attempt to fight him. Oh sure ... Aahil had made it clear: *No one expects you to actually fight him ... you only have to paralyze him with your enhancement shield until he can be taken prisoner.* Really? That's all? Okay then ... fine ... no problem!

She watched as Aahil and Capri spoke in lowered tones in the near distance. She knew they were talking about her

… how utterly crappy a job she'd done in her exercises. She'd yet to defeat anyone. She either ended up flat on her back, or on her bottom, every time. And she was sore. Her whole body was sore. She considered moving off the tree stump's rough seat to the softer, pine-needle-covered ground below. She shifted her bottom, moving from one cheek to the next, but found no comfort on either.

Aahil and Capri approached. They didn't look happy with her. Boomer chewed at the inside of her lip and waited for them to come a bit closer. She'd come to a decision; she was going to let them know she was the wrong person for the job … they needed to find someone else.

Aahil spoke before she could say anything. "Are you ready to continue?"

"No."

Aahil and Capri exchanged a quick look. "Even before trying out that new shield?"

"It's just a shield … I'm just a kid … and I want to go home. You can't make me stay here."

Aahil slowly nodded—seeming to be carefully considering her words. A hopeful sign. "I have to tell you something … um, something I've kept from you."

"What?"

"Your training shield … the one you've been practicing with up until now …"

"Yeah?"

"It was set only to one-third power configuration. You were training at a substantial disadvantage from the start."

"It didn't seem like it," she said, not sure she was buying any of his confession.

"You compensated for the deficiencies of the shield, Boomer. As hoped, you possess certain innate capabilities."

"I don't know what innate means."

"It means natural ... powers you already have but probably don't know you have," Capri clarified.

Boomer shrugged. "I don't really know what you're talking about. I've decided to go home. I want to go home."

Aahil looked bemused. His eyes moved toward Boomer's feet and the enhancement shield he'd earlier given her. "Leaving a shield such as this one lying around on the ground is disrespectful to me, as well as to the shield itself."

Boomer flushed. She'd meant to put the thing back in its fancy box. To give it back to Aahil ... she didn't want it anymore. "Sorry ... you can keep it."

He now held the shield in his hands, flipping it over with his fingers. He stopped and leaned down—the shield only inches from her face. He traced the ridge on the small inside flange, running around the inside perimeter of the weapon. "See here? This section with these tiny raised projections?"

Boomer leaned in closer and furrowed her brow. "I see them ... like little bumps."

"Run your fingertip along those bumps."

She raised her brow. *This is getting stupid.* She did as told, taking ahold of the edge of the shield in her left hand, then doing what Aahil requested. She moved her forefinger back and forth along the little bumps.

"Oh my God!" Boomer stood, holding on to the shield. She continued to make power adjustments—feeling the difference. It was night and day. It was amazing. She looked up at Aahil, then to Capri. "You had me training with a ... a toy!"

"You needed to gain strength from your own innate powers ... it would have been a mistake to have you rely solely on a shield so early on."

Boomer fitted the enhancement shield over her hand and onto her forearm. She set it to its maximum strength.

"You may want to set that down a position or two, Boom-er," Aahil said.

"I want to see what I can do with this thing." She took up the *Kahill Callan* battle stance, and, bowing her head, smiled. Again, Aahil and Capri exchanged glances. Aahil shrugged and attacked without warning.

Chapter 38

Dacci System
The *Charm*, Zoo Habitat 331

Things were already tense within the tight confines of the little vessel. Leon wanted to smack the condescending smile off Stalls' face. It was as if the pirate had anticipated their arrival. Was expecting them. His hands had been bound without the slightest resistance. The guy was a psycho, no doubt about it. He was going to try to screw them all—the very first opportunity—it was only a matter of when.

Stalls sat next to Bristol, three seats up from Leon, within the *Charm*'s narrow cabin. He saw Hanna, seated to his left, one row ahead. Her eyes were on Stalls as well. Her expression said it all: she wanted to kill the bastard. *What in hell had he done to her?* Whatever she planned to do back, Leon wasn't going to get in her way ... hell, he'd even supply the weapon—one of those big multi-guns should do the trick.

Leon saw that they'd reached the habitat's portal, leading back into the *Minian*. Again, he looked toward Stalls. *This is really a bad idea.*

* * *

Five hours later, after an earlier long hot shower, Leon was rousted from a far-too-brief catnap. Sleepy-eyed and disoriented, he told the AI to send whoever it was away. Apparently she didn't take orders from guest passengers, because the energy hatch to his small quarters vanished as a sole military man strode in.

"Rizzo ... what are you doing here? Don't you ever sleep, man?"

"We'll sleep when we're dead ... time to go."

Leon sat up and ran his fingers through his tousled hair as Rizzo stood silently in front of him. He looked like a younger version of the captain ... kinda acted like him, too. "Okay ... I'm ready ... where are we going?"

"To your ship."

That put a smile on Leon's face. *Finally*. "It's a fair distance away ... how we getting to it? Shuttle? Maybe that perky Lieutenant Commander Grimes can pilot us." Leon pulled on his left, then right, boot. He stood and gestured with a hand toward the still-open hatch: "Lead on," he said, with an exaggerated smile.

Three long corridors and two DeckPorts later, they arrived at the flight deck. Considering the size of the ship, it was a massive space, spanning the *Minian*'s width, with gargantuan-sized arched bay doors on both port and starboard sides.

"You could park an ocean liner in here ... hell, several of them, end to end," Leon remarked, taking in various individual spacecraft—hundreds of unmanned mini-fighter drones, their wings collapsed, secured in tight rows onto a bulkhead, reaching high above, and spanning multiple decks—also a complement of royal blue fighters, including several red ones.

There were also a handful of shuttles—the *Perilous* was one, the smaller *Charm* another, secured off to the side. Maintenance drones, some robot-like, others cylindrical, hovered about or were speeding off somewhere—busy at work—doing whatever drones do to keep a fleet this size operational.

Leon, seeing Rizzo had kept on walking while he ogled, scurried to catch up. The starboard bay doors were open to space, an energy field keeping the flight deck's atmosphere contained within. Abruptly, Leon stopped in his tracks. There, situated in the middle of the flight deck, was his ship—the *SpaceRunner*.

"I don't understand ... how is my ship here?" Leon asked, not sure if he should be happy to see it, or angry someone had piloted it here without his permission.

"Didn't you tell someone where it was hidden? How to override the ship's security measures?"

"Yes, but ..."

"You can't provide that kind of information to Ricket, or even to Bristol, without them figuring out the rest. Apparently, they used a shuttle, one capable of phase-shifting, to fetch it ... it was right where you said it would be. I thought you'd be happy to see it."

"I am ... I guess. I just don't like anyone else flying her."

"Uh huh. Well, when you can get over feeling violated maybe you can make sure it's ready for our mission. There's a lot hinging on this ship of yours being everything you say it is ... fast and battle ready." Rizzo turned back toward the *SpaceRunner*. "It's not what I expected—"

"What? You expected a tin can held together with bailing wire and duct tape?"

Rizzo shrugged.

Leon, not expecting an answer, walked around his ship, making sure there wasn't new damage. In truth, it was the most beautiful vessel he'd ever seen. He remembered seeing it for the first time, when his then soon-to-be partner, Petty Officer Sean Doogin, brought him to its hiding place on Palis-Z, a wretched little planet where one could purchase virtually anything—if willing to pay the local space gypsies their exorbitant, over-inflated prices. The *SpaceRunner* had originally been a wealthy intergalactic trader's personal star yacht. On the outside, it looked little different than it had back then; much of the hull was highly reflective, mirror-like, while other areas—design features, with textured, dark-gray panels—were, in reality, not design features at all. Depending on where one looked, either a rail cannon or a plasma gun lay hidden behind various slide-away panels—no less than eight in all. The ship looked surprisingly sleek and aerodynamic, considering its width. At one time, this rich trader's space yacht had fifteen stateroom suites, plus a large storage hold running the length of the vessel below the ship's deck. With the exception of spacious staterooms, the inside of the vessel bore little resemblance now to its former, luxurious, glory days. Excluding seven small quarters, and several heads, most of the *SpaceRunner* had been reconfigured, befitting the requirements of a trading vessel needing, oft times, to get away fast and/or defend itself. Leon reached up high and ran his palm along a portion of the hull. He liked the mirror-like finish. One of the most unique aspects of this ship was its capability to alter its outward appearance. Apparently the original owner's wife wanted a ship that could match her daily attire ... he wasn't sure of the technology behind it, but all of the reflective hull siding could be altered to any number of colors or patterns—but there had also been another option, probably had been added by the husband. Leon called it ghetto-ship gray ... when selected, the *SpaceRunner* looked thirty years older and battered—with simulated dents, scuffs and areas of mismatched paint repairs. For the kind of places Leon had typically been taking this ship, ghetto-ship gray was almost always the most appropriate.

They came to a standstill at the bow of the vessel. Rizzo noted, "It's a nice-looking ship ... how does it do in planetary atmosphere?"

"Cuts through the air like a knife."

"Well, it'll be a lot faster now."

"Faster now? I don't think so," Leon said, not really sure what he was referring to.

Rizzo walked beneath the ship's portside toward the lowered gangway, approximately at the center point of the vessel. "Mind?" he asked, pointing upward.

"Go ahead ... seems everyone else has been on board anyway."

Leon followed Rizzo up the *SpaceRunner*'s gangway into what seemed like a comfortable vestibule, of sorts, but was, in fact, an airlock. The circular compartment had two opposing curved hatchways, one leading to sub-level hold areas, and the other back to Propulsion, where the vessel's powerful antimatter drive was located. Before them, a curved ramp gracefully followed the curved contours of the bulkhead, and led to another curved hatchway, fifteen feet overhead, that was the egress into the main deck area above, on level one.

The hatch leading into Propulsion was open and Leon could hear someone inside muttering something. In three strides, he crossed over the airlock compartment and rushed into the hatchway, where he found Bristol, standing on his tiptoes, using a tool of some kind.

"What the hell are you doing to my ship?" Leon crossed the confined space, grabbed a fistful of Bristol's jumpsuit, and threw him against a vertical support beam.

"He's doing what he's been told to do," Rizzo said behind

him, "and you should be thanking him, not smacking him around."

"Thanking him for what? Nobody messes with my ship without my permission."

Bristol shoved back at Leon, causing him to take a short step back. "Hey, fuckwad … you don't want phase-shift capability on this ship … fine with me. I'll yank it back out." Bristol headed back where he'd been … doing *something*.

"You're installing phase-shift capability? No shit? How much is that going to cost me?"

Rizzo said, "Do your job right and we'll call it even … how 'bout that?"

Leon nodded and looked at Bristol. "Sorry … didn't mean to—"

"Don't you have something else to do? I'd like to finish this and get some sleep."

Leon and Rizzo left Propulsion. Leon headed up the ramp; the level one hatchway opened as he approached. Curious to see what else they'd done to his ship, he made his way forward toward the bow. The bridge interior was approximately the size of two side-by-side minivans and easily spanned upward ten feet. He entered the bridge's rear hatchway, with Rizzo two steps behind. Leon again stopped dead in his tracks.

"What the hell are you doing here?"

"Good morning, Mr. Pike. If you remember, my name is Trommy5."

Leon simply stared at the metallic robot. The mecher was seated in the copilot's seat, in front of the controls.

"I know who you are … what are you doing here?"

"I have been assigned to you. I am your automated mech-er unit … I am at your disposal for whatever functions you deem necessary."

Leon turned back to stare at Rizzo, who held up both palms in mock surrender. "Hey, don't look at me ... this wasn't my idea. I don't think anybody knew what to do with him. You brought him on board the *Minian* ... so he's all yours."

Trommy5 cautiously stood up—reaching for the seatback with one hand to steady itself. "I've been instructed to tell you the others will be here shortly. We only await the one called Boomer to arrive back on the *Minian* ... then we'll be on our way."

Chapter 39

Dacci System
The *Minian*, Bridge

Jason watched the overhead wrap-around display as the stream of warships methodically emerged, one after another, from three separate, simultaneously generated, interchange wormholes. He had mixed feelings about their arrival. In one sense this fleet of two hundred Allied warships would go a long way in curbing outright attacks by the Sahhrain, but in another—it emphasized the fact that Star Watch could not handle the situation on its own.

"Captain, your presence is requested in the flight bay."

Jason glanced up to the display and saw that a white U.S. heavy cruiser had just entered the flight bay and was setting down on the flight deck.

Jason looked over to Seaman Gordon with a sideways glance. "Who the hell gave them permission to come aboard my ship? I don't have time to entertain fleet commanders ... not now ... not with everything going on. Send them away—"

"Captain ... I don't think you want to do that," Orion interrupted, turning in her seat to face him. "You're outranked on this one, Cap."

Jason let out a breath and stood. "Fine ... I'll get rid of him. Somebody find my XO. I'll hand over whoever this is to Perkins ... he can give him a tour of the ship."

* * *

Two minutes later, Jason entered the flight bay. Crew personnel were already coming down the large, bug-shaped cruiser's gangway. Jason looked for the ranking officer, thinking, *he's probably another admiral*. Perhaps hearing of his father's near-death situation, someone was looking to elevate his own position. Then he saw her running down the gangway: Four-foot-something, wearing a bright yellow sundress, Mollie yelled at a junior officer crewmember to get out of her way. Several paces behind her was her ever-faithful droid, Teardrop. Last to appear was Mollie's mother, Nan—his ex-wife.

Out of breath and all smiles, Mollie ran into Jason's open arms. He picked her up and hugged her tight. "What are you doing here ... little one?"

"Okay, okay ... you can put me down now, Dad!"

Jason did as told.

"I think Mom wants to talk to you ... I don't know, ask her."

Nan walked right by him, muttering, "Not here ... and we're taking your quarters ... ten minutes."

Jason called after her, "Where's my son?"

"Back in D.C."

Mollie smiled up at Jason and scurried after her mother, with Teardrop close on their heels.

* * *

As the still-acting President of the United States, Nan certainly outranked him. Nan's sudden appearance took Jason by surprise, and he guessed that was her intention. About to enter his own captain's quarters, he paused at the hatch: "AI, please let the president know I'm here."

A moment later, as the hatch de-energized, Mollie stood inside to greet him. "Can I go play?"

"Hello to you, too," Jason said, stepping into his suite. He saw no sign of Nan.

"Can I?"

"Um … what does your mother say?"

"She didn't. Teardrop will be with me … it looks just like *The Lilly* … well, kinda … a lot bigger."

"Fine … stay out of trouble. Why don't you go see Dira … the AI will direct you—"

But Mollie was already out the hatch and running down the corridor.

"Go with her … keep an eye on her."

"Yes, Captain Reynolds." Teardrop quickly hovered out into the corridor.

Jason heard noises coming from deeper inside his quarters. He found Nan in there, hanging up clothes in his closet. She'd changed out of her navy pantsuit into faded jeans and a pink pullover sweater. Her long auburn hair was tied back in a ponytail.

"Staying long?" Jason asked.

She didn't look up from what she was doing. "No … maybe a few days … I don't know."

"Well, what's going on here?"

She stopped and glowered at him. "Why don't you tell me?"

He saw she was angry. No, not angry. Furious. "What's going on ... what's the matter, Nan?"

"Maybe you can tell me where my daughter is?"

"She just left—" Jason cut his words short. She wasn't referring to Mollie. "What have you heard?"

"Only that she was in some kind of training ... training to go up against some kind of mass-murdering monster. That she isn't even on this ship!"

"Where did you get this information?"

"Who gives a shit where I got the information from? Is it true? Have you gotten my daughter involved in something no ten-year-old should even remotely be doing?"

"Look ... it's complicated. It's not like that. At least, not entirely."

Nan looked to be on the verge of punching him in the face.

He continued, "You need to know that I was just as upset by all this—"

"Upset? That's how you're phrasing this? Of course I'm fucking upset!"

"Just let me finish!" Jason stopped and tried to find a way to explain something he knew he wouldn't be able to explain satisfactorily—most of all, because she was right. There was no way to defend something he never should have allowed to happen in the first place.

"Boomer is not even remotely like Mollie. They may share the same DNA, but that's where all similarities stop. She's ..." he searched for the appropriate word, "she's a warrior."

"Come on ... she's ten, Jason!"

"Do you have any inkling of the things our ten-year-old daughter has accomplished over the last year and a half? How many lives she's saved? Hell, Boomer was sneaking out to learn close-contact martial-art techniques a mere week after she'd come on board *The Lilly*. If you remember, she even helped rescue you from the Craing not so long ago. Yes ... in many ways she's a ten-year-old child. And though that part of her, happily, still exists, a warrior-persona resides within her, too. She lives for adventure ... I couldn't change that part of her no matter what I tried. She'd hate me for trying."

"You think I don't know she's different? That I haven't seen it for myself?" Nan asked. "Don't get me started on the trouble she caused back at the White House. But what you're permitting her to do ... letting her go up against this alien nutcase, just doesn't make sense to me."

"What you ... and I, too, until recently, didn't know, is that Boomer has certain ... um ... other abilities."

"What kind of abilities?"

"I'm not one hundred percent sure, but I've seen her ... watched her train. She's amazing. Hell, it's almost supernatural, what the kid can do."

"You make her sound like some kind of freak, Jason."

"Not a freak ... not at all. She's special and only someone truly special, with her kind of abilities, will be able to get close enough to Shakrim ... subdue him, until he can be taken into custody by my forces."

"I've been briefed on Lord Vikor Shakrim. I know he's a bad one and his dark intentions could easily escalate into the next interplanetary war."

"Then you know he'll never be apprehended by conventional means. His intuitive capabilities will allow him to escape ... only to continue, probably, with greater force later on."

"And you're saying Boomer has these same capabilities?"

"That's where she is now. She's being trained ... learning to fight him at this same skill level. It was either consent to her training, or ready the Allied forces for the next, all too soon, interstellar war."

"So our daughter becomes the sacrificial lamb?"

Jason shrugged. "As if you or I could stop her anyway. If it's not this it will be something else. That ship's already sailed, so to speak. I've come to the harsh realization that it's probably best if she's prepared for what lies ahead. If that involves training by a group of nomad warrior masters, then so be it."

Jason saw most of Nan's anger draining away. He suspected she, too, was fully aware who and what Boomer, in both body and spirit, had become.

Nan sat down on the edge of the bed and looked toward the observation window. Her eyes were wet; a deep sadness, conflicting inner turmoil, weighed on her shoulders. Jason sat down next to her, put an arm around her, and pulled her close.

"I promise you, she'll be fine. I won't let anything happen to our baby, Nan."

She nodded and looked up at him. They stayed there, eyes locked on each other for several seconds. He watched as her eyes searched his and then she kissed him. Her lips were soft and sweet and he found himself kissing her back—pulling her body in closer. Memories of their past passion—their love for one another—rushed back in a flood of bittersweet memories.

She pulled away and stood. "I'm so sorry. I don't know why I did that."

Jason didn't know why she'd kissed him either, or why he'd kissed her back, and probably wouldn't have stopped there. His mind flashed to Dira and a wave of guilt washed over him.

Nan stood at the window, looking out. "I'm no longer the president."

"What? You're no longer ..."

"You and I both knew it would be a temporary position, at best. I never wanted that responsibility and was probably ill-equipped for it, anyway."

"So who's taking over the presidency?"

Nan turned to him and smiled. "Howard's coming around."

"As in President Howard Ross?" Jason said. The president had been taken by the molt weevils, wrapped inside a cocoon like millions of others in Washington D.C. Last he'd heard, doctors were less than optimistic about his cognitive abilities returning to normal.

"So that's it? He's in perfect health and back in the White House, running the country as if nothing has happened?"

"As you know, the rest of his family did not fare as well. He's alone, but wanted to move in right away. Truth is, I couldn't get out of there fast enough."

"Where did you go?"

Nan pursed her lips, looking a bit sheepish. "I thought maybe we'd stay at the scrapyard house."

Jason raised his eyebrows.

"It would be temporary ... while I figure out what I'm going to do next. You'll be here in space for a while, right? Hope it's okay?"

"It's fine. So who's watching little Michael?"

"A close friend. He's in good hands. I didn't think I should bring him here ... probably should have left Mollie home, as well. But—"

"Don't worry about it. Make yourself comfortable here on the *Minian,* too, as long as you like."

She nodded, again looking sheepish. "Sorry about the whole ... kiss thing."

Jason brought two fingers up to his ear. "I'm being hailed ... I have to go."

Chapter 40

Dacci System
Planet Harpaign, Ancient Subterranean
Ruins

Palms flat on the gritty stone surface, Lord Vikor Shakrim leaned down further and kissed the ancient artifact. Naked, and on his knees, his head bowed—prone and submissive—Shakrim presented himself to his Master ... and waited.

Eventually the true darkness came. Hot—with the smell of spoiled meat—it flowed all over him like a shroud: down his back and buttocks, over his head and down his arms and legs. It enveloped him in totality.

Illumination came from one flickering candle. The subterranean vault rested a hundred feet below the surface of Harpaign—or most of it did. The chiseled stone tablet, lying horizontal, was like flooring in the vault. The last third of the tablet floor was missing; only a jagged, uneven edge remained. Shakrim hadn't needed it. Everything he required to call up *Rom Dasticon* was already present, as foretold in these ancient tablet writings ... as was he, Lord Vikor Shakrim, and his approaching destiny.

Shakrim, seated, felt his Master's all-powerful Sachem presence and let his shoulders rise up—his back becoming perfectly erect. The vault, with its stone walls and ceiling, became nothing more than a swirling gray mist. The lone candle flickered out while an amber glow, from a new encircling fire, reflected high up on the walls around him.

Rom Dasticon suddenly stood before him, and Lord Vikor Shakrim again bowed his head.

"Stand, my son … stand and converse with me a while."

Shakrim did as he was told. Dasticon stood three paces in front of him, his overwhelming presence making it hard for Shakrim to breathe, to comprehend. The all-powerful Sachem was old; he looked as old and withered as the ancient tablet lying beneath their feet. His long robe was brown and simple … a nomad's attire. Thin, twisted, angular fingers pulled back his hood, letting it droop onto his back, and exposing a long, narrow face. His dark sunken cheeks, with exaggerated folds and wrinkles, covering millenniums of time, sagged his ancient, grayed, flesh. But the ravages of time stopped there. His blue and intelligent eyes glistened, reflecting the dancing light from the surrounding flames.

Dasticon began to walk the perimeter of their misty-gray surroundings, appearing in deep thought, his fingers steepled together, as though in prayer. "You have made much progress, my son. You honor me with your actions … your devotion."

Shakrim absorbed his master's praise and felt his heart rate elevate—all sense of time and space merging into one. "I serve only to please. Even now, my Lord, my ships and soldiers are poised to attack. Then … I will open the conduit between our realms. Soon, you will move between all realms of reality with the same ease as walking through a door. I will provide access to all realms … I do this for you, dear Master."

Dasticon abruptly halted and looked directly at Shakrim.

Eyes that were calm just moments earlier now burned with fury. "You? You think it is you ... and not me, who does all this? Your ego has truly gotten the best of you, Shakrim!" With the speed of someone much younger, Dasticon leapt across the space separating them. Startled, Shakrim drew in the stench of his master's bitter, foul, breath. Dasticon's face, contorted in rage, was up close; his eyes bored deeply into his very soul. A claw-like hand moved near Shakrim's left cheek. He felt fingertips faintly touching his skin. Suddenly, smoke rose into the air and a horrific, agonizing pain seared him as Dasticon's long discolored fingernails plunged deep into his cheek ... making deep, black, columned tracks as he slowly raked his fingers down ... down ... down ... finally stopping at the base of Shakrim's neck.

Shakrim had not moved, had not made a sound. He stood perfectly still while Dasticon admired his handi-work—drawing in the last vestiges of Shakrim's still-smol-dering, burnt, flesh.

"I must take possession of the magical chariot ... the ves-sel named *Minian*, within the next full rise and fall of the sun. Is that understood, my son?"

"We are ready to attack, Rom Dasticon ... I will not fail you. The ship is as good as yours."

Smiling, Dasticon gave Shakrim an almost affectionate pat upon his now-ruined face. He vanished, along with the mist and fire. The vault appeared now as it first was. The can-dle, relit, again flickered and danced in the darkness.

* * *

High above the vault's tablet floor, up on one of the rock-walled ledges, standing perfectly still, hidden within a deep-shadowed crevice, stood a lone observer. The observer watched as Lord Vikor Shakrim now looked up into the darkness, as if searching for something ... was seeking him out. Shakrim's face, caught in the dancing light of the candle below, exhibited the dark deep tracks upon his cheek and neck. Ricket stepped farther back into the crevice and phase-shifted away.

Chapter 41

Dacci System
The *Minian*, Mess

Jason and Nan entered the *Minian*'s mess, along with Mollie, who was being a motor-mouth—something to do with the Zoo habitats and being reunited with Raja the elephant. Nan literally walked right into Dira, apparently just on her way out. The two hugged and promised to catch up later. Mollie and Dira exchanged smiles, but Jason received nary a glance. Dira passed by him without the slightest acknowledgment he even existed.

"I'm sorry," Nan said, as the three got into a short line in front of one of the food replicators. "I'm sure to her it must look like we're ... I don't know ... a family again," Nan said.

"It's fine, I'll talk to her," Jason said, doing his best to sound unconcerned.

Mollie, the first to reach the replicator, filled a tray to an amount bordering on obscene.

"That's too much, Mollie. Why make such a pig of yourself ... it's not like you can't come back for more if you really need to," Nan said.

Mollie shrugged and headed off to an empty table.

By the time Jason and Nan joined Mollie, she was nearly finished eating.

"I don't know where she puts it all," Nan said to Jason, sitting down.

Jason shrugged. "At that age they're never still ... they're calorie-burning machines."

The three sat side-by-side, on the same side of the table, with their backs to the entrance. So when someone came up behind Mollie, placing two hands over her eyes, it took all three by surprise.

"Guess who?"

Jason and Nan spun around as Mollie grabbed on to Boomer's wrists.

Mollie pulled her sister's hands away and laughed out loud when she saw Boomer. "You didn't surprise me; I knew you were there the whole time."

"Liar ... none of you knew I was here."

Jason was relieved to see her ... seeing that she was safe, and back on board the *Minian*. He watched as Nan hugged Boomer tight, rocking her back and forth. Suddenly Nan pushed Boomer away at arm's length—her face flushed with anger. "Do you know how much trouble you are in? How your selfish actions affect everyone else? Do you have any idea how scared I was?"

Boomer didn't answer. The corners of her mouth turned down and she was on the verge of tears. Again, Boomer was their little girl. She slowly nodded—looking guilty and ashamed. Once Nan had released her hands from her shoulders, she pulled her in again for another tight embrace. Boomer tapped her father on the shoulder, signaling him to scoot down so she could sit between them. She was dressed in her typical spacer's jumpsuit attire. He continued to stare at her—perhaps to confirm she was still the same child she'd always been.

She glanced up at Jason and smiled. "What? Are you going to yell at me too?"

* * *

Jason walked around the perimeter of the *SpaceRunner*, admiring Leon's recently retrieved spacecraft. It was somewhat larger than he'd expected, but it also didn't look like a black market trader vessel someone like Mr. Pike would be captaining. As if on cue, the ship's appearance suddenly changed: Its glistening, highly reflective hull ... a real jewel of a ship ... had morphed into what might best be described as an unremarkable, battered, old space jalopy. Jason smiled as he reached up and ran his hand over what looked to be a charred, fairly deep, plasma crater. It was perfectly smooth— the hull only appeared to be damaged.

Leon came down the gangway in three long strides. "Well ... what do you think?"

"I think that's a useful feature," Jason replied, suddenly becoming serious. "Look ... I don't know you ... not really ... and that makes me nervous. You're taking on an invaluable cargo here, Mr. Pike. *The* most valuable cargo." Jason stared toward the bow of the vessel where a group of people had begun to assemble. Boomer was standing next to her mother and talking to Hanna. Somewhere out of view, inside the ship, Jason heard someone loudly cursing.

Leon shook his head. "Bristol ... he's quite a character. But he knows his shit ... got a feeling he already knows the propulsion system on the *SpaceRunner* better than I do."

"I guarantee he does," Jason said.

Leon gestured toward Boomer. "I'll watch out for her. I give you my word on that."

277

Jason brought his full attention over to Leon. "Know this. If anything happens to my daughter, I'll track you down and kill you with my bare hands. You can take that to the bank." Jason didn't wait for a reply, leaving Leon standing bemused beneath his ship. Jason headed toward the near-complete assembly of team participants.

Mollie and Boomer were playing—clapping each other's hands in a faster and faster, back-and-forth, routine that made everyone laugh. Boomer was the first to screw up.

"You did it wrong!" Boomer barked.

"Shut up! You're a sore loser," Mollie barked back.

Nan rolled her eyes as the girls started playing again. "Tell me we're not making the biggest mistake of our lives, Jason."

"I don't know. I wish I did," he replied.

Hanna said, "Leon's a good guy. Rough around the edges, but a good guy. He saved my life on more than one occasion."

The last of the team was arriving. Stalls had his hands bound in front of him and Jason also noticed the thin silver band around Stalls' left wrist. From what Ricket had previously told him, the custom-made tracker would be impossible to remove. It could also deliver a lethal electrical voltage that would stop Stalls' heart immediately from virtually anywhere across the galaxy. He wore an identical band on his right ankle, if one wasn't enough deterrent.

The two girls stopped playing and watched as Rizzo escorted the now all-too-familiar pirate toward the *SpaceRunner*.

Stalls, all smiles and looking as if he hadn't a care in the world, focused his attention on only one person: Nan. "I'm truly touched … here you are … the beautiful … splendid creature … that you are … and you're here to see me off."

Nan's eyes went wide as she struggled to get the words

out, "What ... what the hell is he doing here?"

Jason froze. She didn't know Stalls was part of the mission and would be on the same ship. *And how could she?* He hadn't told her. Hadn't told her their daughter would be traveling alongside the very person who had, on multiple occasions, tried to kill each one of them, and who'd vowed that someday, he would finish what he had started.

"No ... this isn't going to happen! Jason, you SOB, tell me this isn't going to happen!"

"I don't like it any more than you. But he's the only way they'll be able to gain access into Dacci space ... to get close enough to Lord Shakrim."

Nan continued staring at Jason in angry exasperation.

"Rizzo's never leaving her side. And don't forget, at this point Boomer could turn him inside out on her own, if it comes down to that."

Nan closed her eyes, inhaled, letting her rage out slowly. "This keeps getting better and better."

"If there was any other way—"

Nan brought up a hand. "Just shut up, Jason. Just shut up."

* * *

It felt good to be back in the pilot's seat. Leon completed his pre-flight checklist and everything seemed to be operational. There were several new additions to the cockpit's forward console. Earlier, Bristol had configured the newly installed phase-shift system, as well as the required, beefed-up, deep-space communications system.

"How familiar are you with this vessel, mecher?"

Trommy5, who'd repeatedly been told to speak only when spoken to, and was seated in the copilot's seat, answered with a surprising, all too welcome, economy of words. "I am programmed to pilot similar vessels, but not this specific model."

"Well, I've provided you direct access to Miranda ... the ship's AI. In your downtime, I expect you to tap in and get fully acquainted with this ship's operation. It's probably best if I'm not the only one who can pilot her for this mission."

"Yes, Captain Pike."

Leon watched as the tall robot went quiet—already interfacing with Miranda—and pulling necessary data from her vast storage core.

Leon took hold of the controls and felt the *SpaceRunner*'s drive revving up as the vessel lifted off the flight deck. He saw on the display that the *Minian*'s AI had provided clearance to exit through the portside bay opening. He eased the ship forward and within five seconds was crossing through the invisible energy field separating ship environment from the total vacuum of deep space.

The *SpaceRunner*, now locked on course for the Dacci system, traveled through space at a mere fraction of the speed she was capable of. From here on out, they had to avoid doing anything that would cause suspicion.

Leon got up and left the bridge, with Trommy5 still sitting quietly in the copilot's seat. He exited through the opened hatchway and walked up a small stairway where another hatchway automatically opened on his approach. The *SpaceRunner*'s semi-circular main cabin contained everyone who was part of the mission. Bristol sat alone, tinkering with some unknown piece of equipment on his lap, while Hanna and Boomer, chatting, sat next to each other. Rizzo and Stalls, seated across from one another, were not speaking nor looking particularly happy with each other's company. Rizzo was the only one wearing an initialized battle suit—the muzzle of his multi-gun pointed directly at Stalls' chest.

Leon sat down next to Rizzo. "Let's go over the scenario

one more time."

Everyone stopped what they were doing and looked at Leon.

"We already did this," Hanna said. "I'm the captain's loving and adoring wife."

"I'm their bratty kid," Boomer volunteered.

"I'm the captain's partner," Rizzo said.

"I'm a crewmember," Bristol said, yawning hugely.

All eyes went to Stalls. "I'm a passenger ... a simple trader, hitching a ride into the Dacci system to sell my recently-acquired supply of Targonian spirits ... a known favorite of the Lord Shakrim."

"And I'm the captain of this ship and also a fellow interstellar trader," Leon said.

Stalls smirked. "There's no guarantee I'll get clearance to enter their system ... if I do, we won't get far, looking like this ... dressed like this."

Hanna pulled a large duffle bag onto her lap and unzipped it. One by one she brought out various articles of clothing and tossed them to those around her.

Stalls held up his new clothes and nodded appreciably. "I couldn't have selected better myself."

"Your typical attire is well documented. We simply replicated the clothes," Hanna said.

Leon looked at Stalls' fancy black trousers and frilly, white, button-down shirt. An outfit he wouldn't be caught dead in, but to each his own.

Bristol held up his uniform. "What the hell is this? Some kind of joke?"

Hanna seemed to struggle in keeping a straight face. "It's a simple spacer's jumpsuit ... what's the big deal?"

"It's bright red ... who wears a fucking bright red jumpsuit?"

"Santa Claus does," Boomer said, with a giggle.

Leon stood. "Let's get changed and prepare for what's coming next. Stalls … fifteen minutes and you're making that call. If the Sahhrain don't buy your act, you'll be of no use to us. I have advanced permission to throw you out the airlock."

Chapter 42

Dacci System
Planet Harpaign, Ancient Surface Ruins

Ricket, hiding on the surface of Harpaign, watched as Lord Shakrim returned to the *Assailant*, took off, and headed back into space. Three miles away was the wreckage of his Pharlom fighter—its broken wing, and failing aerodynamic structure had made any kind of atmospheric flight virtually impossible. In retrospect, after the rescue of the admiral, he now realized he should have told the captain his plans to stop off on Harpaign before returning to the *Minian*.

Fortunately, he was able to get close enough to his intended surface destination, phase-shifting out of the cockpit, mere seconds before the fighter crashed.

Ricket also knew he needed to contact the captain and relay what he'd learned—where they were most vulnerable from attack. He briefly wondered why both communications, and most of his suit's sensors capabilities, were so completely disrupted here, while the ability to phase-shift seemed unaffected.

Ricket continued to stare into the hazy sky above him, knowing full well he wouldn't be leaving this desolate world in the same manner the *Assailant* had.

Soon after he'd phase-shifted to this site from approxi-mately one mile out, he'd spotted the parked *Assailant* and knew he had found Lord Shakrim. Then, he'd made his way below ground, utilizing a combination of climbing and phase-shifting—basically trial and error—until he found the Sahhrain leader far beneath the surface within the sa-cred subterranean vault. Between the strange effects this planet probably played on Shakrim's normally high, acutely aware psychic senses, not to mention Ricket's own advanced Caldurian battle suit, which concealed his presence from view, Ricket hadn't been detected by Shakrim.

He got to witness the visitation by the one called Rom Dasticon; obviously, he was some kind of god in Shakrim's eyes. He could see how one so powerful could captivate someone … could even captivate whole societies … to follow after him. Ricket wondered what this demi-god was really selling? He needed time to properly decipher the tablet, now that he knew where it was located. Ricket double-checked his previous drop coordinates and again phase-shifted there.

In a flash, he found himself in total darkness. Earlier, he'd used care with his movements, on his high perch above the vault. The candle Lord Shakrim had relit still flickered be-low. Now, in the dim light, Ricket could make out an old, zigzagging, stairway that led from the surface down to the bottom of the vault. He phase-shifted directly across to the stone steps. Kicking up the intensity on his helmet's spot-light, he peered down to the vault floor. The tablet artifact hadn't been in HAB 7, though that hadn't stopped him from looking for it, and he had concluded it had been removed or destroyed. But this gigantic ancient tablet below him seemed intact. From his high-up perspective, Ricket could still read some of the ancient alien engraved writings upon it; what he couldn't read was being deciphered, floating before his eyes on a virtual layer within his HUD. Ricket read the engraved writings and then read them again:

For the righteous their destiny is foretold. Cometh in time will be the heralding of a magical chariot. Hark the one true God. The malevolent one, Rom Dasticon, will upon HIS return, bringeth into manifestation a new blight of blackness and despair, arising thence from a secret hidden realm. A conscript of a million, mindless, aspirants' spears bringeth forth death and despair onto the non-believer. Submission is salvation. See HIM bringeth destruction to the child warrior in the greatest of battles. Only then will HIS magnificent charge begin for all to witness. Recondite are the words that openeth the gateway for an army of thousands to enter. Harken to thus speaketh twice: Hove Lom Shillo Plum—Hove Lom Shillo Plum. Henceforth upon HIS magical chariot, the river of blackness floweth unhindered unto all realms of heaven's spheres for all time.

Ricket stood there musing. How a society, living over two millennia ago, could foretell the occurrences of current events, or even remote events, was less interesting to him than the actual ramifications of the prophecies. Whoever this Rom Dasticon was ... this demi-god character, he was coming. Seemingly, he was a conquering invader from an alternate, multiverse realm. So what actually was Lord Vikor Shakrim's role in all this? A disciple? *Probably.* And probably someone bestowed with supernatural powers, as an added egoic-bonus. What most disturbed Ricket was twofold: the destruction of the child warrior (Boomer) and no mention given of a great space battle. Everything revolved around a magical chariot (the *Minian)* and the opening of a secret gateway.

Suddenly Ricket felt dizzy. Could the fleet of enemy Sahhrain ships in Dacci space be little more than a diversion? Could HAB 7 be the secret gateway ... one that would allow unhindered access into the *Minian*? *Yes!* Ricket was now sure of it. *Hove Lom Shillo Plum*, entered twice at the portal access panel, was the *backdoor* code that would allow entry into the ship ... and, beyond doubt, was also the same code the two Blues nomads, Aahil and Capri, used to gain access into the various habitats. So not only was Lord Vikor Shakrim expecting Boomer's arrival, he was viewing it as a necessary battle prior to secretly invading the *Minian*, through habitat 7, with his thousands of Sahhrain warriors. Ricket needed to warn the captain and warn Boomer to stay away from Lord Shakrim. *But how?* He first needed to locate the hidden habitat portal—the one Lord Vikor Shakrim, he was sure, had already found.

* * *

Jason entered Medical, crossing in front of a row of unoccupied MediPods, then into the adjacent semi-circle hospital compartment, with its numerous identical, double-railed beds. His father, currently Medical's lone patient, was sitting up in bed. His full attention was on the expanded virtual notepad displayed in front of him. His arms raised, he used both forefingers to peck at the virtual screen.

"You should have learned to type a long time ago."

The admiral looked over the quasi-transparent display. "I had more important things to do with my time."

"How you feeling?"

His father finished whatever he was working on and closed down the display. "I'm fine. Well, I don't know ... Dira tells me I'm back to eighty percent ... where the hell the missing twenty percent went, I'm not sure. Apparently, I was dead far longer than any MediPod could fully repair."

"Do you feel ... impaired?"

He shrugged. "Not to the point I'm going to start drooling or anything ... truth is, I'm still sharper than the majority of the idiot officers in the Allied fleet."

But Jason could see its impact on his father's face. Almost imperceptible ... the slower speech ... the slower eye movement. The admiral hadn't wanted to talk about any events occurring at the hands of Lord Shakrim aboard the *Assailant*. Either they were too awful to remember or his father didn't fully remember them. In either case, Jason didn't want to push it.

"Nan and Mollie are here," Jason said.

"I know that ... they came by an hour or so ago," the admiral said, now looking uncomfortable.

Jason waited for him to continue.

"I assume Nan told you the same bullshit story about her leaving the White House now that Ross is back in the saddle?" said the admiral.

"Made sense to me ... she was only a junior cabinet member before the shit hit the fan with the molt weevil infestation on Earth."

"I've been going back and forth with my contacts in D.C.," the admiral said. "Sure, Ross is slated to return to office ... eventually. But, like me, he's got a ways to go. Nan's still the interim president. So ... no ... there's something else going on with your ex-wife, Jason."

Jason shrugged. "Stress of the job ... isolation ... it could be any number of things. I wouldn't place too much importance on it."

"I don't. But maybe you should. This could be her way of finally reaching out to you before things progress any further with Dira. You two have a lot of history together ... kids."

"That ship has sailed, Dad. I'm with Dira now," Jason

said flatly, but wondered how much of that was true. Did he still have feelings for Nan? Was he really ready to toast a final farewell to the one he'd thought was the true love of his life? He didn't want to think about any of that right now ... not with everything else going on. "Can you do me a favor, Dad?"

"Maybe."

"You've got some R&R coming ... ask Nan to take you back to San Bernardino. I want her and Mollie as far away from this sector as possible."

Jason was being hailed. "Go for Captain."

"Cap, we've got major movement coming from the Sahhrain fleet. Looks like an attack could be imminent," Orion said.

Chapter 43

Dacci System
The *SpaceRunner*, Open Space

Leon noticed Hanna when she entered the bridge. Standing now behind the copilot's seat, she was wearing the casual clothes she'd brought with her. *Are these the clothes a black-market trader's wife would wear?* He averted his eyes, trying not to stare, but failed miserably. Sleeveless and low cut, the outfit showed some skin; her tan slender arms and small breasts briefly captivated his attention.

"You know how to make coffee, mecher?"

Trommy5 looked away from the console, first at Leon, then Hanna. "Yes, Captain Pike. Cream and sugar?"

"Black." Leon raised his brow toward Hanna, questioning.

"Tea, please ... milk and sugar."

Trommy5 stood and moved out of the way as Hanna took his seat. "I don't want you ... anyone, to forget why I'm here."

"I know why you're here, Hanna. I don't know the whole story, but I know you need resolution ... for something."

She nodded but didn't add anything further. Leon, for the first time, noticed she'd put her hair up, emphasizing her long neck. He pictured himself kissing her ... right there, just below her left ear.

"You need to be careful with Stalls," she said.

"I already know that."

Hanna turned in her seat, facing him. "This was a bad idea. You don't know what he's capable of. What this psychopath is capable of."

"You want to talk about it?"

"With you? No!" She added, "Just do as you promised ... get me in front of Ridert."

"I'll do what I can."

Leon saw that they were now approaching Dacci space. "Crap!"

"What is it?" she asked, looking out the front cockpit observation window.

Leon didn't answer; instead, he tapped the console and spoke aloud: "Get up here, Bristol."

Several seconds later Bristol arrived, wearing his bright red spacer's jumpsuit. He'd kept on his own black trousers, which helped diminish some of the Santa Claus effect. "What do you want?"

Leon gestured with his chin toward the tiny lights ahead, too many to count.

"Yeah ... so what? We knew the fleet was close. It's why we're here," Bristol said.

"That's not five hundred ships ... I'd guess, closer to eight hundred. We were already coming into this at a disadvantage—two Sahhrain ships to each Allied ship. Now, I'm really not liking the odds ... I don't care how much firepower the *Minian* has."

Bristol leaned in and brought up a secondary display.

"You're not using the new configuration ... why in hell did I waste my time updating your software if you're not going to use it!"

"What are you talking about?"

Bristol brought up his hands and feigned using sign language. "I'll talk real slow so you can understand me. You need to use the new virtual sensor display I installed."

Leon ignored his antics, and looked at Bristol's new display. "Shit ... those other three hundred vessels ... Parlek Orion warships."

"Bingo," Bristol said.

"Go back and get your brother; we're getting close enough now. We need to make contact."

Several moments later both Stalls and Rizzo entered the small bridge compartment. Hanna moved to the back and leaned against the bulkhead while Stalls took her place in the vacated copilot seat. Rizzo sat in the second row of seats, kitty-corner to Stalls, never lowering the muzzle of his multi-gun.

"Remember what you're here for. Nothing else. No warnings, no funny business," Leon told him.

Stalls flashed a smile and held out his still-bound palms, indicating he was waiting on Leon.

Leon opened a broad-reach channel and silently pointed a finger at Stalls.

"This is Captain Stalls of ..."

Leon silently mouthed the name, *SpaceRunner*.

Stalls continued, "The trader vessel, *SpaceRunner*."

The response was almost immediate. "Divert course. You are entering restricted space."

"Check your logs ... we're expected. Either that, or contact Commander Ridert Douville ... it's his five barrels of Targonian spirits we're delivering." Stalls sat back and leisurely inspected his fingernails.

"There's nothing on record—"

Stalls quickly leaned forward and cut him off, "The barrels are for Lord Shakrim ... can I have your crew designation number so I can tell him who, specifically, turned us away? We've already been paid ... it makes no difference to us."

"The best I can do is connect you directly to the commander."

It was nearly a minute later before the comms came alive again with a deep male voice questioning, "Stalls? That really you?"

Leon glanced back to catch Hanna glaring out the forward observation window to an undefined point in space.

"Of course it's me, my friend. Looks like someone's having a party and forgot to invite me."

"Don't concern yourself with Sahhrain business. What do you want, pirate?"

"As I said ... I'm making a delivery of Targonian—"

"That's bullshit," Ridert interjected.

"Let me finish. It's actually for your illustrious leader. He asked for it specifically, the last time I was in these parts. I was well paid for it. It's a drop-and-go ... in-and-out ... unless, perhaps, you have time to sit and sample some of the brew."

"Look around ... does it look like I have time for any of that? Give me a minute while I try to contact Lord Shakrim."

Leon saw tension on Stalls' face for the first time. "I can see you didn't expect that reply. And there's no way Lord Shakrim's going to grant us access into Dacci space, so you better have a plan B."

Ridert's voice was back on the comms channel. "I'm sending you the coordinates now."

Hanna quickly moved forward between the seats and

reached for the back of Stalls' head, grabbing a tight fistful of the pirate's hair. His eyes narrowed in pain as he tried to look back at her.

Stalls added, "And you too? ... Commander ... you'll be joining us as well?" Stalls asked.

Several long moments elapsed. "Sure. I wouldn't miss it."

Leon saw that the connection had ended. He looked at the newly transmitted coordinates Miranda, the AI, had already transferred onto the logistical display. It showed the planetary system, and the suggested flight vector to a single nearby planet.

"That's Harpaign."

Everyone turned to the back of the bridge, toward the small girl standing in the open hatchway. Boomer was wearing her battle suit, her enhancement shield on her left forearm. Her visor was up and Leon could see the sheen of perspiration on her flushed red cheeks.

"You all right?" Leon asked.

She nodded. "Practicing. I need to be ready."

Chapter 44

Dacci System
The *Minian*, Flight Bay

Jason watched the *Capricorn*, an older, Allied forces transport shuttle, enter the *Minian*'s flight bay, hover forty feet in the air—spin around one hundred and eighty degrees—and gently settle onto the deck. The high-pitched drive leveled out to a low hum but kept running.

"Guess this is *adios* for now," his father said. Jason offered his father a sympathetic smile. The admiral then gave him a rare hug, and stood back, his hands still resting on Jason's shoulders. "Probably best if you let her know that you're on to her … talk to her." With that, the admiral grabbed the oversized satchel at his feet and headed off toward the awaiting shuttle, as Nan, Mollie, and Teardrop entered the bay, looking less than pleased to be leaving.

Mollie gave her father a hug and looked sorrowfully up at him. "Dad … why do we have to leave already? We just got here."

"Mollie!" Nan warned sternly.

"Well … you won't tell me anything."

"Get on board … Keep your grandfather company."

Mollie made a mean face and ran off toward the shuttle.

Nan watched as Mollie, with Teardrop close behind, hurried away in the sudden relative silence. Jason saw her biting her lip.

"Look, I don't know what's going on with you … why you had to come here at this particular time—"

Nan interrupted him, "I can't do it anymore, Jason. I can't run a country. I can't even run my own life."

"You're loved, Nan, by the whole country. The U.S. needs a strong leader like you. And I know you're still in office. Hell, according to the admiral, Ross may never get back to where he can function again in running the country."

Nan looked up and held his eyes.

"You're just overworked … stressed. Understandably so!"

She nodded and looked to be relieved he knew the truth. "Do you really have to do this, Jason?"

"This?" he asked.

"Risk your life in space on this particular mission. You have kids. Don't you owe it to them to stay alive?"

"Come on. This is what I do, Nan."

"You know I have all the information … all the briefings and specifics of what you're up against with these Sahhrain shits. This is different."

Jason shook his head and smiled.

Angered, she kept talking. "I've felt it in my bones … that you're not coming back from this one. That's why I'm here … I had to warn you … had to tell you to come back with me right now … come back to your family."

He continued to stare down at her. Her eyes, full of pleading, looked up at him. *What does she know?* "How about if I come back for a while when this is over? When Star

Watch can spend sufficient time eradicating the rest of those damn *peovils* back home?"

That answer didn't pacify her in the least. Her voice was now soft and barely audible. "Jason ... you need to sit this one out ... please ... come home ... just this once, listen to me."

"I can't ... you know I can't do that."

He pulled her close and wrapped his arms around her. "Watch out for my father. Can you do that for me? Let him hang out at the White House for a while ... maybe convalesce there, before he heads back to California?"

"All right. But I'm not real sure he'll go along with that for very long." Her expression became more serious. "You make sure nothing happens to Boomer. I mean it, Jason ... nothing can happen to her."

He felt her nod into his chest. She pulled away and kissed him on the lips. He tasted her salty tears as she turned away, quickly hurrying toward the awaiting shuttle.

* * *

Jason entered the bridge and scanned the occupants.

Orion caught his eye. "Everyone get off all right?"

"Fine. Where the hell's Ricket?"

"Been meaning to talk to you about that. He never returned to the *Minian,* Cap. I tracked his fighter ... his last known coordinates were near the planet ... Harpaign. Anything entering that world's atmosphere is pretty much impossible to track. I'm sure he's fine, though ... probably needs a new ride."

"Damn ... I remember. Actually saw him and that beat up fighter heading off toward the planet ... what the hell's he up to?"

Orion pointed up to the display. "Captain, the fleet ... it's on the move."

Jason took a seat in the command chair, absorbing the quickly changing dynamics in space.

"Incoming missiles! One thousand and counting. Look to be coming from the Parlek Orion warships."

Jason watched their incoming trajectory on a newly added logistical display segment. He saw the *Minian*'s positioning, sitting approximately midpoint within the fleet of two hundred Allied warships. Millions of miles away, he saw the larger fleet of Sahhrain and Parlek Orion warships heading right for them.

"How much time do we have before the missiles strike?"

"Thirty seconds."

The tiny missile icons blinked and then disappeared. "What the hell just happened, Gunny?"

She continued to work at her console ... her hands quickly moving across the board. She looked up, concerned. "They're cloaked ... gone dark ... sensors don't see them?"

"I thought Bristol fixed that!"

"Only the Parlek Orion warships ..."

Jason continued to stare up at the display. A thousand inbound warheads would be finding their targets within the next few seconds. Nan's departing words replayed in his mind ... *please ... come home ... just this once, listen to me.*

* * *

Ricket had spent hours looking for the habitat portal to no avail. Instead, he discovered other writings, albeit smaller, on engraved walls and tablets. He was well aware now that there were other ancient ruins, where both Blues and Sahhrain societies had once lived, at multiple locations around the planet. Many were buried beneath the surface of Harpaign.

He checked the scrambled, nonsensical readings one more time. Without use of functional data from his HUD, or his internal sensors, it wasn't possible to locate the portal. Simple as that. Ricket sat down upon a larger segment of crumbled column. His eyes looked upward, toward where he guesstimated the current position of the *Minian* and Allied fleet to be. *How do I contact them?*

He wondered, at first, if his eyes were playing tricks on him. All so faint—nearly indecipherable against the dreary backdrop of Harpaign's dark gray sky—were tiny reflections. Hundreds of them arced from high above to a distant location on the world's surface, many miles away. Ricket stood and looked toward the horizon but could see nothing there—too far away.

He checked his suit's power levels—he'd been using his suit's power reserves nonstop—phase-shifting often and discharging his integrated wrist plasma weapons a dozen times to clear away subterranean obstacles. His suit's power reserves were barely holding at five percent. Ricket eyed the distant horizon again and shrugged. *I'm not doing any good standing around here.* He set the phase-shift coordinates for fifty miles' distance and flashed away.

He'd misjudged the coordinates by a mile … maybe two. He phase-shifted again. Closer now, Ricket watched as spherical drones, each highly reflective, descended from high above in a constant stream. One after another they approached the surface below, slowed, and quickly joined row-upon-row formations of other identical-looking drones. He counted fifteen hundred, as many more still dropped from the sky.

No less than twenty Sahhrain warships were haphazardly parked nearby as well. Sahhrain warriors were filing out from one of the vessels and heading off toward a massive, mostly intact, rock archway.

"What do we have here?" Ricket asked aloud, using his HUD to magnify the distant landscape. The vessel closest to the archway was instantly recognizable ... the *Assailant*.

Startled, Ricket first felt the hot wash of thrusters above before looking up and seeing the spacecraft quickly descending. He was directly beneath it. Ricket checked his HUD—suit power levels were at zero. Phase-shifting no longer an option.

He ran.

Chapter 45

Dacci System
The *SpaceRunner*, Entering Harpaign Atmosphere

Leon quickly realized nav-sensors were useless here. As soon as they entered the atmosphere he switched over, manually navigating the *SpaceRunner* to the provided planet coordinates. In the misty-gray swirls of fog hugging the surface of Harpaign below, he spotted the *Assailant*, parked near an old archway. Here and there he saw ruins—several freestanding pillars, a low, crumbling wall, and multiple piles of marble-like stone.

Lowering his ship's landing struts, he slowly settled onto the surface, then shut down the ship's drive. He left the pilot's seat and headed up the stairs, where he found everyone waiting for him in the main cabin.

"It's show time," he said. "Everyone know what's expected of them?"

There were nods all around.

Stalls held up his bound wrists. "You'll need to release my hands."

Leon looked over to Rizzo, who obviously wasn't keen on the idea. Reluctantly, he stepped forward and removed the electronic bindings. He whispered something into Stalls' ear before stepping back away.

Hanna, looking out one of the side observation windows, observed, "We've got a welcoming committee coming."

All eyes went to Boomer. Leon still was having a hard time believing the entire mission hinged on one little girl's ability to confront and immobilize the Sahhrain leader. Perhaps he didn't fully understand things ... but, somehow, it just didn't seem right.

Boomer initialized her battle suit and looked up at Rizzo through her helmet's visor. Once again he instructed, "Remember, kid ... you'll need to get him off by himself, away from his men. Once you immobilize him ... even for a few seconds, I'll be able to bring him down." Rizzo lifted the muzzle of his multi-gun to emphasize his point.

"You're going to kill him?" she asked.

"That'll be up to him. I'm ready to, if it comes to that."

Boomer glanced around at the cabin's occupants, took in a deep breath, and nodded. For the first time, she seemed nervous and unsure of herself. Leon gave her an encouraging smile and a thumbs up. "Watch yourself out there, Boomer."

She flashed away.

Leon turned to Hanna. "You'll need to stay on board— out of your husband's sight, until Lord Shakrim is dealt with." He walked to the back of the compartment and slid open a door-sized panel, which provided access into a hidden compartment. "We won't encourage them to go anywhere other than the hold area below, especially since this posh upper deck wouldn't jive very well with the ship's phony, old-wreck-looking exterior. Just in case you need a place to lay low, there's enough room in there to be comfortable ...

at least for a while. Bristol and the mecher will keep you company."

Hanna looked over to Trommy5. "I don't suppose you have a deck of cards on board?"

* * *

Leon, Stalls, and Rizzo, slinging his multi-gun over his shoulder, exited the *SpaceRunner* and hurried down the gangway, single-file. A welcoming party was waiting for them at the bottom of the ramp.

Leon took in the three tall Sahhrain warriors and the sole human. Wearing leather breastplates, which exposed well-muscled arms, it was clear none had an ounce of extra fat anywhere on him. The human, with an eye patch, was most assuredly Hanna's husband; he was a foot shorter, wearing a silver breastplate, and was no less an imposing figure. Although each was equipped with an enhancement shield, only the three Sahhrain held the shafts of long spears in their grasp. A gust of wind swirled around them and Leon caught the pungent, sour smell of body odor. *Physically fit, sure ... but these guys reek to high heaven.*

Stalls stepped forward, his palms spread wide before him. His smile looked authentic as he approached them. "My good friend ... how have you been, Ridert?"

The human did not return Stalls' smile. "You will address me as Commander Douville, Captain Stalls."

"Of course. Commander Douville, it is. We have your delivery ... you'll need a hover cart to transport the barrels from the hold."

Leon watched the human's expression of mild disinterest turn to contempt. "Enough of this ruse ... we know why you are here." Ridert gestured to the others with the wave of one hand. "Take them!"

Leon wasn't totally surprised by this less than cordial reception. They'd expected just such a possible scenario. Several hours earlier, Rizzo reviewed the procedure involved in initializing Leon's battle suit from the small SuitPac device he wore on his belt.

Leon dove to his right, even as he felt his battle suit expand, one segment at a time, quickly conforming about his body. He hit the ground, his battle suit fully initialized. Rizzo, earlier, had also instructed him on how to access the integrated, wrist plasma weapons via his HUD. But before he could actually do that, bright violet distortion waves filled his vision—multiple bone-crushing thuds hitting him in the chest. He gasped for air, doing his best to spin away on the ground, and getting a quick glimpse of Rizzo in the process. Fortunately, the young Navy SEAL was better prepared. Somehow, he'd already unslung his weapon and initialized his battle suit while remaining on his feet.

Leon suffered several more painful blows to his back and shoulders before he heard Rizzo firing his multi-gun. Two Sahhrain warriors fell to the ground next to him. Leon noticed nearby drones were in the process of encircling his ship. No less than twenty of them. Shiny, lethal-looking, they hovered several feet off the ground, plasma weapons pointed in their direction.

It took a few seconds for Leon to process what happened next. The drones began firing. The first one hit was Captain Stalls. His body blew apart, shredded into a scramble of bloody, fist-sized chunks. Within a millisecond, all three Sahhrain warriors suffered the same messy fate as Stalls. Leon curled into a ball as plasma fire streamed from all directions. He felt each and every white-hot bolt as it hit his battle suit. He glimpsed Rizzo, staggering, but miraculously still on his feet. He pointed a finger toward the horizon and was gone in a flash. Leon got the message. He accessed his HUD's phase-shift menu, then phase-shifted away. He had noticed, prior to the bright white flash, Ridert standing far back ... well behind the still-firing drones' line of fire.

* * *

Lying flat on her belly, sixty-five feet up, atop the broad stone archway, Boomer watched events unfold far below her, near the landing struts of the *SpaceRunner*. She really hated Captain Stalls, but seeing him suddenly die so disgustingly—she almost felt sorry for him ... *almost*. Then she thought of Bristol, safe inside the ship, and how ... in just an instant ... he'd lost his brother.

She wondered where Leon and Rizzo had decided to phase-shift? Rizzo was definitely hurt badly, and if they were smart, they'd stay hidden. She next thought about the human, dressed like a Sahhrain warrior, but wearing a breastplate of silver instead of leather. He'd fled from the scene so quickly—almost as if he phase-shifted—but he wasn't wearing a battle suit. No, he'd used his enhancement shield. Boomer remembered seeing a fleeting glimmer of violet distortion waves. The guy had crazy skills! Thinking about that, her heart sank and she wondered if she should just give up ... surrender right then. This whole plan was turning out to be a bad idea.

Boomer continued to watch the other guy—realizing he was the same person Hanna had spoken about—Ridert, her husband. Trying to visualize them as a couple, a disgusted expression formed on her face. Dust swirled in the distance as scores of marching Sahhrain warriors descended down the alien ship's gangways and, like a funnel, converged into two long lines. Ridert met them, taking up position in front of their formation. In step, they came to a halt in front of the archway below her. As if a silent command was instigated, gazillions of round drones fell in line behind the warriors, extending off almost as far as the eye could see.

So now what? Boomer's question was about to be answered. She spotted him coming down the gangway of the nearby *Assailant*. Her heart skipped a beat and her mouth gaped open when she realized just how *big* he was. But it was more than mere size. The wind pulled at his long black cloak, causing it to flutter wildly behind him. His golden breastplate—the quick flashes of scarlet beneath his cloak—gave eerie, almost super-hero status to his appearance. But she intuitively *knew* this guy was no hero.

Lord Vikor Shakrim walked forward several paces, stopped, and suddenly looked up. *Crap!* He was staring right at her. Boomer quickly lowered her head and did her best to flatten her body against the stone blocks.

What am I doing? He already knows I'm up here. She cleared her mind, took in a breath, and scrambled to her feet. He was still down there—looking up at her. Waiting. *Okay, fine ... so, I guess, this is where it's supposed to happen.*

Lord Shakrim approached the warrior's front line and spoke to Ridert. Both looked up at her. Boomer felt small and stupid just standing there.

Lord Shakrim gave an audible command and Ridert, along with the rest of the assembled warriors, marched forward, into the archway beneath her. Boomer spun around but didn't see anyone emerge from its other side. *That's definitely weird.* She looked back to see Lord Shakrim heading out alone toward the open desert. One hundred yards out he stopped, turned, and stood still, his hands on his hips. *Is he waiting for me?*

New movement. She saw a couple of dozen Sahhrain warriors, different from the others—these were Shakrim's Chosen Spear warriors. Equipped with spears and enhancement shields, they were hurrying toward Shakrim, and began forming in a large circle around him.

Lord Shakrim raised an arm high over his head and gave two quick flicks of his hand: the universal gesture to come forward, and join him within the circle. *Okay, that's it. Do-or-die time.*

What looked like hundreds of warriors, followed by drones, continued to file into the archway beneath her. *Where are they going?* She didn't know, but at some level, she knew they needed to be stopped.

The near-countless number of warriors, drones, then Ridert, and now Lord Shakrim, caused mounting fear to slowly creep into Boomer's subconscious. Breathing had become difficult; she'd begun to hyperventilate. She tried to recall Aahil's voice—the hours and hours of training she'd undergone so panic, like this, wouldn't happen. She was already failing Aahil ... and failing her father, too. *Stop thinking!* One more time, she checked the settings on the enhancement shield, snugly fitted onto her forearm. Even through her battle suit she could feel its tiny protrusions, letting her know it was set to its most lethal setting. Finally, calmness settled over her. *I can do this.*

Poised to phase-shift down to the ground—she stopped when she saw a sudden bright flash. A flash from someone's phase-shift! Rizzo! Unplanned, and unexpected, he nevertheless appeared, standing five feet behind Shakrim, his multi-gun pointed directly toward the back of his head. Rizzo fired.

But Lord Shakrim was already gone, obviously anticipating the attack. Boomer silently cursed Rizzo. Shakrim had skillfully used his enhancement shield in a way she didn't think possible: a maneuver that allowed him to block plasma fire, while simultaneously spinning his body sideways. The move was somewhat similar to her doing cartwheels ... but much, much faster, and much, much more cool.

Lord Shakrim came at Rizzo from behind. He held up one hand—disruptor waves flew through his fingertips. She knew he was *somehow* channeling the enhancement shield's distinct power through his own body. *How does he do that?*

Rizzo's body left the ground, flipping three times into the air before landing, face down, thirty feet away.

Boomer looked down at Rizzo's unmoving body. *Is he dead?* She checked to see if there were active life-icons on her HUD, then remembered most HUD functions weren't working. Shakrim casually walked toward Rizzo's body. *Oh God! He's going to finish him off!*

She screamed the words as she phase-shifted down to the ground, "Don't you touch him!"

She didn't land in front of him or behind him ... she landed *within* him. After hundreds of phase-shifts, and many stern warnings from her father—she knew the perils of phase-shifting in too close, or landing on top of another person. But right then, she knew exactly what she must do. The instant Boomer's physical form, battle suit and all, began materializing sixty-five feet below, three nearly simultaneous things occurred: One, it was determined that the desired end-point was already occupied by another organic mass; two, her own organic mass was determined to hold precedence over the other, pre-existing, mass; and three, Boomer's mass would transpose the mass of Lord Shakrim. In the fleeting moments before phase-shifting, neither Boomer's intentions, or actions, were anticipated by Shakrim, and that was what distinguished her from Rizzo … or anyone else, for that matter.

Shakrim's body flew sideways, with such instantaneous force, such momentum, that his shiny gold breastplate was instantly ripped from his chest and landed fifty yards out in the open desert. His head and neck had been splayed awkwardly—twisted around clockwise, while the rest of his body was twisted around counter-clockwise.

The encircling crowd of warriors quieted down. Lord Shakrim's body lay prone on the ground before her. A trickle of blood seeped from the corner of his mouth. Had she killed him … *had it really been that easy?*

Lord Shakrim's eyes opened to cloudy confusion. Four seconds elapsed and confusion turned to focused intelligence. His gaze locked on to Boomer.

Chapter 46

Dacci System
Planet Harpaign, Ancient Subterranean
Ruins

With his battle suit's power pack completely depleted, Ricket sprinted from beneath the descending space-craft's hot thrusters and headed directly for the stone arch-way. He quickly discovered it was actually the gateway to a wide, subterranean stairway. Down he went, more than a thousand steps, before reaching a broad, cobblestoned thor-oughfare. Internal nano-devices, with specialty enhanced optics, allowed him to perceive basic shapes in the near to-tal darkness. He determined he was in an immense natural cave—perhaps a dried-up aquifer—one that reached a thou-sand feet into the darkness above and extended miles in all directions, though it was too dark for him to be complete-ly sure. He continued walking down the main road, and, in time, reached the outskirts of a city. Ricket marveled at the sheer size of the surrounding, towering stone structures—most were in a remarkable state of preservation. His battle suit's power levels, eventually sufficiently regenerated, allowed him to use his helmet's spotlight to take in his nearby surroundings. He turned his head and noted other buildings—buildings even paralleling the buildings behind these. The size of this subterranean world was far larger than he could ever have imagined.

A thousand rectangular windows, black and vacant, like so many empty eye sockets, followed his movements. He walked for nearly a mile, down the sprawling city's central causeway. *Easily a hundred … maybe two hundred … thousand people once lived here, in the distant past.* Ricket briefly wondered what happened to them. Were they Blues or Sahhrain? Did it matter?

Ricket picked up his pace—well aware the *Minian* was still in grave danger—soon to be attacked by an overwhelming force. Not from space, but infiltrated from within, via one of the ship's habitat portals.

Ricket, at first, didn't notice but now he could clearly see various small icons and readouts coming back alive on his HUD. This far beneath the interferences on the planet's surface, his suit's sensors were slowly coming back to life. He tried hailing Captain Reynolds, then the *Minian*, but neither hail connected. He ran through several other HUD menus until he found, and displayed, the directional locator overlays for a relatively close habitat portal. An amazing bit of Caldurian technology that he'd used successfully in the past, within *The Lilly*'s HAB 12, and other Zoo habitats, it was an indispensable, essential tool when searching for a habitat's entry-exit portals.

The *Minian* possessed one known Zoo portal into this small section of Harpaign, with its ancient ruins and ghastly weather. The habitat, known as HAB 7, was first created by the Caldurians a distant thousand years, or more, ago. Ricket, never aware of the towering stone archway's presence, now so prominent above him on the surface when he was within HAB 7, thought about that—concluding, it must have been built some time after the Caldurians first created the habitat.

A smile spread across Ricket's small lips when an aqua-colored triangle hovered before his eyes. His HUD was informing him where the closest habitat portal was located. He'd need to change direction, but it was close ... less than a mile away. With such good fortune, hopefully he'd be able to access the portal, enter the *Minian*, and warn the captain.

Again, Ricket stopped in his tracks. New life-icons were popping up on his HUD—too many to count. They were coming from behind him, where he'd just been. Sahhrain warriors were on the move. Ricket didn't understand how they could move with such speed. Even if he phase-shifted to the portal ahead, it would be too close—he wasn't sure he'd have sufficient time to give the captain adequate warning. He interrupted setting the coordinates and stepped into an alleyway between two stone buildings as they passed by him in a blur, riding distortion waves of violet light. One by one, they whisked by, in what seemed a never-ending stream of Sahhrain.

Ricket, momentarily paralyzed by indecision, saw the last of the warriors whisk past him. As he stepped out onto the street he saw more coming, but they weren't Sahhrain warriors—they were drones. Over a thousand of them. He inputted his new phase-shift coordinates, based on the location given on the portal directional locator overlay, and flashed away.

* * *

The battle in space continued as the cloaked Sahhrain

missiles bombarded the Allied fleet. "Two Blues' ships just fell off our sensors … destroyed, in that last missile strike, Cap," Orion said.

"We've got more requests to return fire, Captain," Seaman Gordon said, his voice anxious—an octave right below squeaky.

Jason took in the multiple overhead display segments and quickly recognized there was no avoiding the inevitable: this conflict was escalating to all-out war, despite the Star Watch initiative to keep the peace. There was tolerance, reluctance to commence new battles, but such even-mindedness was balanced by an even greater necessity: to face reality. In light of the Sahhrain's blatant attacks, he knew he had no choice; he would have to destroy the Sahhrain in battle. But first he needed to deal with one evident problem.

"Let the Blues' fleet captains, all of them, know we've got this … have them stand down and fall back." Thus far, Jason wasn't impressed with the Blues' capabilities—the way they'd haphazardly assembled their forces. He wondered if they'd ever actually confronted an enemy in space before. If they had, he doubted they won. At this point, they were just in the way. "Gunny, return fire."

The logistical display was already a flurry of movement. Allied warships were strategically maneuvering into well-practiced battle formations. Sure, their assets were outnumbered four to one, but Jason wasn't overly concerned. His fleet was battle-savvy from the many years fighting scores of space battles against the Craing. Added to that, the Sahhrain warships' technology was far inferior. This battle would be over soon.

Jason thought about his father's lofty ideals for Star Watch. He swore under his breath at the futility of it all, as it now seemed a pipedream, to hope there could be some kind of post-Craing War peace within the galaxy. He continued to watch, as the battle unfolded, and listen to Orion's voice communicate in low tones to her counterparts sitting at other bridge tactical stations.

Jason ordered the repositioning of fifty Allied warships—then split these assets into two synchronized attack modes—thereby flanking the enemy and isolating them.

The overhead wrap-around display's views, on all sides and back, gave the impression of looking directly out into open space. Hundreds of brilliant blue, crisscrossing plasma bolts streaked across the black void. On the display's front segments, more and more Sahhrain warship icons could be viewed fading from bright red to non-threatening gray.

"Give me an updated count, Gunny."

"We've lost two more … both Allied light cruisers. Eighty-nine Sahhrain warships have been destroyed."

"Seaman Gordon … open a channel. Request the enemy to surrender. Let them know we have no interest in furthering loss of life … on either side."

"All hails are being ignored, Captain."

Jason pounded a fist onto his command chair armrest. "Damn it!" He stood and glared at the display. "What's their damned end game here? Suicide?"

The question was rhetorical—Jason didn't expect an answer, but one came back just the same.

"They want this ship. I warned you, Captain." It was Granger, the Caldurian scientist. He'd entered the bridge and now stood beside him.

Jason scoffed at that. "Well, it's obvious their attempts have failed miserably."

Granger didn't answer right away. When he did, his condescending smile was gone. "What does this," he gestured toward the display, "accomplish?"

"Not much. Frankly, it's hard to watch."

"Are they directly attacking the *Minian*?" Granger asked.

"For the most part no ... but there again, would you?"

"Perhaps it's something else ... perhaps they've been ordered not to attack."

"Yes, they want this ship ... to keep it in one piece. I know that ... you've already made that clear. But it's obvious they're not going to get her."

"No, not from out there; that's evident. They're wasting—"

Jason turned toward the tall Caldurian and cut him off, "Time!"

Granger nodded. "They're stalling ... I'm betting they're keeping the *Minian* occupied for a different kind of attack." And suddenly Jason knew exactly what was about to go down.

"Gunny! We're being attacked."

She looked up in confusion, then toward the logistical display segment. "Captain?"

"No ... from the Zoo ... maybe from one or more of the habitats. We're being infiltrated ... from *inside*, not *outside*."

He wondered if it was too late—were they already entering the ship? "Granger ... can you turn them off? Close down the habitats?"

Granger shook his head. "It doesn't work like that."

Jason hailed Billy. "Ready your men ... your Sharks. Deploy to the Zoo ... we're being attacked!"

There was a momentary silence on Billy's end. "Holy shit ... okay ... I'm on it, Cap. Let me roust the Sharks."

Chapter 47

Dacci System
The *Minian*, Zoo Habitat 7

Distortion waves don't suddenly emanate from an enhancement shield, as if some kind of mechanical trigger were pulled. It didn't work that way. No, first one needed to communicate his or her intentions—in much the same way one willed an arm to move—or eyes to blink. An enhancement shield was effective, but only to the level the user integrated the weapon into his own state of being. What constituted a master in the ancient martial arts of *Kahill Callan*, specifically, wielding an enhancement shield effectively—came from years, usually many decades, of training. But the warrior's level of mastery in that regard was finite. Yes, he (or she), although certainly masterful—was like a technician—skillful in all the intricate, incredible, defensive and offensive moves.

But there were others who were, typically since birth, bestowed with mental abilities that went far beyond those of master technicians. The few who could tap in to their own inherent, latent abilities—to actually influence their surroundings—not depending solely on the small, three-sided shield worn upon their forearms, were indeed a rare breed. Aahil had spoken about this. Spoken of Lord Vikor Shakrim's level of mastery. Of Boomer's own potential to match his, perhaps even eclipse his, in time. What Aahil had repeatedly conveyed to her was that she didn't need years and years of training. She possessed innate fighting skills that reached far beyond any warrior's he had ever encountered, regardless of age. No, any perceived boundary, limit, to her capabilities was all in her mind. She needed to transcend doubt—believe in the unbelievable. To coax and manipulate the invisible forces of matter, which weren't really matter at all, only pure potential. Boomer didn't quite understand what Aahil meant. He told her that was fine—that actually, in some future—still to be defined at a point in time—she already fully knew, and understood, his meaning.

Lord Vikor Shakrim rose to his feet, without the use of arms or legs. One second he was on the ground, and in the next, standing before her.

Boomer attacked. She unleashed a torrent of distortion waves toward Shakrim's head, while driving forward, towards his legs. He moved aside with relative ease, as a matador would to evade the horns of a charging bull. She flew past him and rolled forward, abruptly using the power of her shield to cartwheel sideways. Behind her, powerful distortion waves plowed a deep trough into the sand, obliterating her footprints.

"It fills my soul with pleasure that my Sachem has finally sent me a somewhat adequate opponent," Shakrim told her. He stood ten feet away, taking up the primary *Kahill Callan* fighting stance. His bare chest looked like two swollen pillows; the muscles on his arms bulged—taut, branch-like veins loomed large in his underarm flesh.

Disgusting, Boomer thought.

They moved at the same time, both manipulating the edge of their shields in a similar motion that propelled them upward—Boomer straight up six feet, and Shakrim even higher—over ten feet. He fired down at her, his hands and fingers extended. Two sets of distortion waves swirled into brilliant violet tornadoes of energy—converging into a single, blindingly white pinpoint on Boomer's chest.

She screamed into her helmet—screamed until her throat felt as if it would rip apart. She grabbed for her chest—for the open, gaping crater she felt certain was there. She fell to the ground in a heap. Opening her still-tearful eyes, she saw that her visor had dug several inches into the sand. She continued to probe the front of her battle suit with her fingers—looking for damage—but found none. Immediately, she phase-shifted fifteen feet to her left with no conscious thought.

He pounced—standing now exactly where she'd been. Boomer arched backward as distortion waves sliced through the air close above her. She continued her reverse movements by going into a modified back flip; two more shield-accelerated flips put her forty feet away from Shakrim. Unable to track his quick, sudden blur of movement, she spun to her left, ready to dive forward, when several consecutive violet waves knocked her sideways, onto the ground.

Boomer staggered to her feet, then immediately experienced a strangling sensation around her neck. Grabbed from the side, she found herself held in the air. Shakrim, one hand tightly gripped around her throat, and holding her at arm's length, partially turned her body around to look into her visor. She tried to phase-shift away. Nothing. He must have damaged her suit with his last volley of distortion waves.

"I want you to know, little girl, your death has not been in vain. And understand, there was nothing you could have done differently … it's a foregone conclusion you would die here today. It's an honor, really. Think about it … chiseled into sacred tablets, two millennia ago, your presence here was foretold. Yes … an honor indeed! *Rom Dasticon* will save an honored place for you in his realms of infinite darkness."

Boomer glimpsed Shakrim slowly bending his elbow—bringing her face in close to his own. He watched her eyes, as if studying her. She felt his grip around her neck tighten, then heard a sound—like the crinkling of a squeezed soda can. *Oh god … I'm going to die here.* Her desperation was turning quickly into fear … then to infinite sadness. She thought of her mother and Mollie and tears filled her eyes. She thought of her father … *I'm so sorry, Dad.*

It was becoming increasingly difficult for Boomer to breathe, and swallowing nearly impossible. Beginning to choke, as violet light pulsed from his clutched hand, Boomer could see her terrified face reflected in his eyes. She knew his muscular strength was bolstered by his enhancement shield's unique power. Alarms sounded in her helmet, warning icons flashed onto her HUD, as the integrity of her battle suit was compromised. It wouldn't be long now.

If she were about to die, she didn't want it to be in her battle suit. Her HUD was crapping out—readouts and icon statistics flashed on and off. As a last conscious act … she disengaged the suit.

Boomer fell to the ground, choking. On hands and knees she gulped for air. She saw her enhancement shield, lying on the sand, no more than five feet away. Miraculously, her battle suit retracted into the SuitPac device on her belt. Somehow, Shakrim had lost his grip … or his concentration. Something must have happened. She continued to gag and gasp for air and, more than seeing him, she sensed his sudden movement. He was bending over, ready to grab her neck again.

In an instant Boomer knew: Some unfulfilled craving, lying deep inside her, was instinctively aroused, attracting the shield toward her. She knew what the shield required, where its need to please emanated from—from some deep void, prompting it to give *everything*, in order to please the one who'd wield it.

She re-routed the direction of the distortion wave energy, letting it consume her ... *become* her. She dove up and forward at a forty-five degree angle—one arm and hand raised over her head like superman; her other arm trailed down, hand open. Like a magnet the shield flew into her palm. She brought the shield up, grasping it in outstretched hands. Downward distortion energy continued to build and enhance into blossoming waves. The throbbing waves of violet turned to vivid red as Boomer ascended higher and higher into the sky. *I'm flying! I'm alive, and I'm flying!*

A half-mile away, she landed imperfectly—coming down feet first. Stumbling, she tried to run fast to match her forward momentum. In the distance, she saw the Sahhrain warriors, still in a circle, and spotted Lord Shakrim standing there too.

Suddenly startled by a brilliant flash of light, Boomer reflexively assumed a *Kahill Callan* fighting stance, ready to go at it again. But it wasn't Lord Shakrim. Instead, Leon stood in front of her and she could see him grinning through his visor. He said, "You've got some pretty cool moves, kid, but it's time to go." He stepped in, wrapped his arms around her, and together they flashed away.

* * *

They phase-shifted into the crew compartment of the *SpaceRunner*. Leon released her and saw Boomer's less than grateful expression.

"What have you done? Put me back! Right now! Put me back in the fight!"

Leon retracted his battle suit. "Sorry, kid … that's not going to happen."

Boomer ran to the observation window and looked out. The last of Shakrim's warriors, riding on violet distortion waves, were entering a stone archway. She continued to watch until there was nothing left to see, only a quickly dissipating cloud of dust remained.

She spun back around. "I have to follow them. I'll need a new SuitPac." Boomer then noticed Rizzo's body, outstretched on the opposite side of the compartment. His tall form lay immobile on a bed of seat cushions. Hanna was kneeling next to him, talking in low tones. Boomer's heart sank.

Leon was gone. He'd probably headed off to the bridge. She saw Bristol sitting alone, tinkering with something on his lap. His cheeks were red and it was evident, by his puffy eyes, he'd been crying. *Of course he'd cried*—he just lost his brother.

Boomer crossed the compartment, settling on the deck near Hanna. She heard the *SpaceRunner's* drive revving up and felt its soft vibration in her legs.

"Are you okay, Rizzo?" she asked.

Slowly, he turned his head and looked at her. Obscured from her view earlier, the left side of his face was a blackened mask of charred flesh. His words were slurred and distorted, coming from a mouth only half-intact. "I think I will be, once I get into a MediPod."

Boomer took his hand and squeezed it. "Thank you for trying to shoot Shakrim. I know you were trying to protect me."

She saw his failed attempt at a smile. "I'll get him next time."

She smiled back at him. *No ... I'll get him next time.*

Boomer noticed Hanna looking out the window above Rizzo's prone body. Her face was taut—angry. Boomer realized that Hanna, too, had not accomplished what she'd come here for. She never even saw Ridert.

The *SpaceRunner* rose above the planet's gray atmosphere and now all Boomer could see was the absolute blackness of space. She thought of Lord Shakrim—picturing him mere inches from her face—the deep, blackened, scars on his cheek, trailing all the way down to his neck ... and his eyes ... those deathless eyes ... staring into hers—into her very soul.

Chapter 48

Dacci System
Planet Harpaign, Ancient Subterranean
Ruins

Ricket phase-shifted into an area beyond the subterranean city—at the cavern's farthest boundaries—where
the rocky ceiling angled down to a mere twenty feet. Before him, a portion of the cave's wall was finely chiseled flat.
He focused the beam of his helmet light there, and could
make out on the wall an intricate engraved pictograph. He
stepped closer and viewed a scene depicting numerous warriors. Blues or Sahhrain? Ricket wasn't sure which. They were
in the process of leaping over some kind of void, some kind
of elongated, roughly triangular platform. Ricket tilted his
head. It looked like a spacecraft ... uncanny, how similar to
the *Minian*'s shape it appeared.

Ricket, again checking his HUD, noted he had less than
two minutes before the charging Sahhrain warriors would
arrive. According to his directional locator, he was standing
before the portal leading into habitat 7. He quickly needed
to find the access panel. Typically, Caldurians made it a point

to hide habitat access panels out of easy view. As the seconds ticked by, Ricket's search became more and more frantic. He placed both hands on the wall, moving them around; perhaps there was a hidden panel, something he could trigger or dislodge, as he'd encountered that sort of thing before. Nothing. He only had forty seconds before the Sahhrain would catch up to him.

Maybe the access panel wasn't on the wall itself? He looked right, then left. Nothing. Wait ... he looked left again. The shadows, showing up on the wall in his spotlight's beam, didn't look right. There was a shadow that shouldn't be there. He quickly shuffled to the left, sliding his hands along the wall's surface as he went. Eight feet over, his left hand lost contact with the wall. An optical illusion? Only now, standing right before it, Ricket could see that an actual wall wasn't there. It was an opening—a doorway—virtually impossible to see unless standing right in front of it. He stepped forward and found that the cave continued on another thirty feet, farther back. And there to the left, where the real back wall was actually sited, hung a metallic box, mounted about four feet off the ground. Ricket ran to the box, opened it, and began entering the appropriate access code. The same backdoor code Aahil and Capri had provided him earlier. Halfway through the code's activation process, a ten-by-ten-foot portal window appeared to his right. He glanced at it and saw another cave, or vault, situated inside the semi-transparent portal window.

Beep Beep Beep! The portal window vanished.

Ricket crossed over the portal's threshold into the dark vault and immediately spotted carved stone steps leading upward. At this point he was leaving the planet of Harpaign and entering a secondary portal into HAB 7, and was one step closer to reaching the *Minian*. Behind him, he heard more beeps, the portal's open time had elapsed, and the portal window reinitiated. Racing up the stairs, he suddenly stopped midway. He sensed movement—or the shifting, perhaps, of a shadow. Ricket turned, seeing a dark form standing outside the portal window. It was too dark to make out who it was … but he, nevertheless, knew anyway.

He called up his HUD portal directional locator overlay and saw the next portal icon hovering close by. Very close. He phase-shifted directly to its designated coordinates.

Ricket flashed onto the surface. Sure enough, the familiar access panel for HAB 7 was before him. But what first caught Ricket's attention was Capri, bent over and entering a code onto the panel. His initial confusion turned to alarm.

While continuing to enter the code, the ten-by-ten-foot portal window directly to her right became visible. The clear window barrier was still in place, but Ricket could see into the *Minian*'s Zoo beyond it. Capri looked over her shoulder, made eye contact with Ricket, then continued entering more digits.

"Stop!" Ricket said, rushing forward and slapping her hand away from the panel. "You can't do this. Capri! … Please stop!"

She flailed an arm out without looking—her enhancement shield smacking the side of his helmet. Ricket felt himself propelled into the air. He hit the side of a stone wall, covering partially buried ruins with enough force to trigger alarms—now blaring within his helmet.

Unhurt, Ricket sprang to his feet and rushed back toward her. At any moment she'd have the portal window open—providing unobstructed access into the *Minian*. He made it back in three steps before a large hand grabbed his upper arm and lifted him off the ground.

Ricket twisted and kicked—tried to free himself from

whoever had come up behind him. He'd never been proficient at fighting; it wasn't in his nature. He called up his HUD's combat menu to access his integrated wrist plasma weapons. He'd shoot his way free, if he had to. But he didn't get that far.

Lord Shakrim flung Ricket forward with enough force, like tossing a small rag doll, that he hit the same stone wall again, face first, with incredible force. His body bounced and flipped over backwards before crashing upside down onto the ground. Everything went black for several seconds before his sight returned. Ricket tried to move—tried to stand, but his arms and legs remained immobile. He realized his spinal cord was severed. He briefly thought about some engineering alterations he could make to the battle suit's design—to better withstand this kind of catastrophic assault. His thoughts turned inward to his labored breathing. Realization set in ... if only his spine had been severed several vertebrae lower.

* * *

Lord Shakrim glanced over at the small crumpled being wearing a battle suit and propped awkwardly, upside down, against a nearby stone wall. He wasn't a threat. He turned toward Capri—this traitor to her people—as she tapped in the remaining code digits. He loomed over her, his eyes traveling over the strange Blues female. He took in the curves of her slender body and felt the beginnings of stirring in his loins. Perhaps he'd take her again ... right here ... right now.

Beep Beep Beep!

She stood up straight and nervously smiled at him. "The portal window is open and will stay open for as long as you'd like, my Lord. You can bring forth your Sachem ... for, in there, your magic chariot awaits." She bowed her shoulders and lowered her head.

"Yes ... you have done well, Capri Sharan," Shakrim said, eyeing the portal, then looking down at her. "I have not forgotten what was promised you." He reached out a hand and lifted her chin—bringing her head up so as to look into her eyes. His hand dropped to her stomach and he held it there. "Even now, my seed has taken hold within you. A future king grows there, thus you will be spared. In fact, you will be revered. Now, step aside, so I can fulfill my destiny."

Capri obeyed him, keeping her eyes fixed on the father of her unborn son ... and now her one true lord.

Commander Ridert Douville rushed forward from the distant ruins. Lord Shakrim waited for the human at the open habitat portal. Ridert, a spear grasped firmly in one fist, momentarily bowed his head as he advanced to his side. "My Lord ... our warriors approach ... and we are ready."

Shakrim knew as much. He saw his warriors—big, strong, and immensely capable, as they one by one emerged from the distant ruins.

Exhilarated, he slowly filled his lungs with air. He stood erect and closed his eyes. *My Lord ... we have reached the very pinnacle of our destiny. Together, we'll bring about ultimate darkness.* Shakrim knew that finally the time had come ... *his* time. He felt the presence of his Sachem, Rom Dasticon, filling the space around him ... pushing him toward the open portal.

"First the drones," Shakrim said aloud. "Let them infiltrate every compartment and corridor within this ship." With a casual swipe of his hand, he signaled for the charge to begin. Both he and Ridert stepped aside as the first of the mirror-like drone spheres came forth from the ruins, moving around and past the warriors without hesitation, and sped into the *Minian's* now open portal.

Chapter 49

Dacci System
The *Minian*, Zoo Rhino-Warrior Habitat
170

Jason had to give Granger his due. Sure, they'd had their differences over the years, and he still didn't completely trust the opportunist Caldurian, but today, he'd actually come through. His knowledge and understanding of the Caldurian technology was unparalleled and had, in this case, allowed him in a matter of minutes to modify the operational configuration of a single habitat portal window. Jason didn't understand all the technical specifics but he didn't need to. Granger had explained it as being a simple crossover patch … a means to bridge one habitat portal to another.

Anyone crossing over the threshold from HAB 7 into the *Minian*'s Zoo would actually be diverted to an alternate habitat—thus bypassing the *Minian*'s Zoo completely.

"How many are coming, Cap?" Billy asked.

"Could be up to a few thousand Sahhrain warriors … and a shitload of attack drones."

"Relax … we're ready for them," Billy said, through a billowing white cloud of cigar smoke.

"It's not my job to relax." Jason was uneasy and knew he had good reason to be. Sahhrain warriors, armed with enhancement shields, opened up uncharted territory for him. He'd put his own multi-guns up against just about any weapon he'd ever come across, but these shield weapons were new to him … an unknown entity.

It was still early dawn within HAB 170, the chosen home of two hundred and fifty, plus or minus, rhino-warriors.

Jason and Billy, both wearing battle suits, stood off to the side of a cluster of house-sized boulders. A stone's throw away was the start of an alternate rocky ridgeline, making this habitat an excellent choice for providing cover. Anyone exiting the portal would be forced to traverse between the boulders on one side and the ridgeline on the other—a fifty-yard exposed span where the enemy would be vulnerable to formidable crossfire.

Jason scanned the mostly hidden positions of Billy's Sharks. Close to two hundred Sharks were left behind, back within the *Minian*, as a precaution if things didn't go well out here—if Lord Shakrim, somehow, found his way inside the ship. That left nearly two thousand heavily armed men and women, strategically placed, holding high-ground positions on the rocks above where he now stood, as well as along the other ridgeline.

Jason felt the ground start to tremble and looked back. Three rhino-warriors running close together were fast approaching. Each, no less than a thousand pounds of hulking muscle and a quick-to-anger temperament, was carrying a four-hundred-pound heavy hammer in a colossal-sized fist, with a multi-gun slung over one shoulder.

Jason recognized Traveler as the rhino in the middle. They slowed, walking the last few yards as they approached. For most, a rhino's expression was just about impossible to read, but that wasn't the case for Jason. He knew Traveler too well and right now he looked like a kid in a candy store. He was eating up the chance to fight ahead … there were very few things the old rhino-warrior enjoyed more than an honorable battle. He'd been going stir crazy and was now back in his favorite element.

He heard all three rhinos snort in excitement; bursts of hot steamy snot blew from some kind of vent hole on their helmets. "Captain … we are in position."

"Thank you, Traveler. Again, this isn't your fight. You don't need to risk rhino lives here today. Allowing us to be in your habitat is enough."

"If it's your fight … it's our fight."

"Where are your warriors? Other than you three, I don't see any of them."

"Good … then we are doing things right."

Jason stared off behind Traveler toward a grouping of distant, mud-colored, domes. The morning sunlight was just hitting their rooftops. He held up a finger: "Hold on," as he answered an incoming NanoCom hail. "Go for Captain."

"I really really want to be there, Dad."

"I told you before, no! That's not going to happen, Boomer. I probably shouldn't have agreed to it the first time."

"But I can beat him this time. I know I can! You need me there … I'm the one—"

Jason cut her off. "There's an army invading us, Boomer. I want you safe and as far away from here as possible. Stop arguing and make yourself useful. Why don't you help Dira in Medical when the wounded start coming in?"

Jason listened to Boomer's breathing as she tried to think of something to say to convince him to change his mind. "I need to go, Boomer. Stay out of trouble." He no sooner cut the connection than another hail came in. It was Dira. "Go for Captain."

"Ricket's in trouble. That, and the Sahhrain warriors are just now heading out of the habitat."

"What? Where are you?"

"I'm standing in the Zoo with about ten others. I just saw a giant warrior dude throw Ricket into a wall. Oh God, Jason … he might be dead." A moment passed before she spoke again. "And they're sending in drones … a lot of them!"

Jason heard Dira's worried tone and tried not to over-think Ricket being injured, or worse, dead. His eyes were leveled on the square habitat portal two hundred yards in front of him.

One of the Sharks yelled, "Incoming!"

"I see them … something's happening at the portal … have to go, Dira."

"But what about Ricket? We just leave him out there to die?"

Jason saw drones through the portal window first—one after another—perfectly spaced as they sped along the ground, then suddenly shot upward, toward the sky. Jason gave Billy a decisive nod. He heard Billy speaking through the open channel over his helmet comms.

Dira, on NanoCom, was still waiting for an answer.

"Talk to Granger, Dira … see if there's a way to get to Ricket without giving the Sahhrain access to the *Minian* in the process." She cut the connection without saying another word.

Plasma fire erupted from both lines of Sharks. As more and more of the shiny small drones filled the air, Jason was reminded of flocks of birds, like geese, which instinctively moved as one when they changed course. Here, the drones were making similar moves, by breaking into smaller units and strategically attacking positions on the boulders, as well as the distant ridgeline, from multiple flanks.

Jason changed his HUD munitions menu from plasma gun setting to tracking micro-missiles. Unlike conventional weapons, multi-guns were tied into the *Minian*'s phase-synthesizer. Even here within the habitat, his multi-gun was constantly fed a wide variety of JIT manufactured munitions, which were continually phase-shifted in. As long as he remained there, and ready to pull the trigger, he would never run out of ammo. He aimed at the tight cluster of drones above him, firing off ten micro-missiles, and watched as they shot toward their intended targets. Soon splitting off, each had tracked its selected quarry. Right off the bat, four missiles were destroyed by drones, while another six drones, focusing on the missiles targeting them, destroyed them in explosive balls of fire. Other drones now changed their targets, tracking missiles instead.

It looked like the Sharks may have been getting the upper hand on the drones. But there'd been a price to pay. According to Jason's HUD, they'd already lost over one hundred Sharks. Jason changed back to a heavy plasma gun setting and aimed toward three approaching low-flying drones and fired. Prior to being hit, they'd fired too—nearly simultaneously—and he took two plasma bolts to the chest. As the three drones exploded, he was bowled over, knocked flat on his back. Traveler was at his side and offered him an outstretched hand. Jason took it, pulling himself up to his feet.

His suit power levels were down, showing fifty percent, and his shields weren't back to full strength either. He'd have to stay out of the line of fire for a while.

Orion was hailing him. "Go for Captain."

"Just checking in. We're basically still mopping up, Cap."

"Status of the enemy?"

"They've backed off … no longer engaging Star Watch warships. But they're still not answering hails and won't let us approach their damaged ships. Won't even let us rescue their wounded."

"We can't force them to accept our help." Jason, back to firing micro-missiles, unleashed seven more into the sky. "Keep me up to date if anything changes."

"Copy that, Cap."

Jason heard Billy's voice over the open channel. "Warriors coming through the portal. Holy shit … these guys are really trucking!"

Jason used his HUD optics to zoom in on the portal and the stream of attacking warriors. The drones entered the habitat in an organized, single-file manner, while the Sahhrain entered six or seven abreast, and at a much faster rate. He saw the telltale strobes of violet light emanating from their enhancement shields and marveled at the warriors' speed as they flew into HAB 170. Already several hundred had emerged. At the front of the formation was a stout-looking human, wearing a silver breastplate and holding a long thick spear. That would be Hanna's husband, Commander Douville … Ridert … *Okay, so where's Lord Shakrim?* Jason wondered.

Chapter 50

Dacci System
The *Minian*, Flight Bay

Hanna found Leon in the flight bay, beneath the forward landing strut of the *SpaceRunner*. The ship was beautiful, back to its former, bright mirror-like finish, with fresh gray accents. Leon stood about midway on the strut, and was reaching with both hands to the outer hull.

"That doesn't look so good," Hanna said, pointing to a twenty-inch gash in the hull.

"Temporary patch ... this is the last of them. Nothing like a bunch of attacking drones to ruin a perfectly good starship." Leon stepped down, and could see that Hanna was carrying a duffle over one shoulder. "Going somewhere?"

"A little birdie told me you were preparing to head out ... weren't you at least going to say goodbye?"

"Um ... I'm not real good with goodbyes. Not so sure my presence would be missed here, anyway." He caught a flash of irritation cross her face, then disappear.

"Look ... do you think I can hitch a ride?"

"With me?"

She smiled at that. "Yes, with you. There's nothing for me here."

"Well, where do you want me to take you ... back to Trom?"

Hanna continued staring at him with attitude.

"Okay ... not Trom."

The shake of her head was nearly imperceptible. She shrugged and chewed the inside of her cheek. Leon, never witnessing any degree of vulnerability in her before, totally knew it was an act. "Knock off the lost puppy routine, Hanna ... I'm not buying it. If you want a ride to parts unknown then just say so."

Her demeanor changed to one of quick indignation. "Hey ... it doesn't mean you and I ..." she used her index finger to point back and forth between them.

"Don't be ridiculous ... you're hardly my type," Leon replied back with a sneer.

She tucked long strands of blond hair behind her ears and made a face, conveying *fuck you* without actually saying the words.

"Seems you aren't the only one wanting to hitch a ride with me."

"Yeah? Who else?" she asked, surprised.

"The mecher ... Trommy5."

She nodded again. "Maybe we can change its name ... Trommy5 is beyond lame."

Leon gestured toward the gangway: "Go ahead and stow your gear. We should be ready to depart within the next few minutes."

* * *

Ricket guesstimated he had about thirty-five minutes

before his bodily functions completely shut down. Lungs, kidneys, and heart were failing, all showing signs of terminal distress. He wasn't giving up yet, but forthcoming assistance from the *Minian* did not look promising. In that moment, time was not his friend, and there wasn't much he could personally do to keep himself alive. Everything from his neck down was paralyzed. About all he could do was swallow, force air into his lungs, and move his eyes about. Theoretically, he could phase-shift somewhere, but where? Physics made phase-shifts possible when inside a habitat, but only within that given habitat's perimeters—not elsewhere beyond an access portal. He brought up his HUD's environmental settings and boosted his oxygen intake to its maximum setting.

Ricket watched as the first stream of drones, followed closely by Sahhrain warriors, moved past him and over to the HAB 7 threshold. There was something odd about it, though. Out of his peripheral vision he could see the portal. He could see into the *Minian's* Zoo. But as warriors and drones rushed past, clearing the threshold, he couldn't actually see them within its corridor. Next came Lord Shakrim, and his twenty-five Chosen Spears—they were the only ones still within HAB 7. But they held back—apparently opting not to follow behind the other forces. Had Shakrim suspected something? Ricket, watching them, wasn't sure. They didn't cross over, and he didn't know where the Sahhrain leader and his warriors went. Perhaps close by? Just out of sight of his upside-down position, at the bottom of a two-thousand-year-old wall?

Ricket strained the muscles of his eyes, catching some movement within the Zoo. At first, he thought it might be sunlight, reflecting off the window—but then he recognized the unmistakable form of a female ... it was Dira! She moved closer to the portal window and placed her open palms on it.

She shouldn't be able to do that, not with an open portal. Or was it? Then it made sense to him. The portal was a bridge to some place else ... probably to another habitat. Clever. Although, apparently, it hadn't fooled Shakrim for long.

Dira lowered her body, becoming more visible to him. He could see her trying to talk to him. Normally, that wouldn't be a problem; NanoCom communications worked fine into most habitats—but not this one. Too much interference. Dira was now trying something else—entering something onto her virtual notebook. He saw her pull at the virtual corners of the hovering display, turn it around, then hold it up to the portal window. Ricket read what she had typed in:

I KNOW YOU ARE ALIVE. HANG IN THERE!

One more bodily function was working—his tear ducts. He blinked away the blur and permitted himself to feel encouraged. But the upbeat emotion lasted only a fleeting moment. If she knew he was still alive, then perhaps Lord Shakrim did, too ... he needed a way into the *Minian* and was waiting, perhaps, for someone to remove the bridge and open the Zoo to HAB 7.

Ricket's heart rate was increasing and he desperately tried to think of a way to warn her ... to stop anyone from opening that portal. He looked at the timer on his HUD and realized his time was quickly running out. He had twenty-seven minutes to live.

* * *

Dira, Rizzo, and Bristol stood in the Zoo corridor in front of the HAB 7 portal window.

"Can't you leave this one alone and add a second portal

into the habitat?" she said to Bristol.

"Perhaps in time ... but we don't have a lot of that going around right now. Best to ask that guy."

Dira saw Granger off in the distance and waved at the tall Caldurian to hurry up—move it—as he ambled down the Zoo corridor. He picked up his pace and joined them at the portal window. Once he'd caught his breath he saw Ricket's upside down, crumpled form within the habitat.

"How do you know he's not dead? He looks dead to me," Granger said.

"He's not ... and could you sound any more detached, Granger?" Dira asked with a furrowed brow.

"I care about Ricket. You know I do ... but look at him."

"I'm a doctor. You haven't noticed what I have. Look at Ricket ... these newer battle suits conform to the body. They give and take, and become almost a second skin. Though it's almost imperceptible, if you look long enough you'll see his chest is moving. Air is moving in and out of his lungs. That typically does not happen when you're dead."

"Excellent! I can open the portal ... temporarily remove the bridge over to HAB 170."

"No. That's not an option. I've already talked to the captain. Lord Shakrim, and some of his personal guard, never crossed over into HAB 170. He may be in there, just waiting for us to provide him access."

"That does create a problem. I don't see how we can help him, then. And being a doctor, you must know the poor fellow has very little time before ..."

Dira held up a hand. "Don't say it." Frustrated, she crossed her arms over her chest and stared into the habitat. "If only there were another way in."

The Caldurian, also gazing into the habitat, shrugged. "There's always more than one way in. I mean, there's the portal down on the planet ... you know, the way they got in there in the first place. But ..."

Dira spun and looked up at Granger. "Wait ... say that again!"

* * *

Leon filled and patched the last of the holes in the *Space-Runner*'s hull—at least to the point it would hold up temporarily, until repaired by a professional. He collected his supplies—a bucket full of tools, and a satchel holding power tools—and headed up the gangway.

"Wait! Leon, wait!"

He turned to see the pretty violet-skinned doctor running into the flight bay with Bristol and Rizzo close behind.

"Dira? What is it?"

"You can't leave yet."

"Okay ... what's going on? What's wrong?"

"I need your ship ... I need you to take me down to the planet."

"No way. I've been on that planet. I just finished patching about twenty plasma burn craters in my ship's hull," he told her as he continued up the ramp.

"It's Ricket. He's in HAB 7, and he's dying."

Leon stopped and looked down at Dira.

She shook her head and stopped him from asking the obvious question. "No ... we can't get to him from the Zoo ... that portal is a bridge to another habitat right now and if we open it to the Zoo Lord Shakrim will be able to get aboard the *Minian*."

Bristol, looking dissatisfied, was looking up at Leon's makeshift patchwork on the hull, while Rizzo, who had recovered from his ordeal with Lord Shakrim without a scrape, stood staring back at him with his hands on his hips.

"We need to save Ricket … He's one of our own."

"So Shakrim's a part of this mix? Now it's definitely no thanks. Have you seen what that maniac can do with that little shield weapon of his? Well I have, so I think I'll pass."

"Please. Please, Leon … Ricket's dying."

He again hesitated and appraised Dira, then Rizzo, then Bristol, who were standing at the bottom of the gangway. Dira's eyes were pleading.

"Shit … shit, shit, shit! Get in … and hurry up!"

Chapter 51

Dacci System
The *SpaceRunner, Minian* Flight Bay

B oomer tried not to move in the total darkness, but something was jabbing her in the back. She reached around and felt the long handle of a broom. She had disengaged her battle suit once she'd phase-shifted into the small space. Perhaps doing so was a bad idea? She felt the spaceship moving and the familiar, elevator-drop feeling in the pit of her stomach—they were off the ground.

Earlier, she had looked for Dira in Medical, as her father had suggested, and learned from a med-tech she and Rizzo were down at the Zoo. She found Dira, Rizzo and Granger in front of HAB 7, and listened to their conversation about Ricket's dire situation. They were planning to go down to the planet and enter the habitat from another side.

"I want to go," Boomer had said.

"That's not an option," Dira told her. "Your father would skin me alive."

Rizzo nodded in agreement.

"Look ... you want to be useful, go tell Bristol he has to meet us in the flight bay. I've already talked to him on comms, but he needs more convincing. Can you do that?"

She'd had just enough time to get to Bristol's quarters and guilt him into helping Dira with her plan to rescue Ricket. Then she needed to get back to her own quarters, grab her enhancement shield, and phase-shift into the *SpaceRunner*'s hidden compartment. She knew she'd probably catch hell for phase-shifting within the *Minian*, but this was too important. She tried to remember the saying her father used on numerous occasions. Oh yeah ... *sometimes the end justifies the means.*

* * *

Jason couldn't help thinking about his father and how—once again—the admiral would be disappointed by his son's recent actions. He looked around the embattled habitat. There were thousands, on both sides, now engaged in battle. Instead of finding a way to manage the situation, following the set directives of Star Watch, he'd done just the opposite: incurring more fighting ... more dying ... more war.

He was standing shoulder to shoulder with Billy and Traveler, waiting for the first of the Sahhrain warriors to reach them.

"Damn, they're fast," Billy said, spitting out his cigar stub and closing his visor.

Now that they were close enough to clearly see, Jason realized the warriors weren't actually riding waves of violet light. They were running at incredible speeds—through the assistance of distortion waves. Abruptly, Traveler rushed forward, meeting head on the first of the six approaching warriors. Like a battering ram, his outstretched heavy hammer plowed into the Sahhrain warrior's face. One down. The warriors abruptly changed course, circling around them. Ja-

son and Billy simultaneously fired their multi-guns at the
remaining five. Two immediately sank to the ground and
didn't get back up. The other three, using their enhancement
shields to block the shots, sent three violet waves spiraling
back at them. Jason found himself catapulted off his feet
onto his back. Although his battle suit took the brunt of the
blow, his chest hurt all the same. Billy, too, lay sprawled on
the ground, while Traveler remained solidly on his feet. He'd
resorted to using his multi-gun too and was fending off the
three warriors on his own. Jason and Billy quickly scrambled
to their feet and rejoined the fight. It took less than a minute
before all six Sahhrain warriors lay dead on the ground.

Billy gestured toward Traveler's battle suit, noting countless blackened streaks. "That's coming out of your paycheck,
soldier."

Traveler didn't get Billy's humor, but he was used to it
enough to know when to ignore him. Jason watched his
HUD readouts and realized their Sharks weren't faring well
against the Sahhrain.

"Let's split up, guys," Jason said. He ran over to a cluster
of rocks to gain higher ground. He looked for a reflective
breastplate, across the battlefield, and finally spotted it, seventy-five yards away, close to the portal window. He set his
phase-shift coordinates and flashed away.

Jason guesstimated there were fifteen Sharks lying dead
around the Sahhrain commander; he was the only human
wearing an enhancement shield. Currently fighting four
Sharks, he easily blocked incoming plasma fire by redirecting
their own fire against them via strategically placed ricochets.
Ridert spun and leapt and flipped with the ease of a gymnast
on steroids.

Jason joined the Star Watch Sharks, watching mutely as
they fell to the ground, one by one, as Ridert expertly ma-

neuvered his enhancement shield, both as a defensive aid and as a weapon. Jason watched his movements—looking for an opening—a weakness in the man's technique. With the four Sharks now out of play, it was now Jason against Ridert. He felt the heat of his multi-gun in his hands as it continued to spew bolts of plasma fire toward his opponent's head, chest, and legs, then back to his head again. Ridert locked out each shot and was smiling. Jason returned his smile, remembering in that instant that he, too, had an unconventional weapon, no less effective. Actually, it was Rizzo who'd showed him that not-so-easily-found HUD menu setting: where, as long as it was initialized ON, the HUD would track your eye movements. Stare at any one location, with eyes exaggeratedly widened, and you'd automatically be phase-shifted to that location in an instant. Because the locations were all close range, one could phase-shift one hundred times or more before the battle suit's power would need regenerating. Jason, locking on the HUD's rapid-eye phase-shift mode, was behind Ridert in a blink. He fired and caught Ridert on his buttock's left cheek, then phase-shifted away, before Ridert could react, and fired again. This time, Ridert held his shield in position and blocked Jason's fire, but he was hurt … his movements less fluid. Jason phase-shifted again, this time right into him. Ridert's mass was transported to the left, but he landed on his feet anyway. He leveled his enhancement shield at Jason and fired off a seemingly endless stream of distortion waves. Jason didn't have time to contemplate his next phase-shift point before being blasted in his visor. He tried to spin with the force, but once again landed on his back. He waited for the next assault—perhaps for life-ending violet waves to strike his body. But they didn't come. Ridert was gone.

Within the last thirty seconds, Jason heard multiple hail

requests coming in. He also heard the open comms channel become more and more congested—voices of desperate Shark command personnel were flooding in. As he got to his feet he took in the battlefield. One thing stuck out more than anything else—they were losing the battle. The dead were strewn across the landscape to the far ridgeline. Shark bodies outnumbered Sahhrain five to one.

Jason answered Billy's incoming hail. "Status?"

"Cap ... we're down to four hundred ... not sure how the rhinos are faring. We need to fall back."

Jason was shocked by the sheer number of men and women lost in one day ... well over a thousand Allied forces had perished; their situation was quickly becoming dire.

"I agree ... have our forces phase-shift at least one hundred miles farther out into the habitat ... convey the coordinates to Shark team leaders. Get everyone the hell out of here!"

Jason saw the new phase-shift coordinates projected onto his HUD. In a flurry of white flashes, remaining Star Watch forces phase-shifted away from the battlefield.

* * *

One hundred miles away in an open, flat expanse of nondescript desert, Jason, Billy and Traveler kneeled before Jason's virtual notebook, looking at the 3D holographic representation of HAB 7.

"We'll definitely need to phase-shift again; perhaps to the foothills over there, at the far end of the habitat. There are trees for cover and somewhat higher ground within the rocks there," Billy said, pointing.

Jason looked to see if there were other, better, options. "It's not enough; we'll only be forestalling the inevitable.

344

They'll cut us down there just as easily as they did back at the portal. No ... what we need are reinforcements."

"I suggest we bring in our own attack drones from the *Minian* ... and the little ship, the *Charm* ... she was designed to pass within a habitat's portal, and she's got excellent fire-power," Billy said.

"Agreed ... with the added airpower we'd be in better shape. Perhaps pull in another hundred Sharks from the *Minian* as well," Jason added.

Traveler grunted, "There are more warriors on the nearby Allied vessels ... yes?"

Jason nodded. "I'll contact Gunny ... have her coordinate the movements of air and ground reinforcements." Closing down his notebook, he spat, "Shit! We still have the same problem ... getting anything into HAB 170 ... as long as it's bridged to HAB 7. We can't chance opening up anything into the *Minian* ... not with Lord Shakrim lurking around."

Jason saw icon movements on his HUD. The enemy was on the move. Even without the problem of bridged portals, everything they talked about—bringing in reinforcements and air support—would take time—possibly hours. The Sahhrain warriors had, somehow, detected their location and were now no more than fifteen minutes out.

Noting the icon movements, the other two became quiet. Jason stood and looked around at their remaining assets—four hundred Sharks and about two hundred rhinos. They were in small groups—some on the ground injured, others resting for the upcoming battle. They all looked tired, and beaten as well. Jason couldn't recall ever being in a similar situation. He wasn't used to losing, being so completely out-matched.

What it came down to was simple: either continue phase-shifting—hiding from the enemy indefinitely—or stand their ground and attempt to defeat a formidable opponent.

Was he willing to sacrifice himself, his men and the rhinos, to ensure the safety of the *Minian*? The safety of the galaxy? Apparently, Billy and Traveler came to the same conclusion.

"Cap ... we always knew this day could come. We've had a pretty good run. We've kicked ass and lived to boast about it."

Jason couldn't argue with Billy's words.

Traveler said, "This is a most honorable way to die ... a worthy opponent. We make a stand ... together. I will shed much of their blood before my carcass falls dead on the ground."

"Christ, Traveler," Billy said, "can we not talk about dying carcasses just yet?"

Traveler snorted, not replying.

"Let's get our forces ready. Billy, you've got about ten minutes to teach six hundred troops how to use that phase-shifting trick Rizzo taught me ... It helped me earlier today ... it might help others." Jason tried to sound upbeat, but as the distant Sahhrain warriors moved closer to their position, he was anything but encouraged.

Chapter 52

Dacci System
SpaceRunner, Planet Harpaign, Ancient
Subterranean Ruins

It didn't take long for the *SpaceRunner* to touch down on the planet surface. Boomer remained still, hidden within the secret compartment, and hoped no one would initialize their battle suits yet, as her life-icon would show up on their HUDs, plain as day. When it was safe, she initialized her own battle suit and phase-shifted over to a recently observed higher location where she figured she'd go unnoticed.

In the gray afternoon light, other than the *SpaceRunner*, the *Assailant* alone remained on the surface. She watched as all five—Dira, Hanna, Rizzo, Bristol, and Leon, bringing up the rear—hurried down the ship's gangway. One by one, as they initialized their battle suits, they continued heading toward the wide archway below her. By checking her own HUD, Boomer noted planetary interferences were making it impossible to detect anyone else in close proximity.

Boomer lowered her head, while keeping an eye on them, expecting any moment for someone to look up and spot her, sixty-five feet above them. But no one looked up—no one noticed her presence. She waited another full minute, then phase-shifted down to the ground.

At the entrance to the archway, Boomer listened for their sounds but heard nothing. She hurried forward and quickly descended the stairs. By step five hundred her annoyance grew ... *so many stupid steps!*

Boomer decided she couldn't afford to lose them. She hadn't been down here before, and didn't have a clue where she was going. They at least had Bristol ... he'd be able to figure out where to find the other portal window. She phase-shifted down the stairs, as far as her helmet light reached, then phase-shifted again. Reaching the bottom of the stairway Boomer took in the enormity of the underground cavern. Still not seeing the others she ran forward, down the wide roadway for a while, until forced to phase-shift again.

She landed right behind the others. If the white flash from her phase-shift wasn't enough to give her presence away, the bright light on her helmet was.

Dira was the first to spin around and look at her. "Boomer? Damn it, Boomer! What do you think you're doing? Get back to the surface ... in fact, get back on the ship ... now!"

Boomer looked back at the five angry faces staring down at her, but kept her resolve. "No!"

"I'll tell your father ... you want me to do that?" Dira threatened.

"I don't care ... you don't know what I know. You don't know what you're up against. Dad would be a lot more upset if you all got killed by Lord Shakrim and his warriors."

Dira, infuriated, continued to stare down at Boomer. Bristol tapped his wrist, reminding her time was ticking by. "I know I'm going to regret this ... stay behind me ... or, better yet, stay behind Rizzo. You do exactly what you're told

... understand?"

Boomer nodded.

"I've got a fix on the first habitat portal down here ... it's beyond some kind of city," Bristol said.

"Can you phase-shift all of us at once?"

Bristol rolled his eyes at Dira's apparently stupid question. "Here we go."

In a flash, they were standing in front of a large, fairly flat wall. Boomer stepped up close, noticing there was an engraved picture on it. "Look, there's the *Minian!*"

No one shared her excitement. Rizzo and Bristol started searching for something while Dira and Leon watched them.

"What are you doing?" Leon asked.

"Looking for an access panel. They're usually hidden," Bristol replied.

"Be faster if we all look for it," Rizzo added.

While the others concentrated on the wall, Boomer held back. There were recent footprints in the dirt, the majority heading off toward the wall's left. She followed after them until, looking up, she could see that the wall wasn't actually solid there—there was an opening.

"Here! It's over here," she called, darting forward into what appeared to be another cave chamber. Boomer heard Dira yelling for her to stop, but she rushed forward anyway. "I found it! It's right here," she said, running over to the ten-foot by ten-foot-wide window before her.

Bristol ran straight to the small access panel on the left and began entering the code.

Dira grabbed Boomer's arm and swung her around to face her. "You can't do that! I'm serious, Boomer. No more running ahead ... do you understand?"

"Okay! But we're running out of time ... look at your HUD ... if you were right about how much time Ricket's got to live, he's got … like … fifteen minutes left!"

Dira glanced over to Leon, then Rizzo, then back to Boomer again. "Just stay close to me."

Beep Beep Beep!

The six darted across the portal's threshold and continued up the stone steps at a run. Leon took the lead while Boomer brought up the rear, directly behind Rizzo. They reached the top of the steps and continued running through a narrow passageway. Up ahead, Boomer saw daylight; the last one to exit the passage into habitat 7, she knew the habitat like the back of her hand. After countless hours of training with Capri, then others, for the first time she felt back in her own element.

"There!" Dira yelled, as she rushed toward the distant portal window and Ricket's body, lying nearby. Hanna and Bristol ran after her as Rizzo and Leon brought up their multi-guns, surveying their surroundings.

"Help me, damn it!" Dira yelled.

Bristol knelt down next to Ricket and gently put his arms beneath his broken body and began to lift him.

"You need to support his head, are you a total idiot?"

Bristol repositioned his arm, making sure Ricket's head was better supported, and stood up. Holding Ricket in his arms, he and Dira quickly headed back toward the passageway.

Dira rushed past Boomer. "Stay right behind me … we're getting out of here."

Boomer did as told, while Rizzo and Leon—walking backwards, their weapons held high—followed closely behind them. Boomer watched Bristol as he struggled with his load, seeming ready to drop Ricket as his skinny legs wobbled.

Bristol disappeared into the black opening. He would be

the only one.

In a mist of violet-charged light, the speed in which Lord Vikor Shakrim appeared took them all by surprise. He stood tall and imposing, directly in front of the passageway gap.

Boomer could not have been more pleased. His eyes quickly locked on to her enhancement shield, then up to her eyes, and he smiled.

Then Boomer realized Sahhrain warriors were standing all around them.

"There is no reason for all of you to die here," Shakrim said amiably. "You are, obviously, far outnumbered. Certain death awaits you ... and for what?"

Boomer moved around Dira and stood before Shakrim. "Let them go ... let them back into the passage," Boomer said.

"No," Dira said, doing her best to pull Boomer behind her.

Boomer used her shield to forcibly push Dira back. "This is my fight! No one else can do it!" she said, keeping her eyes on Shakrim.

"Do what she says, Boomer," Rizzo said. "Get back."

Lord Shakrim's expression turned stern. "The *Minian* is mine. The outcome here has been foretold ... written two thousand years ago. You cannot change the inevitable. Stand aside."

"Kill us and you still won't be able to enter the *Minian*," Dira said. "You've gained nothing."

"Oh, but how wrong you are. You are the captain's woman ... and that young one, Boomer, his warrior child. Do you honestly believe the captain will idly stand by and watch while I rip the very skin from your arms and legs? While his loved ones cry out in horrific agony?"

"He's not on the ship, so you accomplish nothing," Dira

said, desperation in her voice.

Shakrim smiled and looked at her—an expression of reluctant patience on his scarred face. "At this very moment, I'm sorry to inform you, in an adjacent realm, the very last of Captain Reynolds' men are dying all around him ... over a thousand humans beaten by a far superior force. I suppose they fought an honorable battle, but in the end their destiny was written, long long ago. As was mine. Your Captain Reynolds, in a matter of minutes, will be the sole survivor. Soon enough, he will be brought before me."

Boomer listened to Shakrim and tried to quell her rising hatred. She believed him. Sahhrain warriors, enhancement shields on their arms, were an unbeatable force. Boomer's heart pulled in her chest as she thought about those either dead or dying in the rhino-warriors' habitat. She looked around at the towering Sahhrain Chosen Spear warriors—each held a long pratta-shaft, plus an enhancement shield. They were the best of the best—Lord Shakrim's most highly trained personal guard. Boomer looked over at Leon and Rizzo, still holding their multi-guns high, but she noticed no confidence in their eyes. Shakrim was right; there was nothing any of them could do ... perhaps they really had been defeated.

Chapter 53

Dacci System
The *Minian*, Habitat 7, Ancient Ruins

B oomer saw movement at the opening, in the gap leading into the passageway behind Lord Shakrim. She silently cursed Bristol for still hanging around ... *why didn't you get yourself and Ricket to safety!*

But it wasn't Bristol.

Prince Aahil Aqeel stepped into the light and stood right behind Lord Shakrim. He nodded toward Boomer, a brief smile crossing his lips. He glanced first at Lord Shakrim's back, then over at her. The message was clear ... she knew exactly what she needed to do.

Aahil's warriors streamed into HAB 7, in a constant blur of blue skin and violet distortion waves. Boomer and Aahil attacked Shakrim at the same moment.

Boomer anticipated Shakrim's most likely defensive move, positioning one edge of her shield to face both down and inward as she leapt as high into the air as she could. But Aahil's presence must have been detected before the Blues' leader could unleash his own attack. Shakrim spun sideways, diverting most, if not all, of Aahil's bright, lightning-like, violet charge.

Boomer continued to rise higher into the air as her violet waves of light turned red—the power emanating from her shield was far stronger than she'd previously encountered. She flipped over backward as a stream of distortion waves from below sizzled by—just missing her head.

She saw Shakrim and Aahil below her, their shields emitting brilliant waves, crackling swirls, of violet lightning. Boomer landed on her feet and joined in the fight. Shakrim blocked her advances in stride, dodging and spinning with remarkable agility. His cloak, a black frock blowing in the wind, twirled and twisted—making it difficult to see around.

Twice before, Boomer had, somehow, called up the red distortion waves ... waves that were far more powerful than the violet ones. As she spun and leapt away from Lord Shakrim's advances, she consciously surrendered to that same open mindset—that place of allowing—and slowly the shield's violet distortion waves changed hue. She felt the shield on her arm become heavier—stronger. Holding it out before her, and securing its hold with her other hand, she fired wave after wave of thunderous scarlet distortion waves at Lord Shakrim. He spun left and then right, dodging the incoming bombardment from both Boomer and Aahil. With a quick turn of his arm, the face of his shield ricocheted Boomer's distortion waves directly into Aahil. Unprepared, the prince took the red waves directly to his face. He stumbled backward, into the ruins behind him, and slid to the ground.

Unsure if Aahil were dead or only injured, she knew she was on her own against Lord Shakrim, either way. For the first time, she became aware of the fighting going on all around her. Blues warriors were going up against Chosen Spear warriors. Both Leon and Rizzo were still alive and fighting hard as well. *Where are Dira and Hanna?*

Then she saw it … could it be possible? Was Lord Shakrim slowing … tiring? Boomer, who'd been lulled into false assumptions before, remained on guard when he suddenly attacked her. A rampage—first high, then low, then forward bursts of distortion waves came toward her. Boomer dodged twice and blocked the third volley. Bound in a sense together—neither combatant yielding an inch of leeway—both steadily held their ground as crisscrossing streams of light struck the other's shield. Shakrim's stare bore into her. Now anger and hatred emanated from his eyes. But his rage turned to something else when he witnessed her shield's violet waves turning to red, as they flowed toward him. His arms, noticeably, began to tremble before out-and-out shaking took over.

Desperate, he looked around for an escape. Boomer continued her onslaught—bringing the might of her enhancement shield closer and closer to Lord Shakrim's exposed neck. Something flashed in his eyes that Boomer didn't understand until it was too late. Again, Lord Shakrim used his mastery of Kahill Callan: In one fluid, practiced movement he leapt backward, raising his shield over his head, while positioning it face down and to the side.

Boomer marveled at his quick thinking and skill, as once again her distortion waves ricocheted harmlessly away.

No … not harmlessly. Someone was on the ground … someone had encountered the full force of her thunderous red distortion waves. *Oh my God … Hanna.* She'd just killed Hanna! Tears filled Boomer's eyes and she felt her own energy draining away. Shakrim's blows came at her now with renewed ferocity. The scarlet-red hue was gone from her distortion waves. She tried to back away, to fend off the overwhelming power of his attack. She felt something hard against her back … she'd backed into one of the ruin's tall walls. There was nowhere else to go … nowhere to flee. The first of Lord Shakrim's distortion wave blows creased her left shoulder, and her arm fell limply at her side. The same arm that held her enhancement shield.

Lord Shakrim raised his shield, his face now calm. He looked almost sympathetic at what was to come next. He raised his shield and Boomer closed her eyes and waited.

I should be dead, was the first thought entering her mind. It had been too long. *How long does it take?* She opened her eyes, not understanding at first what she was seeing. It didn't make sense … didn't compute. *Dad?*

The fighting around her had ceased. Blues warriors and Chosen Spear warriors and Rizzo and Leon and Dira were all watching her father and Lord Shakrim. *How did you get here, Dad?* More importantly, *How can you fight him?*

In the next instant, Boomer recognized Lord Vikor Shakrim's enhancement shield lying on the ground—the arm straps had been cut. Shakrim was without the use of his shield.

Chapter 54

Dacci System
The *Minian*, Zoo Rhino-Warrior Habitat
170

Jason was surprised to learn most of the Sharks, even some of the rhino-warriors, were already familiar with what had become known as *Rizzo's maneuver*. They even had time to practice the quick phase-shifting move for several minutes before the quickly advancing Sahhrain warriors were near.

What seemed most odd as the seconds wound down, before the final attack came, was the sense of calm he and the others were feeling. One and all they'd come to terms with their inevitable demise within HAB 7, and an almost jovial atmosphere had taken hold.

Jason watched Billy use *Rizzo's maneuver* to flash in and out around Traveler as the big beast swung his heavy hammer wildly—never coming close to hitting him. Laughter echoed across the desert from four hundred Sharks prepared to meet their Maker.

"Incoming!" Jason yelled.

"Lock and load," a younger Shark, standing near Jason's

357

side, yelled in response. Jason spoke into the open channel. "Just like we practiced it … spread out … let's not give them an easy target."

Fast approaching in the distance, Jason saw the reflective breastplate of Commander Douville. *Come to Papa … you fucking traitor.*

As one thousand-plus Sahhrain warriors arrived on the scene, Sharks and rhinos instantly flashed away. But Jason stayed where he was—waiting for Ridert. Dusk had turned to night and, like flitting fireflies, Sharks and rhino-warriors danced in and out, using Rizzo's maneuver. *Would their diversionary tactics be enough to change the tide in their favor? Enough for their outnumbered forces to win the day?* he wondered.

He waited for the overconfident Sahhrain warrior to stride to a halt, two paces in front of him. Jason didn't flash away, but he did raise his multi-gun.

"Time for us to finish this romp, Captain," Ridert said, looking smug. And why shouldn't he be? The battle was nearing its end and his face merely reflected his anticipation of victory.

Jason didn't answer—instead he pulled the trigger on his multi-gun and didn't let up. Somehow, each plasma bolt was blocked by Ridert's quick-moving shield. Perhaps it was his *Kahill Callan* training—but he seemed to know precisely where Jason was going to point his weapon next. In the midst of the ricocheting fire, Ridert steadily moved forward, and eventually used his shield, like a distortion wave battering ram, to propel Jason off his feet and onto his back. While flat on his back, Jason used Rizzo's maneuver to flash away, directly behind Ridert. He fired—this time plasma fire raked the commander's back. His metallic breastplate, which covered his chest, as well as his back, took the plasma fire—

leaving an angled, blackened, foot-long scorch mark. Ridert immediately spun to his left, this time using his shield's edging to propel himself up and away.

Jason jumped back to his feet, doing his best to track the commander's movements. Again, he was struck by more distortion waves. Alarms sounded in his helmet as a warning flashed across his HUD—shields and power levels were falling fast. Jason caught Ridert's life-icon, blinking into view, on his HUD, behind him. Without looking, Jason reacted with a high-angled back kick—delivering a devastating blow to Ridert's face. Immediately, Jason followed up with a spinning-heel kick, delivered precisely to the commander's temple. Ridert spun around one hundred and eighty degrees before falling face first into the sand.

Jason stood over Commander Douville, his multi-gun raised. It took nearly a minute for Ridert to rise from the ground. His eye patch, now askew, revealed a grotesque-looking empty eye socket.

"You're under arrest, asshole. So much as twitch and I'll blow you away."

* * *

There were many casualties within HAB 170. Winning the battle was not easy, but in the end, the Sharks and rhinos prevailed over the Sahhrain warriors. Jason's forces were cut in half—barely two hundred Sharks left—but they'd won, nonetheless.

Jason wasted no time—he phase-shifted directly back to the portal window and hurried across the still open threshold. As planned, he bypassed entering the *Minian*'s Zoo and entered habitat 7, the ancient ruins of a past Harpaign civilization.

What he hadn't expected was to find himself in the midst of another ferocious battle. Plasma fire came from off to his left and violet distortion waves were virtually arcing all around; slain bodies lay everywhere on the ground. Leon and Rizzo still held their own with the assistance of twenty-plus Blues warriors. There were just as many Sahhrain combatants about, but none of that caught Jason's attention.

In the distance, closer to the ruins, he saw a reflective gold breastplate and a black cloak—the unmistakable signature of Lord Shakrim. Who was he fighting? Someone small ... was it Ricket? No ... not Ricket ... he'd been injured earlier ... oh, God ... please not Boomer ...

Jason used Rizzo's maneuver to come up behind Shakrim. Stunned at what he was seeing, Shakrim about to strike down his daughter—Jason realized he didn't have his multi-gun. His battle suit power levels were at zero. Boomer, with her back against a wall, had fear on her face, her eyes clenched closed.

Without conscious thought, Jason slapped the long and slender access panel running down the upper thigh of his battle suit. The Ka-Bar knife was in his hand, thrust forward in less than a second. Jason aimed for the back of Lord Shakrim's head. But, perhaps detecting his presence, Shakrim moved his body away just in time—but not his left arm.

There'd been other times in his life when Jason felt rage, but nothing compared to that moment. The knife, with its razor-sharp blade, sliced into Shakrim's forearm. With Jason's full body weight momentum behind it, the knife's path continued on, slicing through both bands that secured the enhancement shield onto Shakrim's forearm. Once released of their fastenings, both knife and shield flew upward, into the air.

Jason deactivated his battle suit. Even before each segment had fully retracted, his tightly clenched fists began to pound on both sides of Shakrim's head and face. One thing Jason was certain of, he couldn't let up ... not for a second. So he punched—punched until his knuckles cracked and bled. Lord Shakrim was hurt and stumbling to stay upright. Just as abruptly, he took three quick steps backward; he'd somehow regained his senses and was standing up straight.

Shakrim smiled—he smiled the way a parent looks at a petulant child. He thrust out both arms simultaneously—one in the direction of his fallen shield, the other toward Jason. Distortion waves shot out from the shield, into his body, and back out through his other hand. At least ten feet from Shakrim, Jason felt the warrior's fingers begin to tighten, like a contracting vice, around his neck. Unable to breathe and his eyes feeling as if they would bulge from their sockets, Jason began to rise off the ground. Using both hands, he tried to free himself to find some gap to pry open the ever-tightening grip. Jason's feet flailed like a man at the end of a hangman's rope. Without air ... without blood circulating into his brain, consciousness was quickly fading. He was dying. He saw Boomer below him ... eyes wide. She was paralyzed with fear. Jason didn't want her to see him like this. Like a pathetic clown jerking around in the throws of death.

Movement. But not Boomer ... who, then? Dira! She was holding something in her hands ... a stone—part of a crumbled pillar. She was higher than him, up on a raised area of the ruins. Behind Shakrim—she hefted the stone up over her head ... teeth gritted and her face contorted in what could only be described as pure hatred, she leapt from above while bringing the full weight of the stone down upon the back of Shakrim's head.

Jason fell to the ground gasping for breath—his lungs heaving. He looked up and saw Lord Shakrim was still alive.

He'd been driven to his knees and was reaching behind his head. His hand came away bloody.

Jason tried to yell for her to move, but his words came out more like a croak. Dira continued to stand there—as if mesmerized—transfixed. Shakrim slowly rose to his feet, staggered, turned, and looked at Dira. He back-handed her to the face with enough force to knock her off her feet—catapulting her several yards away. She hit the sand and didn't move.

Shakrim staggered again and fell back down to his knees. His eyes lost focus and he wavered there.

What Jason next witnessed froze him in his tracks—Shakrim's body was losing substance, turning quasi-transparent—like an illusion, he was there but *not* there ... fluctuating between some alternate realm where something, or someone, was taking over his place. Now, before Jason, stood the smaller figure of an elderly man, dressed in a simple nomad's attire. Jason knew, beyond a doubt, he was looking into the cold, evil eyes of *Rom Dasticon.*

Jason spotted his knife where it had landed and dove for it. He landed within reach and let his fingers tighten around its handle. But that was as far as he got. A scalding hot, searing bolt shot him in the back of his shoulders. His consciousness faded to blackness, and then slowly returned, as he tried to turn back over twice. He needed to keep Dasticon in his sights. *Where is he?* He needed to protect Boomer. *Is she even alive?*

A blur of movement caught his eye. What he was seeing now didn't make sense: apparently Boomer had regained the use of her arm and her shield. She was back in the fight. But who or what was she fighting?

Jason blinked and again tried to make sense of what he was seeing. It seemed as if Rom Dasticon and Lord Shakrim, now holding his recovered enhancement shield in two hands, were superimposed, one onto the other. They moved as one—but also separately. It was more evident now: Dasticon was the predominant force ... the puppeteer wielding Lord Shakrim's once-powerful warrior body.

Jason watched Boomer quickly duck, evading the Dasticon-Shakrim duo's now bright red distortion wave. It missed her head by inches, while cleaving, in half, an ancient pillar directly behind her. Their combined force obviously multiplied, their destructive power was greatly enhanced.

Boomer was in the air, twirling like a gymnast. As if defying gravity, she rose higher yet, unleashing a stream of crimson-red distortion waves. She missed, turning the sand near Jason's feet to molten glass. He wanted to intervene—get into the fight. Assist Boomer to defeat them, but everything was moving far too fast for his eyes to follow. Even if he had a multi-gun, he'd just as likely shoot her as he would her combatants.

Jason got to his feet and noticed that the battle formerly raging between Blues and Sahhrain was quiet. All eyes were on Boomer and her attackers. She was running on the ground now, going head-to-head with them—blocking their waves of energy and firing off her own, lighting-fast, distortion wave streams back at them. Her hands and shield moved with incredible speed, everything a blur.

Sparks erupted high on Shakrim's breastplate. A portion of his shoulder was no longer there.

Rom Dasticon's form quickly became more predominant, his face distorted in rage. He spat words—phrases Jason's nano-devices couldn't translate.

More sparks erupted, this time at Lord Shakrim's midsection. Dasticon was now unable to control the Sahhrain leader's body; he flailed his arms but Shakrim no longer mirrored his movements. Boomer used her shield's distortion waves to propel herself up and over them in a cartwheel maneuver. She landed behind their co-joined backs and delivered a final killing blow to the base of Lord Vikor Shakrim's neck. He fell to his knees, hesitated there for a moment, before listing over on his side.

Rom Dasticon remained standing. He turned toward Jason, his form progressively becoming more and more transparent, as his eyes stared past Jason, toward the portal, and into the *Minian* behind it. Then he was gone.

Jason felt horrific pain throbbing in his shoulders, where he'd been struck earlier by distortion waves—he lost consciousness.

* * *

He opened his eyes and saw Dira kneeling down beside him. A bruise had formed on her cheek where she'd been struck. She reached out, touching his face, and pushed his damp hair from his forehead. "It's over ... it's over now, my love."

Jason sat up and looked for Boomer. She barreled into him with arms wide open and held on to him, tightly, for long minutes. Eventually, letting him go, she stood back and retracted her battle suit. She again looked like any other ten-year-old girl.

"Are you okay, Boomer, are you hurt?"

"Nope. Not hurt, but tired." She looked over at the unmoving body of Lord Vikor Shakrim. "I guess ... he's dead?"

Jason nodded. "He's gone."

"Good." She sat down next to her father and continued to stare at the body.

Dira had returned to assisting Hanna, who lay unmoving

on the ground somewhere behind him. Jason suddenly detected the unmistakable, and potent, odor of Billy's god-awful cigar, coming from behind him.

"What do you say we get the hell out of here, Cap?"

Chapter 55

Star Watch forces were in the midst of their second, post-interstellar uprising mopping-up process in less than a week. Jason assigned seven fleet assets, all Craing light cruisers, to remain behind within the Dacci system—for an indefinite period of time.

Now that Vikor Shakrim was dead, Commander Douville was in custody, and the Sahhrain uprising squashed hopefully for good, the *Minian* was scheduled to leave the system within the hour and return to Jefferson Station.

Jason rose from the command chair and headed for the exit. "Gunny ... I'll be in Medical. Keep me abreast of any developments with the Sahhrain ... or the Blues ... or anyone else for that matter."

"Aye, Cap. But things seem to have quieted down."

* * *

Jason entered Medical, which earlier had been more like

a three-ring circus than an onboard hospital. For the first few hours, after the dual habitat battles, all MediPods were in constant use; others injured were in an adjoining hospital compartment, lying in rail beds as they waited their turn. Med-techs scurried from patient to patient treating minor injuries, while Dira and two other doctors concentrated their efforts on those more critical.

Jason had waited for things to calm down some, before personally checking on his injured crew. Dira, speaking with another doctor, briefly caught his eye from across the compartment, but just as quickly looked away. She was still frosty from the whole Nan situation. He knew he'd handled it badly ... terribly, in fact. Hurting her was the last thing he wanted to do. Dira probably figured he was well on his way to reconciling with his ex-wife ... reuniting their broken family. At some point, he knew they'd need to talk and clear the air—but the truth was, he wasn't sure how she would react.

The good news, Jason thought, as he looked around, things seemed somewhat more manageable. He approached the first MediPod and looked into the small observation window.

Leon, whom Jason hadn't noticed earlier, stepped up to his side and huffed, "She spends more time in one of those pods than anywhere else."

"She's going to be okay, right?" Jason asked, looking down at the young blonde woman who appeared to be sleeping.

"Massive internal injuries ... got her here in the nick of time. But yeah ... thankfully, she'll live."

"Good. I'd like it if you both stuck around for a while. I may have a long-term proposition for you, unless there's a reason you need to get back into space."

"She'll be convalescing for another few days ... I'll listen to your proposal," Leon replied.

Jason squeezed his shoulder and moved along to the next MediPod. Ricket lay inside it.

"Spinal cord injuries are especially tricky to treat … he'll be in there a while."

Jason looked up to see Dira on the other side of the clamshell lid. Her beautiful face reflected all-business composure—a doctor talking to her boss.

"I'm sure he's getting the best treatment."

"MediPods give everyone the same level of treatment," she answered flatly.

Jason moved over to the next MediPod, closer to Dira, and stood facing a substantially larger MediPod, designed specifically for the bulk of a rhino-warrior or larger-sized patients. Traveler rested inside this one and Jason reflexively grimaced at what he was viewing. He'd witnessed his friend lose his arm, at the shoulder, in battle, as three Sahhrain warriors all together used their enhancement shields to bring down the big rhino. Although half his arm looked restored, the exposed bone, muscle, tendons, and everything else on the rest of it, now in mid-regeneration, wasn't a pretty sight.

Together, they continued to watch Traveler. Jason could smell Dira's soft fragrance and his heart felt heavy in his chest.

"Well, I have things to do," she said, stepping away.

"Wait. Who's in that one?" Jason asked, pointing to the next MediPod in the line.

She paused and looked over to the next MediPod and shrugged. "No one. It's available." She looked annoyed and continued to walk away.

Jason moved to the MediPod and said, "No … there's someone in there."

She let out a breath and joined Jason at his side. They both looked into the observation window. Jason looked at

Dira. She was now staring at what rested on the cushioned bed. "What is that?"

"I don't know … why don't you take a look and see?" Jason nodded to Boomer, who'd been standing in the wings. She activated the pod's lid and the clamshell separated and opened, then came to a stop. Dira's expression became even more serious as realization set in.

Jason reached in and took out the small jewelry box, then opened it. Her eyes were wide and her face had the unmistakable look of one approaching the biggest drop ever on a rollercoaster. Jason opened the small box wider while lowering down on one knee. Dira's hands flew to her cheeks, as her eyes brimmed over with tears. She looked first at the extricated diamond ring now in Jason's fingers and then to Jason. For the first time she became aware that others had joined them: Boomer and Leon and Billy and Orion and, as far as she could see, the whole damn crew were huddled together in Medical. All eyes were on Dira.

She looked down at Jason and, for the first time in quite a while, smiled.

She held out her hand and waited for Jason to put the ring on her finger.

"Marry me?" Jason asked.

She hesitated … looked at the faces around her, and replied, "Of course, I will!"

Cheers filled the crowded small compartment as Jason stood and took Dira in his arms and kissed her.

Epilogue

```
Dacci System
The Minian, Brig
```

Hanna entered the brig section of the *Minian*. Up ahead she saw a corridor with a row of confinement cells off to the right, each behind a grayish blue force field. Leon was walking at her side.

Hanna put a hand on his arm, stopped and said, "Can you wait? I need to do this alone."

"I'll be right here," he said.

She continued on, head high, eyes forward. She passed three empty confinement cells before reaching her husband's. She turned to face the lone occupant.

He looked different than she remembered. Above and beyond the eye patch and even the far more muscular physique than she remembered him having, he looked like a man she might have known in another lifetime. Which he was.

"Hello, Ridert."

"Hello, Hanna."

She continued to look at him sitting there in the white cell, on a white bench, under the all too bright lights. He wore a spacer's jumpsuit with broad horizontal black and white stripes.

He stood and approached the force field. "You've come for answers."

She shrugged and continued to stare at the person she once thought she could never live without. "I used to think it was another woman ... or perhaps even a man ... that stole your heart away."

He didn't respond.

"But I now know it was ... just one more little infatuation with power."

"It's intoxicating, Hanna. I was ill prepared for the effect Lord Shakrim would have on my life. I would never be the same ... nothing ... not even you, would come between me and—"

She cut him off, "I don't ever want to see you again. You can die in here for all I care. Goodbye, Ridert." She turned and headed away. Something caught her attention behind her, back in Ridert's cell. She glanced back and caught sight of something peculiar, perhaps an optical illusion caused by the force field—for an instant, there seemed to be two figures standing there ... one superimposed onto the other. And then it was gone.

"Everything all right?" Leon asked, taking her hand.

"Couldn't be better. Let's get out of here."

The End

Thank you for reading **Star Watch!**

If you enjoyed Star Watch, *please leave a review on Amazon.com — it really, really helps!*

To be notified of the next book in this series, and other books, please join my mailing list — I hate span and will never share your information. Jump to this link to join:

http://eepurl.com/bs7M9r

Thank you, again, for joining me on these SciFi romps into space.

Acknowledgments

I am grateful for the ongoing fan support I receive for all of my books. This book, number ten, Star Watch—came about through the combined contributions of numerous others. First, I'd like to thank my wife for her never-ending love and support. She helps make this journey rich and so very worthwhile. I'd like to thank my mother, Lura Genz, for her tireless work as my first-phase creative editor and a staunch cheerleader of my writing. I'd like to thank Mia Manns for her phenomenal line and developmental editing ... she is an incredible resource. And Eren Arik produced another magnificent cover design—maybe his best yet! I'd also like to thank those in my Tuesday writer's group who have brought fresh ideas and perspectives to my creativity, elevating my writing as a whole. Others who provided fantastic support include Lura and James Fischer, Sue Parr, Stuart Church, and Chris Derrick.

Other books by MWM

Scrapyard Ship
(Scrapyard Ship series, Book 1)

HAB 12
(Scrapyard Ship series, Book 2)

Space Vengeance
(Scrapyard Ship series, Book 3)

Realms of Time
(Scrapyard Ship series, Book 4)

Craing Dominion
(Scrapyard Ship series, Book 5)

The Great Space
(Scrapyard Ship series, Book 6)

Call To Battle
(Scrapyard Ship series, Book 7)

Mad Powers
(Tapped In series, Book 1)

Lone Star Renegades
(Lone Star Renegades series, Book 1)

Star Watch
(Star Watch series, Book 1)